THE QUEST FOR TRUTH

Keep the faith and remain strong.

Mandamus Veritas!

THE QUEST FOR TRUTH

The Allegorical Journey of Youngblood
Hawke—Poet, Philosopher, Soldier of
Fortune, and Professional Adventurer

Poetry, Philosophy, and Lessons in Leadership

Brandon A. Perron

iUniverse, Inc.
New York Lincoln Shanghai

The Quest for Truth
The Allegorical Journey of Youngblood Hawke—Poet, Philosopher, Soldier of Fortune, and Professional Adventurer

iUniverse, Inc.

For information address:
iUniverse, Inc.
2021 Pine Lake Road, Suite 100
Lincoln, NE 68512
www.iuniverse.com

ISBN: 0-595-29951-2 (pbk)
ISBN: 0-595-75162-8 (cloth)

Printed in the United States of America

Appreciation

Appreciation is extended to the philosophers, authors, and publishers who granted permission to utilize their written work.

1. "Thus Spoke Zarathustra" from The Portable Neitzsche by Friedrich Nietzsche, edited by Walter Kaufmann, translated by Walter Kaufmann, copyright 1954 by The Viking Press, renewed (c) 1982 by Viking Penguin Inc. Used by permission of Viking Penguin, a division of Penguin Group (USA) Inc.

2. "A Nietzsche Reader" translated by R.J. Hollingdale (Penguin Classics, 1977) copyright (c) R J Hollingdale, 1977, Reproduced by permission of Penguin Books Ltd.

3. The Revolt of the Masses by Jose Ortega y Gasset. Copyright 1932 by W.W. Norton & Company, Inc., renewed (c) 1960 by Teresa Carey. Used by permission of W.W. Norton & Company, Inc.

4. Aristotle: The Desire to Understand by Jonathan Lear, Copyright 1988 by Cambridge Press, Reprinted with the permission of Cambridge University Press.

5. Plato, Republic, translated by Robin Waterfield, Copyright 1993 by Robin Waterfield, Reprinted by permission of Oxford University Press.

To Sapphire

The nature of truth and all she commands

Contents

Acknowledgments

My own life has been and continues to be a journey and quest. Many obstacles, questions, and trials have tested my resolve and persistence. I have at times been victorious and defeated. Faith and hope have been lost and found and the lessons learned have been invaluable. My quest continues.

The spirit of the solitary warrior resonates within my own heart and soul. It is a state of being that haunts humanity and me personally. The story of Youngblood Hawke is in many ways an allegorical autobiography detailing my own personal quest for truth. I have learned a great deal in my own journey. The lessons of experience continue to enlighten me as I pursue my quest. I have learned that we must all travel our own path but we don't have to travel it alone. Most of all I have learned that I don't really know anything at all. The nature of my existence remains a riddle that will continue to haunt me.

I must extend my gratitude to those favored souls who have believed in me and inspired me to pursue my potentiality. They are special indeed.

A special thank you is extended to my family, friends, and colleagues who supported me throughout the creative process. May the spirit of Youngblood Hawke live within all of you.

Alyssa and Christopher you are my truth.

I am Youngblood Hawke!

Respectfully yours,

Brandon A. Perron
Poet, Philosopher, Soldier of Fortune, and Professional Adventurer.

Foreword

What is truth? It is without question many things to many people but most of all it is an ideal. An ideal that must be pursued while at the same time preserved. Truth is both a predator and prey of humanity. The absolute power of truth remains constant and elusive in respect to the relative ability of humanity to grasp it. The mass majority chooses to ignore the proverbial quest for truth and accept mediocrity as the standard for their existence. They fail to recognize the allure of absolute truth and by doing so settle for far less than their potentiality demands. Fear maintains a powerful hold on our collective conscience and continues to shackle humanity in the chains of ignorance. The desire to understand is all too often replaced by apathy and complacency. The chains of ignorance must be broken and human potentiality freed from a self-imposed imprisonment.

The true fate of humanity is dependent upon intellectual evolution fueled by the desire to understand. It must be understood that the next level of existence cannot be found in the physical realm. Truth exists in an alternative reality and is defined by the human intellect and spirit. Ultimately, humanity is defined by the nature of our spiritual and philosophical existence. The physical reality is just the beginning of the human experience and journey. It is a long and arduous journey that has been and will be led by intellectual warriors seeking the next level of existence. Rebels who find the courage to dismiss the herd mentality and reject the mass may very well determine the future of humanity.

The spirit of the intellectual warrior has traveled the alternative realms of reality and human consciousness for ages. In search of the truth and all it commands, the intellectual warrior has pursued and confronted the most elusive adversaries of humanity. The beasts of ignorance, dragons of mediocrity, and enemies of change have continued to seek retribution against the intellectual warrior and his desire to understand. It has been said that the spirit of the warrior can be ignored but it can never be dismissed or silenced. The warrior in his act of rebellion cries out, "You may not listen but I will be heard!" It is in this spirit that the never-ending battle for truth continues.

Humanity struggles with the questions of life, truth, and destiny within the darkest confines of the human mind, heart, and soul. The battle for truth is often fatal and fought by courageous souls who dare to be different. History is filled with warriors who have pursued the answers to the most daunting questions confronting mankind. The warriors of truth bravely lead humanity to the next level of existence with the hope that one fateful day the truth will be known. We should all look deep into our own heart and soul and ask ourselves if we possess the warrior spirit.

This is the tale of such a warrior. You are about to embark on a journey of wonder and mystery leading to the meaning of our existence as it relates to the punishing brutality of truth and the pursuit of destiny. Open your mind and release your spirit. It is within these pages that you will learn that there is no limit to human potentiality: only obstacles.

A Warrior Indeed!

A warrior's mind is forever free,
    No longer shackled in chains,
Pursuing an unknown destiny,
    Searching for fortune and fame.

A warrior's spirit is wildly alive,
    Riding boldly into the night,
Doing what it must to survive,
    Always prepared for the fight.

A warrior's heart is never soothed,
    Growing old and forever alone,
Close to love but once removed,
    True love he has never sewn.

A warrior's soul is dark & cold,
    Trapped & imprisoned by fate,

Waiting for his future to unfold,
    Forbidden to enter heaven's gate.

—*Youngblood Hawke*

"I know where I am, I know what I am,
I am fully aware of who I am.
But why I am, remains a riddle."

—Youngblood Hawke

CHAPTER 1

The Dispatch

My Armor is robust, my weaponry deadly.
Fearing nothing that dares to confront me.

The road to Ventura was long, and for the most part, desolate. A few weary and somewhat miserable travelers and beggars were encountered along the way, but very little else. Of course, there was that brief encounter with the small band of highwaymen. One of the many hazards awaiting unsuspecting pilgrims, refugees, and Bohemians traveling long distances. The lone voyager was usually the most vulnerable prey for such scoundrels. But Youngblood Hawke was no stranger to such men. On this particular day, the young warrior was keenly aware of his surroundings. He confirmed that the small band of four to five riders was following him when he reached the top of a hill and began his descent. They were following at a distance of about 200 yards, and had been doing so for well over an hour.

Youngblood Hawke learned a long time ago that if one is to be forced into a confrontation, one must at least choose an advantageous place, time, and terrain. He waited just below the crest of the hill behind a large rock cluster providing cover and an elevated position above the road. Hearing the men approach, he removed a ripe and rather delicious-looking apple from his saddlebag. The band of men reached the rock cluster and slowed, engaging in a flurry of discussion and disorder over the apparent loss of their target.

"Good day, gentlemen!" Youngblood said from his lofty position.

They were obviously startled, but soon regained their posture and focused upon their prey. There were four riders consisting of the typical sinister road scum littering such highways. A motley crew if he had ever seen one, and they were all heavily armed. They did not say a word and only stared at their prize like four vicious cobras preparing to strike. Little did they realize they had cornered a most tenacious mongoose.

His characteristic smirk joined the sparkle in his eyes as Youngblood Hawke threw the apple in the air with the confidence of a stage performer and at the same time asked, "Would any of you care for a slice of this tasty apple?"

In what appeared to be one swift motion, he discharged the katana sword strapped to his back with his right hand. Amazingly, he split the apple into four pieces, immediately catching the even morsels with his left hand, and with lightning speed, returned the katana to its scabbard! It was a rather impressive display of swordsmanship. The striking sound of the sword returning to the scabbard only added to the drama.

No doubt the four would-be attackers were impressed as well, as they slowly backed away from their former prey, unsure as to their next move. Three of the four highwaymen appeared to have no further interest, and continued on a slow retreat. The fourth remained steadfast, glaring at Youngblood Hawke, and contemplating his next move. He was assessing the skill of the warrior and comparing it to the fact that they were four and he was one. However, the indecision was short-lived when his three comrades departed rather hastily in the opposite direction, leaving only a cloud of dust and their friend behind.

"It would appear that this contest shall be between you and I alone. Your friends have, without question, deserted you," Youngblood Hawke noted.

The lone highwayman stood, still glancing at the hasty departure of his comrades, and then he glared back at Youngblood Hawke. He continued to evaluate the risk and his chances of success, independent of his comrades.

"No honor among thieves," Youngblood Hawke commented.

Youngblood continued to stare at the lone highwayman, revealing the confidence of a warrior who was no stranger to armed conflict.

The highwayman sneered at the warrior and then turned his horse in the direction of his fleeing colleagues and departed at full gallop.

Only do what needs to be done,[1] Youngblood thought to himself, as he watched the lone highwayman join his band of fleeing compatriots and ride off into the distance. He also recalled the teachings of his second Eastern Master, *"To startle or surprise people is a little device, like hitting at snakes in the grass to scare them."*[2] A lesson learned with a practical application on this day.

"I guess they weren't very hungry?" Youngblood said, as he shared the remaining apple slices with his trusted steed and traveling companion.

Horse and rider continued on their way down the road to the City of Ventura. Once again Youngblood Hawke escaped a very difficult situation through a display of cunning, strength, and a little help from lady luck. He was relieved that the four malefactors opted to make an exit, and not tempt fate on this day.

As Youngblood continued on his journey, he thought of his former master and his teachings, "*Only do what needs to be done. Do not take advantage of power,*"[3] Sifu Lao guided Youngblood through his studies of the Eastern Arts during his time spent in the farthest reaches of the Eastern Kingdom. His words were wise and enlightened, yet the young warrior's own western philosophy constantly struggled with his teacher's. His master told him when he departed his company that he had mastered the arts in respect to the body, but his mind remained clouded, and unwilling to reach the *Tao*.[4] Master Lao provided many lessons for *Chung ts'ai*[5] and Youngblood continued to use them during his own meditations. He spoke of understanding and said that, "*Understanding comes to those who have realized their true self. Realization of their true self comes to those who have gained understanding. To him who has reached the Tao and is master of his true self, the universe shall be dissolved.*"[6] The young warrior always wondered what he meant by those words and spent many hours meditating in search of the meaning. However, the prophecy of his master that truly haunted him did not elude his understanding, "*A violent man shall die a violent death.*"[7]

There she was in all her glory, Ventura, the city of a thousand lights and even more promises. It had been quite a few years since he had seen its city walls. In fact, the last time he entered her gates, he was a member of a column of cavalry being honored with parades, for the glory it had won in the Great War. Youngblood Hawke could never forget the pain he saw during those days. But such painful memories were now behind him, and the city was currently alive and thriving. The City of Ventura was, without a doubt, the shining star of the Western Kingdom.

As the road drew closer, it also grew more crowded and difficult to navigate. Merchants, farmers, and livestock flocked together with the pilgrims and refugees to form a miserable display of civilization. Upon entering the city, Youngblood decided it was time to shake the dirty road from his garments, and wash the dust from his very dry throat. A sign inviting the weary traveler into the tavern hit its mark, catching the attention of the thirsty and hungry warrior. After getting Veritas settled into the stable, along with an ample supply of oats and water, Youngblood entered the tavern.

He almost always caught the attention of patrons when he entered such establishments. His air of confidence combined with the intense stare of his eyes made for a rather interesting first impression. This was especially true when observed in conjunction with the weaponry displayed by the warrior. The battle sword by his side was the envy of every warrior who cast eyes upon it. The katana sword strapped to his back revealed an exotic side of the warrior. A legendary samurai of great distinction gave it to him during his time in the east studying the martial arts. Youngblood Hawke was proud of this weapon, and he was an expert in its use. And when exposed, no one could ignore the menacing ebony-handled dagger concealed beneath his cloak. Youngblood Hawke made his typical entrance, displaying his natural military posture and slight swagger, as he made his way to the bar. Of course, his trademark smirk was always worn with a patronizing air.

A large chalice of ale refreshed the weary warrior so profoundly that he ordered another, saying, "Keep them coming, innkeeper."

The three rogues were loud and, without question, intentionally disruptive as they appeared to stake their claim as the tavern masters. The largest one of the three appeared to be the support mechanism for the other two who were especially annoying and antagonistic to the other patrons. The entry of Youngblood Hawke had not gone unnoticed by the trio as they eyed his weaponry and demeanor.

"That is an interesting weapon strapped to your back," one of the men commented.

The other two just watched and waited for the unknown warrior's response.

"Yes, it is," Youngblood calmly responded without making eye contact as he continued to drink his ale.

"Let me see it," the rogue commanded, as he abruptly approached Youngblood in an attempt to intimidate him.

"I don't think so," Youngblood Hawke replied.

"What? Are you denying my request?" the rogue asked, as he became agitated with Youngblood's obvious lack of interest.

The largest one stood up from the bar, exposing his massive size, and quietly approached Youngblood. He stood behind his colleague in a show of support as he puffed out his chest and displayed the impressive diameter of his biceps. The third man also moved into a potential striking position, gripping the handle of the sword strapped to his side.

"I have no quarrel with you, gentlemen, and only wish to be left alone to enjoy this chalice of ale," said Youngblood Hawke as he continued to stare at the reflection of the men in the mirror located behind the bar.

"Too late, you worthless road trash," the smaller troublemaker said, whose courage was fueled by the support of his comrades and a large quantity of ale.

Youngblood never turned his head to face the band of fools as he continued to watch their reflections and noted the swift attack of the larger enforcer. The back of Youngblood's closed fist immediately met the attacker's advance. The large enforcer was struck down as Youngblood used the man's size and momentum to facilitate his counterattack. The rogue's descent to the hard floor was fast and hard. His fall was followed by the heel of Youngblood's boot to the back of his head. The enforcer's unconscious state left the two remaining rogues in a state of surprise and paralysis.

The patrons had cleared the immediate area of the bar but moved in closer to examine the residual effects of the conflict. Acts of violence were often considered exciting and colorful entertainment in such establishments. The patrons also appeared amused and pleased with the fact that the three rogues had met their match. The humiliation of such a defeat would not be easy to dismiss. The two men attended to their large friend while also guarding themselves against the possible next move of Youngblood Hawke.

"Sheer numbers and brute force are not always a capable opponent for cunning and speed," the man commented as he stepped over the defeated mass lying on the floor.

The man dismissed the two attending rogues as irrelevant as he passed.

"You boys shouldn't play with fire," he added while shaking his head and laughing.

One of the two rogues stood up and was about to respond but remained silent in the face of the elder warrior, who had now raised his hand and said, "Think carefully about what you are about to do, boy."

"That would be very sound advice," Youngblood Hawke interjected.

"Still stirring up trouble and toying with the overinflated egos of local scoundrels, I see," replied the man as he walked away from the young rogue and waved his hand in a dismissive manner.

"Alas! Are you still alive?" Youngblood said, followed by a hearty laugh.

"At least for this afternoon, my friend," the tall, aging man said.

He was much older than the last time he had seen him. His hair had thinned, and his thick beard was completely gray. But his strong frame remained quite impressive and intimidating, considering the mileage and scars it possessed. Horatio Cantrell had been quite the soldier and an accomplished mercenary in his day. But he gave up the life of adventure when he fell in love with a lord's daughter. In addition to his duties now associated with his noble station, his current trade was now that of a discreet provider of rare goods and information. In other words, he was a high-priced smuggler and spy, under the protection of a powerful lord who happened to be his father-in-law. But for the most part, he was a well-respected member of the aristocracy now.

"How the hell are you, old dog?" Youngblood said with an obvious reverence for his old friend.

"I am well," he answered.

The young warrior offered the old warrior a drink, "Join me in a drink and toast the past, my friend."

Horatio looked at his former student and laughingly said, "I remember a time when this was your quest."

"I remember also, but fear not, my search has not changed so drastically. Do you recall the motto of our elite unit?" Youngblood presented the question to Horatio, knowing very well that he did.

Simultaneously, they rang out the words, "*En vino Veritas!*"

"In wine is truth," had been chanted many times following both victory and defeat on the battlefield. The two men stared momentarily into the past and then raised their chalices in a silent salute to fallen comrades. Youngblood Hawke's time in the military was initially spent among the common ranks. However, his obvious skill for warfare shined and it was Horatio Cantrell who recruited him into one of the most elite and feared military units to take the field. It was there that Horatio took him under his wing and ignited the fire within his student. Youngblood Hawke revered his mentor and would deny no task in his favor.

"What brings you to this place, Horatio?"

"I have a message for you," Horatio answered, puzzled that his friend was not expecting the dispatch.

The equally puzzled Youngblood asked, "How did you know I would be here?"

"The place and time was marked on the pouch along with an impressive payment of gold, I might add," he responded.

Youngblood's interest was increasing, "Who charged you with this task, my friend?"

Horatio continued to reduce the contents of his chalice as he said, "I don't know. An old man arrived at my door and handed me the dispatch and the bag of gold insisting that I personally deliver the communication. When I observed that you were my contact, I immediately accepted the assignment. Was I wrong to accept?"

Dismissing the last question Youngblood asked, "Do you have the dispatch?"

"Of course," the now bewildered Horatio said as he handed him the message.

Youngblood opened the document and read it carefully as his long-time friend and mentor waited for a response.

"Do you know of the triangle?" the younger warrior asked of his former teacher.

"Are you speaking of the Temple Triangle?" a very curious Horatio replied.

Youngblood just shook his head and said, "I am to seek the counsel of the triangle."

Horatio was patiently waiting for more information but also knew that it may not come. One of the rules of the mercenary game was that all assignments were confidential. He had played it many times prior to retiring.

"Is that what the letter says? Who is it from?" Horatio asked.

Again ignoring his friend's questions, Youngblood asked, "Tell me of this Temple Triangle."

"It is an ancient temple just outside the city within the mountains. I would estimate about a day's ride from here," Horatio responded.

Horatio assumed the communication contained a very serious mission, based on the grave manner in which his friend now reflected.

"The temple is said to be the home of three wise sages, of the ancient order, I believe?" Horatio added.

Youngblood Hawke turned toward the busy and bustling tavern and continued to drink his ale as he watched the activities of the other patrons. Horatio knew the look and also knew that there would be no more discussion regarding the mysterious message he delivered to his friend. The two men soon took a table and feasted on the finest delicacies that Ventura had to offer as they talked of old times and old friends. The time passed deep into the night with both Youngblood Hawke and Horatio Cantrell enjoying all the city had to offer a warrior that evening. Youngblood Hawke's trademark smirk would be in rare form on this night. He enjoyed the evening but in the back of his mind he knew very well that he was about to embark on a journey riddled with mystery and danger. Youngblood Hawke could only wonder what fate had in store for him.

CHAPTER 2

The Epiphany

Rendering my sword upon demand,
Restrained as a man in solitude I stand.

Youngblood Hawke was still enjoying the glory and rewards of his last mission as he proceeded to his next assignment. Having traveled the majority of the day with little rest, he stopped along the side of the road under an apple tree to take advantage of its shade. Counting the spoils and the wounds resulting from his trade had become a ritual within itself. Both appeared to be adding up quite rapidly. The scars and bruises he carried told a tale all their own. He also provided his war-horse, Veritas, with a drink of water and some well-deserved rest.

"I suspect that we have traveled enough on this day, my old friend," the weary warrior said as he dismounted. "Surely there is an easier way to travel? No offense of course," he added, as he stretched and rubbed his backside, implying the presence of saddle sores.

Veritas and Youngblood had been trusted companions for quite some time. They had not always been together, but for the most part, they were inseparable. In fact, for the past few years, the trusted steed had been Youngblood's closest friend. During their time together, they had shared many experiences involving both danger and adventure. However, they were different beings with different purposes. They both knew their purpose and limitations in respect to the other. The two also knew that they could not accomplish greatness without the other steadfastly by his side. Although Youngblood Hawke was publicly awarded the glory and proclaimed the hero, it was without question Veritas who bore him upon his back to and from the battlefield. It was Veritas who remained by his side and carried him during times of trouble. It was Veritas who remained loyal without question, even when his master was in error. They were one and were bound not by a master-servant doctrine but by common goals and commitment. The other was free to depart at any time.

As they both shared slices of an apple, a ragged old man approached them. He was leading a cart loaded down with baggage and pulled by a very scrawny and tired-looking horse. The man exhibited the oddest air of familiarity to both Youngblood and Veritas.

"Old man...is there an inn nearby where a traveler can purchase food, drink, and perhaps a good night's rest?"

The old man stopped and turned to the young warrior and responded with a degree of confidence and command that startled him.

"That is not what you seek, warrior," the old man said.

"It's not?" Youngblood responded, appearing rather puzzled.

"You seek the one who guards the crossroads," the old man replied.

"What is this nonsense you speak of, old man?" Youngblood asked with his characteristic sarcastic tone veiled only by his equally confident smirk that had been the cause of many problems in the past.

The old man grinned and said, "You fool only yourself, boy. All those who encounter you are very aware of your quest, even if you are not."

Youngblood Hawke continued to bite into the apple and shake his head. "Crazy old man," he said amusingly.

The old man pointed toward a path leading into the dark orchard. Turning toward the path, Youngblood was rather startled to see the path before him, not having noticed it before.

"Travel the path and your quest will be clear," the old man advised.

Youngblood stared down the path, past the trees, beyond the shadows, and into the darkness, feeling a sudden chill that even Veritas appeared to experience.

"Tell me old one...did you deliver the mysterious dispatch?" Youngblood asked.

"What does it matter? Your pockets are lined with gold, are they not? Is that not the nature of your quest?" the old man replied.

Youngblood Hawke turned back to respond, but the old man was gone. He had departed as quickly as he had arrived. He was nowhere to be seen, but somehow the young warrior knew they would cross paths again. Youngblood finished the apple and then climbed upon Veritas, ready to proceed down the road. However, he was unable to ignore a feeling that the path leading into the orchard was calling him, or possibly warning him to turn back. He attributed the feeling to mischievous curiosity and decided he would travel the path for the sake of exploration. After all, he had no destination or appointment to keep this day. His next assignment could wait. At least that is what Youngblood Hawke believed at the time. But he did have an appointment…an appointment with destiny.

The path was long and unusually dark for the hour of day. His sense of the time and distance traveled became unclear as he continued down the trail. Youngblood's instincts were usually on point about such things as time, distance, and direction. But this path was very different and eerily unfamiliar, unlike any he had traveled before. As he traveled down the path he began to think of his historical studies, military history being his primary enjoyment, and engaged in his daily philosophical debate with Veritas.

Youngblood Hawke was many things to many people and had fulfilled many roles successfully. In general, though, he is known as an accomplished warrior, soldier of fortune, and professional adventurer. The lords and other nobles often called upon him to assist them in their conflicts. He offered a service for which he was paid rather handsomely. He was not a rich man, but many would describe him as affluent as his wants were few. His true passion was for history, philosophy, and the pursuit of all knowledge. A very contradictory passion for such a pragmatic soul, but a passion nonetheless.

He often pondered over the nature of truth and the meaning of life, using history's lessons as a guide. Although he enjoyed philosophy, he did so with no formal training in the art of philosophical debate. Unlike his mastery with a sword, which was second to none in its sharpness and accuracy in the art of attack and defense. His combat skills, combined with his bold decisiveness and ability to manipulate the moment, rendered Youngblood Hawke a very formidable adversary. But Youngblood Hawke had not been exposed to the finer art of intellectual pursuit. His station had not provided him the best teachers or the opportunity to devote a life to the study of the finer arts. Without question he possessed the talent and the intellectual prowess, but he was lacking in the understanding of how to hone his natural skill and ability, and most of all, how to take advantage of them. His journey to date had been mostly devoted to accomplishment and glory associated with confrontation and combat.

Although once a soldier of distinction, he ultimately found little reward being one who followed orders as an integral part of the mass soldiery. A culture of honor had been replaced by a culture of mediocrity. Like so many before him he was forced to pursue his own path, alone and supported solely by ambition and self-preservation. The former soldier known as Youngblood Hawke was branded a rebel, a sword for hire offering his services to the highest bidder. Many believe his motivation to be solely mercenary. In fact, he discreetly swears allegiance to no man but to a cause, a devotion to an idea that he finds both noble and good. An idea that must be fundamentally noble and good for it can represent that which many would consider evil.

Youngblood Hawke defined himself as a warrior and advocate of truth! An impartial and objective guardian sworn to defend it wherever and whenever it may come under attack. The ancient code of honor is his proverbial banner. Such an allegiance does not always put a warrior in a popular position or on the side of the collective good. In fact, it often places him in very dangerous situations, staring into the face of very powerful forces. But such odds are the very thing that Youngblood Hawke lives for and dreams of as the perpetual underdog and hopeless romantic facing overwhelming odds and most certain defeat. Thus, when victory is attained, it is sweeter and much more appreciated, for it is earned by merit. Many suspect he has a death wish and call him a reckless fool. But his success cannot be ignored. The years have brought scores of victories to our warrior, resulting in a most impressive record of accomplishment. It was a record that has transcended local recognition to a reputation that stretches across the land and throughout many kingdoms. His youth, combined with his impressive record, earned him the respect of his elders and the most noble of warriors and generals. However, his personal history remains a mystery, and his reputation, that of a charmed soldier of fortune associated with no single kingdom or army. In other words, no one knows what Youngblood Hawke represents other than himself and his most recent employer. It is said that no one truly knows the man, whose professional ideology often remains as much a mystery as his personal history.

Suddenly the orchard emptied out into a large meadow, and the darkness of the forest was replaced by sunshine, rolling hills, and wild flowers. Youngblood stopped and admired the beauty of the meadow and made note of its contrast with the orchard from which he had departed. In the distance he was able to observe a solitary figure standing within the high grass as the wind blew through an array of flowing white garments. The figure was still and appeared to be waiting. Veritas, without prodding, galloped cautiously toward the figure with no complaint from his rider. The wind was blowing with just enough force to generate a slight whistle as it blew through the grass. As they approached the figure, the wind became still, and the air, silent. The sky was blue and expansive and there was not a cloud to be seen. Veritas slowed his gallop and trotted slowly up to the figure that had not moved and remained hidden behind a hooded cloak.

"You…sir…why do you stand here alone miles from anyone or anything?" the young warrior asked.

"I wait for you," the cloaked figure responded. "I have been waiting for quite some time."

Youngblood's expression became both focused and serious as he turned his head with suspicion and placed his hand on the hilt of his sword. "Are you an assassin?" he demanded, suspecting that the old man on the road had been a conspirator and had led him to his current dilemma by luring him with gold.

The mysterious figure spoke in an equally mysterious tone stating, "No, but there will be days when you will consider me your assassin and will wish that I had been successful on this day."

"Who are you?" Youngblood barked in defiance.

"I am your gatekeeper, young warrior," the figure replied.

Youngblood's patience was wearing thin…as was the restraint on his sword. "Gatekeeper to what…strange one?"

The figure remained still and responded, "To what you seek."

"And what is it that I seek?" the sarcasm was now ringing through Youngblood's voice.

The figure moved closer, "That is the question I ask of you."

Youngblood Hawke remained still, staring at the figure, when without warning, he drew his sword high into the air and in a commanding voice declared, "It is knowledge that I seek! You speak in riddles and stand here wasting my time!"

"Yes, but knowledge is a riddle," the figure replied.

Youngblood stepped down from his mount and approached the mysterious figure that remained hidden beneath the cloak, exposing nothing human other than his form and an almost mystical voice.

"You are a sage?" Youngblood Hawke asked.

"I am called by many names," said the sage. In an unwavering tone the mysterious sage added, "You say you seek knowledge. Clarify the knowledge that you seek, young warrior."

Youngblood stood his ground and proudly answered the sage, "I seek the truth!"

The sage once again questioned the young warrior, "Why do you seek the truth?"

With complete confidence and bravado Youngblood responded, "Because I desire it. In fact, I command it to be revealed to me!"

"Answer this bold warrior and you shall find that which you seek, if it is revealed to you, what will you do with it?"

Youngblood Hawke remained still, taken aback by the question, displaying complete bewilderment at its simplicity. He pondered the question and searched his mind for the answer. He was unable to respond with the cunning, sharpness, and accuracy for which he had become renowned. The fearless warrior was speechless. He had no answer and could only lower his head and sword as he accepted defeat.

The sage approached Youngblood and said, "You command nothing and are not ready for that which you seek, young warrior. Now depart here and make it your mission to find that which you profess to protect. Earn it, young warrior, earn it meritoriously."

In a now subordinate tone Youngblood Hawke asked, "Where will I find that which I seek?"

"In experience," the sage proclaimed, continuing with an air of command. "You will begin your journey forthright and will be met along the way by guides, mentors, and prophets possessing great wisdom."

"How will I find them?" the now humbled warrior asked.

"They will find you," the sage said. "Now go and stay your course," the sage ordered.

As Youngblood Hawke climbed aboard Veritas and began to ride away, the sage uttered his last words in a tone that at once disturbed the brave Youngblood Hawke.

"Young warrior," proclaimed the sage, "be courageous while also cautious during your journey. You see yourself as the hunter, but to many you are seen as the prey. Beware! And take care! For the beast pursues you with a mission and hunger to destroy you and all you represent!"

Alarmed, Youngblood Hawke turned and asked, "What beast do you speak of?" But it was too late. The sage had disappeared, as did the meadow, the orchard, and the clear blue skies that were now replaced by darkness and an approaching storm.

"Your quest awaits you, young one," the old man said, waiting for Youngblood's return.

Once again puzzled by the familiarity of the old man, Youngblood asked, "Do you know me, old man?"

"No more than you know yourself, boy. Now go…you have much to learn," the old man said.

The old man responded with the same confidence and command he displayed when Youngblood first encountered him. Youngblood turned toward the mountain pass he was to travel. He turned back to speak to the old man, but found himself alone. *Obviously in the employ of the sage,* Youngblood thought to himself as he watched the old man depart in the opposite direction.

Youngblood Hawke stood alone on the roadside staring off into the horizon as the distant storm rumbled closer. His thoughts drifted as he pondered what lay ahead.

Forbidden Knowledge

Traveling my own path,
A relative truth revealed,
An epiphany of sorts,
No longer concealed.

Truth now confronts me,
I ask—What do I do?
Many paths to destiny,
Now forced to choose.

My future is unclear,
Only the past is mine,
Now aware of my fears,
I live one day at a time.

Absolute truth is hidden,
Unreachable and obscure,
Perhaps I am forbidden,
To possess a truth so pure.

—*Youngblood Hawke*

Reflecting upon his experience, he wondered what fortune or dangers awaited him on his journey. For this was a true test and mission of which he had no knowledge or experience to draw from. In fact, alone on that winding road far from anything or anyone, Youngblood Hawke experienced the familiar and uncontrollable disturbing affects of fear. Little did he realize that it was just the beginning of his journey through the darkness in search of the light he desired so passionately. The path into the mountain pass was without question dark and cold, and the young warrior knew it was his to follow. Perhaps this world of mystery and wonder did have a place for such a warrior.

❦   ❦   ❦

The imaginative world of Youngblood Hawke exists in an alternative reality of sorts. It is a world of wonder and potentiality, but also one of darkness and despair. In other words, it is very much like all worlds—a complete mystery to all its inhabitants.

It was supposed to be a time of perpetual peace and unlimited prosperity. At least that is what the leaders of the Western Kingdom had been promising the population. The world had in fact changed upon the fall of the Eastern Empire and its reigning dictatorship more than a decade ago. The despotism of the Eastern Empire had threatened world domination for many years. The Great War had been fought on many fronts across the globe as the conflicting ideologies continued the struggle for primacy. During the Great War, professional soldiers were in demand and found adventure beckoning their spirit to answer the call to arms.

The warrior's path was evident during such a time of clarity. The question of "good versus evil" was easily answered by both sides, as they viewed their adversary through a filter of propaganda distributed by their leadership. The misinformation provided the necessary fuel required to aggressively continue the conflict. It was almost implausible for anyone to envision an end to the war. However, the end did in fact come in the form of victory for the Western Kingdom, who had allied itself with the Northern Kingdom and the rebel factions within the Eastern and Southern Kingdoms. Victory over the Eastern Empire had not been acquired without great casualties and severe consequences. The result was a final battle of monumental proportions that continues to resonate in the collective conscience of the world's leadership and populace. But as the remnants of the Eastern Empire collapsed, and the evidence of its past began to disappear, a New World emerged. A world where the question of "good versus evil" was no longer clear as it now dwelled within the twilight of human perception.

The fall of such a powerful empire disrupted the balance of power and abruptly shifted it to the young democratic government of the Western Kingdom. The Northern Kingdom remained under the control of a monarchy, but the Eastern and Southern Kingdoms were comprised of small despots, dictators, and struggling city-states. The abrupt shift of power created a false sense of security within the Western Kingdom, allowing the enemies of change to influence the meek and develop a following of misguided disciples. The majority learned to enjoy the lack of responsibility and created a world of entitlements. The leadership became complacent and naïve as they bickered among themselves, focused solely upon trivial matters of special interest and personal gain. Such an atmosphere of self-imposed ignorance allowed the enemies of change to infiltrate the unsuspecting culture and capture the minds of the mass majority.

The lack of awareness allowed them to create the necessary infrastructure required to strike at the very heart and soul of the Western Kingdom. Unlike the threat posed by the former power of the Eastern Empire, the current threat remained obscure and hidden within the shadows. No foreign army threatened the borders, and no navy sailed upon friendly ports in a show of might. The conventional military forces of the four kingdoms had been reduced in accordance with an international treaty. The treaty diminished the sovereignty of the kingdoms and provided the foundation for the creation of a mysterious alliance and shadow government: A shadow government with far-reaching powers within the four kingdoms. The mysterious alliance formed an elite military unit appropriately named the Black Guard, to impose its will. These were dark times and the four kingdoms were ill-equipped to effectively combat the elusive and virtually invisible predator infecting the populace. The resources were available, but scattered across the kingdoms with no organization or ideology to combine their ranks and take to the field of battle.

The one resource necessary to defeat the obscure and powerful enemy was visibly absent. The illusion of perpetual peace had forced the next generation of warriors and leaders to seek personal fortune and adventure as mercenaries and soldiers of fortune. Society no longer required their service and dedication to a code of honor and loyalty. They had been dismissed as irrelevant and obsolete in what was described as the "New World Order." The "warrior hearts" now wandered the four kingdoms in search of glory and honor, offering their services to the highest bidder in exchange for personal reward. Little did they know that a higher calling awaited them, and that destiny would soon be knocking at their proverbial doors. From among their ranks great leaders would emerge to rally the lost warriors and answer the call of eternal destiny in a battle for the hearts, minds, and spirit of humanity itself. The time had come.

CHAPTER 3

The Triangle of Knowledge

A philosopher and poet of sorts,
An adventurer and mercenary by creed.

Youngblood Hawke began his journey through the mountain pass pondering the potential perils of his quest. He also thought of his meeting with Horatio Cantrell and reminisced aloud of their many adventures together. He shared with Veritas stories that had been told hundreds of times while traveling, stories that appeared to change ever so slightly with each telling. But Veritas did not appear to mind hearing the colorful tales of adventure and intrigue again and again.

As Youngblood approached the Temple Triangle he was immediately drawn to the majesty of the structure. It was almost mythical in the way it was elevated above its surroundings, and its marbled walls reflected the sunlight. The tall, majestic columns ran upward into the intricately detailed portico. The road leading to the entrance was marked with statues and busts of great warriors, philosophers, and kings.

The temple structure was classic in its architecture, providing a monumental presence, surrounded by picturesque rolling hills and a colorful array of trees. Interestingly enough, perusal of the grounds revealed that there was not a soul in sight. Youngblood dismounted Veritas and ascended the steps leading up to a large oak and iron door. Upon reaching the door he was not sure what he was supposed to do.

Do I knock or just enter? he thought to himself.

Someone or something else answered the question for him as the two doors slowly opened. He entered the temple respectfully, recognizing that it was a house of wisdom. He cautiously followed a long hallway lined with burning torches that led into a large and dark chamber. With one hand on his dagger, he looked up into a seemingly endless ceiling that reached deep into the darkness.

Youngblood slowly entered the center of the chamber noting the strange writing on the walls around him. The room was dark and as he looked down he noticed that he was standing in the middle of a triangular mosaic inscribed with the ancient and very familiar term—V E R I T A S. His trademark smirk revealed itself briefly when suddenly three figures appeared before him. Each of the figures assumed a position on one point of the triangle. A subtle light projecting from the darkness suggested to Youngblood that they had been standing there when he entered. They were distinguished, older men. Each was older than the next and was adorned only in white tunics and sandals. Except for the older and odd-looking one. He was barefoot and bald, and his tunic was ragged. They appeared to be studying the young warrior and talking among themselves in a faint whisper.

Youngblood was about to speak when the eldest of the sages asked, "Who are you?"

"I am Youngblood Hawke, sir," the warrior pronounced with pride.

"That is your name," a sage replied.

"Do you think you know yourself, merely because you know your name?"[8] the eldest one responded.

The younger sage appeared to be listening intently as he gazed upon the warrior, and then he released with an air of contempt, "So, who are you?"

Youngblood Hawke returned a gaze to the sage and responded with caution, "A soldier of fortune and professional adventurer."

"I did not ask 'What are you?'" the younger sage replied.

"Is that what you are or is that how others see you?" the middle sage asked.

The young warrior was becoming more confused as the younger sage demanded, "I ask you again, who are you?"

Youngblood responded with a somewhat lesser degree of confidence, "I am a truth seeker and have come to find the object of my quest."

"This one does not know who, what, or why he is, and it is quite possible he does not know where he is," announced the youngest sage with complete contempt. "He is like all the young, and we waste our time with him."

Youngblood Hawke listened and pondered the words of the youngest sage.

The Ignorance of the Young

Ignorance and youth, what a truly wonderful blend,
Living life clueless, they have no need to pretend.
Fooling only themselves, they think they are clever.

Pursuing the moment, and the illusion of fun,
Staring at the clouds, and frolicking in the sun.
Laughing and playing, believing it will last forever.

Caring only about today, forgetting their tomorrow,
Unaware of a future, filled with pain and sorrow.
Simple and carefree, trusting things will get better.

What fools are the young, unappreciative of youth.
Dismissing life's lessons, and running from the truth.
Turning away from reality, and the advice of elders.

One day they will awaken, by then it will be too late,
Their time will have passed, having sealed their fate.
Left with wisdom and old age, what a terrible waste.

—*Youngblood Hawke*

"Yes, but he desires to know," the middle sage responded with a tone of compassion.

"*Gnothi Seauton—know thyself*, young warrior,"[9] the elder declared in the ancient tongue.

In an attempt to engage the sage and demonstrate his own skill, Youngblood responded rapidly to the eldest with a question, "Tell me, what is it that you claim to know, sage?"

"*I know nothing except the fact of my own ignorance*,"[10] he responded with confidence.

Somewhat annoyed, Youngblood uttered under his breath, "You can't get this one to answer a question."

"Once again I ask, who are you?" the youngest and least hospitable sage asked.

"Perhaps I don't know."

"Then this is what you seek?" they all replied.

"I seek myself?"

"In this, will you not find truth?" fired back the elder. "It is knowledge, and knowledge is virtue," he added.

The irritable one continued, "*If knowledge is virtue is it not identical with happiness, for a man who is doing what is right is doing that which is for his own good, resulting in happiness, is he not?*"[11]

"Are you happy?" they all asked.

Youngblood responded with a lesser degree of confidence, "I believe I am."

The irritable and younger sage replied, "You obviously do not know thyself, or else you would know if you were happy. *Someone who is able to realize his nature will lead a rich, full, happy life, and he will experience a certain unity and harmony among his desires.*"[12]

Youngblood Hawke remained silent for a moment, evaluating the meaning and words of the younger sage and compared it to the experience of his own life.

Alone and Confused

In search of life's answers, I can no longer pretend,
My life a proverbial puzzle, a maze without end.
From the very beginning, I was alone and confused,
A virtual powder keg of emotion, unable to defuse.

Time passed so slowly, maturing from a boy to a man,
In preparation of my future, and all life would demand.
Entering the world, with raw excitement and ambition,
I ignored the menacing power of fear and inhibition.

No longer imprisoned, mind and spirit wandering free,
Dismissing a painful past, in pursuit of a new reality.
Level after level, I conquered more difficult heights,
Fleeing the cave of darkness, seeking intellectual light.

In command of a world, reserved for the very few,
Yet, I found myself lacking, unaware of what to do.
Detachment and distraction, questions so profound,
Inflicted with paralysis, I was chained and bound.

Suddenly and without warning, a truth was revealed,
The meaning of my existence, no longer concealed.
A vision to tomorrow, the very image of potentiality,
Unveiling the answers to the questions of my destiny.

—*Youngblood Hawke*

"Remember warrior, *nature does nothing in vain*,"[13] the irritable one added.

The eldest once again addressed him, "Explore yourself as you would a new, mysterious land and remember this—*the unexamined life is not worth living.*"[14]

"So, I will find truth in happiness?" the young warrior asked.

"Truth is your quest, young warrior, and if you find truth, you ask if you will be happy?" the youngest sage replied.

"Yes," Youngblood replied.

The sage looked at him sternly and said, "Then ultimately it is happiness that you seek, for once you find truth, the result will be happiness, will it not? Pursue that which you seek, young warrior, and be aware of your potentiality for it coincides directly with your prospect of revealing the truth, and ultimately, with your happiness. You were created for a purpose, and failure to realize that purpose will bring you discontent," he added.

"How do I know what my potentiality is?" Youngblood asked.

"He has many questions and no answers," the younger sage replied, appearing increasingly annoyed.

The eldest shook his head in agreement and in the manner of a pleased grandfather said, "As it should be."

The middle sage, who had remained fairly quiet, interjected, "You must balance your soul and mind to allow your potentiality to reveal itself. By your own admission you are mercenary and ambitious, are you not?"

The young warrior nodded in the affirmative, with a small degree of shame.

"Do not be ashamed. You will find that such traits are the very tools necessary to pursue your quest. In fact, in many ways they define the nature of your existence."

"Perhaps they do," Youngblood acknowledged.

"But what of your philosophical side, young warrior?" he asked. *"Is it not this part that is entirely directed at every moment towards knowing the truth of things?"*[15] The sage continued, "Consider the success you have enjoyed in your life. Would you have achieved this level without all three of these basic human parts—the philosophical, the mercenary, and the ambitious?"

Youngblood Hawke shook his head in acknowledgment, listening intently as the sage enlightened him.

"Potentiality of only one of the three parts would not have allowed you to be who you are at this moment," the eldest sage added.

The middle sage once again interjected, *"If you were mercenary alone would you not only be concerned with making money, finding no profit in ambition or the pursuit of knowledge? Such a man does not value education and in fact dismisses it as useless. And the ambitious person does he not find it vulgar to find pleasure in money alone? Then again, he would also find the pursuit of knowledge as an impractical waste of time. Wouldn't he? And what of the devoted philosopher? Does he not find enjoyment strictly in the use of his intellect and seeking to know the truth of things? Is it not his evaluation of all the facts of experience that will allow him to make intelligent decisions? However, when this part is all he possesses, does he not tend to experience paralysis when it is time to make a practical decision, requiring action? Considering what we have explored would not a philosopher who has experience in mercenary and ambitious endeavors only render him better suited to seek and ultimately find the truth?"*[16]

Youngblood Hawke stood in acknowledgment and replied, "Yes, teacher, a balance of the three parts would appear to make one better suited to seek the truth."

The young warrior remained silent as the three sages engaged in a whispered discussion until finally the eldest spoke, "The world is large and filled with experience far beyond what you believe the world to be."

With less enthusiasm for success the youngest added, "You must open your mind to other possibilities and experiences beyond what you currently believe to be true. Face the fears and beasts that pursue you. Only then will you understand them."

The young warrior was unnerved by the sage's reference to the beasts but listened intently as the eldest commanded, "You must now depart here and proceed directly to the cave."

"What cave do you speak of?" he asked.

"My cave,"[17] the middle sage interjected. "A cave of eternal darkness."

The three sages nodded in acknowledgment, and as the young warrior turned to exit the chamber, the middle sage left him with a final proclamation, "Remember this young warrior and it will guide you during your search—*thinking is the intermediate state between believing and knowing.*[18] Fail to think, Youngblood Hawke, and your mind will close, entombing you in the cave of darkness for an eternity."

Armed with the wisdom and the warnings rendered unto him by the three sages, Youngblood departed the Temple Triangle wondering what awaited him in the cave to which he had been directed. Was it some kind of trial or test? Did the cave contain the truth? Youngblood Hawke—"philosopher, soldier of fortune, and professional adventurer"—would soon enter a cave of discovery and knowledge, or quite possibly, a cave of great danger and peril.

As he departed the temple grounds he directed a question to his trusted friend, "Veritas, do you suppose that this cave harbors the beasts described by the mysterious sage?"

Veritas continued on as Youngblood glanced back at the temple, knowing that he would soon return to this place. At least it was his hope that he would return. For he truly did not know what beasts awaited him in the cave of darkness. He could only wonder…

The Path of the Damned

Tragically inflicted with the desire to understand,
The questions of life, the very meaning of existence,
Asking what is the profound purpose of destiny's plan?
Surely such a question is the reflection of ignorance.

So frail and pathetic is this creature we call man,
Yet gifted with the power of a creative intelligence,
Faithfully searching for truth and all it commands,
Confronted by legions of opposition and resistance.

Burdened by so many perilous and earthly demands,
A servant of nature, forever subject to its influence,
So naïve and idealistic, heroically taking a stand,
Encumbered by a soul and guided by a conscience.

This poor being travels the path of the damned,
Led hopelessly astray by fate's cruel indifference.

—*Youngblood Hawke*

CHAPTER 4

The Cave of Darkness

Haunted by the desire to understand,
Freed from the shackles of the mass man.

Youngblood Hawke's brushes with danger had been many, but they had always assumed human form or that of an animal beast. This engagement was subjecting the young warrior to great anxiety for he was unaware of the nature of the combatant that awaited him. Would his sword be quick enough, his cunning sufficient? As he continued along the primitive road into the mountains, his mind settled into more comfortable thoughts. Many months had passed since his last visit to the "Noble House." It was a house marked with tradition, virtue, and simplicity by its occupants. He was not one of them, but had been accepted as such. Youngblood Hawke did not belong to any one place and the concept of "home" was somewhat foreign to him. However, if he were to call anywhere his "home," it would be within the Noble House. It was without question a place where he could lay to rest his sword and find relative solitude. They did not understand his code of honor or the necessity of his mission. Therefore, the Noble House provided little support and minor opposition in respect to his endeavors. His time amongst them was unsophisticated and comfortable. They did not require or demand that he fulfill his role as "philosopher, soldier of fortune, and professional adventure." In this place he was often able to find refuge from the many storms that littered his life. He had hoped to return soon, but his quest demanded his immediate attention, and he could not even begin to think of such respite. His thoughts soon returned to his destination as the cry of a hawk soaring above him broke his concentration and delivered his attention to the task at hand.

The mountain pass was becoming very narrow and steep as the horse and rider slowly and cautiously made their way upward in search of the cave. Youngblood was now fully aware that although he did not know the path to his destination, Veritas appeared to know exactly where he was going.

"Well, my good friend, it would appear that someone has given you directions to ensure I reach my destination," Youngblood said.

Veritas continued up the path, intent on successfully completing his own mission. The hour of twilight had arrived and upon reaching a plateau, our two, weary travelers came upon a small village. The villagers appeared to be hard at work preparing dinner and finishing the day's tasks as they paid little attention to the visitor. He followed the road into the town, passing a variety of interesting carvings and statues of man and animal. Obviously the stock and trade of the town, as the artisans carried them about with pride. Adjacent to a very busy section of the road was a small wall partitioning the village from a cave. The cave entrance was surprisingly small and was barely visible, as it was overgrown with weeds and vines. The villagers appeared to dismiss its existence. Veritas led the young warrior to the threshold of its entrance. Staring at the less than inviting portal to the unknown, Youngblood let out a sigh, acknowledging his anxiety.

He looked at Veritas and said, "Be it man or beast that awaits me, my friend?" He dismounted Veritas, checking the arrangement of his weaponry and prepared for what was soon to befall him.

As he penetrated the cave his instincts called out in warning to him that he was entering an abyss comprised of great danger. The mystical "sixth sense" that served Youngblood Hawke so well predicted that an enormous creature lurked in the darkness. The cave was cold and damp, with the only sounds being that of dripping water. The muffled sound of the wind could barely be heard blowing through its corridors. Visibility was limited and allowed the young warrior to see little other than the exaggerated shadows reflected from the flickering light of a fire burning further ahead.

Descending into its depths, he became aware of everything around him and was ready to strike when the need presented itself. Suddenly, an ominous sound joined the symphonic harmony of the wind as a disturbing figure appeared in the form of a shadow. It appeared to be approaching from all sides, revealing itself to all of the warrior's acute senses. Youngblood's immediate thought was to extend the business end of his sword, but he could not. Somehow the beast had rendered him spellbound. He could not move and was subject to a state of frozen inaction and indecision. It was as if the beast wanted his prey to contemplate his eternal fate before he struck. It was then that the beast revealed itself, cloaked by shadows and darkness. It was colossal, enveloping everything within its reach including our now helpless warrior. The beast towered over Youngblood Hawke, mocking him and exploiting his mortality. Somehow the beast had gained access to his mind and began to enter his bloodstream.

The defenseless warrior began to tremble from the blinding effects of this powerful creature. Then, without warning, the beast struck the warrior with a devastating blow! It was an inhuman blast the likes of which he had never experienced before in battle. The pounding against his body rang through his very essence, propelling him into the rigid wall of the cave. He landed on the cold, barren floor, disoriented and subject to the whims of his tormentor.

The mysterious sage had warned of such a beast, but the warrior's arrogance veiled the magnitude of the prophecy. Lying on the floor of the cavern, Youngblood was blinded, powerless, and very much alone. The powerful beast crippled the warrior, pinning him to the floor.

He braced himself, believing and knowing that he had met his eternal fate and was now the prisoner of this powerful creature.

The Beast

What is it that pulls me?
Forever dragging me down,
The power of gravity,
Bringing me to the ground.

Struggling against its power,
Fighting day after day,
More difficult by the hour,
Impossible to break away.

This mighty beast lives inside,
Against it I have no chance,

From this monster I can't hide,

For it is my own ignorance.

—Youngblood Hawke

Suddenly the words of the ancient one rang in his head, "*'Thinking is the intermediate state between believing and knowing.'*[19] Fail to think, Youngblood Hawke, and your mind will close, entombing you in the cave for an eternity."

Inspired by those words, the young warrior opened his eyes wide. He lifted himself from the floor and turned to face the mighty beast. He willed the release of the beast's grasp from his mind and body as the spirit of Youngblood Hawke returned, diminishing the creature's power and hold.

"Expose yourself, beast!" the young warrior demanded, extracting both of his swords from their scabbards. Standing defiantly before the creature, Youngblood cried out, "You are an illusion and I refuse to be your prisoner!" The beast appeared to withdraw as our warrior advanced and declared, "I will make it my life's mission to expose you to the light, where you will be rendered powerless!" Then like a bolt of lightning, Youngblood leaped at the beast in a flurry of steel and fire as he screamed the battle cry, "*Mandamus Veritas!*"

The combat raged on for several hours as the young warrior stood his ground against the powerful beast. His swords clashing against the sharp claws of the beast threw sparks throughout the cave. The beast recoiled from the unyielding blows and attempted a futile counterattack. But the warrior's assault was relentless. It was not long before the beast realized that retreating into the darkness of the cave was its only chance of survival. But Youngblood Hawke pursued the creature with the intensity of a comet propelled through the heavens.

However, the cave was deep, and unlike the creature he pursued, Youngblood was unfamiliar with its many passages. The creature withdrew and disappeared into its depths. Youngblood Hawke stood victorious but conscious of the fact that he remained within the beast's domain. He was also very much aware that although he had defeated this creature today, it was by no means dead. This fight was long from over.

Standing within the passage of the cave he heard the sound of human voices. He cautiously followed the faint whispers, arriving in a large cavern inhabited by scores of people. They were bound and tied about their legs, arms, and necks in a manner that kept them in one place and allowed them to look only straight ahead. They were unable to see themselves or those around them. Youngblood Hawke was both shocked and appalled by the site. He could not believe his eyes.

The Fate of Mankind

A fate worse than death?
>Life, some would say.
Better to die young,
>Than to die of old age.

Some will burn brightly,
>While others fade away.
A few achieve greatness,
>But most will just obey.

A truth will be revealed,
>Without further delay.
The promise of tomorrow,
>Yet, a reflection of today.

The weakness of mortality,
>Humanity runs astray.
An undetermined destiny,
>Forced to live day to day.

—*Youngblood Hawke*

Prisoners of the beast, he thought to himself, as he entered the cavern. He approached one of the older prisoners and said, "Don't be afraid. I will free you; I will free all of you and lead you out of this cave."

In a surprisingly contemptuous tone the man responded, "Leave me alone, you fool!"

Youngblood Hawke was taken by surprise, "Do you not wish to be free?"

"Free from what?" the old man asked.

The young warrior gazed upon the old man in puzzlement and said, "From the beast, of course."

The old man laughed asking, "What beast do you speak of?"

"Why, the beast that holds all of you prisoner," he replied.

The old man looked upon the warrior in bewilderment, "Prisoners? We are not prisoners. What you erroneously describe as a 'beast' is in fact our protector."

"Protector from what?" the now confused Youngblood Hawke cried out.

The old man looked at the warrior piously and said, "Why, from the evil creatures and true beasts that live outside the cave, my naïve boy. We have been here since childhood and have watched their shadows as they pass our protected sanctuary."

"Sir, they are not evil creatures, nor are they beasts. In fact, they are just like you but they live in the light and enjoy the fruits of freedom, experience, and creativity. They are not bound and chained like a slave. No sir, the beast does not control them the way it has imprisoned you," Youngblood Hawke responded.

The old man looked upon the warrior with disdain and said, "You are a fool and must represent evil. Perhaps you come here as a demon and attempt to lure us to your underworld."

"But, sir, I only mean to help you," the warrior plead.

"We know of your world. It is a world where no boundaries are in place providing safety and security for our benefit and protection. It is a place where we will be condemned to an eternity of risk, responsibility, misery, and pain. Now go and leave us alone!" he demanded.

Youngblood Hawke walked among the others and asked, "Does anyone wish to follow me?"

The cavern echoed with the response, "No! No! No!"

Youngblood Hawke stood in amazement that they were all refusing his assistance and the benefit of his wisdom.

"Does not one of you have the courage to explore what awaits you beyond this cave?" the warrior asked.

The cavern remained silent with the exception of one voice announcing, "I will follow you, warrior."

He followed the sound of the voice and found very youthful and bright eyes staring at him in a state of wonderment and admiration.

"Do you wish to seek the truth, young one?" he asked.

The child smiled and looked up at the liberator asking, "Are there others like you, warrior?"

Youngblood gazed down upon the child as he removed the chains and said, "We are many."

Youngblood Hawke exited the cave followed by the young child who, at this point, remained very close to the armed warrior. As the light of the outside world became nearer, the child's face lit with excitement and apprehension. Upon exiting the cave, the child ran in circles and jumped up and down, feeling the warm sunlight of a new day. Tugging at the warrior's cloak, the child thanked him. Youngblood Hawke placed his hand upon the child's head and smiled. Just then a group of children ran past them, playing and laughing in amusement. The child looked at them and then returned a questioning glance to the warrior.

Youngblood nodded his head in the direction of the other children and said, "Go ahead, young one. The world is now yours to experience."

On those words the child, filled with anticipation and a newfound desire to understand, ran after the other children. Youngblood Hawke walked over to the waiting Veritas and rewarded him with a cube of sugar from his cloak, "Hello, old friend. I almost didn't make it out of there."

As he made his way down the mountain pass he thought of the child and wondered what would become of those who chose to remain a prisoner of the beast.

The Mass Man

He is the ultimate fool,
    Following all the rules,
That others have set for him.

He will always obey,
    Without further delay,
Avoiding any hint of sin.

He renders no resistance,
    Content with his existence,
Unaware of a future so dim.

He needs no goal or plan,
    No, not the mass man,
Knowing he can never win.

—*Youngblood Hawke*

A beast that would not soon forget or forgive Youngblood Hawke for what he had done on this day.[20]

CHAPTER 5

Reflections

Responsibilities abound, problems profound,
More and more aware of my own mortality.

Youngblood Hawke's return to the Temple Triangle was victorious, but there was no parade or celebratory festivities to honor his triumphant return. He entered the solemn halls of the temple and proceeded to the chamber occupied by the three ancient sages. Once again he found himself standing in the center of the triangular mosaic. The chamber was dark, with only his position illuminated. Youngblood could hear the faint whisper of the sages as they spoke amongst themselves, rudely ignoring the presence of the young warrior.

"Did you find what you were looking for?" the middle sage asked.

"I found experience, and through experience I found knowledge," he responded.

"It would appear that the young one is capable of learning," the youngest and characteristically irritable sage said.

"Did you defeat the beast?" the eldest asked.

"Yes," declared Youngblood, "but it continues to live, and I suspect it will seek revenge."

"That beast will pursue you forever and you will continuously do battle with it," the elder declared.

Youngblood Hawke did not doubt that last statement.

"You were victorious because you remained true to yourself and your convictions," related the middle sage. He continued, "Take advantage of your potentiality and it will guide you on your quest."

Youngblood looked upon the sage and responded, "I understand, teacher, but I have been criticized by many for what I am, or as you stated, what they perceive me to be."

"Very good," the elder responded, "*people who are quick at learning, have good memories, and are astute and smart and so on, tend—as you know—not to combine both energy and broadness of mental vision with the ability to live an orderly, peaceful, and stable life. Instead, their quickness carries them this way and that, and stability plays no part at all in their lives,*' [21] therefore, such people tend to be misunderstood by the masses."

Youngblood listened intently and replied with his trademark smirk. "Sounds like a recipe for a philosopher, soldier of fortune, and professional adventurer."

"So it does," the middle sage acknowledged.

"*On the other hand, a sound and stable character, which makes people more dependable and slow to respond to frightening situations in battle, also makes them approach their studies in the same way,*"[22] the eldest added, as the younger sage studied the young warrior.

"This would appear to be true," Youngblood replied.

"*Then it would appear to be clear that a good and sufficient helping of both sets of qualities is a prerequisite for anyone*'[23] to be allowed such a title as 'philosopher, soldier of fortune, and professional adventurer,' would it not?" the middle sage interjected.

Youngblood shook his head in acknowledgment and reflected upon his own life.

The youngest sage gazed upon the warrior and said, "These lessons must be considered when confronting a crossroad. You will encounter many choices, and failure to act may endanger, if not destroy, your quest."

Youngblood continued to listen to the sage as he lectured him, "*We choose what we know very well to be good, but we form opinions about things that we do not really know to be good. It seems that people are not equally good at choosing the best actions and forming the best opinions; some are comparatively good at forming opinions, but through a moral defect fail to make the right choices.*"[24]

"In other words, think before I choose?" the warrior asked.

"Yes, but do not think too long or you will be subject to paralysis, and your choices will be fewer," the middle sage said.

The young warrior knew this all too well and had been forced to make instinctive decisions without the luxury of deep thought on many a battlefield.

The younger sage interrupted the warrior's thoughts and said, "*Decisions may be made instantly in battle but 'we call actions done on the spur of the moment voluntary, but not the result of choice,*'[25] young warrior."

"Yes, but how do I know I have made the right choice?" Youngblood asked.

The sage looked upon his focused student and declared, "*The man of good character judges every situation rightly; i.e. in every situation what appears to him is the truth.*"[26]

Youngblood Hawke could not help but notice that the sage used the word "appears" and not the word "is" in his last statement.

"But you did not answer my question, teacher," the frustrated warrior responded.

"The question may be the answer," the elder sage replied.

"Riddle after riddle! I just want the truth!" Youngblood reacted in frustration.

"You seek truth. Is it not a riddle?" the middle sage asked. "The truth you seek is absolute?"

"Yes, but to the world truth is relative; it is only a matter of opinion," the young warrior responded.

"You mean that truth is subjective opinion?" the elder asked.

"Exactly, according to the majority doctrine, what is true for you is true for you and what is true for me, is true for me. Truth is subjective," Youngblood countered.

"Do they really believe that? That my opinion is true by virtue of it being my opinion?" the puzzled middle sage interjected.

"Indeed, they do," the young warrior replied with confidence.

"Well then, my opinion is this: *Truth is absolute, not opinion, and that the majority doctrine is absolutely in error! Since this is my opinion, then they must grant that it is true according to their philosophy,*"[27] the eldest sage proclaimed with a certain degree of enjoyment.

"A paradox," Youngblood noted.

"Consider for a moment that we have in our possession an instrument that is capable of detecting the absolute truth," the middle sage said. "Also accept for this argument that the instrument in question is infallible," he added. "We will examine two individual subjects, utilizing the instrument and ask them each the same question," he continued. "Now, the individuals are very similar but they are very different in one significant way. One of the individuals is a very religious man with a strong belief in God. The other is an atheist who knows that God does not exist." The sage paused for a moment to ensure his young student and two colleagues were following along. "I ask the religious man, 'Is there a God?' He replies, 'Yes,' and the instrument confirms he is speaking the truth. I ask the atheist, 'Is there a God? He replies, 'No,' yet the instrument confirms that he also speaks the truth. I ask you, if truth is absolute how can they both be speaking the truth?"

The other sages stood silently in thought as Youngblood Hawke shared his thoughts, "Obviously, the human condition views the concept of truth in subjective terms. Your example examines truth only from the subjective human perspective. It does not address the fact that only one of the individuals is ultimately speaking the truth. In the final analysis, the existence or non-existence of God surely must be an absolute?"

"Perhaps," responded the younger sage, "but will either of the individuals gain the answer to the question while afflicted with the human condition?"

"Absolutely!" the elder sage exclaimed with a chuckle that clearly annoyed the younger sage. "What is the human condition? Life and then death, is it not?" he added.

"I understand, wise one, but is not your philosophy of absolute nothing more than an opinion and therefore, subjective?" Youngblood asked, as he stood, enjoying the banter.

Displaying a look of irritation, the younger sage interrupted, "He leads you in a ridiculous circle of never-ending puzzlement."

"*Thinking is the intermediate state between believing and knowing,*"[28] the elder interjected with a laugh, suggesting he was quite amused with himself.

However, those words immediately brought a chill to the young warrior and delivered him momentarily to the cold floor of the cave before responding, "I understand. Develop the proper questions and they may lead to the answers, or may in themselves be the answer."

The three sages shook their heads in approval. "Be aware of the choices that will confront you on your journey. Remember, '*virtue lies in our power, and similarly so does vice; because where it is in our power to act, it is also in our power not to act, and where we can refuse we can also comply. So if it is in our power to do a thing when it is right, it will also be in our power not to do it when it is wrong.*'[29] Do you understand?"

The young warrior shook his head in the affirmative and replied, "Yes, teacher, I think that I do."

The eldest sage looked upon his worthy student and said, "Your studies have just begun and will continue on your journey."

Youngblood bowed his head, "I understand, teacher."

"You do appear to desire to understand," replied the younger sage. "Now answer this question for me, warrior: Who are you?"

Youngblood pondered the question for a moment and then answered, "I am many things to many people. I am who I choose to be, and who others perceive me to be. I am an illusion, a mere shadow of reality, defining myself by thought and action."

"This question does not puzzle you any longer?" the sages asked.

Youngblood looked at the three sages with confidence and declared, "I know where I am, what I am, and who I am, but why I am remains a riddle!"

The three sages approvingly nodded to each other and then dismissed the young warrior from the chamber, followed by the final words of the middle sage, "You will now ride with those who came before you—those who succeeded, those who did not. You will learn by example the lessons of decision and indecision. Now go and seek the Oracle for guidance," the younger sage commanded, extending his arm toward the door.

As Youngblood departed, he found amusement in the fact that the three sages continued to argue amongst themselves. He also noticed that the eldest and oddest one always seemed to annoy the youngest, and appeared to enjoy it immensely.

The words and advice of the three sages weighed heavily upon Youngblood Hawke as he continued his journey. His mind wandered in an attempt to find the answers leading to the meaning of his quest.

The Riddle

I know where I am, what I am,
And am fully aware of who I am,
Yet, why I am remains a riddle.

This is my puzzle, my own mystery,
Pursuing the question of my destiny,
The answer hidden by the hand of fate.

Forever searching, the ultimate test,
Day and night, leaving no time for rest,
I must find the answer, before it's too late.

Time is my enemy, obstructing my path,
A reminder, I will fall victim to its wrath,
Such is the dilemma, the nature of my quest.

—*Youngblood Hawke*

CHAPTER 6

The Encounter

So beautiful, surely an angel is she,
Sapphire eyes calling out to me.

The very sight of the City of Ventura was a welcomed one. A hearty meal and a good night's rest were in order for the weary warrior. Twilight had arrived and the city's lights illuminated the horizon. Youngblood Hawke found pleasure in the twilight, for in his mind, it reflected the world as it truly was—vague and mystically plagued by shadows and illusions. He entered the city by way of the north gate, bringing him through the Market Square.

The market was crowded with merchants and patrons engaged in the daily exchange and trade of commerce. Ventura was a city that did not sleep. In fact, Youngblood could barely remember being in the city and finding the streets peaceful. The crowd was moving along in one large mass, moving only for carts and men on horseback. It was then that he glanced into the crowd and made eye contact with her.

Sapphires, he thought to himself, as her eyes mesmerized the young warrior.

He was immediately enchanted by the degree of quiet strength and innocence she projected, as she moved through the crowd with an unmitigated degree of grace.

A Vision of Beauty

Look into my eyes, what do you see?
Determination, ambition, and potentiality.
A man with a quest, a future to unfold.

Look into my soul, what do you see?
Loneliness, despair, a desire to be free.
A solitary spirit, lost and out of control.

Look into my heart, what do you see?
Desire, passion, romance, and fantasy.
A lover in waiting, one to behold.

Now I turn to you, what do I see?
Clarity and truth, a vision of beauty.
An image of true love and my destiny.

—*Youngblood Hawke*

He continued to watch this apparition as she was soon engulfed by the massive crowd and disappeared from his sight. Youngblood Hawke shook off the encounter and continued on his journey through the crowded market.

As he made his way through the masses he suddenly found himself crossing paths with the old man and his ragged horse again.

"So we meet again, old man!" the warrior announced. "Shopping? I would suggest you get yourself another cart and perhaps a stronger horse if you wish to add to that collection of baggage you carry," he added with a smirk.

"You travel light, young one, but your cart fills as we speak," the old man responded.

Youngblood was fascinated by the old man and was never quite sure what he was talking about. "Do you know of the Oracle spoken of by the ancient ones?" he asked.

"Very well, very well, indeed," he replied with a surprising smirk.

Looking down upon the old man from Veritas, Youngblood continued, "Tell me, where might I find this Oracle?"

"The Oracle will find you, and you will find the Oracle as the need arises," the old man said, retaining the smirk.

Youngblood shook his head and laughed, "Just what I needed, more riddles!"

"Be alert, young one," the old man advised, as he led his cart in the opposite direction.

"Old man! What do you carry in that cart within all that baggage?" he asked.

"My life!" he responded. "And it is becoming heavier by the day!"

The old man waved as he disappeared into the crowded market. Youngblood Hawke continued on his way, pondering the old man's warning.

The twilight was now gone and had been replaced by darkness. Turning onto a side road, he continued through the city. The road was very narrow, allowing the two men on horseback to block the path of the warrior with ease. At first Youngblood thought they may just be two acquaintances stopping to talk in the night. But as he approached, he was able to see that they were facing him and not each other. Youngblood stopped about ten feet from the men and remained silent. He was hoping that his instincts were wrong, and they would just let him pass.

The exercise in silence was broken by one of the men, "You are the one they call Youngblood Hawke?" His hand was on his sword.

"I am," Youngblood responded sternly.

Without warning the men pulled back the reins of their horses and charged Youngblood, "Your quest is over!" they screamed.

Veritas reacted immediately and charged between the attackers. Youngblood's katana met the larger man's sword with a clash and spark that exploded in the dark alley. Simultaneously he discharged his battle sword from its scabbard and swung it horizontally, striking the smaller man's midsection. The second attacker was immediately thrown from his horse as he howled in anguish. The larger man continued his assault as the clash of steel on steel ignited the darkness. Youngblood's attacker was powerful and he could not help but notice the crimson color of his eyes as they exchanged blows. Surely, this dark warrior would defeat many an opponent with his battle face alone! But Youngblood Hawke was no stranger to battle, and the dark warrior was fully aware of it.

The combat between the two fierce warriors continued as blood began to stain the swords and spill to the ground. Youngblood's speed met every powerful blow released by his attacker with two counter-strikes. The dark warrior was relentless, using his brute strength to enhance his advance. Youngblood responded with a combination of fast and graceful countermoves designed to throw his attacker off balance. The sound of the two warriors echoed through the city like thunderbolts from the gods! It was almost mystical in contrast to the deafening silence between the warriors now engaged in mortal combat.

"Your last moment is near, Youngblood Hawke!" the dark warrior cried out. "The body begins to fail you, young one!" he added while delivering a blow that hurled the young warrior to the ground.

Youngblood immediately regained composure and spun around clockwise, leading his attack with his katana. The dark warrior blocked the strike with his sword but was unable to counter the fatal blow of the young warrior's battle sword that immediately followed.

"Strength of mind my friend…it never fails me," Youngblood Hawke advised, as he stared into the dark warrior's eyes.

The dark warrior slowly slipped into the *sleep of death*.[30] Youngblood Hawke removed his bloodied battle sword from the dark warrior and watched him fall to the ground. The dark and cold crimson eyes had now been extinguished forever. *Assassins*, Youngblood thought to himself, wondering what price had been placed on his head this time and by whom? The list of enemies appeared to be growing by the day.

❦   ❦   ❦

Horatio Cantrell's home was located in a neighborhood of wealth. His was not the most expensive villa, but it was both luxurious and comfortable. A servant met Youngblood at the door and guided him into the foyer.

"Master, a Mr. Youngblood Hawke is here to see you," he announced.

"Well, don't keep him waiting!" shouted the master of the house. Horatio entered the foyer and stood with his hands in the air and jokingly said, "So, you didn't get yourself killed, I see."

His face became more serious as he noticed the blood covering his young friend.

"Not this time, my old friend," he said.

"What in the name of Hades happened to you?" Horatio asked.

Dismissing his appearance as nothing important, Youngblood replied, "It's a long story, my friend, and I am very tired."

After ordering a servant to tend to Youngblood's wounds, Horatio approached his young friend and slapped him on the back and said, "It is good to see you again. They will attend to you and you will be my guest tonight."

"For a short while, I suppose," Youngblood answered.

Horatio stood shaking his head with a smile. "Always in a hurry with something to do and someone to see. You will never change, my friend."

Horatio spared no expense on the night's festivities as the night progressed with entertainment, a feast fit for a king, and a never-ending flow of fine wine. Youngblood was enjoying the evening but his mind continually wandered as he wondered when he would encounter the Oracle. His mind also entertained thoughts of the beautiful woman with the sapphire eyes.

"My sources tell me that a band of men were asking questions about you," Horatio said, breaking Youngblood's train of thought.

"What men?" he asked.

"I am told they numbered a dozen or more." Horatio continued to work on the roasted lamb on his plate. "They must want you badly enough for they are spreading plenty of silver to gain the information they desire. Do you know who they are?"

"Well, I now know who the two were," he replied. Youngblood lifted his chalice and emptied its contents, and with his trademark smirk responded, "Former disgruntled employers or assassins, I would guess!"

Horatio assumed he was speaking of his obvious conflict earlier that evening.

He placed his hand on his young friend's shoulder and advised, "Be careful, my friend…you have made many enemies over the years."

"And I shall make many more before my quest is complete," he replied.

"Surely you do not seek to make enemies?" Horatio asked.

Youngblood continued to watch the entertainment and replied, "I seek only one thing…and that alone will create enemies. For that which I am to expose is protected by a powerful beast. This is a mighty beast with many loyal and devoted followers. Followers who will stop at nothing to protect this beast and the world it rules."

Horatio admired his young friend, but sometimes believed that he created an unnecessarily complicated world for himself.

"It sounds to me like you are ill-equipped for this fight, my friend. I would suggest that you begin raising an army to join you on the field of battle!" jokingly replied Horatio as his chalice of wine was replenished.

Youngblood Hawke was struck by his friend's last words and with a laugh replied, "Perhaps that is exactly what I need?"

The two men continued to enjoy the evening as they talked of old times and old friends. Following the festivities, Youngblood retired into Horatio's library to enjoy the rare luxury of a fine cigar and vintage cognac. He was afforded one of those rare tranquil moments alone and protected as he fell asleep reading a very appropriate classic titled the *Odyssey*.[31] He dreamed much that evening as the alternative universe of sleep captured his imagination and fears. But Youngblood Hawke would soon awaken to the reality of a new day.

Time Alone

Peaceful, reflective, and surreal,
A silence that surely can't be real,
Quietly we sit, we think, and stare.

Such a time is needed to heal,
Our own thoughts—how we feel,
Reminding us why we still care.

These moments we tend to conceal,
For it is often the truth they reveal,
Accept such moments if you dare.

—Youngblood Hawke

CHAPTER 7

The Oracle

Overcome suddenly, by a sapphire sea.
Tossed and thrashed about deaf to my pleas,
Lost in a storm of wonder and mystery.

Youngblood took advantage of Horatio's hospitality, finding a comfortable night's rest in his old friend's library. He was very comfortable among the shelves of books and papers, as well as Horatio's collection of military artifacts. Perhaps it was because he was, in many ways, surrounded by knowledge. His dreams were vivid throughout the night as he slipped in and out of the past and potential future. His thoughts while in slumber delivered him to the Noble House, where he found tranquility, to the mysterious sage, and to the chamber of the three ancients. However, his mind was clear of the beast, of the cave, and of the dark warrior with the crimson eyes. For better or for worse, the young warrior had learned long ago to bury such memories deep within his mind, where dreams did not dare to go. His dream was just delivering him to the one with the sapphire eyes when a banging on the door abruptly awakened him.

"Mr. Hawke? Mr. Hawke? Are you awake, sir?" the servant asked, as he banged on the door.

"I am now, my good man!" he replied. "What is it?"

With a sense of urgency the servant entered, "Sir, a dispatch has arrived for you by royal courier and the master insisted I deliver it to you immediately."

"Bring it here," Youngblood declared as he stood and stretched the sleep from his sore and tired body.

The servant stood patiently, studying with amazement the extensive number of scars and residuals of battle the young warrior had sustained. Youngblood examined the correspondence and immediately recognized its seal. It was a royal correspondence from the Northern Kingdom. He read the dispatch, requesting his services on behalf of the prince. It would appear that Youngblood Hawke's services were needed as a royal bodyguard. *Assassins all around us*, he thought to himself. Acknowledging the fact that his "mercenary" side was in need of nourishment, he responded to the dispatch in the affirmative, and accepted the assignment.

"Well…it would appear that my quest will have to wait a bit," he announced aloud to the servant, who only nodded his head.

The servant darted from the room as Youngblood donned a clean set of clothes and set out to find breakfast. For at the moment it was not the "truth" that called him but, in fact, it was the bellowing of his stomach that cried out.

"I hear there is great trouble in the Northern Kingdom," Horatio said as Youngblood strapped the saddle to Veritas and prepared him for the long journey.

"Of course there is trouble. If there was not, I would not be going," Youngblood replied, laughing sarcastically.

"All kidding aside, my friend, the king is dead and his brother seeks the throne, as well as the queen, from what I understand," responded Horatio with one eyebrow raised. "The young prince may need more than a bodyguard to escape the web of deceit woven by his uncle," he added.

"While under my charge, I am only concerned with his personal protection…not the future of his throne," Youngblood declared. "The royal treasury would be emptied to meet my fee for such a task!" he laughed.

Both men began to laugh as they shook hands and Horatio watched his young friend once again begin another adventure. He observed his determined comrade ride off into the morning. He longed to join him and once again experience the thrill he had experienced as a warrior, but long ago abandoned.

The Reluctant Adventurer

The distant horizon tempts me,
Forever calling out my name,

Gazing out—What do I see?
The allure of fortune and fame.

So far away it appears to be,
A promise of another life,
The spirit desiring to be free,
Dismissing all pain and strife.

A ship suddenly drops from view,
Falling from the edge of reality,
Traveling from the old to the new,
Following the stars seeking destiny.

A ship and crew seek a heroic tale,
Now traveling a course set by fate,
The winds of change fill their sail,
As an unknown future lies in wait.

How I wish to be one of the crew,
Pursuing adventure and mystery,
A journey reserved for a select few,
Such courageous souls—so unlike me.

—Youngblood Hawke

The market was even busier during the morning than in the afternoon. In fact, Youngblood thought that the entire city of Ventura must have decided to shop in the market on this morning. He made his way through the crowded square, understanding clearly why Ventura's economy was the envy of the continent. He noticed the bright colors of the fruits and vegetables and decided he would stock up for his journey. He dismounted Veritas and led him through the bustling crowd. Just as he arrived at the vegetable stand, he turned and found himself face to face with the sapphire eyes.

She is absolutely beautiful, he thought to himself. He was just about to say something, when suddenly he became spellbound and fell deep into the sparkling sapphire eyes, as they illuminated everything around him. He was transported to another dimension as the crowded market was replaced by a radiant assortment of shining blue lights, extending out from the apparition before

him. Silk vestments replaced her worn and colorless smock, and she appeared
to hover before him.

"Beauty, truth, and rarity. Grace in all simplicity,"[32] he murmured to himself,
as he gazed upon the brilliance before him.

She gazed back at him, revealing the most radiant smile he had ever
encountered. The warmth and allure of the sapphire glow shattered the ice
encasing the warrior's cold heart. She rendered him defenseless with her powers, but he experienced no fear. His experience was that of calm, a certain peace
of mind, spirit, and body that was very foreign to him. He had never experienced such feelings before, and they overpowered him.

"Who are you?" Youngblood Hawke asked.

In a placid voice she spoke, "I am your guide."

"Where and what is this place?" he continued.

"An alternative reality…another dimension, if you will," she replied.

Youngblood remained silent, mesmerized by her beauty, and then asked,
"Are you the Oracle that the ancient ones spoke of?"

Her smile grew, providing Youngblood Hawke his answer.

"Does my quest bring me to you?" he asked.

"Yes, it does, warrior," she responded. "Clarity and understanding combined with patience and decisiveness will be your lesson," she added. "You
must understand the contrast and the perils."

"Yet another riddle?" the warrior asked as he stared into the depths of her
eyes.

"Your teacher awaits you. His army marches east where he will be confronted with his riddle, and you quite possibly, the answer to your own," she
said.

"But why must I answer this riddle when my quest awaits me?" Youngblood
asked.

"Your quest may very well be a riddle," she said.

"Nothing is that simple."

"You tend to complicate things beyond necessity, warrior," the Oracle
noted.

"My life is not a simple endeavor," he responded.

"Why do you treat the word simple with contempt?" she asked.

Youngblood shook his head but did not reply.

"Simple is not always a terrible thing," the Oracle advised.

"Grace in all simplicity," he whispered as he gazed upon the Oracle. "But what of my duty to the prince?" Youngblood asked. "I must see to my charge first."

"No time will pass disrupting your service to the prince," she said. "We will transcend time and space, and I will deliver you to the 'Great One.' You will stand beside him and will learn from his example," she added with an authoritative air.

The sapphire lights blinded Youngblood and he suddenly found himself among a large contingent of heavily armed soldiers. He recognized the strange land of the Eastern Kingdom immediately, for he had traveled there in his younger days, during a military expedition. As he inspected the soldiers around him, he could not help but notice the antiquated but very well-preserved status of their weaponry. He found it odd and wondered what army he stood amongst. It was then that he first observed the young, confident general surrounded by his loyal officers and soldiers. He was scrutinizing what appeared to be a fairly complicated knot attached to a wagon.

"An odd problem for a general to concern himself with," whispered Youngblood.

A soldier of rank standing beside him heard his comment and responded, "This is not just a problem, warrior. This is the legendary riddle that has baffled all who have stood before it."

Youngblood stood in disbelief at what appeared to be transpiring before him. His extensive reading of historical events had not gone to waste, as he soon realized that the Oracle had delivered him to history itself. A legendary general and leader now stood before him in all his greatness. His presence was almost mystical as Youngblood Hawke stared in awe. He moved closer to see if he could actually feel the energy and power of the great conqueror. Youngblood Hawke moved among the soldiers to gain a better position directly behind the Emperor.

The "Great One" was examining the complicated knot as he pulled out the pole connecting the wagon to the yoke. He carefully inspected the hidden cords of the knot[33] and then stood upright, turning directly into the direction of the young warrior, now standing beside him.

"What do you think?" the young general asked.

Startled, Youngblood Hawke's eyes opened wide as he shook his head and acknowledged, "Quite a complicated-looking puzzle, General."

"Yes, it is," the great leader responded, shaking his head in agreement.

"Yet, I suspect you could readily attend to the matter," added Youngblood. "How do you intend to solve this riddle, General?" Youngblood asked as he also studied the knot with conviction.

"It depends," the general replied.

"Depends upon what, sir?" the beleaguered Youngblood Hawke asked, as he continued to examine the intricacies of the knot.

"It depends on how much time I have to waste fooling around with such a meaningless complication," the Great One said in a tone befitting a true leader.

"Good point," Youngblood replied with a nod and a smile. "Expediency would appear to be a prudent course of action, sir."

With that, the greatest general known to man approached the legendary knot and looked about with all the drama of a man destined to greatness.

He then looked over at Youngblood Hawke and with a wink and a grin declared, "I have no time for such trivial pursuits! We have an empire to build!"

Upon those words, the Great One discharged his sword and raised it high with all the majesty of a great king. He then brought it down and sliced through the knot, fragmenting it into what appeared to be a thousand pieces.

The act sent a shockwave of cheers through the ranks as the soldiers erupted in a manner typical of the warrior class dedicated to a mystical leader. The general turned to Youngblood Hawke in a manner that left the impression that he appreciated the young warrior's counsel. Youngblood bowed his head in a manner deserving of and befitting the general's status. Not to mention his status and position in history, which he was not even aware of.

The general approached the warrior and said, "I could use a lieutenant with your ability. You have a place in my cadre if you desire it."

"I am honored, General, but must respectfully decline," Youngblood replied with all the military bearing he could muster. "I have my own quest to pursue, and your destiny awaits you."

"So it does, warrior," the general acknowledged.

The two warriors shook hands and parted company, choosing different paths but a common goal.

"Warrior! What do they call you?" the general asked as he mounted his horse.

"I am Youngblood Hawke!" he responded with pride.

"Good luck with your quest, Youngblood Hawke!" the general said as he extended the courtesy of a military salute, bringing his fist to his armored breastplate and then extending outward.

Youngblood Hawke returned the acknowledgment. The Great One then turned his stallion toward the east, led his elite military unit to meet the main force of his army, and ultimately toward his destiny. Youngblood Hawke watched in reverence as the legendary leader disappeared over the horizon.

The Great One

Behold the Emperor! He thinks and stares,
Approach and ask, why? No one dares,
It is said that he contemplates our destiny.

A visionary—he remains deep in thought,
Confronting the riddle of the Gordian Knot,
Discharging his solution—defining our fate.

To the east he leads us to final victory,
Conquering all who would be his enemy,
So swift and exact, his dream cannot wait!

Spreading the light of Hellenic ideology,
It is in our blood that he writes his history,
Liberator or tyrant? Better left to debate.

Centuries to come will speak of his name,
Many more will attempt to achieve his fame,
For they too wish to be known as *"The Great!"*

—*Youngblood Hawke*

Youngblood turned back into the crowd of civilians, who were still examining the remains of the knot, and telling stories of how the Great One solved the puzzle. As he made his way through the crowd, he laughed as the story continued to change with each new telling.

History appears to be but a vague reflection of the truth as well, he thought to himself.

Once again the Oracle appeared before him without warning, the sapphire storm set in her eyes as he was immediately swept into the mystical world of illusion and imagery. Her beauty, innocence, and grace literally brought the warrior to his knees. He bowed before her, acknowledging the contrast of his mortal existence to her divine presence.

"What was the point of this lesson?" the Oracle asked.

"That not everything is as complicated as it appears," he replied.

She continued to cast her radiance upon the young warrior and advised, "Truth and simplicity often mingle together. One should take care not to waste time and energy searching for that which does not exist. For complications that are created from nothing only obscure reality and distort the truth."

"Indeed," Youngblood acknowledged.

"Through experience you have once again gained knowledge," she proclaimed.

Youngblood lifted his head slowly and stared deep into the sapphire light and responded, "*From thine eyes my knowledge I derive…. As truth and beauty shall together thrive.*"[34]

Without warning the sapphire storm returned him to his reality.

"Excuse me! I say, old man, do you mind moving aside to allow others through?" announced the older gentleman, as he moved through the crowded market, and past the daydreaming warrior.

Youngblood Hawke stood before the colorful array of fresh fruits and vegetables, realizing that he was no longer with the one he called "Sapphire." He could feel the blood flow from his heart as he released a sigh that revealed a very uncharacteristic hint of despair and loneliness. Youngblood returned to Veritas, who revealed no indication that he was aware his master had been gone for any length of time. As he turned Veritas toward the city gates, he wondered when he would see Sapphire again.

"Well, my friend, I am sure that she will present herself when the need arises," announced Youngblood in a clearly disappointed tone.

CHAPTER 8

A Royal Dilemma

Crisis, scandal, disaster all around,
Turmoil and calamity are the only sounds.

Darkness was just setting in and the glow of the moon was reflecting off the tin roofs as Youngblood rode into the quaint village. He had ridden most of the day en route to his assignment, and he was looking forward to a hearty meal and a good night's rest.

"I say, good man, would you mind providing a little assistance?" the half-dressed gentleman from a nearby balcony requested.

The gentleman was standing with one foot over the balcony, attempting to pull up his trousers, while buttoning up his shirt. He revealed a certain degree of urgency as he continued to look back into the balcony. Suddenly, a woman appeared and exchanged affections with the gentleman, who appeared to be in quite a hurry.

"What appears to be the problem?" Youngblood asked in a puzzled tone.

"I appear to have gotten myself into a bit of a spot, my friend!" he replied with a grin. "Would you mind bringing that fine horse of mine over here within striking distance?" he added.

A loud bang rang from within the house, followed by an equally loud baritone voice demanding, "Where is that scoundrel? I am going to kill him!"

"Well, my dear, I rather suspect that it is time for me to depart and bid you farewell!" the gentleman said as he once again demonstrated his fondness for the young lady.

The grave nature of the situation did not go unnoticed by Youngblood Hawke, as he immediately retrieved the gentleman's horse and positioned himself directly below the balcony. The man threw down his coat and boots, along with his sword. He then rather gracefully leaped from the balcony, barely evading the reach of a very large and angry man, who was now upon the balcony.

"Bring me back that rogue's head!" screamed the man as a group of equally large men exited the tavern below the balcony with their swords drawn.

The men did not appear to be a welcoming committee of any sort, as they ran toward Youngblood and their intended target like a pack of wild and angry dogs.

"I would suggest departing with great haste, my good friend," the gentleman advised, as he continued to dress himself.

With the group of men approaching, Youngblood extended his trademark grin and shook his head in disbelief as he followed the gentleman who was wasting no time in his escape. The impending trouble was clear enough to the adventurous warrior. He swiftly discharged his katana and in one sweep, cut the cords to the tavern's awning, dropping it around his would-be pursuers. The awning fell around the group of men, who had obviously had too many spirits, which only added comedy to the drama. The scene Youngblood Hawke left behind was suitable for any circus or minstrel show.

"Good show, old man!" yelled the gentleman with a loud laugh.

Youngblood Hawke and the man he had delivered from impending death rode out of the village at a gallop and continued down the moonlit road.

"I suspect your pursuers have lost their motivation," Youngblood said.

The gentleman turned and looked back at the empty road, acknowledging Youngblood's observation. "Your evaluation would appear to be accurate."

The two riders slowed down and caught their breath as they continued along the quiet road.

"So much for a fine meal and a good night's rest," Youngblood said in a rather disappointed manner.

"Alas! Fine food and rest are plentiful and available upon demand, my good friend. But the allure of a beautiful young maiden and the excitement of romance are rare, indeed!" the gentleman declared, as he raised his arm in the air with fanciful pomp and flair.

"I wouldn't call the wrath of that young maiden's father excitement. Suicide maybe, but not excitement," Youngblood Hawke laughed.

"Indeed," he responded in acknowledgment. "What is your name, kind sir?" he asked.

"I am Youngblood Hawke," the young warrior said as he continued to look at his traveling companion and shake his head in disbelief.

"And you, sir, what is your name?" Youngblood asked.

"The Honorable Sinclair Fox at your service," the gentleman proclaimed, as he bowed his head and twisted the end of his well-groomed mustache.

His body appeared to have escaped the balcony, but his thoughts had obviously returned to the company of the young maiden as he continued along with the most sinister-looking grin upon his face. The two men continued down the dark roadway, passing only a few lone travelers along the way. The moon was bright and the night air was crisp. It was a perfect night for riding, as well as for compelling and interesting conversation.

"You appear to live a very dangerous existence, my friend," Youngblood noted.

"Dangerous existence? I have often been warned that *one should never look too deeply into the fathomless abyss of existence, lest one become overly enamored of its dark and intoxicating allure. Such is the case with romance as well, is it not?*[35] he responded.

"Your exit from that last abyss was almost canceled," Youngblood said to his incorrigible riding companion.

"Indeed, it was! Ah! To feel alive is such a wonderful thing!" Sinclair said, whose mind had obviously returned to the young maiden.

"Keep up your manner of existence and you may not be alive for much longer," Youngblood advised.

"*Some choose to flee to the safety of anger and hate. But such flight is in vain, love's allure is too great. Surrender your heart fool, love commands your fate,*"[36] Sinclair replied with the passion and harmony of a poet as he stared at the moon's ominous glow.

"You see yourself in a most interesting, and might I add, favorable light," Youngblood responded with a smirk.

"*Man is nothing else but that which he makes of himself,*"[37] Sinclair replied.

"Are you proposing that man has the ability to define himself?" Youngblood asked.

"*I mean that man first of all exists, encounters himself, surges up in the world, and defines himself afterwards,*" Sinclair said with a nod. "*Before the projection of the self nothing exists; therefore man will only attain existence when he is what he purposes to be, not, however, what he may wish to be,"*[38] Sinclair continued with a degree of confidence, suggesting that he had pondered such questions before.

Youngblood Hawke was quite impressed with Sinclair Fox and asked, "So, are you a professional philosopher?"

"You flatter me. I doubt that I have reached such a level of profound thought. It is my desire, but my purpose remains a mystery," Sinclair replied.

"Sir, your purpose and your desire would appear to be compatible bedfellows," responded the insightful warrior.

"A good friend and kindred spirit of mine said it best, *'This above all, to thine own self be true, and it shall follow, as night the day, Thou canst be false to any man,'"*[39] Sinclair Fox replied with great drama.

"Wise words, yet difficult for most men to adhere to," Youngblood responded as he pondered the words.

"*Nothing remains but to trust in our instincts,*"[40] Sinclair continued.

"It appears that you allow your instincts and emotions to guide you, or should I say, misguide you often," Youngblood remarked with a shake of his head.

"*In the end, it is feeling that counts; the direction in which it is really pushing me is the one I ought to choose,*"[41] Sinclair responded confidently.

"Yes, but your emotions may not always lead you to good, but deliver you to that which is bad."

"*Nothing is either good or bad, but thinking makes it so. Thus, conscience doth make cowards of us all,*"[42] Sinclair responded prophetically.

"Your comrade and friend again?" Youngblood asked.

"Why, yes, it is. I would love to claim originality but cannot," Sinclair acknowledged.

"This friend of yours, is he a philosopher as well?" Youngblood asked.

"In a manner of speaking, yes. I suspect that the role of philosopher may be his wish, but he is torn between what he wishes to be, and that which others demand him to be. His purpose is rather puzzling to all, including the young prince. He is a hopeless romantic with an intellect that is plagued by inaction," Sinclair responded. "Although he is masterful with a sword, he is no warrior such as yourself. His heart also yearns for the allure of the abyss."

"Young prince?" Youngblood asked with a heightened degree of curiosity.

"Why, yes. Did I fail to mention that my colleague and friend is the Prince of the Northern Kingdom?" replied Sinclair with an aristocratic air. "In fact, I was on my way to join him, when I myself was distracted by the allure of the abyss in that quaint village," he added with a grin and another twist of his mustache.

"I too have business with the Prince. He has called me into service," Youngblood Hawke replied.

"Well then, it would appear that fate has allowed our paths to cross for a common purpose," Sinclair said.

The two men traveled through the night, resting briefly at a tavern for food and spirits, as well as the hospitality of a very attractive barmaid. Youngblood dispensed of a great deal of energy restraining his incorrigible friend from his instincts, and the "deep allure of the abyss" that seemingly called out to him from every beautiful young maiden.

The new day brought storm clouds, cold drizzling rain, and a chill in the air that penetrated the bones. Youngblood and Sinclair were relieved when they observed the gates to the capitol of the Northern Kingdom. As they approached the main gates to the city, they could not help but notice that the population appeared to be somewhat depressed. Youngblood dismissed the apparent gloom as a result of the equally depressing weather.

"Good morning, sir," Sinclair Fox announced to a passerby.

"What do you find good about this morning?" the older gentleman replied with a scowl.

Youngblood just looked at Sinclair with a raised eyebrow and said, "I guess your charm doesn't work as well this early in the morning."

"Apparently not!" Sinclair said with a nod of the head.

As the two weary riders entered the city gates, they passed two sentries steadfast at their station, but displaying the same look of despair as the civilians.

"Sergeant, might I ask why there appears to be a proverbial black cloud over the city?" Youngblood asked.

"Have you not heard? The King is dead, the Queen is dead, and the Prince is dead! The throne is vacant and the Kingdom is in chaos!" he replied. "We are not even sure why we stand at this gate and for whom," he added in a tone of great desperation.

Both Youngblood and Sinclair immediately halted their progress as their mouths dropped in disbelief. Sinclair appeared to take the news much worse, as he turned pale and hunched over in his saddle. He was virtually speechless, as he tried to find the eloquence and mastery of words that he usually commanded.

"How did this happen?" Youngblood asked, providing Sinclair with more time to compose himself.

"Treachery and deceit," the sergeant replied as if to say, "What else could it be?"

Sinclair appeared to recover somewhat, as he interjected, "Come with me. I have a friend who can tell us all."

A servant answered the door of the magnificent manor. He immediately recognized Sinclair Fox and escorted them to a grand library. The manor was, without question, the home of a high-ranking noble. Its opulence was breathtaking, as it appeared to reflect every luxury known to man. The library was dark, and the drapes were drawn, forcing the available light to focus upon the young man, who sat staring into the fire burning brightly before him.

"Sir, Mr. Sinclair Fox is here with a colleague," the servant announced.

The man immediately turned and upon seeing Sinclair, smiled and approached him with arms extended. "Sinclair! Where have you been?"

"On the road traveling here. Reginald, this is a colleague of mine, Youngblood Hawke. He is a warrior who was called into service by the Prince," Sinclair said.

"He is too late!" he replied with a hint of anger and despair.

"Reginald, tell me, what has happened?" Sinclair demanded.

"A tragedy of great proportions, my dear friend. The Prince is dead, as is his mother, and his uncle, the King," he replied as tears swelled in his eyes. "The kingdom is in ruin and we know not what will become of it!" Reginald shouted as he placed his face in his hands to conceal the tears.

Sinclair attempted to console his old friend but his grief appeared to be overwhelming. Reginald Quartermain was a member of a very old and noble family, and had been a close friend of the Prince since childhood. His entire life appeared to be turned upside down, as one of his closest friends was now dead, and the struggle for rule would ensue. Members of the aristocracy would be thrown into the turmoil that would end with many more deaths before this storm subsided. Such tragedies resulting in uncertainty can also throw a kingdom into revolution, where no one is protected.

"Reginald, sit down and tell us exactly what happened here!" Youngblood Hawke demanded.

Sinclair appeared to appreciate the warrior's assumption of command under the circumstances. Reginald obeyed the command without question or any sense of resentment. Reginald Quartermain began to tell the story of the Prince and the darkness that had befallen the royal house of the Northern Kingdom, as Youngblood and Sinclair listened intently. He told of the mysterious circumstances surrounding the recent death of the King and how grief-stricken the Prince had become. To add to the misery, the Prince's mother married his father's brother, rather abruptly. This caused great anguish in the Prince. Reginald disclosed that the Prince had been informed by a mystical source that his uncle murdered his father. Youngblood's attention was piqued, as he had more than a few encounters with the mystical realm. Reginald continued as the flames flickered in the fireplace. He told of how the Prince was not sure of the source's loyalty, but knew very well that if the information was true, his uncle would have to be killed. The added uncertainty of impending war created an atmosphere ripe for treachery and deceit, as the King became more suspicious of the Prince and his behavior.

According to Reginald, the Prince spiraled into a state of melancholy, confusion, and indecision. He knew what he must do, but found the act revolting and so failed to act even when provided with the opportunity. The Prince became so confused and misdirected that he accidentally killed the father of his lover. Fearing for his own life, the King ordered the Prince to the Kingdom of the Great Isle with two of the King's loyal subjects. The two subjects were carrying orders to kill the Prince. However, it was Reginald himself who discovered the contents of the orders, and informed the Prince. The Prince altered the orders so that the bearers were killed upon arrival. He explained that it was at this time that he sent dispatches to all his trusted colleagues and to the renowned warrior known as Youngblood Hawke. Both Sinclair and Youngblood looked at each other, recognizing the collapse of an alternative fate.

The tragedy continued to unfold as Reginald told of how the Prince rejected his true love, resulting in her state of madness during his absence. She ultimately defined her fate by taking her own life. The emotional drama was beginning to significantly impact Sinclair, as his entire body appeared to suffer from despair.

"If only I were here to stop all this madness," Sinclair said as his eyes swelled with emotion.

"The decision or lack of decision that set this tragedy into motion was not yours to make, my friend," Youngblood replied as he offered a hand of comfort to his colleague's shoulder.

Reginald continued, as he told of the plot by the brother of the Prince's former lover, and son of the man he accidentally killed. Apparently, the angry son was intent on revenge and had assembled a band of scoundrels to avenge his father's death. The King recruited him and his unholy crew in a plot to kill the Prince. The plot set in motion by the King involved a duel between the Prince and his would-be assassin. Knowing that the Prince was an expert swordsman, the King placed bets upon the Prince, to dismiss any suspicion of foul play. However, the treacherous King placed poison upon the sword of the Prince's opponent. He also placed poison in the cup within the Prince's reach; in the event he became thirsty during the confrontation. If this was not enough, Reginald explained how the Queen, unaware of the cup's contents, drank from it and died. Sinclair and Youngblood listened intently with disbelief, as the tragedy reached epic proportions. The duel was relentless and brutal, resulting in the Prince sustaining a mortal wound by the poisoned sword. However, the two combatants exchanged strikes in the conflict, resulting in the death of the misguided avenger. Prior to slipping into the *sleep of death,*[43] the remorseful avenger told the Prince that the King was responsible for the poisonous sword. With no options left to choose from, the Prince seized upon the moment and stabbed the King before himself dying.[44]

Youngblood Hawke had never heard of such tragedy before. He stared at the fire with Sinclair and Reginald and he wondered if he could have done anything to stop the catastrophe.

"'*To be, or not to be, that is the question: Whether 'tis nobler in mind to suffer the slings and arrows of outrageous fortune, or to take arms against a sea of troubles, and by opposing, end them. To die, to sleep—No more, and by a sleep to say we end the heart-ache and the thousand natural shocks that flesh is heir to; 'tis a consummation devoutly to be wished. To die, to sleep, perchance to dream—ay, there's the rub, for in that sleep of death what dreams may come, when we have shuffled off this mortal coil, must give us pause,*'[45] those were his last words to me," Sinclair noted as his voice drifted into silence.

Youngblood and Reginald sat silently, illuminated by the firelight and the prophetic words of the late Prince.

"Our good and noble Prince appears to have answered his proverbial question," Reginald replied.

"Not so my friend, the question '*To be, or not to be,*'[46] was answered not by fate, nor by the will of the Prince, but by his indecision and pause," Youngblood Hawke explained.

"How could you say such a thing!" the outraged Reginald Quartermain replied.

"Because it is true," Sinclair interrupted in a somber tone. "Our beloved friend and Prince failed to act, and thus, procrastination categorically destroyed his options, until the decision was made for him."

The three men said no more, as they remained throughout the day and night, reminiscing and recalling the life and experiences of the Prince. Staring silently into the firelight, Youngblood Hawke listened as he reflected upon both the past and the potential paths of fate that awaited him.

The Questions of Humanity

So many profound questions, no time for delay,
Society and culture, a proverbial state of decay,
Searching for answers, the truth we are told.

Philosophers and poets, questions of destiny,
Revealing nature's truths, a relative reality,
The value of knowledge, the purpose of a soul.

The temptation of wealth, the fear of poverty,
The pursuit of true love, a quest for immortality,
A desire to remain young, the right to grow old.

A need to be free, the demands of conformity,
The potentiality of man, the flaws of humanity,
The cruelty of time, the allure of silver and gold.

The fate of civilization, the lessons of history,
The hope of possibility, the comfort of mediocrity,
The meaning of life, an unknown future to unfold.

—*Youngblood Hawke*

His thoughts also drifted to the comfort of the sapphire light, wondering if she was aware that the "need" had arisen.

CHAPTER 9

Lessons in Leadership

Commonality replaced by nobility,
Not a birthright but earned meritoriously.

Following their departure from the Northern Kingdom, Youngblood and Sinclair decided to spend a few days in the City of Savill, where they could unwind and put the misery and tragedy of the Prince behind them. They remained in the capital with Reginald for as long as they could. But the atmosphere grew dark and dangerous as the struggle for power and the throne ensued. The jails of the kingdom were filling fast with accused traitors and rebels. As for the aristocracy, anyone who was even rumored as being interested in the throne fell victim to the executioner. Many suspected that the Black Guard would soon be dispatched to ensure security within the kingdom. However, the aristocracy was well aware that the arrival of the Black Guard would only ensure a dark future of controlled mediocrity and despair.

Although the month spent in the capital distracted Youngblood from his quest, it did replenish his personal treasury quite handsomely. Indeed, the services of a soldier of fortune were in great demand in such troubled times. In fact, the Quartermain family retained Youngblood to protect them. Under his protection, the family went unmolested and he personally escorted the entire clan to their estate in the country, where they could remain until the storm of troubles blew over and it was safe to return. Sinclair was given the opportunity to remain within the safety of the estate, but he chose instead to accompany his new friend on his quest.

Savill was a thriving city, with an abundance of culture, entertainment, and taverns to satisfy the appetite of almost anyone. Youngblood and Sinclair found a very comfortable inn with luxurious rooms, gourmet food, fine wine, and many available paths leading to Sinclair's proverbial abyss. On this particular night, the Dragon's Claw Tavern was alive with merriment and song. Youngblood had found himself in the midst of a most interesting philosophical discussion regarding leadership with a local politico. Of course, Sinclair was busy wooing the local maidens with his poetic quotes and outlandish, yet effective, flattery.

"It was a relatively free culture. The one to gain rule of the Northern Kingdom will have to destroy it in order to hold it," the politico said.

"Such action would appear to be rather harsh, wouldn't you say?" Youngblood asked.

"*In truth, there is no sure way of holding other than by destroying, and whoever becomes master of a city accustomed to live in freedom and does not destroy it, may reckon on being destroyed by it. For if it should rebel, it can always screen itself under the name of liberty and its ancient laws, which no length of time, nor any benefits conferred will ever cause it to forget; and do what you will, and take what care you may, unless the inhabitants be scattered and dispersed, this name, and the old order of things, will never cease to be remembered, but will at once be turned against you whenever misfortune overtakes you,*"[47] replied the confident politico.

Youngblood listened intently as he kept one eye on the activities of his incorrigible colleague.

"But what of a leader who rises to the occasion meritoriously and with the respect and support of the people?" the very interested Youngblood asked.

"Yes, a bird of a different feather altogether. What of leaders who acquire power by merit?" the politico asked, suggesting Youngblood's question was almost profound. "Such leaders would possess great wisdom. And for the most part would *follow in the footsteps and imitate the actions of others, and yet are unable to adhere exactly to those paths which others have taken, or attain to the virtues of those whom they would resemble, the wise man should always follow the roads that have been trodden by the great, and imitate those who have most excelled, so that if he cannot reach their perfection, he may at least acquire something of its savor.*"[48]

Youngblood Hawke shook his head in acknowledgment and immediately thought of his encounter with the Great One.

"Such leaders are very few and very fortunate, my friend," Youngblood said.

"Perhaps, but *while it was their opportunities that made these men fortunate, it was their own merit that enabled them to recognize these opportunities and turn them to account, to the glory and prosperity of their country,*"[49] the politico said as he raised his finger and squinted his eyes to make a point.

"It truly is a noble leader who can accomplish such success and loyalty. However, such a leader will also be subjected to fierce opposition from those who oppose him. Conspirators will be behind every shadow," noted Youngblood.

"The enemies of change are many, young warrior," the politico said approvingly. "Therefore, such a leader must be strong and decisive unlike the popular and now deceased Prince of the Northern Kingdom," he added. "*Whenever the enemies of change make an attack, they do so with all the zeal of partisans, while others defend themselves so feebly as to endanger both themselves and their cause.*"[50]

"So what you're proposing is that a strong leader must retaliate immediately when attacked by the enemies of change."

"Absolutely and without fail! *When they depend upon their own resources and can employ force, they seldom fail. Hence it comes that all armed Prophets have been victorious, and all unarmed Prophets have been destroyed,*"[51] replied the politico enthusiastically.

Youngblood continued to engage the politico, "I would imagine that it would be very important for such a leader to have a loyal following?"

"Yes, he must be *held in reverence, and having destroyed all who were jealous of his influence, they remain powerful, safe, honored, and prosperous,*"[52] the politico answered. "Now you spoke earlier of such a leader being 'fortunate,' did you not?"

"Indeed, I did."

"Let us then consider the leader who acquires power by the aid of others and by good fortune alone, shall we?"

Youngblood could not help but notice that while Sinclair was amidst a group of rather interesting young women, he was listening intently to the politico as well. Sinclair was truly amazing; he could create sincerity from thin air. An attribute the young ladies appeared to enjoy.

The erudite politico continued, *"Leaders who attain power from private station by mere good fortune, do so with little trouble, but have much trouble to maintain themselves."*[53]

"I say, why do you suppose that is, my good man?" Sinclair Fox interrupted with his aristocratic tone.

"Simply because they lack the knowledge, unless they have great parts and force of character, it is not to be expected that having always lived in private station they should not have learned how to command. They lack the power, since they cannot look for support from attached and faithful followers,"[54] the politico explained in an equally aristocratic voice.

Sinclair and Youngblood shook their heads in understanding, as the politico continued enjoying the interest of his audience. "Now, *he who is provided power by favor of the nobles, has greater difficulty to maintain himself than he who comes to power by aid of the people, since he finds many about him who think themselves as good as he."*[55]

"I see how that could be a problem. For a leader to be successful, his followers should not see themselves as his equal," Youngblood said with Sinclair nodding his head in agreement.

"To make the matter clearer, *I pronounce those to be able to stand alone who, with the men and money at their disposal, can get together an army fit to take the field against any assailant; and, conversely, I judge those to be in constant need of help who cannot take the field against their enemies, but are obliged to retire behind their walls, and to defend themselves there,"*[56] the politico advised gravely.

"So, what you are saying is that the strong assume an offensive posture and the weak maintain a defensive posture," Youngblood said.

"Your counsel should have been sought by the late Prince," responded Sinclair.

"There will be many more princes, and all should heed these words," he answered with the confidence of a prophet.

Sinclair began to further engage the politico as Youngblood once again took notice of the two men in the black cloaks that had entered through the rear door. They appeared to be acknowledging the three at the bar. Another was standing guard at the front entrance and was not as inconspicuous as the others, as he continued to stare at the young warrior.

Youngblood was distracted by Sinclair who asked, "What of the use of mercenaries, my good man?" With a raised eyebrow and that sinister grin, he looked to Youngblood for a reaction, "Do you have any use for such malcontents?"

Youngblood shook his head and glared back at Sinclair, who appeared to be amusing himself at the expense of his colleague. But his attention was immediately drawn back to the three men at the bar, who were making their way through the crowd of patrons.

"Mercenaries are at once useless and dangerous, and he who holds his State by means of mercenary troops can never be solidly or securely seated. For such troops are disunited, ambitious, insubordinate, treacherous, insolent among friends, cowardly before foes, and without fear of God or faith with man."[57]

"Yes, a faithful cadre of loyal warriors are more advantageous than a sword for hire," Youngblood noted.

By this time Sinclair had become aware of Youngblood's concerns and advised the politico, "Sir, I would recommend highly that you 'solidly and securely' be seated as you say. For a mercenary is about to demonstrate his—what is it you called it—'cowardice before foes,' yes, that was it!"

Sinclair could see the dagger drawn from the third man's cloak as he approached Youngblood from the left. The second attacker was moving directly at Youngblood as the first man moved in from the right. Sinclair was blocked by the table and was unable to gain a position to help his friend as the situation exploded!

Youngblood unleashed a devastating spinning jump kick that struck the third attacker with such force you could hear his jaw snap! The attacker's dagger fell to the ground and was immediately kicked across the room by Youngblood. The two remaining attackers were somewhat stunned by the display, as was the entire tavern, to include Sinclair Fox, who raised both eyebrows in amazement. However, the astonishment turned to rage as the attackers drew their swords and lunged at Youngblood Hawke. Their attack was met horizontally by Youngblood Hawke's katana as it ripped through the first attacker's midsection, causing the inside of his stomach to spill onto the floor. Enraged by the response of his intended victim, the second attacker moved in for the kill. Youngblood Hawke responded to the assault, thrusting his katana with the force of a battering ram. However, the attacker's reflexes repelled the strike as he deflected the katana from its intended target.

The man at the door had entered the fray and the two men at the rear door were moving through the gathered crowd to join the attack. However, they were met by the business end of Sinclair's sword, as he rolled over the table blocking their path and landed directly in front of the men, halting their advance! Sinclair stood with his sword extended and his free arm well into the air, wearing his most sinister grin. He even took a bow as the men realized their predicament.

"Gentleman, please, let's not be rude, shall we?" he announced. "I suspect that the odds are satisfactory just where they are. Wouldn't you agree?"

The men just stared at Sinclair, deliberating whether or not to accept the challenge. However, the sword was too close to risk action even for these two, battle-hardened rogues.

Youngblood continued to defend against his attackers, but they were delivering a dauntless assault, pushing Youngblood to his limits. The second attacker met his fate as the katana pierced the man's heart. However, the strike momentarily delayed Youngblood's ability to defend from all corners.

The cold sting swept through Youngblood's body as the blade penetrated his left shoulder. He attempted a futile counterattack and then quickly withdrew to avoid another devastating strike. The blood dripping down his arm was distracting as the pain increased in harmony with the numbness. The assailants, aware they had wounded their prey, increased the intensity of the attack. The severity of the wound had now rendered Youngblood's left arm totally useless. He used all his strength and will to defend himself against the onslaught as he felt the velocity of every strike of their swords rip through his body. The experienced Youngblood Hawke knew that unless he went on the offensive, he would almost certainly be defeated.

Youngblood's struggle did not go unnoticed as the younger attacker became wild and out of control. The fact that he had inflicted the wound upon his adversary and drew first blood appeared to ignite his desire to kill. The wild one could smell death and wanted to experience this kill as his eyes turned crimson with rage. He knew it was a kill that would elevate him to that of a legend, considering the reputation of his potential prey.

The sudden intensity of pain delivered by the second strike, penetrating Youngblood's defenses, crippled him momentarily. Falling to his knees in pain, the warrior exposed a window of opportunity that was not lost on the wild one, who was now possessed by the crimson rage in his eyes. A rage that did not go unnoticed by Youngblood Hawke. The determined attackers continued to bear down upon their falling prey as the wild one's eyes lit up, believing he was soon to reach legendary status. Fortunately, the situation was being closely monitored by Sinclair Fox.

Holding the two other would-be assassins at bay, he turned to them and said, "Gentlemen, I regretfully bid you goodnight."

Sinclair swiftly and without reservation extracted their last breaths. He immediately responded to his fallen comrade's aid and directly engaged the wild one.

"I say, good man, your temper and ambitions appear to be getting the better of you!" Sinclair said as he intercepted the sword bound for his weakened colleague.

The relief had arrived just in time as it allowed Youngblood to regain his faculties and respond, focusing his attention on the remaining and somewhat less aggressive attacker.

"I must say I am rather enjoying this fencing lesson, young man! Of course, you do realize that you are the student?" Sinclair said as he continued to taunt the wild one with all the annoying oratory of a true aristocrat.

"Surely you can do better than that? Have you learned nothing today?" Sinclair asked as he toyed with the powerful, yet inexperienced combatant.

"Your head will soon be mounted on a pike, you pompous peacock!" replied the young and now very frustrated attacker.

Sinclair appeared to be enjoying himself as he displayed both speed and grace, combined with tenacity. He was full of showmanship and, like a dramatic thespian, appeared to be fueled by the fact that he was impressing the young maidens who watched intently. Sinclair even found it necessary to stop momentarily and kiss the hand of a young lady who was captivated by the unfolding drama—an act that appeared to infuriate his adversary. However, Sinclair also took notice as he became aware of the crimson rage in his opponent's eyes.

Youngblood Hawke was struggling with his own dilemma as he continued to search for the strength to change the tide and gain the offensive. His attacker responded to Youngblood's attempts with unyielding power. However, it was the unwelcome actions of a stranger in the crowd that dropped Youngblood to the floor as the bottle struck his head. The attacker took advantage of the assistance and stood over Youngblood, glaring down at him in a manner clearly revealing that he would be taking his life.

Suddenly, a "sapphire" storm exploded in Youngblood's eyes so intense that it caused alarm in his executioner. It was then that the opportunity presented itself to the young warrior as he leaped up, releasing the roundhouse kick that struck its target with amazing accuracy. The unexpected counterattack dazed his opponent and knocked him to his knees. Youngblood Hawke took advantage of the momentum as he spun his katana sword counterclockwise. The katana soared through the air and in one swift motion decapitated the former predator! The shock and brutality of the kill stunned the crowded tavern including Sinclair Fox and the wild one. As all stood silent, Youngblood Hawke stood holding his bleeding shoulder and looked down at the results of his fury. His katana, dripping with blood, appeared to absorb the rogue's remaining life force and add it to the many that had met a similar fate. Youngblood lifted his head, directing the intense "sapphire" storm brewing in his eyes toward the now bewildered and only remaining assassin. The look in his eyes was a haunting display of inspiration as the sapphire glow appeared to engulf the room and diminish what was left of the crimson rage.

"You will not make a name for yourself on this day. Perhaps another day, but clearly not today, my young disillusioned friend," Sinclair said to the lone remaining adversary.

The wild one's eyes were no longer lit with fire. They were now replaced with indecision in the face of the approaching storm.

"Run, you imbecile! Before that violent storm overtakes you and denies your very existence!" Sinclair shouted.

The young one looked around the tavern at the mutilated bodies of his former clan and then bolted out of the door, dropping his sword as he ran in panic.

Youngblood Hawke closed his eyes and was momentarily delivered to the Oracle. "Thank you," he said as she returned the sapphire smile and then expelled him from her domain. The sapphire storm diminished from his eyes as he fell to his knees in exhaustion and pain.

As Sinclair approached his depleted friend, Youngblood looked up and nodded, extending his gratitude.

"Think nothing of it," Sinclair acknowledged, as he lifted him to a chair.

"Do you think he will return?" Youngblood asked, referring to the hasty departure of the remaining assassin.

This was a question that he feared would be answered soon enough.

The Wild One

So violent and aggressive,
Dangerous—out of control,
A hatred dark and deep,
His heart empty and cold.

Such a blinding ambition,
Freely selling his soul,
Trading duty and honor,
For mere silver and gold.

He desires with such envy,
For his story to be told,
A vision of his greatness,
Daring, brave, and bold.

Soon his time will come,
The grim future to unfold,
A foolish spirit so young,
Destined never to grow old.

So behold his greatness!
His spirit does swiftly run,
To the cover of his hatred,
Beware of this Wild One!

—*Youngblood Hawke*

"*You gave him an opportunity of showing greatness of character and he did not seize it. He will never forgive you for that,*"[58] Sinclair replied. "Tell me, how did you know of their intentions?" Sinclair inquired of Youngblood.

"*The first sword,*"[59] Youngblood replied, "*I do not refer literally to a sword but to 'incipient movement on the part of opponents. The expression "the critical first sword" means that seeing what opponents are trying to do is the first sword in the ultimate sense,*"[60] understand?"

"Yes, what you are saying is, the warrior must anticipate the first move of his opponent in order to be victorious," Sinclair said, as Youngblood nodded his head in acknowledgment. "Tell me, Youngblood, how do you control your anger?"

"In close combat, as in debate, one must avoid strong emotional responses. Emotions often translate to weakness and clouded judgment. However, do not confuse passion for raw emotion. One can be passionate, strong, and calculating in thought, and at the same time, dismiss emotional distractions," Youngblood explained.

"So what you are saying is that anger and strong emotions will cause loss of control?" Sinclair asked.

"Yes, and in response, a calm demeanor will almost always temper an emotional one. The result will certainly be a superior position for the calm and collective combatant or negotiator."

"Therefore, the calm and collective approach is superior?"

"Not always, passionate debate rarely succumbs to the emotional or the calm approach. In fact, both emotion and lack of emotion tend to fuel passion. The reason, passion begins from a position of strength. It is often a strategic and aggressive approach that can be pursued and controlled with a calm mind, yet passionate spirit."

"Passion translates to strength," Sinclair noted.

"Indeed, it does, my friend."

The tavern's patrons were still in awe over the display they had witnessed. The crowd gathered to gain a better look at the victorious warrior as a physician attended to Youngblood's wound.

"A reputation was not made this day, but another was multiplied ten-fold," Sinclair said as he surveyed the room.

The now very excited politico approached Youngblood exclaiming, "Who were those men?"

Youngblood looked the politico in the eye and said, "I believe you would call them enemies of change."

"Ah yes…the mass," replied the politico knowingly.

"The mass?" Youngblood asked before being interrupted by the oratory of Sinclair.

"So much for your theory that a mercenary is useless," Sinclair interjected with a smirk.

"You are in error, young aristocrat. This friend of yours is no mercenary. No, he has all the makings of a prince!" the politico responded.

Youngblood laughed at the politico's assessment and responded, "I am a warrior, nothing less and nothing more; I am certainly not royalty."

"Exactly! *A Prince should have no care for thought but for war, and for the regulations and training it requires, and should apply himself exclusively to this as his peculiar province; for war is the sole art looked for in one who rules, and is of such efficacy that it merely maintains those who are born Princes, but often enables men to rise to that eminence from a private station; while, on the other hand, we often see that when Princes devote themselves rather to pleasure than to arms, they lose their dominions. And as neglect of this art is the prime cause of such calamities, so to be proficient in it is the surest way to acquire power.*"[61]

"I understand your theory, but should not a prince be pure and good?" Sinclair asked while also apologizing to his friend. "No offense, my friend."

"None taken," Youngblood responded with a grin and a grimace from the pain ripping through his arm and shoulder.

"*It is essential for a Prince who desires to maintain his position, to have learned how to be other than good, and to use or not use his goodness as necessity requires,*"[62] the politico added.

Sinclair raised his brow and responded, "Are you saying that a prince must lead by fear as opposed to goodness? Surely you are jesting? Such leadership will only generate fear as opposed to love by one's subjects."

"*It is far better to be feared than loved. Moreover, men are less careful how they offend him who makes himself loved than him who makes himself feared. A Prince should inspire fear in such a fashion that if he does not win love he may escape hate,*"[63] the politico said with a raised finger to make his point clear.

"Perhaps, my cynical friend, but you cannot argue that a prince must be honorable and a man of his word?" Sinclair noted, believing he was baiting the politico into agreeing with him.

"*A prudent Prince neither can nor ought to keep his word when to keep it is hurtful to him and the causes which led him to pledge it are removed. If all men were good, this would not be good advice, but since they are dishonest and do not keep faith with you, you, in return, need not keep faith with them; and no Prince was ever at loss for plausible reasons to cloak a breach of faith,*"[64] the politico said, knowing he once again made a valid point.

"Clearly such a reputation will only destroy his ability to rule," replied Sinclair, as Youngblood sat back and listened to the debate, while the bandages were wrapped around his wounds.

"*Nothing should ever escape his lips that would be replete with five specific qualities, so that to see and hear him, one would think him the embodiment of mercy, good faith, integrity, humanity, and religion. In other words, everyone sees what you seem, but few know what you are,*"[65] the politico advised.

"I cannot help but believe that such a ruler would be swiftly overthrown," Sinclair said.

"*The prince who inspires such an opinion of himself is greatly esteemed, and against one who is greatly esteemed conspiracy is difficult; nor, when he is known to be an excellent Prince and held in reverence by his subjects, will it be easy to attack him.*"[66]

"You have thought out this argument well, my esteemed friend," Sinclair acknowledged.

"*As I said, your friend here has all the makings. Nothing makes a Prince so well thought of as to undertake great enterprises and give striking proofs of his capacity,*"[67] the politico said.

"Perhaps you do have a greater destiny than you are aware, my friend," Sinclair said as he looked upon his weary friend.

"Do not count yourself out of the equation," responded the politico to Sinclair. "*The choice of lieutenants is a matter of no small moment to a Prince. When they are at once capable and faithful, we may always account them wise, since he has known to recognize their merit and to retain their fidelity.*"[68]

Sinclair nodded his head in acknowledgment as Youngblood continued to listen intently.

The politico turned his attention to Youngblood Hawke and said, "*Be leery of flattery from would-be advisors, for there is no way to guard against it but by letting it be seen that you take no offense in hearing the truth: but when every one is free to tell you the truth respect falls short. Choose certain discreet men from among your subjects, and allow them alone free leave to speak their minds on any matter on which you ask their opinion, but on none other.*"[69]

Sinclair shook his head in agreement and stated, "Yes, a ruler should be surrounded by wise men who may even be superior in thought."

"*A Prince who is not wise himself cannot be well advised by others,*"[70] the politico declared firmly. "Do not deny your destiny, warrior. You have many paths to choose from and you should take care to choose wisely," the politico noted as he studied Youngblood Hawke as if seeing something no one else could see. "Gentlemen, I bid you farewell and wish you good fortune on your quest," he added as he departed the tavern.

Youngblood found the politico's last comment interesting in as much as he had never spoken of a "quest" during their conversations.

Another sage? he thought to himself as he watched the wise man exit with an air of confidence, suggesting he was pleased that he had accomplished his task.

Youngblood examined his wounds realizing that the obstacles and tests found along the path of his quest were becoming more and more difficult.

CHAPTER 10

The Mass

Command of the truth wherever it may stand.
In defense of honor and the select man.

Youngblood was looking forward to returning to Ventura and seeing his old friend, Horatio Cantrell. The stay in Savill was fairly restful, following what Sinclair continuously referred to as his "near-death experience." Youngblood had now become accustomed to his new friend and rather enjoyed their witty conversations and insightful discussions. However, he had spent the last leg of the trip telling the story of the tavern encounter over and over again. He did so under the pretext of highlighting Youngblood's exploit but in fact, he spent the majority of the time recounting his own participation. In fact, the most recent version of the conflict revealed absolutely no mention of Youngblood Hawke at all.

"Veritas, do you remember the old days when we would travel the lonely roads of the continent in tranquillity?" Youngblood said to his old friend sarcastically.

Sinclair completely ignored the comment as he once again embellished in the art of storytelling, focusing upon his heroism. Youngblood began to believe that he was just practicing and perfecting the tales of his conquest and preparing for his next excursion to the proverbial abyss.

The two weary travelers were only about ten miles from Ventura when they came upon the old man and his cart coming from the opposite direction.

"Well, hello, my friend!" Youngblood said, greeting the old man. "I get the oddest feeling that you are following me."

"Perhaps it is you who follow me?" the old man responded with a grin.

"Sinclair, I would like to introduce you to…what is your name, old man?" Youngblood asked.

"What is in a name, young one? It does not identify who I am nor does it identify what I am. It is merely a label for the sake of identification," he responded.

"This one speaks in riddles," Sinclair Fox noted.

"The riddle you see is merely the reflection of your own life," responded the old man.

Both Youngblood and Sinclair exchanged a roll of the eyes as the old man continued to cast his grin upon them.

"The guardian of the crossroads waits for you," the old one declared.

"Where?" Youngblood asked.

"Follow the path through the darkened forest and you will find the light," he responded.

"What path? And who is the guardian?" Sinclair inquired.

"The one behind you," the old one said, as he pointed to a path that had now appeared in the forest.

Both Youngblood and Sinclair turned to find the path opened before them. Of course, it was no surprise to Youngblood, but Sinclair stared in amazement.

"I say, I don't recall this path being here when we arrived," he said with a most puzzled face.

They both turned back to the old man but he had already departed.

"What is this all about, my friend?" Sinclair Fox asked.

"I don't have the answers, only the questions," Youngblood responded, as he surveyed the path leading into the darkened forest.

"Your quest?" Sinclair inquired.

"It would appear to be our quest. Are you coming?"

"I don't appear to have any pending engagements. Lead the way, good man!" Sinclair responded.

The path once again opened to a large meadow, sunshine, rolling hills, and wild flowers. Sinclair looked around in amazement and surprisingly, had nothing to say. Both men noticed the solitary figure standing in the distance as the white garments flowed with the wind.

"Remain here," Youngblood commanded as he rode to greet the Gatekeeper.

"I believe I will do just that!" Sinclair responded, remaining puzzled by the spectacle before him.

Youngblood dismounted Veritas and humbly approached the Gatekeeper.

"Is your quest complete?" the Gatekeeper asked.

"Far from complete," Youngblood responded. "As the ancient one said, '*I know nothing except the fact of my own ignorance*,'[71] meaning, I know less now than when I started," added the warrior.

"Knowing that alone is a wealth of knowledge and far beyond what most know," the Gatekeeper said approvingly.

"Am I traveling in the correct direction?" Youngblood asked.

"There are many paths leading to that which you seek. And along those many paths you will find many answers and many more questions. Take care, and beware of the beast that waits for you."

"I am aware."

"Remember this, warrior, the beast takes on many forms," the Gatekeeper added.

"Man?" asked Youngblood, thinking of the assassins.

"The mass!" replied the Gatekeeper, as he disappeared along with the meadow, returning Youngblood and Sinclair to the road leading to Ventura.

"I cannot even begin to understand this day, my friend," Sinclair said.

"Nor I. I have decided only to continue this quest wherever it may lead me," the determined Youngblood Hawke replied.

"So be it, my friend. And you shall have a companion for as long as you wish."

Youngblood nodded in acknowledgment as the two continued along the road, reflecting upon what has been and what was to be.

Horatio Cantrell's house was alive with excitement and the sound of music as Youngblood and Sinclair approached.

"It would appear that your friend is having some sort of a celebration," Sinclair said.

"Indeed, it does," Youngblood replied.

"Excellent! I am in the mood for a party. This is a rather affluent manor. I would gather that your friend Horatio has invited many a beautiful maiden, don't you think?" he said as he twisted his mustache and checked the manner of his dress.

"I suppose you are going to fall into that abyss again," Youngblood remarked.

"Why, what do you mean, my good man?" Sinclair asked with a most sinister-looking grin.

"Well, just make sure the abyss does not have a large and angry father," Youngblood said with a laugh.

"I believe I will consider that advice very strongly," Sinclair replied laughingly.

The affair was in full swing as Youngblood and Sinclair released their horses to the stableman. As they approached the front door, Horatio noticed their arrival and immediately greeted his old friend and companion.

"Youngblood! How are you, my friend?" Horatio announced as he approached with his hand extended. "I see that you appear to have returned with all of your body parts intact, and even picked up an extra body as well," he added, referring to Sinclair.

"Actually, he may be missing a few pints or so of blood," Sinclair responded.

"What blood? 'Tis not blood that runs through this one's veins! Steel maybe, and sometimes wine!" laughed Horatio.

Youngblood listened as his comrades laughed at his expense, but paid no bother. He was scanning the crowd and thinking of Sapphire.

"Sinclair Fox. At your service, sir," Sinclair said, introducing himself as he caught the eye of a lovely young lady passing by.

"Welcome to my home. Rest assured that any friend of Youngblood Hawke is certainly welcome in it. I am sure you will find your stay most enjoyable," Horatio said as he noticed Sinclair's preoccupation with the young woman.

"*Ah yes, the devil hath power to assume a pleasing shape,*"[72] Sinclair commented, once again revealing that sinister grin.

"Could that be Mr. Youngblood Hawke who blesses us with his presence?" the elegant and very gracious lady of the manor announced as she gracefully approached the men.

Elizabeth Cantrell was the refined and beautiful, first-born of Ventura's leading aristocrat. A blue blood born into affluence, learned in the classics, demonstrating the etiquette of royalty in her manner. It was quite an event when she revealed to her father that it was Horatio Cantrell who she wished to marry. He was no aristocrat, nor was he born into a noble or wealthy family, but he was an accomplished soldier who had made a name for himself. Without question, Elizabeth had elevated Horatio Cantrell to the rank of a noble, and he wore it well.

"And who might be this gentleman who accompanies you?" she asked.

"Sinclair Fox at your…," Sinclair replied before being interrupted.

Before Sinclair could utter another word, Youngblood responded, "He has the tongue of a serpent and twice the bite, so be very careful, my lady."

A Warning

A knight in shining armor?
Now don't you be fooled,
More a rogue without honor,
The very definition of cruel.

Yes, charming and handsome,
Also so very brave and bold,
Appearing kind and wholesome,
Claiming a heart of pure gold.

Be careful my beautiful princess,
For your heart he will surely take,
Return to the safety of your fortress,
At once! Before it is too late.

—*Youngblood Hawke*

"Does he, indeed?" she replied as she cautiously approached Sinclair.

"Madam, the beauty and majesty of your home is surpassed only by your own," Sinclair said as he bowed and kissed the hand of the impressed mistress of the house.

"Would you be of any relation to the distinguished Remington Fox who resides in the Northern Kingdom?" Elizabeth Cantrell asked.

"My father," replied Sinclair with pride.

"I have heard of his debonair and somewhat incorrigible son," Elizabeth said with a raised brow. "How are your father and your wonderful mother?" she asked.

"They are well. But I must confess that I have not been home for quite some time," responded Sinclair with a tinge of shame.

"The prodigal son? You will not find a dire path home in the company of this professional adventurer," noted Elizabeth as she placed her hand on the shoulder of Youngblood.

"I suspect I will not, but his path is terribly exciting," replied Sinclair.

"And dangerous as well!" Horatio interjected.

"Gentlemen, I have quarters being prepared for you as we speak. Show them to their rooms, please?" Elizabeth Cantrell said as she directed a servant to attend to her guests.

Youngblood and Sinclair settled into their rooms before they dressed for the party and met in the hallway to join the festivities. Youngblood was very comfortable in Horatio's home, and it was one of the few places where he could roam without his weaponry, although his dagger always remained concealed and close to his side. As Sinclair exited the room, Youngblood just stood in amazement at the scarlet attire donned by his aristocratic colleague. His manner of dress was in drastic contrast to Youngblood's simple and characteristic black.

"Is that satin that you are wearing?" Youngblood Hawke asked, wearing an expression of amazement.

"Why, yes, it is, my good man. I do look rather dashing, do I not?" Sinclair responded as he caught a glimpse of himself in the mirror.

Youngblood just shook his head as they walked down the hall to join the festivities. The gala was as grand as the aristocracy itself. All the powers-that-be appeared to be in attendance for an event that had no particular purpose. As the two men made their way through the revelers, Sinclair was immediately lured to the expansive "abyss." Without question, all the beauty and grace of Ventura had been invited to the gala. Youngblood took a path directly to the display of delicious foods, revealing every delicacy one could imagine. Not to mention, one of the finest arrays of fine wines he had ever encountered.

"Youngblood Hawke, I would like to introduce you to Mr. Jonathan LeClair," Horatio announced as he stood near the tall and very distinguished-looking man with the graying hair.

Horatio's father-in-law was the epitome of the ruling class, demonstrating all of the courtesies consistent with his rank. In addition to being one of Ventura's leading citizens, Jonathan LeClair was somewhat of a revolutionary and a legend. In the early days, he was instrumental in elevating the Western Kingdom to its present stature and affluence. LeClair was also instrumental in creating a parliament and voice for the people.

"It is my honor to meet you, sir," Youngblood said as he shook the hand of the influential leader.

"It is my honor as well. I have looked forward to one day meeting the renowned soldier of fortune they call Youngblood Hawke. I have often heard of your exploits during conversations with my son-in-law. Quite an honor, indeed," Jonathan LeClair replied diplomatically.

"You flatter me, sir," Youngblood humbly responded.

"So, tell me, what brings you to our fine city?" LeClair asked.

"He is on a quest. A quest for truth, he says," Horatio answered.

"A noble task, to say the least. As well as a very difficult and dangerous one, I would imagine?" LeClair said. "Have you found what it is that you seek?" he added.

"I have found that which is relative."

"But you seek the absolute?"

"The absolute! Is there such a thing?" Horatio interjected.

"It is an ideal," LeClair said.

"An ideal, indeed. *I personally just give up the absolute. I take moral holidays; or else, try to justify them by some other principal,*"[73] Horatio replied in a dismissive manner.

"You are a pragmatist, and your lifestyle requires you to be such," LeClair noted as he continued to direct his attention to Youngblood. "Are you a pragmatist as well?" LeClair asked of Youngblood.

"In many ways I suppose that I am, but I tend to use my own brand of pragmatism as a tool to guide me to the absolute."

"My young, delusional friend, I am not sure how such a philosophy can coincide," Horatio said.

"What do you mean?" Youngblood asked.

"Simply this, *the greatest enemy of any one of our truths may be the rest of our truths. Truths have this desperate instinct of self-preservation and desire to extinguish whatever contradicts them. Your belief in the absolute, based upon the good it does you, must run the gauntlet of all your other beliefs,*"[74] Horatio explained, prodded by the effects of his array of fine wine.

"Horatio, I suspect that your friend here rather enjoys the 'gauntlet' as you so appropriately put it," noted LeClair. "'*Humanity is that which splits into two classes of creatures: those who make great demands on themselves, piling up difficulties and duties, and those who demand nothing special of themselves, but for whom to live is to be every moment what they already are, without imposing on themselves any effort toward perfection; mere buoys that float on the waves.*'[75] The mass crushes beneath it everything that is different, everything that is excellent, individual, qualified, and select. Anybody who is not like everybody, who does not think like everybody, runs the risk of being eliminated. I think it is clear which creature stands before us."

"Nothing is so clear as the elusive nature of truth," Youngblood Hawke noted.

"Does the elusive nature of your prey disturb you?" LeClair asked.

"The elusiveness and inconsistency of my prey confound me!" Youngblood replied passionately, as his thoughts pondered the nature of his quest.

A Most Elusive Prey

Love and Truth, arguably one and the same.
Sharing a destiny, differing only in name.
Dismiss one, and the other would remain.

An eternity spent together, a history to reveal.
The secrets of humanity, profoundly concealed.
Pursued by so many, always refusing to yield.

Possessing the power of vision, the gift of clarity.
Blessed with eternal life, in command of reality.
In defense of the other, unleashing fear and brutality.

Love and Truth, the proverbial partners in crime,
Enjoying an abstract existence, impossible to define.
Eluding capture and the understanding of mankind.

—*Youngblood Hawke*

"Inconsistency and contradiction. Your truths do battle with each other. It is an internal struggle that only pragmatism can counter," Horatio responded.

"Your devotion to pragmatism may work well for you, my friend, but it is not what I ultimately seek," Youngblood replied.

"Horatio professes only his opinions, which like his truths, change, based upon the need of the moment," LeClair noted.

"*The individual has a stock of old opinions that cannot be ignored, and they constantly meet a new experience that puts them to the strain. Somebody contra-*

dicts them; or in a reflective moment he discovers that they contradict each other; or he hears of facts with which they are incompatible; or desires arise in him, which they cease to satisfy. The result is an inward trouble to which his mind till then had been a stranger, and from which he seeks to escape by modifying his previous mass of opinions,"[76] Horatio said with conviction.

"Such a philosophy has served you well, Horatio, but it will not satisfy the lofty ideology of Youngblood Hawke. It is too final for him," LeClair said.

"Sir, circumstances dictate our actions, which in turn require a pragmatic and practical philosophy," Horatio insisted.

"Horatio, it is false to say that in life, 'circumstances decide.' On the contrary, circumstances are the dilemma, constantly renewed, in the presence of which we have to make our decision; what actually decides is our character,"[77] LeClair replied calmly.

"Horatio, I must agree with your father-in-law, yet you are correct in your assessment that my 'truths' do battle with each other. In fact, they engage in a most violent internal struggle against each other on a daily basis," Youngblood added.

Horatio continued his argument, defending his philosophy of action, "The most violent revolutions in an individual's beliefs leave most of his old order standing. Time and space, cause and effect, nature and history, and one's own biography remain untouched."[78]

Jonathan LeClair directed his comment to his son-in-law and said, "Physical space and time are the absolutely stupid aspects of the universe!"[79]

"A lofty ideology," Horatio replied in attempt to finish his thought before being interrupted.

"Revolution is not the uprising against pre-existing order, but the setting up of a new order contradictory to the traditional one!"[80] LeClair responded with spirit.

Youngblood was beginning to realize that this was not the first heated debate between father-in-law and son-in-law. They were from two different schools of thought. He continued to participate in the conversation as he noticed Sinclair Fox entertaining the ladies with the mastery of his dance.

"Is there no end to the number of useless skills that man has?" Youngblood whispered, only to be overheard by LeClair.

"All the talents except the talent to make use of them,"[81] LeClair said as he took note of Sinclair's gracefulness.

"Well said," Youngblood responded in agreement.

"The plague of the children of aristocracy," LeClair advised. "Don't worry, my friend, a man such as yourself is plagued with an entirely different affliction."

Youngblood shook his head in acknowledgment, aware of exactly what LeClair was speaking of, and often felt more cursed than blessed with his desire to understand. Horatio was about to comment when LeClair excused himself from the discussion.

"A very interesting man," Youngblood commented as he observed Jonathan LeClair navigate the room of power brokers with ease and command.

"Yes, he is," responded Horatio before turning his attention to the antics of Sinclair Fox who now had all of the women waiting for a dance. "Your friend appears to be quite the ladies' man, I see," he added.

"Yes, quite, but don't let his fanciful demeanor mislead you," Youngblood replied.

"What do you mean, my friend?" Horatio asked.

"He is as deadly with a sword as he is with his charm," Youngblood said.

"I will be sure to keep that in mind," acknowledged Horatio.

"Horatio, who is that man over in the corner speaking with your father-in-law?" asked Youngblood as he was drawn to the slight tint of crimson in the man's eyes.

"You would be wise to maintain a safe distance from that one, my good friend," Horatio responded with all seriousness.

"Who is he?" Youngblood asked, with his curiosity now piqued.

"Rather, what is he? A snake by the name of Kirsan," Horatio answered with contempt. "If it is criminal or an act of sabotage, Kirsan is surely behind it," he added with a very high level of disdain.

"A noble?" Youngblood asked.

"Hardly, more like a wolf in sheep's clothing! Kirsan is nothing more than a pirate parading as a representative of the people. He is a sophist with a masterful ability to twist the truth. Kirsan leads the mass and control's a shadow army of cutthroats known as the Black Guard," Horatio angrily replied.

"A shadow army? Yes, I am familiar with the Black Guard," Youngblood acknowledged.

Horatio continued, "Yes, an army that operates within the shadows. Officially, of course, the units do not exist. They are not sanctioned, and the four kingdoms do not officially recognize its existence. Failure to recognize its existence allows the leadership to dismiss the Black Guard's atrocities."

"I was under the impression that the Black Guard was an official military unit endorsed by the kingdoms to function as a multi-jurisdictional force," responded Youngblood.

"It is multi-jurisdictional to the point that it does what it pleases and wherever it pleases!" denounced Horatio.

"Surely the commanders of the Black Guard answer to some higher authority?" Youngblood asked.

"Kirsan is the leader, and it is suspected that he answers to some secret high council. Maintain your distance, my friend, for he denies existence to anyone who contradicts his will. In other words, stay away from him!" Horatio advised as he led his friend into the privacy of his library, quickly changing the subject.

"Sometimes these pretentious events annoy me no end!" complained Horatio.

"Yes, but I would imagine that they are a necessary component of your station," Youngblood said.

"I am no prince. I am a soldier," declared Horatio as he poured two glasses of his best cognac.

"I understand completely," Youngblood agreed.

"That is where you are wrong, my friend. You are a prince, but are not ready or willing to accept it."

"I am nothing more than a soldier of fortune and an average man, certainly not a noble," Youngblood responded.

"*For me nobility is synonymous with a life of effort, ever set on excelling oneself, in passing beyond what one is to what one sets up as a duty and an obligation,*"[82] announced Jonathan LeClair as he entered the library. "For once I agree with my pragmatic and sometimes cynical son-in-law."

"You are too kind with your words, sir. I am but a warrior, a barbarian for hire, who, for a price, lays waste to whatever stands in his way," Youngblood replied.

"*Barbarism is the absence of standards.*[83] You, young warrior, set the standard and lead by example. Your destiny is that of a prince. You now need only to accept your destiny," LeClair proclaimed in his most powerful orator's voice.

"A flattering theory, but I personally see no evidence to support it," Youngblood responded.

"Then why does the mass wish to destroy you and those like you?" LeClair asked.

"The mass? What are you talking about?" Youngblood replied.

"The assassins, my friend. They are agents of Kirsan and the mass, and it is their mission to destroy you before you realize your destiny," Horatio interjected.

"Why do they wish to destroy me?"

"*The mass crushes beneath it everything that is different, everything that is excellent, individual, qualified and select. Anybody who is not like everybody, who does not think like everybody, runs the risk of being eliminated.*[84] You, Youngblood Hawke, represent all that is not the mass. You represent the Select," LeClair said.

"You said they wish to destroy me and those like me? Who do you speak of?"

"*I speak of the select. In those groups which are characterized by not being multitude and mass, the effective coincidence of its members is based on some desire, idea, or ideal, which itself excludes the great number.*[85] They are many, but are few, in comparison to the mass. They are like you," LeClair replied as he sat in the large leather chair by the fireplace and sipped his cognac.

"What defines the Select man?" Youngblood asked as he sat in the chair across from Jonathan LeClair.

"*As one advances in life, one realizes more and more that the majority of men—and of women—are incapable of any other effort than that strictly imposed on them as a reaction to external compulsion. And for that reason, the few individuals we have come across who are capable of a spontaneous and joyous effort stand out isolated, monumentalized, so to speak, in our experience. These are the select men, the nobles, the only ones who are active and not merely reactive, for whom life is a perpetual striving, an incessant course of training,*"[86] LeClair said with great intensity.

"Very few people evolve to this state of existence, my friend," Horatio interrupted as he looked with reverence upon his military memorabilia and thought of his fallen comrades.

"*They are the minority. They are individuals or groups of individuals, which are specially qualified. The mass is the assemblage of persons not specially qualified. By masses, then, is not to be understood, solely or mainly, 'the working masses.' The mass is the average man,*"[87] LeClair said, attempting to convince Youngblood of his destiny.

"I find it difficult to believe that average men are all joined together in one large conspiracy to destroy the Select, as you call them," Youngblood said with reservation.

LeClair got up from the chair and poured himself another glass of cognac. "It is not an overt conspiracy. It is perpetuated by leaders such as Kirsan, by telling and giving the mass what they want. By lowering the standards, they effectively provide an illusion that they are elevating the mass," he said.

"This I have seen evidence of," Youngblood replied in agreement.

"*Imagine a humble-minded man who, having tried to estimate his own worth on specific grounds—asking himself if he has any talent for this or that, if he excels in any direction—realizes that he possesses no quality of excellence. Such a man will feel that he is mediocre and commonplace, ill gifted, but will not feel himself 'mass,'*"[88] LeClair said just as Sinclair Fox entered the room, dramatizing his level of exhaustion.

"It is extremely difficult to imagine a humble-minded man when Sinclair is within reach," laughed Youngblood, who was joined immediately by both Horatio and LeClair.

"Alas! I hear my name on the lips of such scholars and assume the discussion has been elevated to the highest intellectual levels!" Sinclair said.

"What is wrong, my friend? Have you been expelled from the abyss?" Horatio asked, resulting in more laughter.

Youngblood continued his conversation with LeClair as Sinclair took up a seat near the fire as well. "So what you are proposing is that the mass man does not know that he is a member of the mass?"

"*The mass man regards himself as perfect. The select man, in order to regard himself so, needs to be specially vain, and the belief in his perfection is not united with him consubstantially, it is not ingenuous, but arises from his vanity, and even for himself has a fictitious, imaginary, problematic character. Hence the vain man stands in need of others, he seeks in them support for the idea that he wishes to have of himself. So that not even in the diseased state, not even when blinded by vanity, does the "noble" man succeed in feeling himself as in truth complete,*"[89] continued Jonathan LeClair.

"I apologize for imposing on your discussion, but are you implying that the average man is devoid of ideas?" Sinclair Fox interjected with his aristocratic concern for all that is average.

"*The average man finds himself with 'ideas' in his head, but he lacks the faculty of ideation. He has no conception even of the rare atmosphere in which ideas live. He wished to have opinions, but is unwilling to accept the conditions and presuppositions that underlie all opinion. Hence, his ideas are in effect nothing more than appetites in words,*"[90] LeClair replied.

"Certainly, you would have to agree that the average man has a desire to become Select?" Sinclair Fox asked.

"Desire inhibited by fear!" Horatio answered as he continued to examine his military artifacts.

"Yes, Horatio! *For life is at the start a chaos in which one is lost. The individual suspects this, but he is frightened at finding himself face to face with this terrible reality, and tries to cover it over with a curtain of fantasy, where everything is clear. It does not worry him that his 'ideas' are not true, he uses them as trenches for the defense of his existence, as scarecrows to frighten away reality*,"[91] LeClair added in agreement.

"Becoming aware that one's life is the epitome of mediocrity is a terrible reality, indeed," Youngblood Hawke acknowledged as he stared into the fire.

"Yes, it is," Sinclair agreed somberly.

Jonathan LeClair stood up from his chair and approached Youngblood Hawke. He placed both hands on his shoulders and looked him straight in the eye and said, "You are the Select, and your quest is evidence of that. It is truth that you pursue, is it not? Destiny is truth, young warrior. Failure to follow your destiny will lead you away from the truth, and not to it. You will never become one with the mass. You will never be owned in either mind or spirit by anyone. That is not your way. You are a soldier of fortune who has rented his services to others, but has never sold himself into bondage. For you, my young warrior friend, cannot be owned by any man or beast."

Youngblood Hawke nodded his head in acknowledgment as Jonathan LeClair began to depart the room.

Before leaving, LeClair stopped abruptly in the doorway and said, "But remember this, the mass pursues you with a vengeance and will stop at nothing to destroy you. You have many supporters and will gain the support of many others. But you must accept leadership willingly and execute your mission with passion and determination. Good luck, young warrior."

Jonathan LeClair departed the room with all the stately manner of a true aristocrat.

CHAPTER 11

The Next Level

Pursuing my quest, forever to be.
Following fate wherever it may lead.
Adventure, fortune, and discovery!

Youngblood Hawke retired to the comfort of his quarters, to ponder the enlightening and thought-provoking discussion with Jonathan LeClair. Of course, Sinclair decided that his pondering would be better served in the deep midnight hours of the epicurean abyss.

As Youngblood fell to sleep, he dreamt of the Oracle and was slowly delivered to the sapphire realm of an alternative universe. The dream appeared to border the thin line between reality and imagination. It is a place where Youngblood was free to be himself, and not what others required him to be. His skill as a warrior was respected, but not required, in this peaceful place. The sapphire storm engulfed this world but left a calmness of mind that was foreign to the battle-hardened warrior. He found peace of mind and spirit when in the presence of the Oracle, but he knew it was fleeting. *If only*, he often thought to himself.

"You struggle with the demands of your quest?" the Oracle asked.

"My struggle is internal, and conflicts with the demands of reality."

"A reality that you have created, warrior. A reality that you alone can destroy or defend."

"I experience no such struggle in this reality," Youngblood said as he stared helplessly into the sapphire storm.

"This is not reality," the Oracle answered.

"It is a reality, is it not?" responded Youngblood.

"Yes, it is a reality for the moment. Created for the purpose of clarity," declared the Oracle.

"Clarity in respect to my quest?" he asked.

The Oracle gazed upon the young warrior who stood before her and announced, "Clarity is power."

"I don't understand."

"Accept your destiny and you will attain clarity. Once you have attained clarity, you will have obtained the power," replied the Oracle.

"What will this power provide?" Youngblood asked.

"Wielded correctly, it can lead you to the truth. In error, it will destroy you," the Oracle said. "Do you accept it? Do you accept your destiny, Youngblood Hawke?"

"I will accept it when and if it is time."

"You have doubts?"

"Many," Youngblood acknowledged.

"When the time comes, you must dismiss such doubts. You must engage the beast directly, or it will haunt you forever," she declared.

Youngblood stood before the Oracle, raised his head and asked, "How will I know when it is time?"

"You will know, and when it arrives, you must accept your path," commanded the Oracle. "But first, you must seek the next level," she added.

"The next level? Where will I find the next level?"

"Internally and externally, with clarity as your guide," proclaimed the Oracle as she called him closer.

"Clarity equals power?" he asked. "Can you provide me with such clarity?"

"Yes, now render your sword unto me," she commanded.

Youngblood Hawke approached the Oracle as the sapphire storm increased all around him and appeared to consume his very existence. The steel blade of his battle sword was converted into a powerful array of sapphire shades of light. The blade then ignited like ice on fire as the magical forces of the Oracle expanded through the sword and into the dark reaches of the warrior's mind, spirit, and heart. He fell to his knees as the euphoric energy swept through him like a whirlwind reaching out to all of his senses. He suddenly became aware of his very existence and the destiny that was now before him. Youngblood

Hawke had transcended his own reality and was prepared to travel to his next level of existence. He knew what he was and who he was, and for the first time in his life, he began to see the possibilities of why he was. He stood before the Oracle revealing a sapphire glow to his own eyes as he raised his sword in acknowledgement of his new strength of mind and spirit. He was now more than a philosopher, soldier of fortune, and professional adventurer. He was a man with a mission.

"You are ready," announced the Oracle.

"Where shall my quest take me now?" Youngblood asked with a renewed sense of purpose and determination.

"To seek the wisdom of the Prophet," she said.

"Where will I find this Prophet?"

"Nowhere and everywhere. He resides alone in a world that very few understand. The journey will be littered with peril and danger, but you must overcome every obstacle that obstructs your path. If you do not…you will fail," added the Oracle.

"You ask much of a mere mortal."

"You are capable of much, and must demand as much of yourself," responded the Oracle as she looked upon the warrior with a venerate affection.

"You have great faith in me?" he replied.

"Yes, I do," acknowledged the Oracle.

"Why do you have such faith in me?" he inquired.

"I have clarity of vision and see your destiny clearly even if you do not," said the Oracle with a level of understanding Youngblood Hawke had never encountered before.

Youngblood directed his eyes to the Oracle, as the luster of the sapphire storm escalated and then suddenly vanished, as he was returned to the comfort of Horatio Cantrell's home. He lay awake all night gazing out the open window at the stars, thinking of the Oracle and the destiny he had accepted. He knew that the challenges and dangers that lay ahead were beyond anything he had encountered before. But he also felt the presence of the new power and confidence that the Oracle had instilled in him. It was more than the motivation to continue his quest at the highest level. Youngblood Hawke was now permeating with the mystical power of inspiration. His mind and spirit pondered the nature of his quest.

Just Another Day

Darkness slowly arrives,
The clouds run for cover
Day disappears with the sun.

This day I did survive,
It was like all the others,
So thankful that it is done.

The pain I cannot deny,
Waiting, suddenly it is over,
Another day has just begun.

—*Youngblood Hawke*

Sinclair was awoken the next morning by the banging on his door.

"I declare what could possibly be so urgent at this hour!" cried out Sinclair.

"It is almost noon! Get up! Now drag yourself from that bed. We must go…now!" Youngblood said in a commanding voice.

Sinclair dressed and headed down to the kitchen to fill his belly when he was intercepted in the hall by Horatio who said, "Youngblood waits for you outside. He is ready to go."

"Ready to go? I do say, what is his hurry? And where are we to go?" Sinclair asked.

"I don't know, my friend, but he is determined and has the strangest look in his eye," replied Horatio. "I must ask you a favor, my friend," he added.

"By all means," allowed Sinclair.

"Watch his back and send for me if trouble magnifies beyond control," requested Horatio.

"I will without fail be ever present at his rear guard," promised Sinclair Fox.

"Very good," Horatio acknowledged.

❦   ❦   ❦

Youngblood was unusually quiet as the two adventurers rode through the market place. Sinclair was busy discussing his evening, recalling one woman in particular that appears to have gained his fancy.

"Did you see that beautiful flower, Youngblood?" Sinclair asked as he gazed up at the sky.

"What? Flower? What flower are you speaking of?" responded Youngblood, who was not really paying attention.

"My poor, poor, misguided colleague. Your quest blinds you to the beauty the world has to offer," noted Sinclair Fox as he pulled a flower from a passing merchant's cart and drew it to his nose.

"It is my quest that blinds?" Youngblood replied sarcastically.

"My dear friend, *her touch, her kiss, magical to me, by her side I must forever be, without her love a tragic end,*" [92] Sinclair cited poetically.

"I will give you this, Sinclair, you do have a way with words, which in turn gives you a way to the ladies," Youngblood noted.

"Alas, my days of wandering are over! I have found the one I seek and will pursue none other," responded Sinclair.

"No sooner will the cock crow and you will be falling into another abyss, my friend," said Youngblood with a grin.

Sinclair raised his hand and turned to Youngblood and said, "My heart suffers and I ask you in the most desperate manner, what is love?" He then lowered his head to heighten the drama.

"My friend, the theater appears to call you as much as the abyss I think," said Youngblood.

"Indeed, it does. Indeed, it does," acknowledged Sinclair, as he let out a sigh followed by a profound laugh.

Youngblood and Sinclair continued to ride as they both pondered the proverbial question.

What is Love?

What is Love? But a poisonous blend,
A mixture of passion and romance,

An infliction to which we must attend,
The outcome often left up to chance.

What is Love? Not so innocent and pure,
Coming to us cleverly disguised as a friend,
Beware of the power of its intoxicating allure,
Promising a beginning, it will deliver an end.

What is Love? Sadly it is just an idea,
Fully aware, but we continue to pretend,
Created by humanity to dismiss our fears,
A broken promise, we will forever defend.

—*Youngblood Hawke*

Youngblood and Sinclair were approaching a village when they came upon a traveler making his way into town. He was dressed rather poorly and was riding atop a mule. The man's relative position within society was clearly defined as he passed by the two distinctive warriors and their impressive steeds.

"Good day, gentlemen! A wonderful day for traveling, wouldn't you say?" the man said as he passed the warriors.

"Yes it is, friend," responded Sinclair as Youngblood nodded his head in acknowledgment.

"Enjoy it for there shall never be another day exactly like it!" the man added as he continued upon his journey.

Youngblood gazed upon the traveler as he passed. "I am not sure what would be worse…a lifetime of confinement or a level of existence that forced me to travel upon such an animal?"

"You do appear to be very hard upon the common man, my friend," observed Sinclair.

"Please be perfectly frank and don't hold anything back. I am sure what you intend to say is that I am mean-spirited. Am I correct?"

"Brutally honest, some would say," Sinclair noted with a smile.

"I just happen to point out the obvious. You and those like you tend to ignore humanity's failings."

"I cannot help it if I am in love with the human spirit and more gracious and sympathetic than yourself," Sinclair noted in an attempt to annoy his colleague.

"Interesting, you see yourself as such a caring and kind spirit," pointed out Youngblood.

"Hawke, my good man, you state your observation as if it is a negative state of being?"

"Perhaps it is," Youngblood responded. "Consider the man we just observed riding that mule. He was middle-aged and appeared to be able-bodied in respect to his physical condition. Furthermore, based upon our brief encounter he appeared to be a rather intelligent man, wouldn't you say?"

"Yes, I would agree with that assessment," Sinclair said.

"Now, when I pointed out that I would rather be imprisoned than find myself in a state of being where I was riding such a mule, you became rather upset and defended the man."

"Well, I wouldn't say that I was defending the man. I was just pointing out that you should not be so harsh in your criticism. After all, perhaps that mule and his current lifestyle is the best he can do," Sinclair responded.

"Ah yes, and you would characterize such a statement as kind, wouldn't you?" Youngblood asked.

"I suppose that I would, and if the reputation I am forced to endure is that of a kind man, then so be it!" acknowledged Sinclair sarcastically.

"Not so fast, my friend. I wouldn't want you to drown in the milk and honey of your own kindness. What would you say if I were to submit to you that you are not being kind at all? That in fact, you are being condescending, displaying absolutely no faith in your fellow man, and therefore actually insulting the man?" Youngblood asked.

Sinclair returned a look of puzzlement and said, "Indeed?"

"Consider the facts. You defend the man on the basis that he is doing the best he can, correct?" Youngblood asked.

"This is true, and we should hardly penalize the man for doing his best," Sinclair agreed.

"Yes, but what if what you describe as his best is not his best at all? What if the man's potential has not been tapped and he is capable of achieving much more?"

"His potential may be greater," acknowledged Sinclair.

"Maybe? Now who is being mean-spirited?" Youngblood asked. "You state that I am unfairly harsh in my criticism, when I am merely pointing out that the man appears to be capable of achieving a much higher level of success. Yet you defend his miserable state by submitting he is functioning at his optimal level."

"I can see there is some merit in your perspective," noted Sinclair reluctantly.

"Some merit? My good man, your defense of the man's poor performance is nothing less than an insult by a member of the aristocracy and intellectual elite," Youngblood declared.

"I must say you appear to have no trouble holding back," countered Sinclair. "I am not insulting the man…I mean…come now…I am supporting him."

"Yes, but if you truly had faith in your fellow man you would support them in a manner that would encourage them to pursue a greater level of performance. You would recognize that such a man is capable of much more, and has but to recognize his own potentiality. But instead, you choose to support his lack of confidence in himself and lower the standard by which he lives. You, my friend, have paid such a man no favor. In fact, you may very well have engaged in a behavior that is supportive of the mass. You, my well-intentioned friend, are no better than Kirsan himself. In all actuality, you are in many ways facilitating his imprisonment within the cave of darkness," Youngblood said.

"I hardly think that you could call me his jailer," Sinclair responded.

"Yes, but I would hardly describe you as the man's benefactor either," pointed out Youngblood. "Is mediocrity the highest goal we can offer to our fellow man? We must raise the standard and lead by example."

"But surely there are those who are not capable of achieving such high levels of performance and success?" Sinclair interjected.

"You are quite right. Those who put forth their best effort should be commended for doing so. However, those who become complacent and idle should be exposed."

Sinclair shook his head and asked, "What is it we are exposing such individuals to be?"

"They are simply individuals who do not care and quite frankly…individuals who don't care…don't matter," Youngblood replied.

"You, Youngblood Hawke, do in fact raise the standards to new levels. Yet I am not sure many people can reach, never mind maintain, such a level," Sinclair said.

"Perhaps you are correct for it is possible that such levels are reserved for the Select, and such a designation must be earned…meritoriously," Youngblood replied.

"Such high standards will undoubtedly separate society," Sinclair noted. "Is it fair to dismiss the weak from the group and so clearly define their inability?"

"By contrast, is it fair to restrict the strong and limit their potential?" Youngblood said.

"Are you suggesting that human beings should not be treated with equality?" Sinclair asked.

"*Human Beings are inherently unequal; to treat them otherwise is not to affirm but to deny their humanity,*"[93] Youngblood declared.

Sinclair shook his head, acknowledging his colleague's point as the two warriors continued on their journey.

Youngblood and Sinclair traveled for five days as they rode higher and higher into the mountains. Sinclair was unaware of their destination but never asked his friend where it was they were going. He knew that Youngblood was following his quest. To Sinclair, it was a journey of fulfillment, and he found it most intriguing. Sinclair Fox had, for the most part, spent his days following the course of no other. He enjoyed the freedom of existence, but for some unknown reason he felt compelled to follow the path of Youngblood Hawke. In many ways the quest of Youngblood Hawke had now become his own. He admired his colleague's determination and found Youngblood's newfound clarity of vision astonishing.

The pass was darkened by the storm clouds as the men continued higher into the mountains. Civilization was not to be found, as they had passed the last remote village several days before. The air was becoming much colder as it began to bite at their bones. Suddenly, the men halted their advance as they became aware of the shadow cast over them. It was mammoth in dimension, suggesting the existence of a most menacing creature.

"What is that?" Sinclair asked as he, without hesitation, drew his sword.

"I don't know, but whatever it is, it appears to be hungry," Youngblood responded.

"With all due respect, my good man, I don't believe this is a time for humor," Sinclair said.

"Don't worry, my friend. I am not laughing," Youngblood replied as he drew his battle sword from its scabbard. "I believe that the appropriate strategy at the moment would appear to be a retrograde departure," Youngblood said to his worrisome friend.

"A what?" Sinclair asked.

"In other words my, good man, run away!" Youngblood Hawke commanded.

"Very good. I am in complete agreement," Sinclair agreed.

The two men without hesitation rode to the left of the predator in an attempt to escape confrontation. But the way they had chosen led them back to the shadow of the creature, as it obstructed their path.

"This way," cried out Sinclair as he sped through the trees, breaking his own path as he went along.

"No use, my friend. Look!" Youngblood cried out as the shadowy beast once again appeared before them.

"How many are there?" shouted Sinclair desperately.

Youngblood immediately turned back and returned to the main road, followed closely by Sinclair. Upon reaching the road, they were immediately confronted by the beast obstructing the mountain pass.

"We have no choice but to turn back, my friend," Sinclair noted, believing it was the obvious choice.

Youngblood stood staring at the shadow of the creature, attempting to imagine the reality that it represented.

"I cannot turn back, nor can I remain still. I have but one choice and without doubt, it is to move forward!" Youngblood Hawk declared as he charged into the direction of the shadow.

"Youngblood, what in God's name are you doing!" Sinclair shouted.

"This is my fight! Remain here!" Youngblood Hawke commanded as he continued his advance into the darkness and mist of the shadow.

The shadow grew near as Youngblood continued toward his target. The great predator was waiting for its prey, and Youngblood became keenly aware of what it was before him.

"A dragon!" Youngblood Hawke proclaimed boldly as he increased his charge and engaged the mighty beast with a blow from his battle sword.

The thunder of steel against its mighty claws rang out beyond the universe of reality as the young warrior engaged the beast to the death! The end would, without question, be near for one of the combatants. The hellish creature continued to spew foul, poisonous venom intended to reduce the warrior to ash.

Yet he fought on, a mere mortal, fueled by the newly found power of his destiny! He thought to himself that surely the magic of the Oracle was no match for this beast? Yet, the heat of battle began to vanquish his strength. The dragon was powerful, exhibiting the might of a hundred men, as they battled in the mist. Youngblood continued to strike the beast with relentless force only to be forced back into a defensive position. The sudden power of the blow pounded Youngblood, forcing him from his mount. He was sent in one direction as his battle sword landed far from his reach. The creature continued its attack as Youngblood drew his katana, with an eye on his battle sword.

"I must retrieve that sword!" he said to himself.

The dragon was relentless, countering every attempt of Youngblood to gain an avenue to the battle sword. Unexpectedly, Veritas charged the beast, drawing its attention away from Youngblood. Seizing the moment, he leaped past the beast as he rolled to the ground, and in one motion retrieved the battle sword. Youngblood then charged the dragon, deflecting its attention from his trusted friend. The battle continued as beast and man engaged each other, drawing blood from the other with each strike.

The dragon appeared to be gaining an edge when the exhausted warrior found renewed power within the sapphire storm that ran through the very essence of his mind and spirit. In fact, Youngblood Hawke began to feel the storm increasing as he raised his sword through the mist, illuminating everything before him.

"It is time!" he cried out as he unleashed the power within, and in one mighty strike destroyed the dragon, sending it to its eternal death!

He stood silently over the beast, acknowledging the majesty of his victory and now, fully aware of his destiny and the path that waited for him.

Veritas approached the battle-weary Youngblood who looked at his trusted friend and said, "Thank you. I am beginning to learn that these beasts cannot be fought alone, my friend."

Youngblood returned to greet the very anxious Sinclair Fox, who was still waiting with sword in hand.

"Youngblood!" cried out Sinclair with enthusiasm.

"Hello, my friend," Youngblood said as he approached, and the two men shook hands. "I want to thank you, Sinclair," he added.

"What could you possibly be thanking me for? I did not assist and should apologize for failing to do so," Sinclair replied.

"That is exactly why I am thanking you," Youngblood acknowledged. "It was my fight and my fight alone."

"Yes, this is true," Sinclair said.

"Shall we proceed on with this quest?" Youngblood asked of his friend.

"Indeed, we shall," Sinclair replied approvingly.

The two warriors camped for the night at the base of the mountain. It was a mountain that was menacing in stature. This was a mountain that Youngblood Hawke also knew he had to climb. It was no ordinary mountain as its pass was riddled with obstacles and obstructions designed to test his faith. Successful ascent of this mountain would lead him to the Prophet, and closer to his quest.

As the two men rested by the fire the sounds of nature abounded. Youngblood attended to the minor wounds inflicted during his battle with the dragon while Sinclair spoke once again of his encounter in Ventura. Youngblood actually found Sinclair's storytelling soothing as he had become accustomed to his friend being by his side. Youngblood slowly drifted into sleep and was immediately delivered to his sapphire world.

"Do you understand?" the Oracle asked.

"Clearly," Youngblood responded.

"It is your destiny. Do you accept it?" the Oracle replied as Youngblood continued to lose himself in the sapphire glow of her eyes.

"Willingly. I will travel whatever path destiny reveals to me," Youngblood acknowledged.

"Destiny will reveal many paths to you, warrior. Choose them wisely for they are for you alone to choose," the Oracle said.

"You will continue to guide me?" Youngblood asked.

"Wisdom and clarity will guide you."

"Yes, you will," Youngblood Hawke acknowledged with a smile.

The sapphire storm set in the Oracle's eyes and in a twist of fate, Youngblood Hawke was returned to sleep. He lay restfully illuminated by a slight sapphire glow. The Oracle's image appeared translucent over him as she listened carefully to the whisper of his dreams.

If Only For A Moment

If only for a moment, I could feel your tender touch,
I would thank the stars, for giving me just this much,
For surely such a gift, would be sent from up above.

If only for a moment, I could hold your lovely hand,
The woman that you are, I might begin to understand,
A mystery to unravel, all that I have dreamed of.

If only for a moment, I could hold you in my arms,
You would soon realize, I could never do you harm,
The object of my desires, you are the one that I adore.

If only for a moment, I could experience your kiss,
Please let it last forever, this would be my only wish,
Your lips, so sweet, would leave me wanting more.

If only for a moment, you would look into my eyes,
A lonely soul you would find, much to your surprise.
A heart filled with sadness, just waiting for your love.

—*Youngblood Hawke*

The glow diminished as she returned to her own realm, leaving the warrior to the trials of his quest.

CHAPTER 12

Thus He Spoke

Lost in a world of chaotic conformity.
My heart and soul grow weary,
Longing for a time of relative sanity.

The weather continued to change for the worse as Youngblood and Sinclair continued their ascent up the mountain. The elements were beating on the two men as the cold wind ripped across their faces. Sinclair had been quiet for over an hour and Youngblood began to worry about his friend.

"How are you holding up?" Youngblood asked.

"Perhaps this quest of yours could lead to a warmer and much friendlier climate?" responded Sinclair, as his teeth chattered from the intensity of the cold.

"I will keep that in mind, my friend," Youngblood acknowledged as he was also suffering from the extreme temperatures of the mountain. "And what to do we have here?" Youngblood asked as he stopped to survey the path ahead.

"It would appear that your quest has led you astray. The road ends here," Sinclair Fox said.

"The road may end, but the journey continues," Youngblood responded.

"Listen to me, Hawke, there is no road to follow," Sinclair insisted.

"Roads are built for the mass. They narrow as they are traveled less, and become obscure paths for the few. And sometimes, Sinclair, a new path must be cleared where no one has traveled before," Youngblood said as he dismounted.

"What is it you hope to find on that mountain?" Sinclair asked.

"Answers? But I suspect I will find more questions," replied Youngblood. "Sinclair, we will tie the horses here within this protected area carved into the mountain. Then we will proceed on foot," Youngblood said decisively.

"I think not, my good friend. This is as far as I go. For this quest is your own, and I am not prepared to encounter that which you seek on that mountain. No, I will wait here for your return, warming the chill from my bones with a fire," Sinclair said.

"I understand," Youngblood acknowledged. "I will return shortly."

"Please do," replied Sinclair with a grin. "And remain alert!" Sinclair added as he watched his friend disappear into the trees.

Youngblood Hawke proceeded on foot, making his way through the thicket and the difficult terrain leading up the mountainside. Slight remnants of a path could be seen. At least Youngblood believed he could see the remains of a path.

A Difficult Journey

What is life, after all?
  A tangled thicket,
Obscuring your view.

An impassable path,
  A maze of sorts,
Forever delaying you.

Impossible to travel,
  Slowing your progress
Difficult to break through.

Such is your journey,
  So difficult at times,
Yet, you must continue.

—Youngblood Hawke

An ancient path. And rarely traveled from the looks of it, he thought to himself as he worked his way up the mountain.

The course he was traveling was difficult, often requiring him to lift himself higher and higher as he gripped the rocks and ledges in an attempt to lift his own body weight to the next level. The wind continued to howl and thrash him about, attacking his balance as he ascended. A cold rain and sleet often accompanied the wind, grinding into his face and diminishing his ability to breathe and see clearly. Youngblood thought of all the things he had done to get to where he was, wondering if it was worth the suffering he now experienced. Nature appeared to be sending legions of her forces upon the warrior, who drew all his strength just to sustain the punishment. He had no counteroffensive available, other than to push on and move up in the hope that he would break through to the next level.

Youngblood stood below the sheer cliff and gazed upward as the wind and cold rain virtually cut into his humanity. His body was shivering from the continued onslaught, but his mind and spirit remained focused upon his quest. As he looked up at the cliff, he contemplated turning back, but his proverbial stare suddenly caught a glimpse of something beyond the mist and rain. It appeared to be a man positioned above the cliff, looking out into the distance. The man did not appear to be aware of Youngblood's presence.

The Prophet? Youngblood thought to himself as he began to climb the steep cliff leading up to the man standing high above him.

The cliff was straight, leading up to a point approximately one hundred feet, if not more. It was treacherous, to say the least, and one mistake in his footing could cause the warrior to fall to his death. His climb was painstakingly slow as he was forced to fight the winds and elements, as well as the sharpness of the cliff. He possessed no rope, no guide, and no support as he climbed higher and higher. Youngblood would stop momentarily to rest, and then he would look down to where he had started. He thought of how far he had traveled, but he could not help but note that if he were to fall, it would take only seconds to return him to his point of departure. Youngblood began to approach the summit, while also feeling the increase in intensity as the wind attempted to derail him from his climb. He reached up and caught hold of a rock as he lifted himself over the top and onto the summit. The wind and rain continued to rage on, but he could only hear it, for it now raged below his lofty position.

The man stood silent, staring into eternity, revealing no indication that he was aware a visitor had arrived. Youngblood remained quiet, catching his breath as he recovered from his climb. He was puzzled by the strangeness of the Prophet, who stood silent before him, and Youngblood dared not interrupt his meditation.

Several hours passed before Youngblood, in frustration, finally stood and said, "A mysterious force has delivered me to the height of this perilous mountain."

Without moving or turning to address the warrior, the Prophet spoke, "*Why should that frighten you? But it is with man as it is with the tree. The more he aspires to the height and light, the more strongly do his roots strive earthward, downward, into the dark.*"[94]

"Yes, the darkness haunts me. I seek the light but these heights are new to me. I am no longer the man I once was, and fear what it is I may become," Youngblood responded.

"*Some souls one will never discover, unless one invents them first,*"[95] the Prophet said as he continued to look into the far distance. "*I no longer trust myself since I aspire to the height, and nobody trusts me anymore; how did this happen? I change too fast; my today refutes my yesterday. I often skip steps when I climb: no step forgives me that. When I am at the top I always find myself alone. Nobody speaks to me; the frost of loneliness makes me shiver. What do I want up high? My contempt and my longing grow at the same time; the higher I climb, the more I despise the climber. What does he want up high? How ashamed I am of my climbing and stumbling! How I mock at my violent panting! How I hate the flier! How weary I am up high!*"[96] the Prophet continued without looking at his audience.

"Is it possible to climb too high?" Youngblood Hawke asked.

Pointing to a solitary tree the Prophet said, "*This tree stands lonely here in the mountains; it grew high above man and beast. And if it wanted to speak it would have nobody who could understand it, so high has it grown. Now it waits and waits—for what is it waiting? It dwells too near the seat of the clouds: surely, it waits for the first lightning.*"[97]

"I understand the dilemma, Prophet. But I cannot control my desire to understand. I am unable to inhibit my desire to seek new heights," Youngblood replied wearily.

"*It tears my heart. Better than your words tell it, your eyes tell me of all your dangers. You are not yet free, you still search for freedom. You are worn from your search and over awake. You aspire to the free heights, your soul thirsts for the stars,*"[98] the Prophet added.

"Yes, I am weary, Prophet, but I continue my quest," Youngblood said.

"*I am a wanderer and mountain climber, he said to his heart; I do not like the plains, and it seems I cannot sit for long. And whatever may yet come to me as destiny and experience will include some wandering and mountain climbing: in the end, one experiences only oneself,*"[99] the Prophet said as the warrior listened intently.

"Why do I wander so?" Youngblood asked.

"*One must learn to look away from oneself in order to see much: this hardness is necessary to every climber of mountains,*"[100] the Prophet answered.

Youngblood continued to contemplate the Prophet's words and asked, "But where does it lead me?"

"*You are going your way to greatness: now that which has hitherto been your ultimate danger has become your refuge,*"[101] the Prophet noted.

"A refuge from what?" Youngblood asked.

"The mass!" replied the Prophet with indignation. "The mass thrives on mediocrity and darkness," he added. "*Behold, how it lures them, the all too many, and how it devours them, chews them, and ruminates!*"[102]

"I have been told, and in fact, have witnessed that the mass seeks to destroy me," Youngblood said.

"*Indeed I know your danger. But by my love and hope I beseech you: do not throw away your love and hope. You still feel noble, and the others too feel your nobility, though they bear you a grudge and send you evil glances. Know that the noble man stands in everybody's way. The noble man stands in the way of the good too; and even if they call him one of the good, they thus want to do away with him. The noble man wants to create something new and a new virtue. The good want the old, and that the old be preserved. But this is not the danger of the noble man, that he might become one of the good, but a churl, a mocker, a destroyer.*"[103]

"Will the mass ever cease to pursue me?"

"Never! But remember this, *what does not kill you makes you stronger,*"[104] the Prophet declared. "What is it you desire from your quest?"

"The truth," Youngblood announced. "The absolute truth!"

"The truth! Why do you seek the truth?" the Prophet asked.

"For the good of all," Youngblood Hawke replied.

"*There is no pre-established harmony between the furtherance of truth and the well-being of mankind,*"[105] the Prophet noted. "If you seek it, you do so to satisfy your own hunger."

"Indeed, I do. But will mankind not also benefit from my quest?" Youngblood asked.

"*Do not throw away the hero in your soul! Hold holy your highest hope! And if you cannot be a saint of knowledge, at least be its warrior,*"[106] the Prophet proclaimed.

"A warrior I am!" Youngblood Hawke proclaimed.

"*Brave, unconcerned, mocking, violent—thus wisdom wants us: she is a woman and always loves only a warrior,*"[107] the Prophet added.

"If only this were true," Youngblood said as the Oracle came to mind.

"It is true! This is why the warrior is at a disadvantage," responded the Prophet. "*Free-doers are at a disadvantage compared with freethinkers because people suffer more obviously from the consequences of deeds than from those of thoughts.*[108] But this you have already learned," he added.

"Yes, but free-doers can also reap the benefits of action, something that freethinkers cannot, if they fail to act and only think about doing," Youngblood countered.

The Prophet remained silent and continued his gaze out into the midnight sky. As he looked into the heavens he appeared to be pondering the response of Youngblood Hawke. The skies behind the Prophet were alive with celestial activity as the stars glistened, interrupted intermittently by a falling star. Several hours passed as the Prophet remained silent, and Youngblood waited patiently for some sign or indication that he would once again speak. The warrior was beginning to wonder if this was in fact a signal that his time upon the mountain was complete. However, something deep inside told him to remain.

Just as Youngblood was beginning to fall asleep, the Prophet raised both his hands toward the skies and proclaimed, "*To you, the bold venturers and adventurers and whoever has embarked with cunning sails upon dreadful seas, to you who are intoxicated by riddles, who take pleasure in the twilight, whose soul is lured with flutes to every treacherous abyss, to you alone do I tell of this riddle that I saw—the vision of the most solitary man!*"[109]

Youngblood remained still, unsure of how to respond, or if he should in fact respond at all. The Prophet continued his stare into nothingness. Suddenly, he turned to Youngblood Hawke for the first time and directed his stare into the warrior's soul.

"Do not remain here high above the clouds where only the solitary man resides. This is no place for a warrior. This is the end of a quest, but not of your own. You must move forward and upward!" the Prophet declared.

"Higher than this mountain?" Youngblood asked.

Youngblood pondered the words of the Prophet and reflected upon his own quest.

Seeking New Heights

The heights of success are almost mystical when viewed from the depths of mediocrity. Represented as a majestic mountain, its summit is barely visible to the naked eye. To many who dwell in the valley, it can only be seen with imagination and wonder. To some, it cannot be seen at all.

The summit towers high above the clouds of insecurity and fear. The majority has no desire or ambition to scale its steep cliffs. For them, the perils are too real, the risk of falling too great. However, a select few are unable to resist the summit's powerful and intoxicating allure. The select accept the challenge of the mountain. Prepared and unprepared, planned and unplanned, as a member of a team, and often a solitary climber, they all share the same quest.

Every minute, every hour, of every day, a new expedition departs. Climbers, beware! This treacherous mountain is loyal to none. Many dedicated climbers have fallen and many more remain stranded, unable to climb higher and reach new heights. What torture it must be to clearly see the summit, but remain unable to reach it?

How can a climber get so close, yet remain so distant from the object of his desire? Paralysis can inflict the climber with the power of a plague. The symptoms are clearly defined: inadequate supplies and provisions, the absence of a strategic plan, the lack of resolve and vision, and the inability to control fear. This disease can be avoided and is not always fatal. It can be overcome by some but for many it is the end. The tragic and unforgiving end of a life's dream.

Why do they climb this mountain riddled with danger? The simple answer resonates within our collective conscience. Echoing from the depths of reality, our minds, hearts, and souls understand that humanity demands no less. The climber of mountains seeks the next level of existence, maintaining faith that the summit is near and within reach.

A very select few will break through the clouds and reach the summit. A truth may be revealed to those who succeed. They may realize that success was achieved when the courage was found to actually begin the journey. The pain, the suffering, and sacrifice endured during the climb will become revered memories. Their past life in the valley will no longer be treated with contempt. In fact, it will remain a humbling reminder of who we are and where we come from. The climber will begin a new life, high above the clouds, upon the heights of this proverbial mountain.

One must take care, for living at such heights can be as difficult as it is rewarding. The perils of the mountain do not disappear upon reaching the summit. The dangers are enhanced, as the winds of competition and change grow stronger. The elements of nature will work harmoniously to push them from the heights. More and more climbers will come, friend and foe alike, seeking a place on this majestic mountain. The summit will become crowded as the majority seeks to secure their positions. Vision and ambition will be replaced by mediocrity and fear.

A select few will become restless and begin to once again look up into the clouds. A fateful few will see through the clouds and catch glimpses of an even higher summit. They will realize that the next level calls out to them. Such climbers will embark on a new expedition into the heights of human potentiality, inspiring others to follow and join in their quest. They will continue to climb higher and higher, never looking down, always seeking the next level. The future of humanity demands no less.

—Youngblood Hawke

Youngblood sat in awe as the Prophet continued to unveil his thoughts. *"You should seek your enemy, you should wage your war—a war for your opinions. And if your opinion is defeated, your honesty should still cry triumph over that!"*[110] the Prophet cried out.

"War? You speak of my internal battle?" Youngblood asked.

"Yes, but your external enemy awaits you as well!" he said.

"But war? You suggest I raise an army and declare war on those who consider me their enemy? Is my quest worthy enough to justify war?" Youngblood asked.

"You say it is the good cause that hallows even war? I tell you: it is the good war that hallows every cause,"[111] he said.

"But surely waging war against the mass will not bring me closer to the truth, nor the mass closer to enlightenment?" Youngblood asked.

"War and courage have done more great things than charity. Not your pity but your bravery has saved the unfortunate up to now,"[112] the Prophet declared.

"Then I must not only follow my quest but I must also bring the fight to the mass?"

"Yes, they are one in the same. Many Select lay hidden within the mass. You must uncover the Select, show them the light, and lead them out of the darkness. You have done this before, but you are one, and you need many to fulfill your destiny," the Prophet acknowledged.

"I think I understand," Youngblood replied.

"You must think to understand," he said. "Now go! You may visit this mountain, but you may not remain! For if you do, you will surely go mad!" the Prophet ordered as he turned and faced the heavens for answers high above the reality from whence he came.

"But what of your fate, Prophet?"

"*I spoke my teaching, I broke upon my teaching: thus my eternal fate will have it—as prophet I shall perish!*"[113] the Prophet declared.

"I will return, Prophet! And I will speak the truth from atop this mountain! I will declare it for all to hear!" Youngblood proclaimed as he began his way down the sheer cliffs of the Prophet's mountain.

A Fool's Quest

Will this tribulation ever end?
A fool's quest, cleverly disguised,
In God's name, we often pretend,
A destination never to be realized.

A cynical thought, you so often say.
Open your eyes! What do you see?
Suffering and pain rules the day,
Closing your eyes, ignoring reality.

Oh what a cute faithful little clown!
Hoping and praying, always in pain.
Unaware you are chained and bound,
Seeking forgiveness, hiding your shame.

Break those chains! Open your eyes!
Life is a journey, not a trial or test,
Pursue the truth; expose all the lies,
Such is the nature of humanities quest.

—*Youngblood Hawke*

❦   ❦   ❦

"Youngblood! I feared that you had fallen to your death, my friend!" Sinclair said as his warrior friend approached from the depths of the path leading from the mountain.

"Why, what do you mean? I was only gone for a day," Youngblood replied.

"Have you lost your wits, man! You have been gone for almost a week! I was running out of provisions and feared I might have to leave for assistance," Sinclair Fox said as he greeted his friend, very happy to see his safe return.

"Really? A week? Time and space appears to be suspended high above the daily doings of reality," Youngblood remarked as he looked up into the clouds to the summit of the Prophet's mountain.

"Sinclair, we must go for we have an army to raise!"

"My goodness. You have gone mad!" Sinclair replied in amazement. "What will you do with an army?"

"Why, wage war of course."

"War? Against whom?" Sinclair asked.

"The mass."

"I must say you have without question returned from that mountain with a very ambitious agenda. Very ambitious, indeed!" Sinclair said. "What leads you to believe you can defeat the mass?"

"Faith in the truth, and faith in oneself, as well as the faith of human potentiality. I must succeed, we must succeed, humanity must succeed."

"Your ambition and drive to succeed is most remarkable," commented Sinclair. "A gift I would imagine?"

"A gift for some, perhaps, but in many ways, a curse for others," Youngblood noted.

"A curse? Why, what do you mean? How could such traits as ambition, vision, and the desire to succeed be a curse?" a puzzled Sinclair asked.

"Perhaps when the desire to succeed, as you call it, becomes the need to succeed."

"Are they not the same?" Sinclair asked.

"To many they would appear to be the same. But in reality, they are very different, and are often separated by the level of adversity and difficulty presented by those challenges that test one's abilities," Youngblood replied.

"Intriguing. Please elaborate, Hawke."

"Consider for a moment that an individual with the traits you describe is a pugilist."

"A prize fighter?" Sinclair asked.

"Indeed, a prizefighter, and a rather gifted one as well," Youngblood offered.

"Please continue."

"Our gifted prize fighter is, without question, a dedicated professional pursuing every challenger with the resolve of a true warrior. He finds himself winning contest after contest with ease within his weight class, and defeating all that challenge him," Youngblood said.

"Yes, I can see this warrior, a true champion," Sinclair noted.

"Our champion soon finds himself desiring more of a challenge. The weight class he currently competes within is no longer a contest," Youngblood said.

"In other words, the lack of quality challengers capable of defeating him and testing his abilities begins to bore him?" Sinclair asked.

"Yes. Our champion no longer finds fulfillment competing at this level. Therefore, he decides to move up to the next level. He adds weight to his frame and trains harder in order to compete at the higher level," Youngblood explained.

"Indeed, of course, he will find the competitors within the next level much more of a challenge," Sinclair agreed.

"Yes, much more of a challenge, at least for a time, that is until he conquers this level, and must now move on in order to find the challenges that will satisfy his hunger," said Youngblood.

"But if he continues to move up into the heavier weight classes, will he not eventually engage competitors and challengers who can defeat him?" Sinclair asked.

"Indeed, he will, my good man, indeed, he will! As our champion continues to climb level after level in search of a challenge, he will inevitably be defeated, and find fewer victories."

"The sensation of victory until now has driven our champion, but now he must contend with the suffering effects of defeat," Sinclair noted.

"Sinclair, my good man, you are almost profound to a fault!" Youngblood replied with a hearty and somewhat sarcastic laugh.

"Ah yes, I do often surprise even myself," Sinclair said as he twisted the end of his mustache rather proudly, while also acknowledging his colleague's sarcasm.

"The true test of a champion is defined by his ability to cope with defeat, and not his ability to deal with victory. Of course, a gracious winner is always an indication of a noble warrior. However, accepting loss and transforming such an experience into a positive lesson is a true test of character," Youngblood Hawke said.

"Indeed, it is," he noted.

"Many who call themselves champions, remain at the lower level, finding glory in victory after victory. But is such an individual a true champion?" Youngblood asked.

"Well, of course, he is winning and defeating all of his challengers," Sinclair noted.

"They may be challengers, but are they a true challenge?" Youngblood asked. "Does his failure to seek the next level and test his abilities against stronger competitors diminish his identity as a champion?"

"I understand your point. A true champion would seek out new challenges, continuing to test his own limits," agreed Sinclair.

"And what of the prize fighter who is unable to deal with defeat? What of this individual who is demoralized by defeat and unable to find fulfillment and motivation without victory? Is this the sign of a true champion?" Youngblood asked.

"I suppose not," Sinclair replied.

"Would not a true champion use defeat as a lesson in humility and perhaps human mortality? One would expect a true champion to engage in a stricter regiment of training, both physically and intellectually, following defeat. A true champion would find motivation in failure and reveal a stronger desire to succeed and reach the next level. Adversity and difficulty would no longer be an enemy, but would now be a most powerful ally," Youngblood said.

"That, my good friend, is a very interesting concept," Sinclair acknowledged.

"It is a state of mind, it is a philosophy; indeed, it is necessary in order to succeed," Youngblood responded.

"Indeed, *the greatest test of courage on earth is to bear defeat without losing heart*,"[114] Sinclair quoted.

"Well spoken, my friend," Youngblood said.

"I suspect that one would have to take care and not allow defeat to kill nor cripple one on the road to success?"

"The effects of failure can be very crippling. In many ways, more devastating than the defeat itself," Youngblood said. "But we should not let fear of failure derail our quest or deter us from our goals and dreams."

"I suspect that even the most confident warrior has doubts," Sinclair said.

"We all have doubts, Sinclair. Anyone who does not experience doubt or fear is only fooling themselves. It is the paralysis that can be the result of extreme doubt and fear that one should take care against."

"Yes, your thoughts bring to mind a passage I once read, '*Our doubts are traitors, and makes us lose the good we oft might win, by fearing to attempt,*'"[115] Sinclair said as he raised his hand for dramatic effect.

"Attempt we shall, succeed we must," Youngblood replied.

The two warriors proceeded down the pass as Youngblood continued to share with Sinclair the tale of his experience on the mountain's summit. He told him of the Prophet and the "Solitary Man," as well as the prophecies told to him regarding future conflict with the mass. Youngblood explained to Sinclair the need to organize the Select Warriors into a force capable of meeting and defeating the mass on the field of battle.

The climate became friendlier as the two men made their way down the mountain. The warmth of the sun, combined with the comfort of a soft breeze, was in significant contrast to the harshness of the mountain. Youngblood and Sinclair were in high spirits and had just turned onto the main road. Suddenly, without warning, Youngblood was knocked from his horse!

The attacker had been concealed in the trees and caught Youngblood completely by surprise. Sinclair attempted to intervene, but found himself confronted by two assailants as they charged him with swords drawn. Youngblood Hawke was struggling with his attacker as the man attempted to bury his sword into the warrior's heart. Unable to gain access to his battle sword or katana, Youngblood focused all of his energy on holding back the sword of his opponent. He was able to struggle to his feet and then he fell backward, flipping the attacker over and rolling him in the opposite direction. The toss and hard landing dazed his assassin, allowing Youngblood an opportunity to draw his dagger. He immediately charged his opponent and lunged the dagger into the man's heart! The attacker fell silent as Youngblood drew his katana and finished him. Youngblood turned, and found Sinclair holding his own against the remaining pair of assassins, but Youngblood wasted no time as he lessened the odds with one strike. The man screamed in pain as the katana delivered a fatal blow and penetrated deep into his shoulder. The remaining attacker attempted to eliminate Sinclair, but found himself overmatched, as Sinclair's sword penetrated the man's chest and relieved him of his miserable existence.

Sinclair looked over to Youngblood with a great sense of accomplishment and said, "Good show, old man! Now, why in the world would you need an army to deal with the likes of such untalented scoundrels as these?"

Youngblood stood, looking off into the distance as he listened to the pounding roar that approached and nodded his head to Sinclair stating, "That is why, my friend."

Sinclair turned to see the dust being kicked up by the horses as the mass approached.

"My goodness! There must be at least one hundred or more of them," declared Sinclair as he wasted no time to remount his horse.

"I would say about fifty would be accurate," noted Youngblood Hawke, as he studied the approaching mass, in true military fashion.

"Without question, it is time to go! I believe you called it a retrograde departure!" Sinclair said anxiously.

Youngblood continued to stand by Veritas and study the approaching mass.

"Youngblood! We must go now!" Sinclair cried out desperately.

"You go! Depart at once! It is not you that they seek to destroy," Youngblood instructed as he turned to look at Sinclair.

"Have you gone mad? Do you honestly believe that I would leave you alone to face that?" Sinclair replied, gesturing to the approaching herd.

"You have no choice in the matter, Sinclair. I am ordering you to depart!" Youngblood commanded as he stared at the horizon and the incoming threat.

Sinclair looked at his friend in puzzlement. He was not sure how to take such a command but knew that his friend was a soldier and a leader. He also knew that in the heat of battle, you did not contest a command from a superior leader. You just followed it exactly as it was given, or die.

"I want you to travel west and I will go east. It is me that they seek, so I will allow them to get closer. Close enough to know which rider to follow," Youngblood said calmly as he climbed onto Veritas.

"Are you sure this is the correct course of action?"

"Trust me, my friend. I know what I am doing. I have many friends in the Eastern Kingdom," Youngblood said as he shook his colleague's hand. "Now go!" he ordered.

Sinclair began to ride west, but stopped suddenly and turned his horse in the direction of his friend and comrade. "Don't worry, my friend, I know what to do!" he shouted and then rode off at full gallop.

Youngblood assumed a higher position, allowing his silhouette to be seen clearly against the backdrop of the sunset. He wanted the approaching mass to clearly identify their target and feel the closeness of their desired kill. The higher ground also allowed him to ensure that Sinclair was not being followed.

"Come on, you blind mass of nothingness!" Youngblood screamed as they drew closer.

The Race

>My life runs a gauntlet,
>Ignorant of the fact it will fail,
>Against the powers of nature,
>>So meek, so weak, and so frail.
>
>Setting sail so boldly,
>Weathering every storm,
>So often thrown off-course,
>>Battered, beaten, and worn.
>
>Running the path to destiny,
>Pursued by fate's evil twin,
>A mad dash against time,
>>It is a race I can never win.
>
>If only I could rest a moment,
>Some time to catch my breath,
>A chance to stop and realize,
>>That I am racing to my death.

—*Youngblood Hawke*

He waited for only a short time longer and then said, "I would say that is about close enough. Wouldn't you agree, Veritas?"

Youngblood pulled back on the reins, raising Veritas up on his hind legs. He turned his trusted steed toward the east and departed at full charge. His gallant departure did not go unnoticed as the mass immediately changed its course toward the east and pursued the lone warrior.

Sinclair Fox had escaped without detection. He stopped in an attempt to see if he could assess the plight of his friend. However, all he was able to see was the cloud of dust billowing to the sky from the determined pursuers. Sinclair looked upon the site with despair and wondered what fate would befall his friend.

"Be careful, my friend," he said to himself and then rode off, at full speed, toward the west and the City of Ventura.

CHAPTER 13

Know Thy Enemy, Know Thyself

Relentless pursuit of an ancient ideology,
Emptiness and loneliness has unto now defined me.
Shrouded by my quest, cloaked in darkness,
A self-imposed exile from the majority.

Sinclair rode long and hard as he continued to drive on toward Ventura. He rarely stopped and when he did so, it was only to rest his horse. He barely slept, as he thought of nothing except the fate of his friend. Sinclair had never taken anything as seriously as he did this mission. He knew that any delay could be fatal for Youngblood Hawke. Sinclair was weary and tired as he pushed himself to the limit night and day. Dismal thoughts ran wildly through his mind as he considered the possibilities of Youngblood's fate.

"He may already be dead," he continually said to himself as he traveled in solitude, acknowledging no one along his path. "What if he has been taken prisoner and his being tortured at this very moment!" he cried out.

He thought of his friend, the Prince, and how he failed him. Sinclair continued to blame himself for the Prince's demise. He constantly questioned himself and wondered if he had only left earlier or traveled faster.

"Could I have saved the Prince from his tragic death?" Sinclair asked himself.

Such thoughts only made him more determined, as he pushed onward to the City of Ventura. Sinclair Fox would not allow a similar fate to fall upon the Prince, known as Youngblood Hawke.

Sinclair arrived in Ventura in the early morning hours. His ride through the city streets was almost frantic as he charged up to the manor of Horatio Cantrell.

"Horatio! Horatio! Come at once!" the tired and worn Sinclair Fox cried out as he approached the estate.

Two stableman were awoken by the uproar of Sinclair's arrival and, at first, thought him to be a madman. They attempted to physically restrain him and keep him from entering the house.

"Unhand me, you fools, or I will kill you where you stand!" Sinclair said as he struck one down and pulled away from the other.

"Sinclair? Is that you? What in the name of heaven are you doing?" Horatio asked as he exited his home with a sword in his hand. "Release him at once!" Horatio ordered to the servants, who were more than happy to comply.

"Horatio, its Youngblood, he...he is certainly doomed if you don't...," Sinclair said as he tried to catch his breath.

"Spit it out, man. Tell me of Hawke!" Horatio commanded.

"It is the mass! They ambushed us about ten days ago, from here to the east. We fought off the first three, but then...," Sinclair said.

"Then what! Tell me now!"

"They attacked in force. There must have been a hundred of them," he said as he dropped his head. "Horatio, I did a terrible thing. I left my friend alone to be pursued by those demons," continued Sinclair as his face dropped into his hands.

"Nonsense! I know Youngblood well. He probably ordered you to depart, aware that you would come to me!" Horatio said. "I taught that boy well. He is a good soldier," he added.

Horatio directed his servants to bring Sinclair inside the house and ordered the stableman to prepare two of his best horses for departure at first light.

"What shall we do, Horatio?" Sinclair asked as he rested in the library and watched Horatio pace back and forth across the room.

Horatio stopped and stared at the collection of military honors he earned hanging on his wall and then said, "We will find him and fight by his side."

"But what if he is already dead?" Sinclair asked, shaking his head in shame that he had even thought of such a thing.

"Then we will avenge his death to the last man and finish his quest!" Horatio declared as he pounded his fist against the wall. "This is now our fight as well, my weary friend!" he added as he stared into the fire with the look of an eagle in search of its prey.

"When do we depart, Horatio?"

"At first light. Now get cleaned up, put some food in your belly, and get some sleep," Horatio Cantrell commanded as he pulled his old battle sword down from above the mantle and marched out of the room.

Sinclair did exactly as Horatio recommended. However, sleep was not on the agenda as he stared all night into the crackling fire until morning, wondering of the fate of his friend.

Sinclair found Horatio ready to depart, as promised, at first light. He was giving instructions to his estate manager and staff, in anticipation that he might be away for an extended period of time.

Elizabeth Cantrell was standing near her husband with a look of sadness about her. She was concerned for her husband and feared that he may not return unharmed. Her concerns were well placed, for she knew that Horatio was a warrior at heart and missed the thrill of battle. Elizabeth also knew that Youngblood Hawke was like a son to Horatio and that he would not stop until he knew of his fate.

Sinclair walked over to inspect his horse as Elizabeth approached him. "Stay by his side, Mr. Fox."

"I will, my lady," Sinclair responded with as much sincerity as he could muster, in an attempt to ease her mind.

"There are forces at work here that I truly do not understand," Elizabeth said as she continued to watch her husband.

"With all due respect, Mrs. Cantrell, I suspect that as the daughter of Jonathan LeClair, you are well acquainted with the mass," Sinclair said respectfully.

"This is the work of Kirsan?" she asked with a tremble in her voice.

"Kirsan is a pathetic excuse for a human being!" Horatio snapped as he approached.

"You are very generous in allowing him a place in humanity," Sinclair replied sarcastically.

"Do not worry, my dear. You will be in fine hands with your brother while I am gone, and your father, as always, will watch out for you," Horatio said, embracing Elizabeth and bidding her farewell.

Horatio was fortunate in that his brother-in-law, William LeClair, would remain at the manor to ensure that all remained well. William was a loyal son to his father and had become a trusted lieutenant of Horatio. However, he did harbor some resentment of the fact that his father placed more power and faith in Horatio than in his own son. An unfortunate situation for William, but actually quite common among the aristocracy. Nonetheless, Horatio treated William as a brother, and trusted him as one as well.

"William, if you should receive word from Hawke, get a message to him. Tell him I will be proceeding to the village of Steepleton," he said.

"It will be done, Horatio," William replied in a manner demonstrating his loyalty.

"William, be sure to watch over matters, my friend, and keep a watchful eye upon your sister while I am away," Horatio said with a wink and a smile to Elizabeth.

"I will, Horatio, and good luck," William replied.

"Be careful, my love," Elizabeth said as she embraced her husband one last time before he departed.

Horatio did not respond and only placed his hand upon her face, acknowledging her plea. From atop his horse, Horatio Cantrell looked over his homestead before turning and riding off in search of Youngblood Hawke.

Ventura was always busy in the morning hours, and this day was no exception. Horatio and Sinclair decided to avoid the calamity of the market, so they just passed through the government square, in order to facilitate their travel. The government square was very active with local politicos and administrators going about their business and that of the state. A large crowd was gathered in front of the judicial building where citizens often assembled to hear the speeches of the city leaders.

"Such a large crowd, at so early in the morning," Sinclair noted as they passed by the group. "Who do you suppose they are waiting to see?" he asked.

"Kirsan," he said as he observed the dark figure make his way through the crowd with his usual entourage of assistants and bodyguards.

Kirsan was a master politico, sophist, and manipulator, displaying his skills as he navigated through the crowd. He stopped only to speak with those who mattered, and waved his hand to the majority of those who did not. He controlled the mood of the crowd with his every glance. His facial expressions appeared genuine, but were in fact, by design. The mass openly exhibited reverence for him, but it was fear that motivated their loyalty. Kirsan was a tall man with striking features whose eyes projected power and greed. The darkness of his stare resembled that of a cobra, preparing to strike everything that crossed its path. Kirsan was no ordinary man, but he continuously made such claims and much to the approval of the mass, as they cheered his arrival. "Kirsan! Kirsan! Kirsan!" The crowd chanted as he continued through the crowd with a false presentation of humility that was happily consumed by the herd.

"Well, good morning, Cantrell. What brings a man of your distinction out so early in the morning?" Kirsan asked with a sinister smile and a tint of crimson in his eyes. "Are you going somewhere? You appear to be dressed and packed for a long trip," he added.

"My destination should be of no concern of yours, Kirsan," Horatio replied with a significant degree of contempt.

"Not a morning person, I see," Kirsan noted, referring to Horatio's attitude, as his bodyguards stared at Sinclair in an attempt to intimidate him.

"Apparently, neither are your colleagues. They must become more pleasant looking as the day passes, I am sure?" Sinclair interjected in an attempt to annoy the bodyguards. "No one could possibly be so ugly for the entire day?" he added with a grin.

"The incorrigible Sinclair Fox," Kirsan said.

"At your service, sir," Sinclair replied as he bowed and tipped his hat in acknowledgment of his apparently dubious reputation.

"Enough of these useless pleasantries! We must go!" Horatio ordered as he passed Kirsan without stating another word.

"Cantrell! You waste your time!" Kirsan said.

Horatio stopped and turned to look at Kirsan and replied, "What do you speak of?"

"He is dead," Kirsan said calmly, which immediately caught the attention of both Horatio and Sinclair.

"Who is dead, Kirsan?" Horatio asked with his perfected military stare.

"The one they call Youngblood Hawke. I believe he is a friend of yours, is he not?" Kirsan replied.

"You scoundrel!" Sinclair interrupted as he went for his sword, triggering the same reaction from Kirsan's bodyguards.

"Stand down," Horatio ordered sternly as he listened to Kirsan, paying no attention to the bodyguards. Horatio knew that the government square was not the place, nor was this the time for such a confrontation.

"A sad story actually. The man was a fraud, you know? Yes, a complete and utter fraud. Nothing but a common criminal, if you will. He ambushed three unsuspecting farmers and killed the poor souls. He and another unidentified coward," Kirsan continued as he watched Sinclair slowly lose his composure.

"Easy, Sinclair," Horatio instructed.

"Yes, but justice did in fact prevail. A group of concerned citizens witnessed the despicable event and chased the coward down. From what I understand, he was captured in the village of Stonehaven and tried for his crime. I believe that his head is displayed on a pike as we speak," Kirsan said with his pompous air and a sinister grin, designed to irritate.

"Dead? Can it be, Horatio?" Sinclair asked desperately.

"Kirsan, if what you say is true, you would be wise to wish for divine intervention," Horatio advised.

"Intervention in what, may I ask?" Kirsan replied, with a somewhat puzzled look on his face.

"In stopping me, if I find that you were in any way responsible for the death of Youngblood Hawke," Horatio promised in a clear and intentional tone.

Kirsan wiped the grim from his face as he and Horatio just stared at each other. Horatio clarified his position and intentions and without uttering another word, Horatio and Sinclair continued past Kirsan. They made their way through the mass crowd and departed the City of Ventura in search of their friend.

"Do you believe Youngblood to be dead? Could Kirsan possibly be correct?" Sinclair asked.

"That one has a twisted tongue, my friend. It goes well with his twisted mind," Horatio replied.

"Where will we look first?" Sinclair asked.

"The ancient ones who dwell in the Temple Triangle," he said.

"Youngblood has spoken of them," Sinclair agreed.

"We shall see how wise they are," Horatio added.

Horatio and Sinclair arrived at the Temple Triangle and walked up the steps leading to the large iron and wooden door. The grounds were quiet, revealing no indications of people or activity of any kind.

"There does not appear to be anyone attending this magnificent property," said Sinclair as he surveyed the area for any signs of life.

Sinclair was about to knock on the door when Horatio just threw the door open and walked in.

"Unannounced? Very poor manners, Horatio," Sinclair said.

"I am not here for a dinner party," Horatio replied as he walked down the torch-lit hall leading to the chamber room.

Horatio and Sinclair entered the dark chamber and stood silently in the center.

"Hello, I say, is anyone at home at the moment?" Sinclair announced.

"What knowledge do you seek?" the ancient one asked.

He was without his two colleagues. The older and younger did not appear to be within the chamber.

"I say, do you know of Youngblood Hawke?" Sinclair asked.

"It is what they call him," the sage replied.

"We are searching for him," Horatio said.

"You search for one that searches for himself," the sage replied.

"Do you know where we can find him?" Sinclair asked.

"He follows truth, and deception and treachery follow him," the sage responded.

"Yes, but how do we find him?" Sinclair asked.

"Follow the path left by deception. It is often more visible than that which is left by truth," the sage added.

"Exactly what do you mean, wise one?" Sinclair inquired.

"He speaks of Kirsan," Horatio noted.

"Do you speak of the politico known as Kirsan?" Sinclair asked.

"*There are those who delude themselves into believing they're true statesman simply because the masses think highly of them,*"[116] the sage said.

"He is without question speaking of Kirsan," Horatio added.

"*Do you suppose there's any way in which a man who is incapable of measuring can avoid thinking that he is seven feet tall when others, who are just as ignorant, are frequently telling him he is?*"[117] the sage asked.

"No, I would imagine that he could not," Sinclair answered. "Surely such a man as Kirsan is knowledgeable?" Sinclair continued, as Horatio became more impatient.

"*Such individuals call it knowledge, every one of those they call sophists teach nothing but the attitudes the masses form by consensus,*"[118] the sage said.

"He feeds them what they want to hear, and they worship him for it," Horatio interrupted.

"Excellent! *Imagine that the keeper of a huge, strong beast notices what makes it angry, what it desires, how it has to be approached and handled, the circumstances and conditions under which it becomes particularly fierce or calm, what provokes its typical cries, and what tones of voice make it gentle or wild. Once he's spent enough time in the creature's company to acquire all this information, he calls it knowledge, forms it into a systematic branch of expertise, and starts to teach it, despite total ignorance, in fact, about which of the creature's attitudes and desires is commendable or deplorable, good or bad, moral or immoral,"*[119] the sage explained.

"Kirsan has turned the beast loose on Youngblood Hawke and his quest," Horatio replied.

"It is his way. His usage of the truth simply conforms to the great beast's attitudes, and he describes things as good or bad according to its likes and dislikes, and can't justify his usage of the term any further, but describes as right and good things which are merely indispensable, since he hasn't realized and can't explain to anyone else how vast a gulf there is between necessity and goodness,"[120] he added.

"Yes, he tells them what they wish to hear and they love him for it," Horatio said.

"I understand your words, sage, but Kirsan maintains an impeccable reputation, and is very popular. Could he deceive so many for so long?" Sinclair asked.

"He would probably ask himself, 'Is it honesty or crooked deceit that enables me to scale the higher wall' and so live my life surrounded by secure defenses? What I hear is people telling me that, unless I also gain a reputation for morality, my actually being moral will do me no good, but will be a source of private troubles and public punishments. On the other hand, an immoral person who has managed to get a reputation for morality is said to have a wonderful life,"[121] the sage responded.

"Appearances can deceive even the most perceptive of men," Horatio noted.

"Such a man would know this and continue to tell himself, since the experts tell me that 'appearance overpowers reality' and is responsible for happiness, I must wholeheartedly devote myself to appearance. I must surround myself with an illusion of goodness. This must be my front, what people see of me, but behind me I must have on a leash that cunning, subtle fox,"[122] the sage said.

"But it's not easy to cloak one's badness forever,"[123] Sinclair remarked.

"That's because no important project is easy, nevertheless, everything we hear marks this as the road to take if we are to be happy. To help us with our disguise, we shall form clubs and pressure groups, and we can acquire skill at political and forensic speaking from teachers of the art of persuasion. Consequently, by a combi-

nation of persuasion and brute force, we shall dominate others without being punished for it,"[124] the sage added.

The youngest sage entered the chamber and added his own observations, "*Conscience of their own ignorance, most people are impressed by anyone who pontificates and says something that is over their heads.*"[125]

"Judgment day will come for Kirsan," interjected Horatio Cantrell sternly. "The knowledge I seek is the location of Youngblood Hawke, not an analysis of Kirsan," he added.

"To follow the one you seek, you must understand the nature of his quest and those who seek to destroy him," the sage noted.

"Then Youngblood is alive and continues his quest?" Sinclair asked.

The elder sage suddenly appeared and stepped in from the darkness, "The spirit of his quest lives."

"Are you suggesting the quest is over and Youngblood Hawke is dead?" Sinclair asked.

"I don't understand this one; he speaks in riddles," Horatio said.

"I understand," Sinclair replied as Horatio looked on in puzzlement. "Youngblood lives, but he has strayed from his quest," he noted.

"Passion! *The strong passions work like a drug, which shuts judgment down, just as does wine or sleep.*[126] *The man overcome with passion has knowledge in a more attenuated sense than the healthy man who is contemplating; only the healthy man can exercise his knowledge at will. The passion-ridden man has knowledge only because when he recovers from his state he will then be able to exercise it,*"[127] the younger sage interrupted.

"Are you saying that one should not be passionate in regards to one's quest?" Sinclair asked.

"Passion causes conflict, ethical conflict, which will ultimately disrupt the quest. There is no room for ethical conflict," the younger sage demanded.

"Then there is no room for the quest," the eldest sage noted.

"*Once one has the relevant premises in mind, it seems one must act, regardless of what beliefs and desires one has. Of course, that is all things considered,*"[128] the youngest sage said.

"*Of course, the premises you speak of are relative to one's own knowledge, are they not?*" the elder asked. "*A bad act must be done in ignorance, under a false belief that it is for the best, don't you think?*"[129] he added.

"Gentleman, let us return to the question at hand, shall we?" the middle sage said, in an attempt to moderate the discussion.

"Yes, let us return to the question at hand. What of Youngblood Hawke, does he live?" Horatio demanded. Horatio was growing tired of the philosophical discussion tainted with riddles.

"Does the spirit ever really die?" the eldest sage asked.

"What of his mind and body? You speak as if he is dead. No more riddles. I desire answers," Horatio commanded.

"'*Desire is the only motivating force for human action.*'[130] Do you desire to find your friend?" the youngest sage asked.

"Yes!" Horatio Cantrell replied in frustration.

"As do I," Sinclair Fox added.

"*If there is some one good, then knowledge of it will have a great influence on our lives,*"[131] the youngest sage said.

"In fact, it can have an influence on many lives when it becomes known to those have a desire to understand," the middle sage added.

"Do you understand?" the eldest asked.

"I do. I understand with a very high degree of relative clarity," Sinclair responded with the confidence that he had just been enlightened.

Sinclair turned and departed the chamber, followed by a very confused Horatio Cantrell.

"Sinclair! What is it you claim to understand from that maze of oratory?" Horatio demanded.

"Horatio, one of the last things Youngblood said to me before being ambushed by those cowardice scoundrels was, 'We have an army to raise.' Do you understand now, my soldier friend?" Sinclair asked.

Horatio stood silent, nodding his head in acknowledgment and agreement, as he too had now been enlightened.

"Yes, my wise, young friend, now I do understand," Horatio replied.

The two men climbed onto their mounts and road east to find Youngblood Hawke with a renewed sense of purpose and urgency. However, both men were plagued by the suspicion that although the spirit of Youngblood Hawke may be alive and thriving, his physical existence was near death, if in fact it had not already passed.

CHAPTER 14

The Wilderness

Slowly detached, my mind loses control,
Wandering in the wilderness alone and cold.

"You know of his whereabouts?" asked the leader of the band of men who had just ridden into the village.

"I haven't seen nor heard from Hawke in years," the older man replied as his teenage son watched with concern.

"He is lying! Let me make an example of him!" shouted the younger man with the wild eyes.

"Now, now, I don't believe that will be necessary. Will it?" the one in charge said as he directed his stare at the old man.

"I tell you the truth," the old man responded as the concern for his son grew. "What does it matter? Rumor has it that he was killed," he added.

"He has more lives than a cat! But he is running out!" erupted the one with the wild eyes.

Zacharia was an old friend of Youngblood Hawke and everyone in the village of Steepleton was aware of that fact. He often told stories of his time spent in the military with his former colleague and now famous soldier of fortune. However, the tales gleefully told by Zacharia appear to have reached the ears of Youngblood Hawke's pursuers. The band of men were obviously members of the Black Guard, and the henchman of Kirsan.

"I want to know more of this friend of yours. Where is he from?" the leader demanded.

"I really don't know. His history is a mystery to even his closest friends," Zacharia said.

"Surely he has a family, a clan of some sorts that he protects?"

"If he does…he has never shared such information with me," Zacharia insisted.

"I am growing tired of this game. Tell me what I want to know, and the boy lives," said the leader as he looked over to the boy and then to the wild one.

"I don't know where he is!" a very emotional and concerned Zacharia insisted.

"Too bad. Take him!" the leader of the Black Guard ordered as two men grabbed the boy and dragged him out into the street.

"No! Leave him be!" the father shouted as he watched his son being taken away to face a certain death.

Just then the wild one struck the old man down and said, "You will be the first in a long line of examples to come. You fool, you sacrifice your son for a coward like Youngblood Hawke?" he turned, wildly tossing everything in his path as he withdrew in anger and frustration.

"We must draw this Hawke out," the leader said.

"He is a coward, and will continue to run and hide," replied the wild-eyed one.

"You are a fool if you believe that to be true," the leader countered. "It is the very fact that he is not a coward that will be his downfall," he added. "Spread the word throughout the province that the boy will be executed for the sins of Youngblood Hawke. Set the execution five days from now at daybreak. He will, without question, attempt to intervene, and then we will execute them both."

"It will be done," the wild one acknowledged.

Horatio and Sinclair traveled fast and hard toward the east in an attempt to locate their missing friend. Horatio contacted every resource he could muster, trying to uncover information leading to the whereabouts of Youngblood Hawke. His seemingly endless number of sources, developed as a mercenary and smuggler, impressed Sinclair, as they visited every tavern and obscure gambling den along their route of travel.

"I must say, your network of friends within the darkest shadows of civilization is most impressive, as well as contradictory," Sinclair said.

"Contradictory?"

"Indeed, when I first encountered you, my impression was that you were a man of the aristocracy who would sooner throw himself from a cliff than socialize with such malcontents," Sinclair said.

"I wouldn't call my interaction with the fringe cultures of humanity socializing. It would be better described as a necessary aspect of doing business," Horatio explained.

"Ah yes, if there is one thing I have learned about your philosophy, it is that everything you do is based upon the necessity of the moment," Sinclair noted.

"Interesting, how my own philosophy is completely contradictory to your own."

A puzzled Sinclair looked at his traveling companion and asked, "Why, what do you mean?"

"Simply that everything you do appears to be unnecessary," Horatio commented with a sarcastic smirk and laugh.

"Touché, my good man," acknowledged Sinclair. "Horatio, may I ask you a question regarding our good friend Hawke?"

"I am quite sure you will ask me whether I agree to answer you or not. So we might as well get it over with," Horatio replied.

"What do you know of him?" Sinclair asked inquisitively.

"I know what everyone else who knows him knows. That he is a philosopher and poet of sorts, a distinguished soldier of fortune, and without question, a professional adventurer intoxicated by the allure of danger and mystery," Horatio responded.

"Where does he hail from? Is he a commoner or a man of noble bloodlines?" Sinclair inquired. "I have heard him speak of the 'Noble House.' What is he speaking of? I have suspected he was speaking of his home or perhaps your own?"

"Interestingly enough, I really don't know what he is speaking of, but I don't believe he is speaking of my home," he replied.

A puzzled Sinclair asked, "Is it his home?"

"I suspect that it is, but he does not elaborate," Horatio responded. "I only know that he protects its identity and location with great caution and resolve."

"His family perhaps?" the inquisitive Sinclair Fox said as he attempted to learn more of his mysterious colleague.

"Hawke is a complex individual, who shares little of his personal history with anyone."

"Yes, indeed," Sinclair acknowledged.

"It is my impression that Hawke conceals the details of his personal history in order to protect those who are close to him. Of course, my impression is based solely upon speculation. Many believe that the man is incapable of being close to anyone," Horatio said as they continued their ride into the Eastern Kingdom.

"One thing is certain about our friend and colleague, Youngblood Hawke. It is that there much more to the man than meets the eye," Sinclair responded, noting his observations. "Tell me, Horatio, when did you first meet Youngblood?"

"I first met him on the battlefield, during the Great War."

"Tell me of this meeting," the very interested Sinclair Fox said.

Horatio's eyes appeared to drift off into the past as he reminisced of days gone by. "I was leading an elite force of cavalry during a brutal campaign against the Eastern Empire. My unit had suffered great losses and I recruited replacements from the rank and file. Hawke was one of them. He held no rank at the time and was just a common soldier, or so it appeared. During a mission, our unit was trapped by enemy forces in a canyon with no apparent avenue of escape. We were being overwhelmed by the onslaught as the enemy forces continued to attack our defenses. We entered the canyon with sixty warriors, but as the battle raged on, we were reduced to about fifteen. It was a sad day and I feared that all was lost. We had all prepared to die when suddenly this young warrior climbs onto his mount, raises his sword in his hand, and cries out, 'I shall not die on the defensive, but choose to perish engaged in the attack! Who is with me?' The determination and courage displayed in that young warrior's eyes inspired us to fight on!"

"Bravo! What happened next? Please do go on," Sinclair begged.

"The young warrior's resolve and courage appeared to increase as his combat skills exploded in the face of the enemy. He led a charge directly through the enemy's point guard and cleared an avenue of escape!" Horatio continued, with a degree of excitement in his eyes that was rarely displayed.

Sinclair listened intently, encouraging Horatio to continue. "Outstanding! Please go on."

"Nothing more to tell, really. I, to this day, remain in awe over what Youngblood Hawke did on that day. He saved the unit from a certain death and turned a defeat into an epic victory in the face of overwhelming odds," Horatio said.

"Now that is exactly the level of heroics I would expect from our colleague," Sinclair said. "Incidentally, why did he not remain within the military? Such a reputation could have easily elevated him to the rank of a general."

"Youngblood Hawke is no bureaucrat. His success has to this day been exclusive of the mass and the herd mentality. He is a creative and critical thinker, who is willing to engage in unorthodox methods in order to succeed. The mass has created a system that does not reward, but in fact, punishes such innovators," Horatio explained.

"Please, do go on, Horatio," asked Sinclair.

"The truth is that I know nothing of the young warrior prior to that fateful day. From that day forward the name Youngblood Hawke became synonymous with honor and valor."

The peasant man entered the tavern, dusty and dirty, wearing worn-out clothing to match his scraggly and overgrown beard. He appeared to be nothing but a homeless tramp and a nuisance. As he approached the bar, the innkeeper was suspicious and immediately asked if he had any money. The tramp dropped a few coins on the counter and asked for food and drink. The tavern was bustling with activity and merriment. The large group of ten to fifteen men were reveling and enjoying the spirits delivered by the ale and wine that they were consuming. They were loud and consumed everything and everyone around them. The other patrons were careful not to even look at them, as it might stir trouble. One of them approached the bar, with an empty pitcher, demanding more ale.

"Innkeeper, more ale! Our throats grow dry!" the intoxicated rogue demanded.

The innkeeper quickly replenished the pitcher as the rogue turned and bumped into the tramp.

"Watch yourself, you filthy peasant! How dare you touch a member of the Black Guard!" he shouted in anger.

"My apologies," the tramp responded humbly.

"Your apology is not sufficient," the rogue replied as he glared at the tramp. "Look at me when I am speaking to you," he demanded.

"Leave him be. He is not worth your time," interjected the innkeeper. "He is not even armed. He is no warrior, and certainly not worth your troubles," he added.

"Yes, nothing!" the rogue acknowledged as he threw the tramp's food to the floor and pushed him down to retrieve it. "Eat on the floor, you human plague."

The rogue was joined by another of his band and they kicked the tramp and then pushed him out onto the street. The tramp picked himself up from the muddy street and looked back into the tavern. His eyes swelled with anger, but he only turned and walked away. He stopped and stared into the night sky, searching for the brightest star. But the sky was filled only with darkness and nothingness.

"Coward," he said to himself as he led his weary horse out of town.

The days and nights were running together as the lone traveler made his way through the many villages leading east. He traveled along back roads and took indirect routes as he continued deep into the Eastern Kingdom. The desperation was growing by the day as all else became secondary to survival. The Eastern Kingdom was alive with tales that Youngblood Hawke had been executed as a common thief. The lonely traveler also began to believe that Youngblood Hawke was dead. And if not, he might as well be dead. What use was he if he were to run the rest of his life? What use was he if he were to continue an existence of nothingness with no purpose but survival? *Of no use*, he thought to himself.

Alone and unsure of himself or the path he should take, he thought of the words of the Prince of the Northern Kingdom, "*To be or not to be, that is the question: whether 'tis nobler in mind to suffer the slings and arrows of outrageous fortune, or to take arms against a sea of troubles and by opposing end them.*"[132] *Troubling words for a troubled soul*, he thought to himself as he continued to wander through the night, aware for the first time in his life how completely alone he really was.

He had grown used to his friend and traveling companion and wondered what became of him. "Was he able to evade the pursuers?" he asked himself. "And what if the Black Guard set a trap for him?" he continued, imagining every tragic scenario possible.

He also wondered if his old friend had just ridden off, leaving the threat of the mass and the allure of the quest behind him.

Questions of faith, loyalty, and commitment continued to ravage his mind as he began to see conspiracy in the eyes of every traveler and an assassin behind every tree. The mass man was everywhere, and anyone of them could be a member of the Black Guard. No one could be trusted. *No one*, he thought to himself. The desperation was overwhelming as the hours turned into days and the days into weeks as he traveled with no particular destination in mind.

A Daily Reminder

Tell me, why do I hate you so?
For so many years, taunting me,
Yet, who you are, I do not know,
Show me mercy, just let me be.

Day and night, living inside of me,
From you I have no place to hide,
Bringing so much pain and misery,
Forcing me to live this tragic lie.

Who are you? Such a miserable soul,
Reveal yourself, disclose your identity.
Wait! I know you, eyes angry and cold,
It is my own image in the mirror I see.

Now I understand this fatal connection,
Forever bound, you will never let me go,
The horror of an image, my own reflection,
A daily reminder of why I hate you so.

—*Youngblood Hawke*

The old man was waiting under a large willow tree. As always, his cart was full and his horse was weary. "Are you lost?" the old man asked.

"Do I appear lost to you?" the lonely traveler said.

"You appear hopeless," he replied.

"Hope is not what I seek. I need answers. Can you provide answers?"

"Only questions, young one," the old man said.

"Then you are as I," the traveler replied.

"And what would that be?"

"Useless," the desperate traveler said.

True Understanding

You tell me you understand?
There is no need to explain,
Compassion and comfort,
Sympathy—feeling my pain.

Do you truly understand me?
The deep sadness of my soul,
The suffering and heartache,
Such a memory to behold.

Into the depths of your heart,
So very deep you should go,
Scars of torment and anguish,
Revealing a common sorrow.

Are you beginning to understand?
Only empathy allows you to see,
Your own woeful tears must flow,
To share my pain and cry with me.

—*Youngblood Hawke*

The old man just looked at the traveler with a sense of pity and concern. "The one who guards the crossroads is waiting for you."

"Let him wait for another. My quest is over and Youngblood Hawke is dead!" he replied.

"If you truly believe that your quest is over, than you are most certainly dead," the old man said somberly.

The traveler continued past the old one and did not look back as he continued east, with no destination in mind. The past weeks had been spent eluding pursuers intent on securing the prize of Youngblood Hawke's head. Any desire to stop and confront the mass was overruled by reason, as he was continuously outnumbered. The weeks had passed with many close calls as he was forced to live like an animal, hunted by a superior predator. But they were not superior, and he knew it. They were just many, and if he were to engage them directly, his quest would surely be terminated, along with his life. So, he continued to run and hide, much to the dismay of his own conscience and pride.

Refuge Within

I must withdraw and escape,
To the confines of my mind,
To a most spiritual state,
Peaceful, reflective, sublime.

From reality I must hide,
The daily trial and grind,
A calmness deep inside,
The only refuge I can find.

Retreating to relative safety,
So solitary—alone and cold,
Hidden in virtual obscurity,
Such a lost and lonely soul.

—*Youngblood Hawke*

The road was dark as the moon was shadowed by the array of clouds across the midnight sky. The traveler continued along the roadway, avoiding contact with other travelers who were moving into the darkness as they approached from the opposite direction. However, he was very aware of the group of men that followed closely, and had been doing so for several hours. He was not sure of their number but estimated them to be seven to eight men.

Too many, for any successful intervention, he thought and then questioned whether or not it was fear that directed his inaction. Once again he was forced to move off the road and wait for the assassins to pass.

He entered deep into the woods and found a secluded location several hundred feet off the main road, beneath a sprawling oak tree. Resting his head on the grass, he stared up at the stars as his thoughts wandered through his past and then drifted to the sapphire storm.

"What had become of her?" he said to himself. In his most desperate hour he wondered why she had abandoned him so. "Was his quest over? Had he failed?" he did not have the answers and feared he no longer had the questions to continue his quest.

The lonely warrior's eyes continued to travel upward, deep into the midnight sky, as he found the brightest star adrift in the darkness.

"Was she on that particular star?" he asked himself.

As his thoughts continued to wander into the heavens, far from the loneliness and suffering of his heart and spirit, his mind drifted aimlessly, deeper into the inner confines of his mind...

Drifting To You

I suffer in a world of complete totality,
Wallowing within the great depths of my own reality,
Yet my mind drifts to you.

In vain, I commit myself to this mundane neutrality,
So keenly aware of time's punishing brutality,
Yet my mind drifts to you.

Responsibilities abound, problems profound,
More and more aware of my own mortality,
Yet my mind drifts to you.

Crisis, scandal, disaster all around,
Turmoil and calamity are the only sounds,
Yet my mind drifts to you.

This quest must come to an end,
For only then, will time become my friend,
As I spend an everlasting eternity,
Drifting with you.

—*Youngblood Hawke*

As he slowly fell to sleep, the sapphire glow appeared before him, illuminating the darkness that now consumed the warrior's world. Her translucent image appeared and gazed down upon him for several hours, maintaining a watchful eye.

"You continue to falsely believe that this quest is all your own," the Oracle said softly as she moved closer to the troubled warrior. "You need only call for truth and it will remain by your side," she added, moving even closer. Whispering in his ear she said, "Truth does not abandon you. You abandon your faith in truth." Her gaze continued as she added, "Renew your faith and you shall renew your quest."

The Oracle paused momentarily and said, "*Truth possesses not nor would it be possessed; for truth is sufficient unto truth. And think not you can direct the course of truth, for truth, if it finds you worthy, directs your course. Truth has no other desire but to fulfill itself.*"[133]

In an instant, Youngblood opened his eyes and was immediately drawn into the sapphire storm he had longed for so desperately. For a moment their two worlds collided and became one as they stared deep into each other's eyes, dismissing the reality around them. Briefly, they shared a realm not of the physical or of the mystical. It was a world all their own. Slowly Youngblood Hawke rose up and stood before the Oracle as her inspiration renewed his sense of purpose.

"I thought you abandoned me," he said.

"You abandoned yourself," the Oracle replied. "You have lost faith in yourself and those around you," she said. "*Our doubts are traitors, and makes us lose the good we oft might win, by fearing to attempt.*"[134]

"Am I worthy of this quest?" he asked.

"Action and not words will answer that question," she replied. "Do you still desire to understand?"

"Yes," he said.

"What is it that you wish to understand?" she asked.

"The truth in its purest form," the weary warrior responded. "Is it written by the ancient's to be disclosed to but a few?"

"It has been written but never understood," the Oracle acknowledged.

"What has been written?" Youngblood Hawke asked.

"H M L I L Y F E. Decipher this riddle Youngblood Hawke and truth may very well be revealed to you," the Oracle said, recognizing she had once again confused the warrior who stood before her.

"I do not recognize this language," the puzzled warrior responded.

"You will, and when you do, reveal it to no one, for it is your truth and your truth alone," the Oracle commanded. "What are you?"

"I don't know," Youngblood replied desperately.

"You do know," the Oracle insisted. "I ask you once again. What are you?!"

He struggled with the question but then cried out, "I am a philosopher, soldier of fortune, and professional adventurer!"

"Who are you?"

He paused and looked deep into the Oracle's sapphire eyes and proclaimed, "I am Youngblood Hawke!"

"Why are you?" she continued, knowing that the heart of the warrior was now returning and the ultimate question was once more being presented to him.

Youngblood Hawke continued to gaze into the sapphire storm, searching for his answer. "The answer to that question remains a riddle. I seek the truth, and my quest is the riddle!" he cried out as he drew his battle sword and raised it high into the darkness of the midnight sky.

"You are wise," he said as he continued to gaze upon the Oracle and bask in the sapphire glow.

"I am wisdom," she replied warmly.

"Yes, and *wisdom loves only a warrior*,"[135] he replied, recalling the words of the Prophet as the Oracle disappeared into the abyss.

Although Youngblood's sense of purpose was heightened and renewed, he remained cautious as he continued east. He pondered a visit to the Noble House of his past but once again found himself dismissing the chains of reality. Once again, the power of his quest beckoned him. His first stop would be to visit his old friend Zacharia. Waiting for cover of darkness, Youngblood rode into the village of Steepleton, arriving at the home of his old friend. The village was quiet, actually, too quiet.

The two men were concealed across the street in the shadows. They were definitely members of the Black Guard as they maintained a watchful eye on Zacharia's home. The small cottage was very quiet, with only a flicker of candlelight from inside. Youngblood slipped into the back and entered through a second-story window. The man was sitting in front of a fire, staring into the flames as Youngblood stealthily approached and placed his hand over the man's mouth, to muffle any potential outcry.

"There was a day when no man could approach you without detection," said Youngblood quietly.

"Hawke?" Zacharia responded with surprise.

"Hello, my friend. Why is your home being watched by those scoundrels?"

"They are watching for you. I thought you were dead?" he said.

"Hardly, yet many wish it to be so."

"Hawke, they took my son," Zacharia said in desperation.

"What do you mean they took your son?" Youngblood inquired with concern.

"They came looking for you and I told them I did not know where you were. Then they took him, stating that they would make an example of him. You must help me...they are to execute him in the morning," Zacharia pleaded, as his eyes swelled with tears and his face fell into his hands in despair.

"They will not execute your son, my friend. I promise you," Youngblood replied.

The two henchmen continued to watch Zacharia's home as they discussed their escapades in the tavern on a previous night. They were both large, menacing-looking men and typical of Kirsan's Black Guard.

"I want you to wait five minutes and then walk out the front door and smoke your pipe," Youngblood directed firmly.

"A diversion?" Zacharia asked.

"Indeed," Youngblood said.

Youngblood slipped out the rear window and into the night as Zacharia watched the clock, waiting for his cue. Five minutes passed and then Zacharia walked out the front door and lit up his pipe. He walked to the corner of the cottage. His exit immediately drew the attention of the two watchers as they stopped talking and observed the activity of their target.

"Is he alone?" one of the men asked.

"Not really," Youngblood Hawke interjected from the shadows.

The two men were startled and turned to find the silhouette of an armed man. Immediately, one of the men noticed the katana sword strapped to the warrior's back.

"Who are you?" one of the men asked with apprehension and a hand on his sword.

"I am Youngblood Hawke!" the warrior proclaimed with his trademark stare that appeared to pierce the very souls of the men.

"Youngblood Hawke!" one of the men shouted as his eyes ignited in fear.

"At your service, gentlemen!" Youngblood said as he drew his katana and attacked with frightening speed.

The first man went down immediately as his sword was drawn and necessity required his swift elimination. The katana was lunged directly through his mid-section as Youngblood pressed on and withdrew his sword from his opponent. The dying man fell to the ground as his comrade backed away and drew his sword in a futile attempt to respond. But it was too late as Youngblood used the momentum of withdrawing his sword from his first kill to spin clockwise, penetrating his adversary's defenses. The Black Guardsman was killed instantly as he fell silently beside his comrade.

Youngblood called out to Zacharia, "Come here quickly."

Zacharia ran over to the shadows and observed the two men on the ground. "I didn't hear anything. How did you do that so quickly?" he asked.

"A lesson, compliments of my old mentor, '*When an opponent is startled and the feeling of opposition is distracted, the opponent will experience a gap in reaction time,*'[136] such was the case here, my friend," Youngblood responded.

"Your time in the Far East was spent well." Youngblood and Zacharia concealed the bodies and then returned to Zacharia's cottage. "What will we do now?" Zacharia asked.

"Do you have trustworthy friends who will help you?"

"Yes. Just tell me what you need."

"When is your son scheduled to be executed?" Youngblood asked reluctantly, knowing the thought would be painful to his old friend.

"Tomorrow at daybreak," Zacharia said as he stood trembling at the thought.

"Assemble your friends tonight and meet me in the old mill just outside of the village," Youngblood instructed.

"It shall be done, my friend," Zacharia acknowledged.

"Zacharia, the men you assemble must be armed and prepared to fight," Youngblood noted sternly.

"Of course," Zacharia replied.

"Which also means they must be prepared to die," he added.

"I understand," Zacharia responded, noting the grave look of his warrior friend who was wearing the battle face he had been witness to so many years ago.

Zacharia watched Youngblood Hawke slip into the darkness, assuming that his mission tonight was one of intelligence gathering. But Zacharia had his own mission to attend to, and his time was running out as the midnight hour passed and daybreak approached. Zacharia had great faith in his old friend. He had no choice but to have faith. For if Youngblood Hawke were to fail, he would lose his only child and the living reminder of his late wife.

Youngblood Hawke will not fail, he thought to himself as he moved through the shadows of the village.

CHAPTER 15

Lessons In Captivity

The heart suffering and confined,
Trapped in a world of its own design.

The darkness continued to envelop the sky, but daybreak was not far away. The group of twelve or so men gathered within the mill, waiting for the arrival of the warrior they had heard of so many times.

"Zacharia, where is this warrior friend of yours?" one of the men asked as they all grew anxious and impatient.

"He will be here," Zacharia replied nervously.

Just then the dark figure stepped out of the shadows, "Good morning, gentlemen. I am Youngblood Hawke."

"Hawke! Thank goodness you are here. I was beginning to worry," Zacharia said. "What is your plan?" he added.

The group of men just looked at the warrior, noting his cold stare, as he moved among them and approached Zacharia.

"The plan has changed, my friend," Youngblood responded.

"What do you mean?" Zacharia asked.

"There are approximately fifty Black Guard members surrounding this mill as we speak," Youngblood noted as the group of men began to panic. "Calm down. It is me they want," Youngblood Hawke interjected sternly.

Youngblood climbed the ladder leading to the second floor and approached the window. "I say, which one of you tyrants would be in charge here?" Youngblood shouted into the darkness. "Come now…it is not as if I am not aware of your presence!" he added.

Suddenly, three men stepped out of the shadows and into the light. "That would be me," the leader responded, accompanied by two lieutenants. "Youngblood Hawke, I presume?"

"Your presumption is correct," Youngblood replied as he glared down from the second story. "And who might I be addressing?"

"Major Constantine of the Black Guard," he replied confidently. "We appear to have you at quite a disadvantage."

"I guess you would see it that way, Major," Youngblood responded with a smirk as he continued to cast his stare upon the men.

"You and your band of criminals are to surrender immediately," the major demanded.

"What was that?" Youngblood asked as the major approached with his two lieutenants.

"Surrender now, you coward, or we will kill you all!" one of the lieutenants shouted in anger.

Without warning, Youngblood slid down the rope hanging from the window, making him land directly in front of his would-be captors. "Yes, that's better. Now I can hear you more clearly," Youngblood said as the men stood in surprise.

"Youngblood Hawke. You are a bold one, aren't you?" Major Constantine said.

His lieutenants stood alert, unsure as what to do, as the warrior now stood only a few feet from them.

"We meet again," he said, recognizing the wild eyes of rage.

The Black Guard lieutenant had not forgotten his last encounter with Youngblood Hawke.

"Now, I am willing to discuss terms of surrender," he added.

"Terms? You are criminals, not an army," Major Constantine laughed as his two lieutenants joined in the humor.

Youngblood remained expressionless, "I alone will surrender and in exchange, you will allow safe passage for the men inside the mill. In addition, you will release the boy and give your word that no further harm will come to him."

"Now why in the world would I agree to such a preposterous proposal as that? What would I gain from such an agreement, when I can just take all of you prisoner right now?" Major Constantine asked as his lieutenants continued to laugh.

"Your life," Youngblood Hawke said as he projected his cold stare deep into the eyes of the major, completely ignoring the presence of the two lieutenants.

The two lieutenants stopped laughing as the leader responded, "My life?"

"Before your two colleagues can blink an eye, my sword would have pierced your heart. I will not be victorious against your entire collective, but it will be of no concern to you," Youngblood Hawke replied coldly and with complete seriousness.

The leader, afraid to respond, just squinted his eyes as the blood rushed from his face.

"It will be of no concern to you because you will be dead," Youngblood Hawke added in a clear and decisive tone.

The four men stood silent, facing each other, as the warrior Youngblood Hawke continued his glare into the eyes of Major Constantine, without a blink of the eye or a flinch of a muscle.

"Let it be done," the major agreed.

"What!" the wild-eyed one shouted in anger.

"Silence! Now do what I tell you and clear the men from the rear of the mill!" the major commanded.

"The boy?" Youngblood interjected.

"Yes, of course. Bring the boy here now!" the major ordered nervously.

Zacharia's son was delivered before Youngblood. He was frightened and shaken but otherwise appeared to be in good health.

"Did they harm you?" Youngblood asked.

The boy responded and indicated that he was not harmed.

"What is your name, boy?" Youngblood Hawke asked.

"I am Remo," he responded.

"You are very brave, Remo," he said. "Zacharia! Come get your son!" Youngblood ordered as he continued to cast his stare upon Major Constantine.

Zacharia ran out of the mill and placed his arms around his son. He stood up to turn as the wild-eyed lieutenant nodded his head in acknowledgment.

The nod did not go unnoticed by Youngblood Hawke. "Have the other men departed safely, Zacharia?"

"Yes," he responded.

"Excellent. Now, get out of here," Youngblood Hawke ordered.

"Thank you," Zacharia replied.

"The boy and his father have safe passage?" Youngblood asked.

"Without question," Major Constantine said. "I will keep my word."

"So be it!" Youngblood Hawke decried as he instantly and with lightning speed drew both of his swords and spiked them into the ground before him.

The demonstration was an obvious message that even then he could have killed Major Constantine but chose the path of honor instead and kept his word.

The wild-eyed one and the other lieutenant seized their prisoner and basked in the glory of having in custody the warrior known as Youngblood Hawke.

Zacharia began to walk away with his son but stopped and just stared at his now imprisoned friend.

The wild-eyed one glanced once more at Zacharia and said, "You made a wise choice."

Zacharia did not know what to say as he looked at his friend in shame. Youngblood just looked at his old friend, acknowledging that he was aware of his betrayal.

"Youngblood, I am sorry," Zacharia said.

"I understand. I would have made the same choice. Now take your son and depart at once," he commanded.

Zacharia remained still and watched as the Black Guards dragged Youngblood Hawke away in chains. He was relieved that he had saved his only son from being executed, but his conscience was now plagued with the guilt of having betrayed his friend. It was he who was responsible for sending him to his death. A fact that he would be forced to live with for the rest of his life.

The following morning the crowd gathered within the Village Square as the gallows were prepared for the pending execution. All was quiet as the Black Guards escorted the doomed warrior within the prison walls. He was chained like an animal and stripped of his personal belongings. The crowd was hungry for an execution, and the death of Youngblood Hawke was sure to satisfy their appetites. Youngblood was brought down into the darkest corridors of the prison and thrown into a cold and damp cell. As the door closed behind him he thought of the words of his old master, "*If all your life you remain with a clear conscience, you need not fear a knock at the door at midnight.*"[137] Youngblood knew that the "knock at midnight" was soon approaching, and he had nothing to fear.

The cell was dark, allowing very little light, but immediately Youngblood knew he was not alone. The figure was sitting against the wall, observing the new visitor.

"You are Youngblood Hawke?" the aging man asked.

"I am. And who would you be, sir?"

"Merely a shadow of a past life," he responded.

"Have you been a prisoner long?"

"Long enough to have been forgotten," the prisoner replied.

"Well, my friend. I shall not be taking up much of your time, for soon I shall be making use of those gallows being built in the square," Youngblood said.

"You find humor in your death?" the small and elderly prisoner asked as he stood and stepped into the light.

He was a native of the Eastern Kingdom, with a very distinguished manner about him, revealing a reserved yet very confident demeanor as he gazed upon Youngblood with interest.

"Just making an observation, my friend."

"Perhaps you are not as close to death as you suspect," the fellow prisoner noted.

"What are your crimes?" Youngblood asked.

"Like you, I was a warrior and declared an enemy of the mass," he replied.

"You look familiar. Have we met?" Youngblood inquired, attempting to recall the familiarity.

"Perhaps. I have met many over the years," he acknowledged.

Suddenly Youngblood recalled where he had seen the man before. "General Chang?"

"At one time many called me by that title," he responded.

General Chang was one of the most renowned military leaders of the Eastern Kingdom. He had attained legendary status in the Great Wars and had defended the Eastern Kingdom against many enemies at the request of kings and emperors. Only once had Youngblood seen the general, when he was a young soldier and member of the Western Kingdom's most elite military unit. It was during a joint military operation against the Eastern Empire that he recalls seeing the general, mounted upon a white stallion, as he called out orders to his men. He was respected, loved, and feared all at once by his armies. He was a pure genius in the art of war. But most of all, he was known for his unorthodox military strategies. One could learn much from him.

"General, why have they imprisoned you?"

"I refused to enter into service on behalf of Kirsan and the mass. If I am not his ally, then I am his enemy," the general replied.

"We appear to share more than a cell," Youngblood noted.

"Indeed, we do," the general acknowledged.

"But what of your armies, your officers, and soldiers? Have they not attempted a rescue?" Youngblood asked.

"My loyal comrades are long dead, and I am but a footnote in the history books. But you represent the present and the future," the general said with the confidence of a sage.

"I have no army," Youngblood replied.

"This is where you are wrong. You need only call them to service and an elite army of the Select will appear before you, prepared to fight by your side and join you in your quest!"

Youngblood Hawke remained in awe of the general and was puzzled by his comments and prediction of the potential future he envisioned.

"Your words are flattering, General," Youngblood said.

"My words reflect the truth, and you should take heed of them. You have much to learn as a general. What better time than the present?" the general replied.

Youngblood walked over to the window providing a clear view of the gallows, which were being prepared for an execution.

"I will promise you this, General, if I should live another day, I will accept your offer and your prediction," Youngblood offered. "However, by the looks of things, my last day passes as we speak," he added.

The following morning, the crowd gathered within the square as the gallows were prepared for the pending execution. All was quiet as the Black Guards escorted the doomed warrior from within the prison walls. He was chained like an animal and stripped of his personal belongings. The blood and scars present on his body were evidence of the severe beating he had suffered at the hands of his captors. His mind was weary, his heart broken, but fragments of his spirit remained. The crowd was hungry for an execution, and the death of a warrior was sure to satisfy their cruel appetites.

The young warrior was slowly delivered to the gallows as the inhabitants watched in silence. As he walked up the stairs to the hangman, the only sound that could be heard was each step as he ascended to his demise. Once upon the platform, the young warrior just stared out into the crowd in search of a friendly face. He begged in silence for just one more glimpse of the one he loved. Slowly, the hangman slipped the noose over his head and tightened it around his neck. He remained still, continuing to search for some sign that she was watching. The warrior wondered if perhaps his entry into the realm of death would deliver him to her for an eternity.

The hangman turned to him and asked, "Any last words?"

The young warrior continued to look out into the crowd and proclaimed with pride, "I am a warrior and shall die as a warrior!"

"Anything more?" the hangman asked.

"*The superior man when he stands alone is without fear. If he must renounce the world, it does not matter,*"[138] the young warrior said with conviction. "I stand alone," he added, standing tall with pride, while one solitary tear passed down his cheek.

The hangman slipped the black hood over his head as the warrior continued to think of her. His thoughts wandered and followed his heart to her, but she was unable to receive it. Within seconds, the gallow doors dropped beneath his feet and the rope snapped, extinguishing his life force forever. The crowd let out a gasp and then remained silent. It became clear that the warrior was in fact dead, as his body continued to swing from the gallows. His quest was now over, and his pursuit of truth had now been accomplished or possibly extinguished forever.

The majority of the cells within the prison maintained a window with a view of the gallows. The prisoners were encouraged to watch the executions as a deterrent and a form of cruel punishment.

"Another member of the Select punished for the crime of individualism and accomplishment," General Chang noted.

"Who was he?" Youngblood Hawke asked, bowing his head in honor of the fallen warrior.

"Just another Select Warrior with no general to lead him," responded the general. "You made a promise to me yesterday," the general noted.

"Indeed, I did," Youngblood replied as he continued to stare at the warrior's body swinging from the gallows, the words of a Great Emperor came to mind, "*Cowards die many times before their deaths. The Valiant never taste death but once.*"[139]

"How very true," the general agreed.

"Lesson one?" Youngblood inquired.

"Lesson one! The Select are few, and always will be few therefore, *when employing a few, concentrate upon the narrows.*"[140]

"The narrows?" Youngblood asked as he moved closer to the general, concentrating on his every word.

"*In warfare, if you oppose numerous enemy with only a few, you must do so when the sun is setting, through ambushes, concealed by deep vegetation or by intercepting them on a confined road,*"[141] the general explained.

"I understand this principle. I have utilized it in respect to personal combat and now what you are saying is, it must be extended to warfare as well. In other words, choose the terrain and utilize the advantage of surprise, focusing upon the weakest parts of your adversary," Youngblood noted.

"Yes, but what if you are the stronger? On such an occasion *although capable, display incapability,*"[142] the general responded as he raised a finger in the air to make his point.

Youngblood Hawke was captivated by the knowledge of the general and listened intently as he revealed his secrets.

"*If you want the enemy to engage your stronger, more numerous troops in battle, you should feign fear and weakness in order to entice them into it. When they carelessly come forth, you can suddenly assault them with your elite troops and their army will invariably be defeated,*"[143] the general said with the utmost confidence.

"Sensible strategy," Youngblood acknowledged.

"If you are the weaker, you should remember that *strength and weakness are a matter of disposition,*"[144] the general remarked. "Deceive the enemy into believing that you are stronger and more numerous than he," he added.

"This is another strategy I have employed successfully on many an occasion," commented Youngblood, shaking his head in agreement.

"Of course you have," the general acknowledged. "Such strategies do not have only one application. They may be and should be employed in every situation where strategy is required to gain the advantage and attain victory. They are as useful to a merchant competing for silver as they are for a general in the field of battle!" he added. "Arrogance!" the general shouted with fire in his eyes.

Youngblood raised an eyebrow as the general became more animated in his discussion. "It has been the downfall of many a general," he noted. "*When the enemy's forces are exceedingly strong and you cannot be certain of defeating them, one must be speak humbly and cultivate obsequious behavior in order to make them arrogant. Wait until there is some political pretext that can be exploited, then with a single mobilization you can destroy them! Remember, be deferential to make them arrogant,*"[145] the general said as his eyes became more excited and wide with every passing word.

"Yes, one should never underestimate the enemy," Youngblood agreed.

"Exactly! And do not dismiss the necessity of strategic power," the general said as he looked directly into his student's eyes.

"Strategic power?" Youngblood asked, seeking more of the general's wisdom.

The general was now standing and moving his hands about.

"*Whenever the enemies are in a situation where they can be vanquished and destroyed, you should follow it up and press an attack on them, for their army will certainly crumble. Rely on strategic power to destroy them,*"[146] the general declared as he pounded his fist into his other hand.

"A general must be wise and knowledgeable," Youngblood interjected.

"The wisdom of a sage and the knowledge of a philosopher, my boy! But knowledge from a practical perspective is important as well. *If one knows the field of battle and knows the day of battle, he can traverse a thousand miles and assemble to engage in combat,*"[147] the general said, now standing at the window and looking out into the square and the gallows.

Swiftness and rapid deployment. The strategy of another great general, Youngblood thought to himself, thinking of the Great One.

"Knowledge must also be gained covertly. *There are no areas in which one does not employ spies,*"[148] the general added as he turned slowly toward his attentive student. "*The means by which enlightened rulers and sagacious generals moved and conquered others, that their achievements surpassed the masses, was advance knowledge. Advance knowledge cannot be gained from ghosts and spirits, inferred from phenomena, or projected from the measures of Heaven, but must be gained from men for it is the knowledge of the enemy's true situation.*"[149]

"Spies…really? I would not have thought that a general would use such deceptive tactics," Youngblood said in surprise. "A soldier of fortune, yes…but a general?"

"*In many respects the effective utilization of spies requires a Philosopher General. Unless someone has the wisdom of a Sage, he cannot use spies; unless he is benevolent and righteous, he cannot employ spies; unless he is subtle and perspicacious, he cannot perceive the substance in intelligence reports,*"[150] the general noted, trying to make his point on the subject.

Youngblood Hawke just shook his head in agreement, drawing upon his own experience as a spy in the service of many a general and king.

"Initiative! Are you listening? *One who precedes others seizes their minds. Whenever engaging an enemy in battle, if after arriving they have not yet decisively deployed their power or put their formations in order, should you be the first to urgently mount a sudden attack, you will be victorious!*"[151] the excited general declared.

"Your strategy is fascinating, General, but I would imagine few others can employ such tactics?"

They are unorthodox and designed for only Select forces," the general responded. "*Unorthodox simply means attacking where the enemy is not prepared and going forth when they do not expect it!*"[152] he added.

"I understand, General. Such strategies will almost always certainly require the use of Select forces."

"*Whenever engaging in combat with an enemy, you must select courageous generals and fierce troops, forming them into an advance front. An army that lacks a properly selected vanguard is termed 'routed,'*"[153] he replied, noting that it was an army of the Select that was required against the mass. "I have provided you with only a few lessons of a hundred!" the general proclaimed.

"I desire to know them all, General," Youngblood requested humbly.

The general walked over to his sleeping area and pulled an old and worn journal from beneath his belongings.

"Take this. I have no need of it anymore," the general offered as he handed the journal to his student.

"What is it?" Youngblood asked as he studied the journal.

"My thoughts and my experience, young warrior. My time in this place has allowed me to write down—*100 Lessons in the Art of War,*"[154] the general responded. "You are a general now, and will need it more than I," he added.

"Thank you. I hope I will be able to use it," Youngblood remarked.

"It is late. I will sleep now and we will continue your studies in the morning," the weary general added as he lay down on his bed of straw and closed his eyes.

Youngblood sat beneath the window and took advantage of the moonlight to read the journal reflecting the general's genius. It covered every area he could imagine, from estimates of enemy strength, to forgetting warfare altogether. If Youngblood Hawke were to lead an army, the journal would be his most trusted advisor. As he struggled to read with the very limited light, he drifted off into sleep. He was keenly aware that it could be he who would climb the steps of the gallows next.

A Virtual Prison

Life—such an elaborate web,
Reaching out so distant and far,
Yet, we remain within bounds,
Self-confined to where we are.

Why do we live so afraid?
Fear is not what we need,
Tangled in our complex web,
A life we have chosen to lead.

We trap and confine others,
Our web does not discriminate,
In every direction it restricts us,
Holding us in this limited state.

A virtual prison of our own design,
Nothing but an abstract boundary,
Imaginary walls keep us confined,
Tragically—we choose not to be free.

—*Youngblood Hawke*

The opening of the cell door shattered the quiet as both the general and Youngblood were awoken. The guards entered the cell carrying shackles, and one had a bullwhip strapped to his side. His grin and the look in his eyes said all that had to be told.

"What do you want?" the general demanded in a commanding voice that at once startled the guards.

The men just stared at Youngblood Hawke as he stood up before them and returned a rebellious gaze.

"It is my knock at midnight," Youngblood said as the guards approached him and he became fully aware that it was he would be climbing the steps of the gallows at daybreak.

CHAPTER 16

The Shadow of Death

Eternity was revealed to me, dismissing reality
Forgiving the weakness of my mortality
Could it possibly be? Is this my destiny?

The corridor was masked by the shadows with only the flickering of torchlight to illuminate the darkness. Due to his limited mobility, the two guards dragged their prisoner with contempt. He was completely restrained by the iron shackles on his legs and hands. They entered another room that was damp and cold, displaying little but the dirt floor and the chains on the walls.

A torture chamber, Youngblood thought to himself.

He was brought to the middle of the room and the shackles on his hands were attached to a chain hanging from the ceiling. Upon being connected to the chain, his shirt was ripped away and he was immediately hoisted in the air, allowing his feet to barely touch the floor. The pain shot through his arms and shoulders as the complete weight of his body was felt on his wrists and arms. The two guards just stared at Youngblood and then spoke quietly to each other as a third man entered the chamber. The two other guards departed, leaving the third man alone to attend to his task. Youngblood was no stranger to punishment and torture. Raising his head in defiance, he made eye contact with his punisher.

Sentenced to Life

Why do you punish me?
I have committed no crime.
Suffering in my humanity,
Facing the brutality of time.

I am a prisoner of fate,
Serving a life sentence.
Locked in a solitary state,
Confined to my existence.

Waiting alone in my cell,
I plead for my release.
Trapped in a living hell,
Begging for some peace.

One day you may forgive,
Freeing me from my chains.
Perhaps then I will live,
Freed from my sins and pain.

—*Youngblood Hawke*

Youngblood Hawke remained silent, continuing to remind himself that although his body would soon be broken, his spirit would remain intact. The pain of the whip continued to ripple through his body, reaching down into the very depths of his soul as he searched for refuge within the farthest confines of his mind. He thought of friends, colleagues, and the long-forgotten memories of his youth. His mind traveled through time, leading him on a virtual tour of his adventures, exploits, and failures. He found himself focusing, not upon accomplishments, but on the more humble moments of his life. He dared to visit the comfort of the Noble House, but immediately dismissed the thoughts in order to protect its very existence.

"What of Sinclair and Horatio?" he asked himself, as he once again wondered if Sinclair had escaped the mass.

His mind slowly drifted toward the sapphire storm and the allure of the Oracle's beauty. *If ever I needed her guidance, it was now*, he thought to himself, as he closed his eyes and drew her image in his mind.

He could feel the warmth of her glow soften the dampness of the chamber. "Come back to me, come back to me, come back to me," he pled for her return, as he found himself drifting farther and farther away from the pain being inflicted by reality.

The shackles continued to tear into his wrists as the punisher ripped into his back. The warrior called upon all of his remaining strength to ignore the pain. He continued to focus upon the image of his Sapphire and the fading sparkle of her eyes as she gazed upon his withering mortality. He wondered if she was with him or if it was merely his imagination searching for comfort from the pain.

He recalled the words of the Prophet, "*Thoughts are the shadows of our sensations—always darker, emptier, simpler.*"[155]

"Don't be saddened," he uttered softly, as he traveled to the edge of her world, "it is my time and I must go. Fear not, for you will find another."

A solitary tear rolled down his cheek, mirrored by the tear displayed by the Oracle's desperation that she was unable to enter his world and assist him. The Oracle appeared to reach out to him, but their worlds were not one. She was unable to touch him and relieve his suffering but could only watch the mortal warrior that had touched her heart suffer a slow and painful death at the hands of his enemy. She could not help but wonder if it was loneliness that was, in reality, his true executioner. Youngblood knew his time was coming to an end and in an attempt to ease her pain, he regained his composure and masked the suffering from his face as his soul slipped away into the emptiness of approaching death.

"Do not mourn for me. I am Youngblood Hawke and I shall die a warrior's death," he said boldly.

The depths of the warrior's soul opened to reveal the desperation of the moment and the shattered dreams of a precocious, yet undetermined, destiny.

Lost in the Realm of Reality

Lost in a world of chaotic conformity
My heart and soul grow weary,
Longing for a time of relative sanity.

I awaken from my dreams
>An angel appears before me.
Is this a dream or reality?

This vision, such clarity!
>Touching me momentarily,
Continuing to elude me.

Eternity was revealed to me,
>Dismissing reality,
Forgiving the weakness of my mortality

>>Could it possibly be?
>>Is this my destiny?

—*Youngblood Hawke*

As the intensity of pain increased, Sapphire's image began to fade from his thoughts with every strike of the whip. His thoughts drifted to her as he pondered the meaning of his existence and the painful struggle of his quest. The paradox of his existence and his quest continued to taunt his spirit, soul, and heart. Youngblood's mind drifted toward the sapphire angel as he whispered to her.

With Or Without You

With or without you,
>My mind wanders,
To a destination unknown.

With or without you,
>My spirit retreats,
Creating a world of its own.

With or without you,
>My soul seeks comfort,
For a place to call home.

With or without you,
>   My heart aches,
Desiring a love of its own.

With or without you,
>   My life will continue,
Desperate, dark, and alone.

—Youngblood Hawke

He slowly opened his eyes and was immediately returned to the cruel reality that she was no longer with him.

Suddenly the door to the chamber opened as the guards stepped in, followed by a third man. The man raised his hand to halt the punisher but remained in the shadows. Hiding his face from the light, he stood silent and stared at his weakened prisoner.

"Youngblood Hawke—philosopher, soldier of fortune, professional adventurer, and would-be prince," the unidentified figure said.

Youngblood could barely maintain his focus as his eyes strained into the darkness, as the pain continued to pulsate through his body.

He reached down and with all his energy acknowledged, "I am Youngblood Hawke."

"Interesting, Mr. Hawke. You don't look like much of a prince," the man noted from the shadows. "In fact, you don't look like much of anything," the mysterious figure added with an obvious tone of disdain.

The failing warrior continued to fight the pain as he strained to identify his captor, noting only the vague familiarity of his voice.

"Your end is near, and soon you will be nothing more than a mythical criminal and enemy of the state, executed in the name of justice," the man said with a tone of triumph in his voice.

"*Time shall unfold what plaited cunning hides,*"[156] Youngblood quoted.

"Yes, I suppose it is comforting for you to remain true to your philosophy, when confronted with your end. I will leave you with that, Youngblood Hawke. But that is all I will leave you with. For within the hour you will cease to exist and will no longer matter," responded the man with contempt as he exited the room, leaving his prisoner to contemplate his approaching death.

❦   ❦   ❦

Zacharia and Remo continued to travel west, departing the dangers of the Eastern Kingdom. The thought of his friend's execution was just too much for his conscience to bear, but the safety of his son was paramount. The battle within his conscience raged like a violent storm as Zacharia searched for a way to justify his actions.

The road was darkened as the end of the day approached and the sun dipped below the horizon. The small band of about twenty men approached on horseback, presenting an intimidating sight. The sound of the hooves pounding on the road created the impression of an approaching menace.

The Black Guard, Zacharia thought to himself, as he moved to one side of the road, allowing plenty of room for them to pass.

As the band drew closer, he could not help but notice the silhouette of the lead figure and the strange familiarity surrounding the image. The manner in which the band was assembled reminded him of an earlier day. Zacharia thought it strange that the Black Guards would display such a disciplined presence. As the group passed, Zacharia peered up at the leader, careful not to draw their attention.

"Major Cantrell?" he cried out in disbelief as the leader raised his hand and halted the band of men.

"Zacharia? Is that you?" Horatio Cantrell responded, noting that he was being called by his former military rank.

"Yes, Major. It is I!" Zacharia replied happily and relieved.

"How are you, old man?" Horatio inquired with a faint smile, vaguely hiding the concern and determination in his eyes.

"It is Hawke! You have to help him…he is…," Zacharia rambled before being interrupted.

"Speak up, old man! What of Youngblood Hawke? Come now…you are ranting like a madman!" Sinclair Fox interjected, as he also noted the boy was riding Veritas.

"Calm down, both of you!" Horatio commanded. "Now, Zacharia, tell me what you know about Youngblood," he ordered.

"The Black Guards hold him prisoner, and he is to be executed at daybreak!" he exclaimed.

"Daybreak! I say, he is to die within the hour," Sinclair said.

Horatio remained silent as he wrote a dispatch and handed it to one of the men. "Take this to William and waste not a moment's time," he ordered. The obedient soldier rode off immediately.

"Zacharia, where is the execution to be held?" Horatio inquired.

"The provincial prison. Within the village of Steepleton," he responded.

"How many prison guards?" Sinclair asked.

"Maybe fifteen. But there is also a contingent of at least fifty Black Guards, under the command of a Major Constantine," Zacharia added.

"Constantine? Kirsan has spared no expense in his hunt for Youngblood Hawke," Horatio noted, who was obviously familiar with the major.

"He is a scoundrel and I will have his head!" Sinclair shouted in anger.

"That day may come, my anxious friend, but we have more pressing matters at the moment," Horatio said. "Gentlemen! Follow me. We have a mission and require a plan," ordered Horatio.

The band of professional soldiers followed by Zacharia and his son disappeared into the night.

The darkness of the chamber was emptied as the door opened and the sunlight entered the room, blinding the prisoner. As his eyes adjusted, he looked to see the wild one standing before him, with two other Black Guard members. He was grinning and appeared to enjoy the miserable state of his captive. Youngblood immediately noticed his katana sword, now being worn by the angry and wild-eyed one. He wore it like a trophy, presenting the false impression that he had won it meritoriously in battle.

"You wear that as if you earned it," Youngblood Hawke said.

"I did," the wild-eyed one replied.

"*Some rise by sin, some by virtue fall,*"[157] Youngblood responded, as he looked upon his captor with pity.

"To Hades with you, Youngblood Hawke!" he replied. In anger he approached his prisoner and struck him across the face. "You see yourself as above us all. But where are you now?" he asked with hatred.

"You hate my accomplishments for they are a constant reminder of your own failures," Youngblood responded.

The anger within the wild one increased as his eyes glowed with the crimson shade of hatred.

"Bring him! It is time for this one to die!" he ordered, as the guards lowered their prisoner to the floor. "Shall we carry you to your death or would you prefer to walk with some degree of dignity?"

"He will walk like a warrior," Major Constantine ordered as he entered the chamber.

The guard provided Youngblood with water as he struggled to his feet with every intention of walking to his death, in a manner befitting a true warrior.

The morning air was crisp and the sky was clear as the sun began to make its mark on the new day. The crowd that had gathered for the execution was unusually large. Executions regularly drew a large crowd, but this day had delivered a crowd of massive proportion. The streets were filled with people who appeared to have traveled great distances just to see the execution of the well-known philosopher, soldier of fortune, and professional adventurer known as Youngblood Hawke. Vendors were already working the crowd as people scurried up the walls and onto roofs in an attempt to gain a good vantage point to witness the execution. The large crowd clearly made the prison guards nervous, but their fears were eased somewhat by the presence of the Black Guard unit. They assembled near the entrance to the town's square, adjacent to the crowd and the gallows.

When the door to the prison opened and the guards escorted the doomed man from within, the mammoth crowd grew silent. Youngblood Hawke did his best to hide the pain, walking through the crowd with his head held high, his eyes remained focused in a deep, cold stare. He looked straight ahead and intentionally ignored the ominous presence of the gallows erected before him. He knew his destination and that his quest was about to end.

The Exceptional Being

Surrounded by many,
I remain standing alone,
A self-imposed exile,
No place to call home,

A dark and lonely heart,
The most desperate soul,
Ruled by fear and doubt,
In command and control.

The moment is coming,
I can no longer pretend,
The world is watching,
This is surely the end.

—*Youngblood Hawke*

"Is everyone in place?" Horatio asked.

"Indeed," Sinclair responded, as both of the men moved their way through the crowd and toward the gallows.

"My God! What have they done to the man?" Sinclair inquired, catching a glimpse of his friend's wounds as he was being delivered to the gallows.

"A futile attempt to break the warrior spirit," Horatio noted. "Follow me," he added as Sinclair and Zacharia followed.

Horatio led them into a doorway that led to another door opening behind the gallows. They moved to a position about twenty-five feet from the gallows and within ten feet of the Black Guard.

The crowd became uncharacteristically silent as Youngblood Hawke climbed the steps, leading up to the platform, where he would be hung from the neck until he died. He found himself thinking of Sapphire once again and wondering if she was aware of his fate. Once he reached the top of the platform, he was escorted to a position atop the trap door, and the rope was placed over his head.

"Do you require a hood?" the executioner asked gravely.

"No, I shall die with my eyes and mind opened wide."

Horatio watched as his men secured their positions, but he was concerned with the location of the Black Guard unit. The proximity of so many to his position could cause a problem. He was concerned that their sufficient numbers could stop him or his colleagues from reaching the platform before the door is dropped.

"What is this we are standing upon?" Sinclair inquired, breaking Horatio's concentration.

"It is a bone pile," Zacharia responded.

"Indeed, it is a bone pile. Human remains, I suspect? How utterly interesting," Sinclair remarked, as he picked up a human skull and began to examine it as if he were attempting to recognize its former owner.

"Silence, you fools. We need a diversion of some kind to draw the attention of the Black Guards," Horatio said.

Sinclair just looked at Horatio, then looked at the Black Guards, and then down at the human skull in his hands and said, "Leave it to me, my old friend."

"What is that madman up to now?" Horatio asked as he watched Sinclair disappear into the crowd, carrying the skull with him.

Major Constantine ascended the stairs and approached Youngblood Hawke, accompanied by the new owner of his katana sword.

"Do you have any last words?" Major Constantine asked.

Youngblood directed his eyes toward his executioners and said, "My death will not result in the death of an idea. An ideology grounded in truth shall never be defeated, nor will it be extinguished by the hand of ignorance. My quest is about to come to an end and the truth will be revealed to me."

"Your faith in the truth is admirable, but naïve," Major Constantine commented, immediately startled by the crack of the thunder and the strike of the lightning on one of the prison towers.

In fact, the abrupt interruption of nature alarmed everyone as the crowd erupted and broke the silence.

"What an odd storm?" Major Constantine noted.

He looked up at the approaching storm forming above them, intrigued by the variety of color glowing from within.

"Sapphire," Youngblood Hawke said, as a smile formed on his face and his eyes brightened at the sight of the setting storm.

"Yes…you are correct. A sapphire storm, the likes of which I have never seen before," Major Constantine agreed, as he continued to study the sky.

Suddenly, a figure was revealed standing atop a tower within the square. He stood tall, as his cape blew in the wind, while the sapphire storm formed behind him, providing an almost ghostly presence. The man held up what appeared to be a human skull, as he waved his other hand with the majesty and drama of a stage actor.

"Alas, poor Yorick! I knew him, Horatio; a fellow of infinite jest, of most excellent fancy: he hath borne me upon his back a thousand times; and now, how abhorred in my imagination it is,"[158] the figure recited aloud, projecting his voice across the square.

"Is that Sinclair?" Zacharia asked in amazement.

"Indeed, it is," Horatio replied, shaking his head in disbelief.

"Who is Yorick?" Zacharia inquired with puzzlement. "What is he talking about and what in the world is he doing?"

"Probably some poor gentleman that he bored to death," Horatio said with a grin. "As to what he is doing? That, my good, man is what one calls a diversion," he noted approvingly.

Youngblood began to laugh as he recognized his good friend and comrade, providing a wonderful exhibition of pompous declaration. The crowd turned to observe the spectacle that had now caught the attention of all the Black Guards and their leader.

"Get him down from there immediately!" the major ordered.

The Black Guards forced their way through the crowd and ordered Sinclair down from his lofty position. However, he continued his recitation and ignored their commands. Several of the Black Guards began to climb the tower in an attempt to remove the nuisance, but were met with the most graceful sweep of a boot, knocking them back to the ground. It was a sight to behold as Sinclair Fox continued to address the crowd and perform to their delight, while simultaneously physically dismissing his attackers. It was truly comical and very frustrating, as well as embarrassing for the Black Guards, who were being humiliated in front of hundreds of people by the antics of the interloper. The distraction of Sinclair and the approaching storm was just what Horatio needed.

"Now is the time," Horatio ordered, as he drew his sword and passed a signal to the other men standing at the ready within the crowd.

Horatio and his men moved swiftly and decisively as they attacked the Black Guards without warning and caught them completely unprepared. The crowd reacted with complete confusion, unsure of exactly what was occurring. Black Guard members were falling at their feet as the avengers struck with deadly accuracy, leaving the unmistakable mark of professional soldiers. Major Constantine noticed that something was wrong, as did the wild-eyed one, who drew the katana and attempted to rally his men for a counterattack. However, his attempts were futile as the roar of the crowd drowned his orders and his men faced superior warriors and certain defeat. Sinclair Fox, who had descended the tower in all the confusion, was now making his way up the stairway of the gallows. He was immediately recognized by the wild one, who exhibited nothing but raw hatred and revenge.

"You! The peacock!" the wild one shouted in anger, as he blocked the stairway and engaged Sinclair.

"I have no time for you, boy!" Sinclair responded, as his steel blade was met by the defensive reply of the katana.

The three other Black Guard members responded to assist as Major Constantine realized what was occurring. "A rescue attempt. How noble," he remarked, immediately gesturing to the executioner to drop the trap doors below Youngblood Hawke and send him to his death.

Youngblood reacted immediately as he leaped up instantly and kicked Major Constantine off the platform. A move that was no easy feat, considering that his feet were shackled, his hands were bound behind his back, and his neck was set within a noose! As the major fell into the crowd, the executioner released the lever, dropping the door below Youngblood. The door dropped instantly but stopped short of the distance necessary to snap Youngblood Hawke's neck. Fortunately, Horatio responded immediately by maneuvering below the trap door and holding it up before it could fall completely through. However, the weight of the door and the warrior would soon become too much, even for the strength of Horatio Cantrell.

"Sinclair! Get him out of there!" Horatio commanded, struggling to hold the trap door up.

"I say, good man! I am doing the best I can!" Sinclair Fox replied, as he navigated the narrow staircase, doing battle with four members of the Black Guard. "Incidentally, I could use your help at the moment."

"Is that so? I just happen to be a little preoccupied."

Meanwhile, Youngblood remained on the tips of his toes, attempting to keep the rope from doing the job for which it was intended. He watched helplessly as Sinclair fought ferociously against overwhelming odds in an attempt to break past the defenders. Suddenly, the small, cloaked figure slipped past the confusion and moved directly toward Youngblood.

Assassin or friend? Youngblood thought to himself, preparing to react in some manner.

The figure revealed a dagger and reached for Youngblood's neck. Youngblood was unable to react due to his current dilemma, and braced himself for the strike. Suddenly, the identity of the cloaked one was revealed.

"Sapphire!" Youngblood Hawke cried out in complete surprise.

The sparkle of her eyes captured his complete attention as the dagger cut the noose from his neck and dropped him to the floor. Just then, the trap door fell and she grabbed onto the warrior. They both fell through to the floor, landing in each other's arms on the ground below. Horatio stood in amazement as he realized his friend was alive.

"Remove those shackles!" Horatio ordered as Youngblood lay on the floor, staring into the eyes of what appeared to be the very mortal Sapphire.

The shackles were removed and Youngblood stood, prepared to join the combat of the moment.

"Come with me," he said, grabbing Sapphire's hand, as she nodded in agreement. Youngblood removed her to a location beneath the gallows, safe from the ensuing battle and ordered one of Horatio's men to remain with her. "Guard her with your life!" he commanded.

Horatio responded and attempted to assist Sinclair as he pushed his way up the stairs. "Sinclair, Youngblood has been freed. Let's go," he said.

"I am not finished with this one!" Sinclair replied, as he continued to attack the three defenders.

One had already fell victim to his sword, and it was the intention of Sinclair to deliver the wild one to his eternal fate.

Youngblood Hawke had not dismissed the situation atop the platform, as he climbed up through the trap door with the intention of recovering his katana. Once he was upon the platform, the unarmed Youngblood Hawke wasted no time as he directed his attack upon the Black Guard defenders. Sinclair continued his assault as Horatio joined in the fight, adding a powerful ally to the precision of Sinclair's sword. The defenders were completely consumed by the attack of Sinclair and Horatio as well as overwhelmed by the carnage surrounding them. Therefore, the first strike by Youngblood was not only lethal but also unexpected as their comrade collapsed instantly from the strike directed to the back of the head. The double jump kick unleashed by Hawke was devastating as the second defender was propelled forward and directly into Sinclair's sword. The man was killed instantly and fell down the stairs to his final resting place. Horatio and Sinclair lowered their swords as the wild-eyed one remained standing alone. Confused by the attack to his rear flank, and the standing down of Horatio and Sinclair, he turned to find his destiny standing before him. His eyes captured the sight of Youngblood Hawke, who had now assumed a posture of a warrior on the verge of attack. The determination in Youngblood's eyes was undeniable as he prepared himself to strike and recover that which belonged to him. The wild one's confidence grew as he became aware that his opponent was unarmed. After all, it was he who held the deadly katana in his hand. However, he did not fully realize the ability of his adversary, and he was about to enter the contest of his life.

"How appropriate that you would die by your own sword," the wild one said, as the hatred in his heart fueled the crimson glow of his eyes. "Soon the fear will overcome you and the coward within will be revealed."

"A great man once said, *True nobility is exempt from fear,*"[159] Youngblood responded, maintaining his stare upon the man that had now become his prey.

He was utilizing the pause to examine the strengths and weaknesses of his armed adversary. The moment was important, for the warrior must be "*aware of his opponents' sword and yet not look at the opponent's sword at all.*"[160] His old master had taught him the martial arts, and he was trained to deal with his current predicament. "*Swordlessness is the attitude whereby you let others have the swords, while you engage them using your hands as instruments. So, since swords are longer than hands, you have to get close to an adversary, within killing range, in order to be successful.*"[161]

Youngblood knew he would need to deflect the attack while at the same time move quickly into killing range, where he could arrest the sword and return it to its proper owner.

"You are not exempt from death," the wild one cried out.

"No, I am not. But another great man once said, '*Death, a necessary end, will come when it will come,*'"[162] Youngblood replied, continuing to carefully study his opponent. "Your time has come!"

The wild one laughed loudly as he extended the sword, "You are a fool, indeed."

He lunged at Youngblood with all his might and anger fueling his assault. Youngblood's response was immediate. He deflected the sword with his left hand and spun clockwise, striking the attacker directly in the face with the momentum and blunt force of his right elbow. The move was employed with lightning speed and accuracy, allowing Youngblood Hawke to dislodge the katana from his adversary's grip and strike him down. The wild-eyed one fell to his knees, aware momentarily that his fate had indeed arrived, and its deliverer now stood over him. The steel sheen of the katana, now in the hands of its rightful master, cast a radiant glow upon the platform that drew the attention of all in the square. Staring up at Youngblood Hawke, the wild-eyed warrior felt the life escaping his body as the katana penetrated the depths of his cold heart. As he fell forward, the crimson glow slowly diminished from his eyes, extinguishing the hatred from his heart, and ending his misguided quest in failure.

Horatio and Sinclair just stood in awe as they observed their leader ascend to the next level of a warrior's existence. He stood upon the platform surveying the massacre that had taken place, as the remnants of the Black Guard lay strewn across the village square. Youngblood Hawke's presence was of epic proportion, standing boldly as the scars of many a battle were exposed upon his shirtless body. The blood of his adversaries, which had mixed with his own, created a most intimidating image combined with the presence of the now legendary katana sword that has returned to the hand of Youngblood Hawke. The Select Warriors had been victorious on this day, and they cheered and saluted their anointed leader, basking in the glory of their decisive win over a force of superior numbers.

"*Mandamus Veritas! Mandamus Veritas!*" they chanted. The ancient motto

"We command the truth!" was repeated as they raised their swords and extended the traditional military salute to their revered leader.

Horatio and Sinclair joined in the salute and cheers, noting that their friend and comrade would now be forced to accept his fate. They reveled in the moment and welcomed the arrival of the Warrior Prince they know as Youngblood Hawke.

Youngblood Hawke acknowledged the praises of his colleagues, raising his katana in salute. Zacharia approached the platform accompanied by his son, who was leading Veritas. Remo ascended the stairs and presented the battle sword of Youngblood Hawke, the Warrior Prince.

"I kept good care of this, and Veritas for you," Remo offered with the admiration of a young boy meeting his hero.

"As I knew you would. Thank you," Youngblood replied, bowing his head in gratitude and placing his hand upon the boy's shoulder. Perhaps someday you will carry this sword as I do."

Remo just smiled as his imagination pondered such a possibility.

Youngblood Hawke now turned his attention to the crowd of the Select Warriors and the mass who had now joined the cause of truth.

"The valor displayed here today will not soon be forgotten, my friends. In fact, it will never be erased, as history will write that, on this day, the truth conquered and declared war upon the culture of deception and mediocrity. I will forever be in your debt. Truth will forever be in your debt. Accept my invitation to continue this quest together. The struggle will be difficult and the obstacles great. However, the Select Warrior shall overcome all opposition and assume a position of prominence, meritoriously! Now, raise your swords high and if you are with me, swear your allegiance to the truth!" Youngblood Hawke proclaimed.

The crowd erupted in the declaration of *"Mandamus Veritas!"* and raised their swords in an expression of allegiance.

The Warrior Prince once again raised his sword in acknowledgment and declared proudly, "I am Youngblood Hawke!"

Youngblood descended the platform greeting his most trusted friends and advisors. Horatio and Sinclair were both alive with excitement as they exchanged the warrior salute with their young leader.

"Well said, good man! Your words rang of the truth and inspired the darkest corners of the heart and mind," Sinclair said in his most aristocratic manner.

"These men will follow you through the gates of Hades now," Horatio commented.

"This fight has just begun, my friends," Youngblood noted. "We must prepare for the next battle. Kirsan will respond quickly and send in the next wave in an attempt to destroy this insurrection. He will deploy the best the mass has to offer when he hears of this. I will need my two best generals steadfastly by my side."

"It goes without saying," Sinclair said, as Horatio nodded his head in agreement.

"I will assemble the men immediately," Horatio said with a renewed sense of being and command that had eluded him for the past several years.

"Excuse me, gentlemen," Youngblood said, as he proceeded under the platform in search of Sapphire.

Sinclair watched in amazement as his colleague walked away with a most impressive command presence. *"Some are born great, some achieve greatness, and some have greatness thrust upon them,"*[163] Sinclair said aloud.

"Indeed," Horatio agreed, as he watched his former apprentice depart.

Youngblood approached the man who was left to protect Sapphire, "Where is she?"

"What? I don't know. She was here just a moment ago, sir," he responded with panic in his voice. "I assure you she was not harmed."

Youngblood just turned to the crowd within the village square as his eyes and thoughts searched for her presence. "Your mystery continues to elude me," he said to himself as he searched the crowd for her.

Once again he found himself feeling the emptiness of her absence.

"Where are you?" he asked. "How is it you always seem to be there when I need you? Yet, you always seem to slip from my grasp and remain out of my reach."

The chaos continued within the Village Square as Youngblood pondered the mystery of the Oracle and the sapphire storm that continued to elude him.

Taunted By True Love

> Romance, passion, the heart's desires be told.
> The allure of happiness punishes my soul.
> The suffering and pain of an unknown destiny,
> Pursuing so many yet choosing me.
>
> True Love as written in the days of old,
> Teasing, taunting, demanding to be told.
> All that I have dreamed of delivered to me.
> What game is this? Fate toying with humanity?
>
> Slowly detached, my mind loses control,
> Wandering in the wilderness alone and cold.
> A soul mate, friend, and lover is she,
> An alternative universe, an escape from reality.
>
> Time will pass, and all will grow old,
> Capture what is yours! Lovers be bold!
> Searching for answers, my quest will be,
> Ignoring the truth, for the answer lies within me.
>
> —*Youngblood Hawke*

"Youngblood, we must go!" Horatio interrupted with a sense of the utmost urgency.

"Indeed, we must," Youngblood Hawke replied, as he climbed onto Veritas. "Sinclair, take a band of men and free all of the political prisoners. Take care, my friend, and politely request that General Chang accompany us."

"Politely is my only way, my dear Hawke!" the incorrigible Sinclair Fox replied.

"You don't mean the General Chang?" Horatio asked with a raised brow.

"In the flesh, my friend," Youngblood said.

Wasting little time, Youngblood Hawke led his elite unit of Select Warriors from the village. He was fully aware that the battle of this day was just the first of many more to come. A prospect he did not relish but accepted, as a necessary means to an end.

CHAPTER 17

The Initiative

Searching for answers my quest will be,
Ignoring the truth, for the answer lies within me.

Moving away from the scene of the battle, the unit of Select Warriors had gained strength, under the command of their new leader. The victory was one of glory and honor as they had proved themselves worthy against some of the best that the mass had to offer. The Select Warriors consisted of approximately fifty of the finest warriors, assembled from all four of the kingdoms. They all had one thing in common—a sincere reverence for truth and a noble loyalty to their new commander.

"Shall we be continuing east?" Horatio Cantrell asked.

"That would be wise, considering the danger is in the west," Sinclair Fox noted with a hint of sarcasm in his voice.

"We will go west and confront the enemy," Youngblood Hawke said.

"What? Youngblood, have you gone mad? We have but fifty warriors," Horatio said, shaking his head in disbelief.

Youngblood Hawke looked to General Chang who was now by his side for advice.

"General, would you agree with my assessment that the strategic initiative should be taken?" Youngblood asked his mentor.

"Without question! *One who proceeds others seizes their minds!*"[164] the general replied.

He then proceeded to inspect the force of warriors assembled around him.

"I see that you paid attention to our lessons." General Chang added.

"Indeed, I did, General," the confident Youngblood Hawke responded, as he took note of the pleased look on his mentor's face.

"Lessons? Exactly what topic would that have been? Insanity, perhaps?" Horatio barked in disagreement.

Horatio was displaying serious misgivings regarding the strategy being offered as he had always been a cautious tactician.

"Horatio! You, my friend, are very near what one could describe as insubordinate. Surprising behavior from a military man such as yourself, wouldn't you say?" Sinclair Fox said in an attempt to temper Horatio's passionate display.

"Gentlemen, please! If we run now, we will be running forever. Therefore, we will confront Kirsan and the mass on our own terms," Youngblood Hawke interjected.

"Sounds like a brilliant plan, General," Sinclair Fox acknowledged, as he nodded his head as a gesture of respect and as a reminder to all that Youngblood Hawke was the commander of this expedition.

Sinclair's actions did not go unnoticed by Horatio as he also nodded his head toward his commander and said, "A bold plan, indeed."

"We will do exactly what the mass would not expect us to do. That is, we will stay on the main roads, which will provide us with a more direct travel route to our destination. Horatio, send two scouts ahead to warn us of any approaching Black Guard units," Youngblood instructed.

"Yes, good idea, Youngblood. The warning will give us time to move off of the road and time to allow them to pass," Horatio remarked.

"On the contrary, my old friend. The warning will give us time to prepare for an attack!" the bold commander replied as the cold stare and the trademark smirk electrified his face.

"That's the spirit, Hawke! *Screw your courage to the sticking place!*"[165] Sinclair shouted out approvingly as he waved his fist in the air.

"If we are not careful, Kirsan will be screwing all of our heads on a pike!" Horatio Cantrell noted with a pessimistic tone.

"*There are more things in heaven and earth, Horatio, than are dreamt of in your philosophy,*"[166] Sinclair countered. "We must think positive, my good man!"

"You think too much, my naïve friend," Horatio said, as he kept his eyes forward.

He was attempting to maintain his military bearing in order to diffuse a potential argument with the always prepared, and all too willing to debate Sinclair Fox.

General Change interjected, "The next battle is inevitable. *A tactical principle from the art of war states: 'If I want to engage in combat, even though the enemy has deep moats and high ramparts, he cannot avoid doing battle because I attack objectives he must rescue.' When they reach the point that combat becomes unavoidable, you should strike them with your fiercest troops, for then they will be defeated."[167]*

"In other words, my fellow soldiers, we will bring the fight to Kirsan. And when it is over, it will not be our heads that are resting upon a pike," Youngblood Hawke added in a tone clearly intended to end any further debate.

The unit continued west, traveling well into the darkness of the night. Upon reaching the crest of a hill, Youngblood ordered the unit off of the road and set up camp for the evening. No fires would be burned, and every other man would remain awake while the others slept. The night was restless for the band of elite warriors, and it was no different for their commander. Youngblood Hawke tried to sleep, but only stared up into the sky, searching the stars for inspiration and answers. The heavens were filled with bright stars, and the moon cast an ominous glow upon the hillside, creating a most surreal atmosphere. A very appropriate environment, considering the monumental task that lay ahead. Youngblood stood from his resting place and walked to an elevated point upon a nearby hill. His position afforded him with a view of both the camp and the road leading to Ventura.

The night appeared to grow darker as the number of stars decreased, and the moon disappeared behind the clouds forming overhead. Youngblood continued to gaze off to the horizon when he noticed the slight glow coming from a patch of trees in the distance.

A small campfire perhaps? he thought to himself.

Youngblood decided to investigate and so he proceeded down the other side of the hill, raising his hand in acknowledgment to a sentinel standing watch nearby. As he approached the patch of trees he realized that his position was no longer visible from the camp or by the sentinel. Good sense told him to turn back and return with a larger force to investigate, but it was not good sense that was motivating him.

The small fire was burning just enough to maintain a slight glow when suddenly the coals burst into a large blue flame, igniting the enclosed area in a powerful display of colors!

"Sapphire!" the surprised warrior shouted, as she appeared before him. "Where have you been? Why did you disappear from beneath the gallows?"

"My ability to remain in your world is limited," the Oracle responded with a hint of despair and sadness in her voice. "Limited by your own desires, wants, and needs."

"I don't understand. Why can you not remain here with me by my side at all times?" the desperate warrior inquired.

"I suspect only you can answer that question," the Oracle said, as she continued to gaze upon Youngblood Hawke with both reverence and concern.

"You continue to answer my questions with questions," the frustrated warrior noted.

"That is because the answers to your questions lay deep within yourself. Only you can shed light upon your questions, dilemmas, and internal conflicts. Look to your philosophical side and search the darkest and deepest confines of your being. It is there that you shall find that which you seek and desire the most," said the Oracle.

"You speak of my dark side?"

"It remains dark only because you choose not to expose it to the light," she noted. "Do you fear your dark side?"

"No, but others do. Therefore, it remains hidden and confined to the shadows where no man shall be exposed, except in my most desperate hours. And only then it is due to necessity, and the price paid for such exposure is always very high."

"I have seen your dark side and experienced no fear from exposure. In fact, I find your dark side to be nothing more than an extension of your enlightened side. Do not dismiss it nor be ashamed of it. For it is as much a part of you as any other. In fact, without it, you would not be Youngblood Hawke," the Oracle replied, as she moved closer to the object of her affections. "Do you remember the words of the Prophet?" she asked.

"Which words do you speak of? He recited many."

The Oracle looked upon the warrior and said, "*I know the hatred and envy of your hearts. You are not great enough not to know hatred and envy. So be great enough not to be ashamed of them.*"[168]

"Yes, I know those words and I know what lies deep in the darkness of my heart," the warrior acknowledged.

For a moment Youngblood's demeanor intensified as he drew closer to the Oracle.

"Know this for certain, you shall forever be subjected to the illumination of my enlightened side and protected by the shadows of my dark side. To my eyes, you are absolute, and I have sworn to protect you at all costs! I shall protect you with my last thought, my last drop of blood, and my last dying breath!" Young-blood proclaimed, as he stared deep into the sapphire storm brewing before him.

The Oracle continued to gaze upon the warrior, returning his intense stare and moving closer to his mortal existence.

Youngblood Hawke continued to be drawn to the warmth and comfort of her sapphire glow.

"Upon my death, my spirit will follow you and provide a shroud of protection against all who would do you harm. You, my dearest Sapphire, shall for all eternity be under the protection of Youngblood Hawke and those loyal to the cause!"

"And you shall be under mine," she responded, as the distance closed between them and they exchanged the tender expression of their affection and desires.

The moment was beyond anything either had ever experienced before. The simplicity and truth revealed by their connection was absolute and undeniable. Yet the moment was also brief as she began to fade into the darkness, leaving the softness of her touch as a reminder that she would be by his side during the approaching battle.

"Absolute truth," he whispered to himself, "shall it ever be attained or shall it forever be out of reach? Alas! I suspect that like all quests it will require much bloodshed, heartache, and sacrifice to find the answer."

Youngblood Hawke pondered the purpose of his quest. He once again recalled his time with the Prophet and recounted the wisdom of his words. *"You should seek your enemy, you should wage your war—a war for your opinions. And if your opinion is defeated, your honesty should still cry triumph over that!"*[169]

He pondered the consequences of the approaching battle and war that would most likely result. The sacrifices that would be made, the loss of life that would result on both sides, and the tears that would be shed for years to come. He questioned the means to the end as the words of the Prophet continued to ring in his thoughts. *"You say it is the good cause that hallows even war? I tell you: it is the good war that hallows every cause. War and courage have done more great things than charity. Not your pity but your bravery has saved the unfortunate up to now.*[170] Youngblood sat alone, the solitary man, considering the future and what it held in store for him and his comrades.

Youngblood returned to the camp as dawn approached so he could prepare his men. The distraction of "absolute truth's" powerful allure remained entrenched within his thoughts. It was a welcome distraction, and in many ways, an inspiration and motivating force for the young general. Its powerful presence was apparent by the sapphire tint of his eyes.

"Alas! I have been looking for you. Where did you disappear to, my good man?" Sinclair asked.

"Into the darkness," Youngblood said.

"Indeed, but you have returned unscathed I see," Sinclair noted.

"The deepest wounds and most terrible scars often remain invisible to the naked eye," Youngblood said, as he gazed up at the stars.

Sinclair looked upon his friend and colleague, shaking his head in acknowledgment, "*He jests at scars that never felt a wound.*"[171]

❧   ❧   ❧

Within the city walls of Ventura, Major Constantine stood before Kirsan, attempting to explain the massacre. "We were overwhelmed by superior numbers, my lord. There must have been at least three hundred warriors. There was nothing we could do."

"You lost your entire unit! Yet you survived? Explain to me how you miraculously escaped death, yet your entire unit was destroyed?" Kirsan demanded.

The crimson glow of his eyes increased, penetrating the very soul of the man before him.

"Hawke took me prisoner and was going to execute me, but I escaped!" Major Constantine explained.

"Youngblood Hawke is many things, you prevaricating little toad. But an executioner of an unarmed prisoner, he is not," Kirsan said with what was left of his patience, diminishing quickly. "Now get out of here, you worthless worm!"

Kirsan turned to the commander of the Black Guard, "General Santiago, how quickly can you have one thousand men take the field?"

"Immediately, upon your command," the general responded eagerly.

"Excellent! Make it so and ensure that they are the best that the Black Guard has to offer."

"It shall be so. I will lead them myself," General Santiago replied.

"You shall accompany me, for I will be leading the Black Guards onto this victory. A victory that will be sure to elevate me to the level of a god! I shall assume the rank of Supreme Commander!" Kirsan proclaimed, as he stood and imagined the triumphant parades, feasts, and festivals that would be thrown in his honor for defeating the criminal and enemy of the people, known as Youngblood Hawke.

❧   ❧   ❧

As the sun began to rise over the horizon, the small band of Select Warriors broke camp and continued on their journey west toward the City of Ventura.

"Sinclair, I want you to take twenty of the best horseman and form a small group, capable of assuming the role of a strike and pursuit unit," Youngblood ordered.

"Very well. Consider it done. Shall they be armed with any special weaponry?"

"Yes, they will need an ample supply of courage, cunning, motivation, and most of all, honor," Youngblood Hawke replied.

"Ah yes, the greatest weapons of them all," Sinclair remarked.

"Indeed, a warrior armed with such weapons can never be disarmed," Horatio noted.

"Horatio, you must take twenty of the strongest and most disciplined veterans and form a unit that will not break lines, no matter how difficult or desperate the situation may become."

"Consider it done," Horatio acknowledged, looking over the men and contemplating the nature of their mission in battle.

As they continued to discuss the potentiality of battle, a rider approached at full gallop, leaving a trail of dust visible for quite a distance. The rider was one of the scouts that had been dispatched to act as an advanced warning, announcing the approach of hostile forces. He rode directly up to Youngblood Hawke and rendered the appropriate military salute.

"Sir, a large force of about two hundred men approaches from the west."

"Black Guard?" Youngblood inquired.

"Unknown, sir, but I assume they are the mass."

"Odd that Kirsan would send such a relatively small force, considering what is at stake?" Youngblood pondered aloud.

"It does seem odd," Horatio agreed, accompanied in agreement by Sinclair and General Chang. "There is another possibility."

"What would that be?" Youngblood asked.

"Let me take a few men and check this approaching force out for myself. I will return shortly," Horatio requested.

"Take what you need, old friend. I will wait for your return," Youngblood Hawke said. Watching Horatio ride off, Youngblood acknowledged that a much larger force now approached him, and he would once again be tested.

"Sinclair, do you see that high ground on the west side of the road?"

"Indeed, I do," Sinclair acknowledged approvingly. "Say no more, Hawke, my unit and I will wait patiently for your command, and upon being given the signal, will swoop down upon our prey with lightning speed!"

"Very good, my friend. Wait for me to draw my battle sword and assemble the men in a line formation. When this is done, I want you to charge into their ranks," Youngblood Hawke commanded.

"It shall be done!" Sinclair Fox acknowledged with great enthusiasm.

Sinclair led his unit of Select Warriors to the higher ground as Youngblood Hawke continued to travel south along the main road. He was just beginning to become concerned for the plight of Horatio, when the approaching force became clearly visible. Youngblood halted the column of about twenty-five warriors and stood firmly by as the much larger force continued to advance in their direction. He was patiently waiting for the ideal moment to unleash Sinclair's unit, to smash into their left flank. As he prepared to draw his battle sword from its scabbard, the approaching force suddenly stopped. Two riders broke from the group and galloped toward Youngblood's position. As the riders approached, Youngblood Hawke began to recognize his old friend and mentor.

"Horatio, now don't tell me you have captured an entire unit of the Black Guard single-handedly, have you?"

"Not that it couldn't be done, my old friend. But what you are looking at is not representative of the mass," Horatio responded, as the identity of the second rider became apparent.

"It is good to see you again, Youngblood Hawke," the second rider said graciously.

"You do remember my father-in-law, Jonathan LeClair, don't you, Hawke?" Horatio added.

"Indeed, I do," Youngblood replied with a visible degree of astonishment. Jonathan LeClair's arrival was a welcome surprise.

"We have come to join your cause," LeClair offered. "I submit to you two hundred of Ventura's finest warriors. At your service and now under your command."

LeClair's sense of diplomacy had now been replaced by the determination of a veteran soldier.

"What has become of Sinclair and the other men?" Horatio asked.

Youngblood pointed to the high ground as Sinclair and his force revealed itself, following word from a dispatch that the approaching menace was in fact, Horatio Cantrell.

"Why, that rascal," Horatio said, as he realized that Sinclair had successfully concealed himself and his men from such experienced soldiers.

Youngblood Hawke shook Jonathan LeClair's hand and thanked him for his support. The elite unit of Select Warriors had now grown to about two hundred and fifty strong men. It was now a military unit of considerable size and quite capable of engaging several units of the Black Guard. It was now more than a nuisance...it was now a real threat.

The City of Ventura was alive with activity as the Black Guards assembled. Their commander, General Raphael Santiago, was a soldier of considerable skill. He had proven himself quite capable many times during his long military career. However, his thirst for glory was not quenched by the sanctity of honor. General Santiago had little use for such concepts as honor and loyalty. His thirst for power was so powerful that he was willing to take any course of action that would deliver to him a resounding personal victory—a personal victory capable of propelling him to absolute power. General Santiago had become Kirsan's enforcer and commander of the infamous Black Guard. Under the command of General Santiago, the Black Guard was successfully utilized for political gain by Kirsan, and the leaders of the mass. Much to the dismay of political opponents, the Black Guard operated under the protection of a covert order that granted the unit with special diplomatic powers. Therefore, the Black Guard was able to cross into the four kingdoms, unmolested by provincial authorities. In fact, they were often supported and endorsed by the local authorities. The four kingdoms were all subjected to the influence of the mass. Therefore, the Black Guard enjoyed the freedom to do as it pleased.

The threat presented by the Select had never been greater than it was now. The mass had always been able to control the Select, who tended to think too much and act too little. In addition, the mass had always benefited from the Select's lack of dynamic and effective leaders, capable of mobilizing them into a cohesive and organized force. Generally speaking, the Select could always be relied upon to pursue lofty ideals and pursuits that generally ignored the plight of the common man. Such a perceived indifference forced the mass majority to look upon the Select with contempt. An attitude that was perfect for manipulation by men such as Kirsan and General Santiago. However, attitudes were changing as a new Select Warrior offered himself to the common man. Youngblood Hawke was no ordinary member of the Select. He was not Select by birth, but had in fact been born a member of the mass and earned his status as a Select Warrior meritoriously. Youngblood Hawke was extremely dangerous. He was living proof of potentiality and an example that if one desired to understand, a greater destiny was available to all. Therefore, he was the greatest threat to the leaders of the mass, and would have to be destroyed at all costs. No price was too high to pay for the absolute defeat of Youngblood Hawke. Kirsan and General Santiago had no intention of achieving anything less than a complete victory—a victory that would require the death of Youngblood Hawke and his loyal cadre of Select Warriors. This was war.

The population of Ventura watched in awe as one thousand soldiers representing the Black Guard were led out of the city gates by Kirsan and General Santiago. Elizabeth Cantrell was among those who watched as she surveyed the frightening show of force depart for war. She was painfully aware that the men passing before her were on a mission to secure the death of her husband, her father, her brother, and a very close friend. Her potential for loss was as great as anyone involved. The world that she knew would be changed forever.

The much smaller force of approximately two hundred Select Warriors continued their journey west toward Ventura. The elite unit had now been formed into two main bodies. The units consisted of one hundred men under the command of Horatio Cantrell and seventy-five men led by Jonathan LeClair. In addition, the cavalry unit commanded by Sinclair Fox was increased to fifty men. The remaining twenty-five warriors were hand picked by Youngblood Hawke and were to serve with him as a strike force and personal security unit. Among the men were William LeClair and Will MacLeod. Will MacLeod was a battle-hardened veteran of many wars and battles. MacLeod was a man of undeniable courage and resolve. He served with Youngblood in the Great War and had developed a reputation as a very capable and deadly soldier of fortune. He was ferocious on the field of battle, and distinctive in his wielding of his Claymore Sword. Will's sword had a reputation of its own, as it had been passed down from generation to generation within the MaCleod clan. He was one in a long line of courageous warriors. Youngblood Hawke trusted Will MaCleod with his life, and owed his life to him on the battlefield. He was in Ventura and answered Jonathan LeClair's call to arms, when he heard he would be once again fighting side by side with Horatio Cantrell and Youngblood Hawke. Youngblood Hawke was honored to have both him and William LeClair as part of his personal cadre, who adopted the name of the ancient elite order of the *"Praetorian Guard."*[172] It was the intention of Youngblood Hawke to lead by example and personally strike at the heart of the mass.

As the force of Select Warriors continued toward Ventura, the conversation between the commanders began to reflect the general level of anxiety among the men.

"I say, good man, do we have any idea what it is we will be doing when we get to Ventura?" Sinclair asked of Horatio.

"Youngblood informed me that he has a plan and will brief us this evening, when we make camp," Horatio replied.

"Will we be holding a council of war?" Sinclair inquired with a raised eyebrow.

"I suppose you could call it that," Horatio acknowledged.

"Good show! I have always wanted to sit in on one of those affairs. My father often spoke of them with great reverence."

"Sinclair, a council of war is not a gala where there will be wine and exotic dancing girls! It is a serious strategic meeting," Horatio said in a tone that did not conceal the rising level of his aggravation.

"Horatio, have you ever attended a council of war, directed by our general, Youngblood Hawke?" Sinclair asked with a grin.

"I can't say that I have, Sinclair."

"Then it would be best not to dismiss the presence of wine and dancing girls as a very real possibility," Sinclair declared as the other men responded with a hearty laugh.

"Sinclair, only the depraved mind of a true existentialist would find the need for dancing girls during a council of war," Jonathan LeClair noted.

"Well, thank you, sir. It is indeed a pleasure to be appreciated," Sinclair responded with a nod and a tip of his hat.

"Ah yes, here comes our young, energetic general now," Jonathan LeClair observed, motioning to the approach of Youngblood Hawke and a small band of scouts.

"Gentlemen, nightfall approaches, and we shall make camp. We will eat and then I would enjoy the presence of my commanders to discuss our mutual destiny," Youngblood Hawke said.

"You have news for us?" Horatio inquired.

"Indeed, I do. Just this morning I stood upon what shall for eternity be considered, hallowed ground," Youngblood responded.

"Of what do you speak?" Sinclair asked.

"He has chosen where we shall make our stand against the forces of the mass," General Chang interjected approvingly.

Youngblood Hawke respectfully addressed General Chang and said, "*Whenever you engage an enemy in battle, you absolutely must secure the advantageous terrain; only then can the few contend with the many and the weak attain victory over the strong.*[173] Isn't that right, General?"

"Yes, without question you must choose the place where this fight will take place!" the general acknowledged.

"Make them bring the fight to you," Horatio Cantrell noted.

"Exactly! The location is perfect for the feat that we must accomplish. My sources tell me that as we speak, the mass advances toward us with one thousand Black Guardsmen, led by Kirsan himself and the notorious General Santiago," Youngblood said.

"Santiago! He is a clever one and should not be underestimated, my good friend," Horatio advised.

Having once served with Santiago, Horatio was no stranger to his strategic abilities and capacity for cruelty. Santiago was known as an oppressor, but he was also a very capable and accomplished military tactician.

"I am aware of his reputation and his accomplishments, Horatio. His presence will not be taken lightly, especially at the head of such a large and formidable military force," Youngblood acknowledged.

"That would be wise," Jonathan LeClair said in agreement.

Sinclair Fox looked about at that column of two hundred and fifty warriors and then turned to his colleague and commander and said, "Did I hear you correctly? Did you say one thousand?"

"Give or take, my good man," Youngblood noted, accompanied by his trademark smirk.

After making camp the commanders joined Youngblood Hawke in a secluded area protected by the Praetorian Guard. In addition to Youngblood Hawke and General Chang, the commanders in attendance included General Horatio Cantrell, General Jonathan LeClair, Colonel Sinclair Fox, Major Will MaCleod, and Captain William LeClair. In order to maintain an effective chain of command upon the battlefield, the group of commanders agreed that they would require the application of appropriate rank. The commanders also agreed that each individual commander would choose a capable deputy and assign the rank of lieutenant.

"We must dedicate our limited resources strategically," Youngblood said.

"Youngblood, have you considered forming an alliance with one or more of the many political groups who also oppose the mass?" Jonathan LeClair asked.

"I have, but one must take care, for successful and lasting alliances require all parties to benefit from the agreement. Failure to maintain such a balance will only result in delay, failure, and ultimately opposition and paralysis. In addition, generosity and compromise are key elements required to sustain an alliance. This is especially true for the most powerful member. The position of strength will be maintained not through oppression, but through the practice of compassion and humility," Youngblood explained.

"Understood, a victory may be required before we discuss alliances," Jonathan LeClair said.

"Indeed, reputations are built upon what one has accomplished, not what one promises to accomplish," Youngblood continued.

"Upon securing a victory, we will be in a better position to negotiate an alliance," Jonathan LeClair said.

"Yes, for then we will be negotiating from a position of strength," Youngblood agreed.

"What is your plan to secure such a victory?" Horatio asked.

"The location where we will confront and defeat the Black Guard is only a day's ride away. The road from Ventura becomes very narrow at this point, providing little room for maneuverability. The road encounters a bend with a hillside covered in tall grass on the south side and a river on the north. It is ideally suited for our purpose. The river is deep and cannot be forged. Therefore, no route of escape is possible across the river," Youngblood Hawke explained.

The commanders all listened intently and nodded in agreement as the young general announced his plan of battle.

"General Cantrell, your unit of one hundred Select Warriors will represent the main body of our force. They will stand in waiting just beyond the bend. It is crucial that your men do not break ranks under any circumstances. The Black Guard must be contained within this area," Youngblood Hawke commanded.

"We will do our part," General Cantrell acknowledged.

"General LeClair, your unit will cross the river at daybreak and proceed to a location five miles beyond the point we are discussing. The river may be crossed there. You will wait in hiding for the mass to pass and then you will cross the river and pursue the Black Guard from a distance that will not reveal your presence. Upon command, you will block any attempt to retreat or rally by attacking their rear guard," the commander instructed.

"It shall be done in the most effective manner," General LeClair replied.

"Colonel Fox, your unit of cavalry has been assigned a most daunting task," Youngblood Hawke said in a most grave manner.

"I would expect nothing less," Sinclair Fox acknowledged graciously.

"Your elite unit will be required to lay in waiting in the most stealthy manner. Men and horse shall set themselves down, hidden within the high grass upon the hillside. Upon command, they shall rise up, mount, and charge the enemy's left flank with lightning speed, smashing their ranks and sending them into a panic!" Youngblood Hawke ordered as he pounded his right fist into his left hand.

"Very good. In fact, excellent! We will, without question, create an image of death itself reigning in upon them!" a very excited and motivated Sinclair Fox responded. "Commander, where will you be during the thick of this encounter?"

The very intense young commander stood before his officers and with confidence, declared, "I shall be the prey that lures the misguided predator into the snare that awaits his overconfidence. I will lead the Praetorian Guard directly into the mass. We will taunt them and cause them to give chase. They will pursue us in full force and when they approach the bend, we will seek refuge up the hill in what will appear to them as panic. They will follow, believing victory is near. However, when we reach Colonel Fox's position, we shall join him and charge their left flank. At the very same time, General Cantrell will lead his force from the east and strike them a most devastating blow. They will be forced to fight on two fronts. Of course, their attempt to retreat will be met by General LeClair's force, which will be attacking the rear guard. Gentlemen, we will strike them, contain them, and then systematically destroy them on the battlefield. There will be no escape. The day will be difficult, and we will suffer losses, but in the end, the day will belong to the Select."

The commanders all stood nodding their heads as they contemplated the battle plans that had been laid out before them. Youngblood Hawke surveyed his command staff but waited for a response from his skeptical and cautious former commander, Horatio Cantrell.

General Cantrell stood silently as he pondered the plan presented by his former lieutenant. Suddenly, he raised his head and cast his eyes upon Youngblood Hawke.

"I remember when I first saw you on a battlefield. You were spirited and bold, thirsty for the taste of honor. I knew at that very moment that you were destined to be a general. I will always remember this day, as it is the very moment that you proved me to be correct. Your plan is brilliant!" Horatio Cantrell proclaimed.

Youngblood Hawke stood proudly as his mentor rendered him the highest honor of respect. The other commanders all raised their arms and extended the ancient warrior's salute to their commander. A commander known and to be forever known as Youngblood Hawke.

"Gentlemen, I suggest that you return to your units and brief your men. A good night's sleep is in order as well, for at daybreak we shall set this plan into motion. Tomorrow, I shall address the men. Therefore, they should all be assembled, befitting that of an elite military unit," Youngblood Hawke requested as the commanders returned to their men and prepared for the fight that awaited them.

Youngblood returned to the camp with General Chang by his side. "General, your assistance would be most beneficial serving with the main force alongside General Cantrell."

"I shall serve wherever I can be of assistance. The opportunity to be on the battlefield one last time is a gift that will not be forgotten," the General said.

"Did you ever become accustomed to the dreadful duty of sending such fine men to their deaths?" Youngblood Hawke gravely asked his mentor.

"Never! And if you ever do, you will know that you have gone completely mad!" the old general shouted. "It will never become easier. The souls of thousands haunt me to this day. It is the price of leadership."

"Indeed, a man I respected greatly as a young warrior once told me 'Uneasy lies the head that wears a crown,'[174] Youngblood Hawke responded, acknowledging that the responsibility of the Select Warriors was his and his alone.

He exuded nothing but determination and confidence in front of his colleagues, but deep within his soul, the demons of doubt and indecision were engaged in a deadly battle for control of the warrior's spirit.

A Reflection of A Man

The spirit of a warrior, I am sworn to protect.
No life of my own, only exile and neglect.
The weight of responsibility, chained to my neck.

The mind of a philosopher, wandering and free.
In search of the truth, wherever it may lead.
The ultimate riddle, tempting and taunting me.

The heart of a poet, desperate, alone, and cold.
Dreaming of romance, passionate and bold,
A lasting true love, a story to be told.

The soul of a fool, forever living in pain.
A punishing ignorance, driving me insane.
This cry for help, I can barely contain.

My spirit, my mind, my heart, my soul.
A warrior, a philosopher, a poet, and a fool.
I am unlike any other, an exception to the rule.

—*Youngblood Hawke*

CHAPTER 18

The Moment of Truth

Mastering a world of unlimited potentiality,
Honor, fortune, and the allure of glory.
Sacrifice all and you shall be one with me.
Risk nothing and mediocrity will be your destiny.

The young general surveyed the impressive military force before him as they assembled in classic military formation. Each commander stood before his unit with pride, demonstrating the finest example of military bearing. The two main bodies led by General Cantrell and General LeClair formed the center. The cavalry of Colonel Fox maintained the left flank and the Praetorian Guard assumed the right, led by Major MacLeod. Captain William LeClair accompanied Youngblood Hawke, who remained silent, examining the faces of each individual man as he passed. The men that stood before him were each prepared to give his life for a greater cause. Prepared to follow him through the proverbial gates of hell, fully aware that it could very well be a one-way trip. He stopped briefly to take note of his old Friend Zacharia and his young son Remo, who were assigned to General Cantrell's unit. He could see the determination in Zacharia's eyes—the determination to redeem himself for what he believed to be the betrayal of an old friend.

The young boy's eyes displayed something else. They revealed a sense of loyalty and a much greater potentiality. Youngblood Hawke had seen that look before. Many, many years ago it was revealed to him from the depths of younger eyes, staring back at him from a reflection in the water.

Youngblood climbed atop his powerful steed and trusted friend, Veritas, and rode before the ranks, acknowledging their impressive and inspiring presence. The young general reciprocated the level of determination that they inspired within him. The warriors appeared to be renewed with confidence and pride as he moved among their ranks. He then positioned himself on higher ground, where they could see him, and where he had an unobstructed view of the entire force. Youngblood Hawke took a moment to just survey the impressive unit of men that stood before him. His sense of pride was unquestionable.

Youngblood Hawke paused momentarily and then said, "Men of your caliber deserve words befitting the monumental task you are about to undertake. You will soon encounter a military force renowned for its power and ruthlessness. One thousand Black Guardsmen approach, representing the darkest elements of the mass."

The rumbling of concern could be heard form the ranks. The announcement that the enemy force outnumbered them—four to one—was unsettling, even among the most experienced warriors. The commander continued raising his voice in an attempt to motivate the men and quell the voices of doubt.

"They will soon test your courage and resolve by engaging you in combat. Fear not for you embark on a most noble cause. This day reminds me of another day: a day that continues to live in history as one of gallantry and honor. I am privileged to have been there on that day as well. A young soldier, facing almost certain death, following a brave King, who led a noble cause. We too faced overwhelming odds, but he reminded us of honor, and the price one must pay for glory and the pursuit of truth, the noblest of all causes," Youngblood Hawke said.

Horatio Cantrell nodded his head in acknowledgment as the young commander spoke for he also accompanied Youngblood Hawke in the service of the King on that fateful day.

Youngblood Hawke continued as the commanders and their men listened silently. "I would like to share with you some of his words. They were great and inspiring words that cannot be improved. In fact, I would not dare attempt to improve upon such honorable words. Remember these words as you enter the field of battle, my friends. Remember these words and the men that stand beside you on this day. For the memory of both shall live eternally from this day forward. *'If we are marked to die, we are now to do our country loss: and if to live, the fewer the men, the greater the share of honor. God's will, I pray thee wish not one man more. By Jove, I am not covetous for gold. Nor care I who doth fed upon my cost: it earns me not if men my garments wear; such outward things dwell not in my desires. But if it be a sin to covet honor, I am the most offending soul alive. That he which hath no stomach for this fight, let him depart, his passport shall be made, and crowns for convoy put into his purse: we would not die in that man's company that fears fellowship, to die with us. He that outlives this day, and comes safe home, will stand tiptoe when this day is named. He that shall see this day, and live old age, will strip his sleeve, and show his scars. Old men forget; yet all shall be forgot, but he'll remember, with advantage, what feats he did that day. From this day to the ending of the world, but we in it shall be remembered; we few, we happy few, we band of brothers: for he today that sheds his blood with me shall be my brother: be he never so vile, this day shall gentle his condition. And gentleman now a-bed shall think themselves accursed they were not here; and hold their manhood's cheap, whiles any speaks that fought with us upon this day.'"[175]*

An ominous silence inflicted the ranks as the warriors contemplated the words recited before them.

"Remember the words I have just spoken, my friends, my colleagues, my brothers. Remember these words during your struggle, for you will be fighting alongside the spirit, the hearts, and the souls of the greatest warriors of all time. *Mandamus Veritas!*"

The unit of Select Warriors raised their swords and cheered the commander, chanting the Select battle cry of "*Mandamus Veritas*"!

The Praetorians were prepared and anxious to confront the enemy on the field of honor. Youngblood Hawke surveyed the small army of Select Warriors, fully aware of their path and where destiny had delivered them. The moment was one of unity and clarity as the Select Warriors defined themselves as individuals and free thinkers.

The Select Warrior

My armor is robust, my weaponry deadly.
Fearing nothing that dares to confront me.
Rendering my sword upon demand,
Restrained as a man in solitude I stand.

A soldier and philosopher of sorts,
An adventurer and mercenary by creed.
Haunted by the desire to understand,
Freed from the shackles of the mass man.

Commonality replaced by nobility,
Not a birth rite but earned meritoriously.
Command of the truth wherever it may stand.
In defense of honor and the Select man.

Relentless pursuit of an ancient ideology,
Emptiness and loneliness has unto now defined me.
Shrouded by my quest, cloaked in darkness,
A self-imposed exile from the majority.

Mastering a world of unlimited potentiality,
Honor, fortune, and the allure of glory.
Sacrifice all and you shall be one with me.
Risk nothing and mediocrity will be your destiny.

—*Youngblood Hawke*

Youngblood Hawke's attention returned to the situation at hand. "General LeClair, are your men ready?" asked Youngblood as the commanders approached for final orders before embarking.

"Indeed, they are, sir," General LeClair responded.

"Excellent. Our scouts tell me that the Black Guard should approach the bend by early morning," Youngblood Hawke said.

"If the timing is right, the sun will be rising to the east and they will be running directly into it as General Cantrell's forces attack!" Colonel Fox said with his usual degree of enthusiasm. "I can actually visualize the battle now. Rather romantic, really."

"Romantic! This is war we are talking about, not one of your adventures into the abyss!" Horatio said with a sense of outrage about him.

Youngblood interjected immediately, noting that the stress of the impending battle was wearing on everyone. "General Cantrell, I am sure that Colonel Fox is fully aware of the seriousness of the matter. However, I would like to note that it is quite possible that his adventures into the abyss have been as dangerous and lethal as any battle in history."

The entire command staff broke out in laughter, including Horatio Cantrell. It was just the thing needed for everyone to relax and put things in perspective.

Youngblood Hawke looked at General LeClair and shook his hand as he was about to set out with his force of Select Warriors.

"Farewell and Godspeed," Youngblood said.

"Please keep a watchful eye on my only son," LeClair respectfully asked of Youngblood Hawke.

"Of course I will. He is one of my most trusted lieutenants," Youngblood replied.

The unit under the command of General Jonathan LeClair departed, as all observed over one third of the entire force set out across the river and headed south. Captain William LeClair watched as well as his father stopped briefly and nodded to him. The nod was returned as an acknowledgment to be careful and a reminder that they would see each other when the battle was over. At least that was the hope of Jonathan LeClair, as he observed his only son prepare for battle and meet his destiny on the most violent of terms.

"Gentlemen, the Praetorian Guard shall take the lead, followed by Colonel Fox's cavalry, and then the main body led by General Cantrell. We shall arrive at our destination by midnight. We will not be making camp. There will be no campfires and little rest. General Cantrell and Colonel Fox will position their forces in preparation for battle. The Praetorian Guard will continue on and raid the Black Guard's position, prompting them to give chase. We will lead them to you like a camel to water," the commander explained as the intense sapphire tint of his eyes pierced all those who made contact with them.

The Black Guard was advancing east with no opposition as they prepared for a long and arduous pursuit. Little intelligence was forthcoming and they had not received any information indicating a force of two hundred warriors was on a collision course with their current position.

"I find it troubling that we are not receiving any reliable information regarding the current location of Youngblood Hawke and his band of criminals," Kirsan said.

"Our field operatives give us conflicting information. According to our sources, he is everywhere and he is nowhere," General Santiago responded.

"I believe it would be safe to say that he and his ragtag force of criminals are heading east. They will most likely hide among the sympathetic peasants of the Eastern Kingdom," Kirsan said confidently.

"Perhaps, sir, but I would not underestimate the cunning of this one. He has surrounded himself with very capable officers. Jonathan LeClair and Horatio Cantrell to name just a few," General Santiago said with a very cautious tone in his voice. "Not to mention, it is my understanding that General Chang is now in their company."

"Chang? I thought he was dead?" Kirsan asked.

"No Kirsan, he escaped from prison with Youngblood Hawke," Santiago explained.

"No matter, Chang is a relic, LeClair is nothing more than a diplomat, and Cantrell is a common criminal and black market smuggler. They are certainly no match for the Black Guard. We will overwhelm them in sheer numbers," Kirsan said, displaying his renowned arrogance and attitude of superiority.

General Santiago listened as Kirsan rambled on, discussing his political plans and ambitions that he believed would be available to him, following a great victory over the Select. However, Santiago was not as sure of their success as Kirsan. He had studied the record and reputation of Youngblood Hawke and refused to underestimate him or his loyal followers.

"Kirsan, let me send a force of about three hundred ahead to act as an advance guard. This would allow them to engage the enemy, if contact was made, and provide the opportunity to send reinforcements if necessary," General Santiago advised.

"What? Divide our force? And what would such a move accomplish, other than weaken our current level of superiority in numbers? Absolutely not! General Santiago, sometimes I do not understand how you military men think. This is as much a political mission as it is a military one, and I will not do anything that could inflict a political defeat upon us. We are taking no chances! We will strike the Select in full force and nothing less! Do you understand? Do you understand?" the outraged and clearly frustrated Kirsan responded.

"I understand perfectly, sir," General Santiago replied, making every effort to refrain himself from telling Kirsan that he was a fool and was making a fatal mistake.

However, General Santiago was all too familiar with Kirsan's disposition. He knew that any suggestion of insubordination would result in his being relieved from command.

❧   ❧   ❧

The Praetorian Guard continued west, ahead of the main force, led by General Cantrell and accompanied by Colonel Fox's cavalry. It was the intention of Youngblood Hawke to surprise Kirsan while he was camped, and then lure him to the trap. However, in the event the Praetorian Guards were to be detected by scouts, Youngblood wanted to draw their attention away from the larger Select Warrior force. It was crucial that the main force remain undetected. The element of surprise was critical to the success of Youngblood's strategy.

As the end of the day drew near, the Praetorians approached a cart drawn by a ragged horse and an old man. Youngblood Hawke immediately recognized the old man. He further noted that he had dismissed the old man at the time of their last encounter. Youngblood allowed the Praetorians to travel on as he stopped and addressed his old friend.

"Hello, old one. What a coincidence that I should find you on this road, on this day, and at this particular hour?" Youngblood said.

"Coincidence? I suppose…if one were to believe in such a thing," the old man responded.

"Can I ask you a question?" Youngblood asked.

"If you wish," he responded.

"Where is it that you are traveling to exactly? I have encountered you many times and you always appear to be on the move. Where are you going and why have you not yet arrived?"

"I have been where you are going and yet my final destination remains unknown."

"What? You continue to travel, yet you don't know where you are going?" a very puzzled Youngblood Hawke asked.

"That is correct," the old man said with a grin.

"Why do you continue this pointless journey?"

"You ask why? The answer to that question, my boy, remains a riddle," he responded.

Youngblood was somewhat caught off-guard by the response as he realized its significance. "A most difficult riddle," Youngblood replied.

"Yes, it is," the old man acknowledged, as he pointed to the path that had opened before him, leading into the dark forest. "*Are you intoxicated by riddles? Do you find pleasure in the twilight? Are you lured with flutes to every treacherous abyss, young warrior?*"[176] he asked.

Youngblood turned immediately toward the old man, having recognized the words of the Prophet.

"Answer the question. Are you?"

Youngblood Hawke pondered the question for a moment and responded, "I suppose that I am, old man. I suppose that I am."

"Enjoy the journey, my boy. For it may very well be the destination and answer to the riddle. Now go to the one who guards the crossroads," the old man said as he gestured toward the path and then turned and continued slowly but steadfastly down the road.

Youngblood noted that his cart continued to gather a greater load with the passing of time. It was obvious that although the old man's journey continued to a destination unknown, the baggage he gathered along the way was a heavy load, and without question, slowed him down.

"Old man, I have but one question for you before you depart. Why do you bother to struggle with the weight and hassle of carrying all that baggage?" Youngblood asked.

"It is the very essence of who I am, my boy. It can neither be dismissed nor forgotten, and it can never be completely left behind." The old man smiled and then continued on his path, without looking back.

Youngblood just nodded his head in agreement and considered the words of the old man as he stared out into the expansive sky.

Looking Toward the Sky

Heaven—a clear blue sky,
Clouds floating and drifting,
Above this barren wasteland,
And humanity asking why?
A lonely creature is man,
This state he cannot deny,
Searching for the truth,
Living such a mortal lie,
Walking and wandering so,

Hopelessly he does try,
Unaware of where to go,
And having no idea why.

—*Youngblood Hawke*

Youngblood instructed Will MaCleod to take the men ahead a few hundred feet and set up camp in a secure position off the road. He then followed the path revealed to him, knowing that he would once again stand humbly before the sage who introduced him to the significance of his quest. The darkness of the path remained as cold and mystifying as the first time he had traveled it. The path once again opened up before him onto a large meadow, where the sage was revealed to him, waiting in the distance. However, his approach on this occasion was now humbled by the experience of his quest and the many tests and trials he had encountered along the way.

"Good day, sage," Youngblood said, extending a greeting and gesture of respect to the mysterious sage.

He dismounted Veritas and approached.

"My quest has brought me far, but I suspect no closer to that which I seek."

"What is it you seek?" the sage asked.

"My quest has not changed since the first time we spoke. I continue to seek the truth. However, the nature of truth continues to redefine itself in the most curious fashion," Youngblood Hawke responded.

"Redefine itself?" the sage inquired in a steady tone.

"Yes. It is very peculiar. I find the truth to be a very fascinating and elusive prey. It has the ability to change and alter itself at will. Just when I suspect I am close to its capture, it slips from my grasp. Astonishing, really," Youngblood acknowledged.

"Interesting. Perhaps it is you who continue to redefine yourself. Changing and altering yourself, just as you are about to be captured by not a prey but a very powerful predator. Is it possible that the absolute truth pursues you and wishes to capture you and confine you forever within its walls? Have you considered the possibility that you are the prey and have not been pursuing the truth, but in fact, eluding it?" the sage said.

Youngblood Hawke stood silent, contemplating the questions presented to him.

"I suspect that it is very possible. I often find myself feeling like the prey and not the predator that I am made out to be," Youngblood said.

"What is it that you are running to? What is it that you are running from? Have you answered the question presented to you during our first meeting?" the sage asked.

"I have not answered that question at all," Youngblood responded. "If I were to be presented with the absolute truth at this very moment, I would have no idea what to do with it. Therefore, I suspect that I am not worthy of being given such a gift. My inability to recognize it is the cause of great internal suffering."

"Perhaps you should ask another question," the sage asked.

"What question would that be?" Youngblood responded.

"Upon being captured, what will absolute truth do with you?" the sage continued.

"Whatever it wishes I suppose," Youngblood Hawke acknowledged. "Tell me, sage, what does my destiny have in store for me? Is this a time for action or delay?"

"There are many paths and you must choose wisely. You must choose your own path and accept responsibility for your own destiny. Your failures will be your own, but your successes will be shared. Do not squander your most valuable and priceless commodity," the sage declared.

"What commodity would that be?" Youngblood inquired.

"Time. It passes swiftly, and with it travels opportunity. Once it has passed, it is gone forever. It is the one thing that can never be recovered in its original form. When you began your journey, time was an ally. However, as your journey continues, time begins to betray you. Slowly it becomes not a friend, but a foe. Beware! Take heed of my words, warrior! For eventually, time will turn on you. It will pursue you, capture you, and ultimately destroy you. Without question, it will kill you!"

"This beast you call time, it cannot be defeated, can it?" Youngblood asked.

"No, warrior, it cannot. You can fight it courageously and hold it at bay for many years. But in the end, it will be the death of you. '*Time is the King of men, He's both the parent, and he is their grave, And gives then what he will, not what they crave.*'[177] Therefore, you should learn not to fight it but to work with it. As I said, it is a commodity and not an unlimited resource. Therefore, you should not waste what little you have been given. Take advantage of your time and make the best of it!"

"I shall make the best of it. '*This quest must come to an end, for only then, will time become my friend.*' I shall with all my heart try!" Youngblood Hawke exclaimed. "Will I see you again, sage?"

"The answer to that question remains to be seen. Rest assured that when you come upon your next crossroads, I shall be waiting," the sage replied.

The sage disappeared and Youngblood Hawke was returned to the road, where he encountered the old man. He immediately proceeded to the camp and joined the Praetorian Guard. Will MaCleod met him and advised that William LeClair took three men on a scouting mission to locate Kirsan's encampment. The moment of truth was approaching and the ability and determination of the Select Warriors would soon be tested.

Youngblood sat quietly within the darkness waiting for the return of William LeClair. His thoughts drifted toward Sapphire as he wondered what she was doing and whether or not she was near. Youngblood focused upon the object of his quest, while also constantly managing the distraction of Sapphire's mystical allure. In many ways, Sapphire had become the object of a quest as well. In fact, Youngblood's ability to separate the two was becoming more and more difficult as time passed.

The darkness cloaked the indecision embodied upon Youngblood's face. His mind was playing tricks upon him as he ran over the battle plans again and again. He could share his lack of confidence with no one. Youngblood Hawke was the leader, and the Select Warriors looked upon him with admiration. Any indication of weakness or doubt would surely infect the force like a plague.

"I am alone. Surrounded by others yet completely alone in a world of profound riddles," he murmured to himself.

Youngblood was unsure of himself and the pressure of command appeared to be taking a toll upon him. The conflict waging within his mind, heart, and spirit was nothing less than mortal combat. His ability to sleep had long disappeared and was beginning to take a physical toll. He was unable to turn to anyone for advice or counsel, fearing that his words would betray his thoughts and reveal the fear resonating deep within his soul.

"Why am I? Why?" he continued to ask the proverbial question of his very existence.

His current path called for, if not demanded, that he release the past and ascend to the next level in order to fulfill his destiny. A frightening thought, as the past was comforting and known to him, yet the future remained uncertain. The approaching battle was a monumental task that was certain to change his life forever, no matter what the outcome. In fact, it could very likely be an unholy alliance of fate and time delivering the ultimate and final blow. Youngblood's thoughts continued to betray him as he questioned his decision to pursue a path that was sure to influence the lives of so many for so long.

If this is my destiny, why do I fear it so? Why does that which is supposed to be my closest ally, appear to be my greatest threat? Alone in the darkness, detached and isolated from his comrades, Youngblood Hawke suffered, drowning in the toxic flow of his deepest thoughts. He continued to battle his greatest enemy. An enemy that without question, was able to counter his every move without hesitation. For at this very moment, the enemy engaging Youngblood Hawke was none other than the famous Youngblood Hawke himself. It was not the first time that this adversary has reared its ugly head. Youngblood Hawke was well aware that he was his own worst enemy, and that no one was more capable of destroying that which he had become, and that which he was destined to be.

"Very good my, old friend. Tell me of this path that we have chosen. Is it a road to self discovery or is it the road to self destruction?" he hesitated after asking himself the question, and pondered the potential answers.

"I suspect only time has the answer to such a question. Time…that elusive adversary who is determined to destroy me, holds the answers to my future." Youngblood laughed aloud and stared off at the stars, with his arms stretched out, as if to call upon them for guidance. "If only time would take the form of a sage and share its wisdom. Then and only then would there be no risk in choosing one's destiny. Alas! I suspect that such a request is too much to ask. Youngblood Hawke, my good man, I am sure of only one thing. Your destination is unknown."

Youngblood spent the evening talking and walking among his men. He reached deep within his spirit to mask his fears and exude the confidence and determination of a warrior prince. His position as a leader demanded nothing less. The shadows of darkness allowed him the opportunity to seek the guidance of the stars and define his existence. The inspiration of Sapphire was ever-present and continued to chart his course of self-discovery.

The deafening silence of thought was broken by a young lieutenant.

"Commander? Captain LeClair is approaching," announced a young warrior, returning Youngblood's attention to the task that lay before him.

"Excellent! Let's go," Youngblood responded, as he followed the warrior.

He met with William LeClair who had already been joined by the ever-ready-for-a-good-fight Will MacLeod.

"Did you find them?" Will MacLeod asked.

"Indeed, I did," responded LeClair accepting the approving nod of his commander.

"Captain, you have done well," Youngblood acknowledged.

"Thank you, sir. They are just three miles west of our position. Their arrogance is obvious from the manner of their encampment. They have but a scattered number of sentinels, guarding entry to the camp. In addition, they have set up their tents in a rectangular formation with a path leading right up to the tent of Kirsan himself! I know you instructed me to be careful, Commander, but I was able to get within twenty feet of Kirsan's command tent," Captain LeClair said.

"Outstanding! Did you encounter any patrols or scouting parties along the way?" Youngblood asked.

"No, sir! Not one single patrol or scout," the excited Captain LeClair said.

"Youngblood, they don't have a clue," the eager MaCleod interjected.

Youngblood Hawke stood silently as he pondered the information presented to him. He stared into the darkness of the night sky and searched for the sapphire star. He immediately captured the brilliance of the brightest star and gazed upon it, fully conscious of the fact that opportunity had presented itself. Time was passing swiftly but not fast enough, as Youngblood Hawke turned to his commanders, revealing the mysterious sapphire tint of his eyes.

"Gentlemen, we shall seize the moment! Mount up…we are attacking the mass now!" he commanded.

"Yes, sir!" Major MaCleod and Captain LeClair responded together, as they assembled the men and prepared them for the midnight strike, directly into the heart of the beast.

"Captain LeClair, may I see you privately for a moment?" Youngblood asked.

"Why, yes of course, sir," he replied.

"You have done well. I would like to give you something as a token of my appreciation for your loyalty to our cause," Youngblood said.

"That will not be necessary, Commander," William LeClair replied.

"Please, I would like you to have this," Youngblood said, as he presented William LeClair with his personal dagger. "The handle is ebony. It was given to me by a very trusted friend, and this dagger has served me well."

"Thank you. I am honored and will use it wisely," he replied graciously.

General Cantrell and the incorrigible Colonel Sinclair Fox were busy preparing their forces for battle. They had arrived on schedule and were able to assume their positions without incident or detection. However, they had no way of knowing whether or not Youngblood Hawke or General LeClair had been successful with their missions. In fact, all anyone of them could do is hope and trust that the battle would unfold as planned. It was now a matter of faith: a common faith and belief in each other and a noble cause. All were well aware that their shared quest did not come without great risk to all.

❧   ❧   ❧

The flickering heat of the large campfires, defining the encampment of the mass, occasionally interrupted the crispness of the night air. The mumbling sounds of men talking, combined with the snoring of others, was suddenly overwhelmed by the pounding of hooves. The mounted attackers crashed the camp without warning! The Black Guardsmen scattered in panic as the Select Warriors tore through the camp with lightning speed, striking down anything and anyone caught in their path. The surprise attack caught the camp completely by surprise, as the twenty-five bold warriors gave the impression of hundreds, driving through the camp and toward the command tent of the notorious Kirsan.

A startled General Santiago was awakened by the commotion and a lieutenant screaming, "Ambush!"

"Settle down, you idiot!" General Santiago ordered, as he attempted to evaluate the nature of the attack and the size of the penetrating force.

Kirsan's personal security force responded to his tent and stood their ground as the Select Warriors approached at full gallop. Youngblood Hawke led the charge down the main corridor, directly toward Kirsan. Youngblood's katana sword was extracted from its scabbard, striking as it passed en route to its intended target. Kirsan exited his tent in full battle dress, with the arrogance of a pagan god. Kirsan directed his stare toward his nemesis as he approached at full speed. The crimson glow of his eyes met with the sapphire storm brewing within the spirit of Youngblood Hawke. The Black Guardsmen stood, ready to strike the attacker, with an emphasis upon the leader.

"A fortune to the man who kills Youngblood Hawke!" Kirsan screamed, as General Santiago watched in amazement from a distance.

The Black Guards charged Youngblood Hawke, attempting to strike him down from his mount, but the bold warrior crashed their protective line, striking down two of the defenders as he passed. Attempts by the remaining Black Guardsmen to respond were defeated by the powerful and determined Major Will MaCleod. Kirsan's fate was almost sealed as he attempted to run from the attackers when suddenly, he was saved by General Santiago and a force of about twenty Black Guardsmen. Youngblood Hawke could almost taste the blood of his fleeing foe but also realized that he had succeeded in what he had set out to accomplish. Momentarily acknowledging that he almost had the head of Kirsan, he turned and led the Select Warriors out of the camp and into the darkness of the night. Not a single man had been lost in the attack, and the Black Guard was sure to pursue him now.

As the force of Select Warriors departed the camp, General Santiago turned to Kirsan, who was still shaken from the attack, as well as from the near-fatal results.

"I want him! Do you hear me? Get him now! I want the head of that criminal on a pike by morning!" Kirsan was screaming frantically in a rage as the camp was still recovering from the attack.

"A ruse," General Santiago interjected.

"What? What are you saying, Santiago?" Kirsan asked, who continued to bark commands.

"A ruse cleverly designed to lure us into a trap," he declared with the calm and confidence of a veteran soldier.

"Ridiculous! That was an intentional attack designed to assassinate me!" screamed Kirsan. "My death would be the one thing that would ensure his safety," he added.

"Think as you will, Kirsan, but you are doing exactly as he commands," General Santiago replied.

"You are coming very close to crossing that line with me, General. Do not question my leadership again!" Kirsan commanded. "Now, bring me that criminal's head on a pike or I will replace you with someone who can."

"My apologies, Kirsan. I did not mean to question your authority or your leadership," General Santiago said, in an apologetic tone, veiling only slightly his true contempt for the man.

"I understand, General. This Youngblood Hawke intimidates you. For he is a threat to your military genius."

"He is no threat, Kirsan. He is nothing more than a nuisance, and I will bring him to his knees," the general said with a sense of determination that did not go unnoticed by Kirsan.

The general turned to his aides and mounted his horse, leading an advance guard in pursuit of Youngblood Hawke. Kirsan remained behind, assembling the remaining force. He would follow the attackers, with every intention of destroying the remnants of the Select Warriors and securing the death of their leader.

❧   ❧   ❧

The Praetorian Guards continued to travel east and well ahead of the pursuing mass, led by General Raphael Santiago. The Select Warriors had no time to enjoy the sweet taste of their initial victory as the true test of their resolve was awaiting them. Youngblood raised his hand, commanding the unit to slow down as they had gained too much ground and were in a position to actually lose their pursuers.

"Will, have the scouts reported yet?" Youngblood asked of his deputy.

"No, sir, but they are expected at any moment," he replied, searching the early morning twilight for their arrival.

"I want a full report, identifying the size of the force that pursues us," Youngblood said.

"You shall have it, Commander."

"We must be pursued by the main force and not just an advanced guard. Do you understand?" Youngblood asked.

"I understand, Youngblood, but what if they have not mobilized the entire force?"

"Then we will be forced to turn and fully engage the advance guard!" Youngblood's response was heard clearly as his words resonated throughout the ranks of the Praetorian Guard. "We must not fail, gentlemen!"

The approach of the scout had come not a moment too soon as the effects of their raid remained unclear. Major MaCleod immediately approached the scout and then proceeded directly to his commander to provide a full report.

"The scout reports that the pursuing force is approximately fifty men, led by General Santiago himself," the scout said.

"Quite an honor to be pursued by the likes of Raphael Santiago," William LeClair interjected.

"He is a prize, but not the one we are seeking on this day," Will MaCleod responded.

Just as Youngblood Hawke was about to react with disappointment, Major MaCleod added, "Allow me to finish. The main force is only a few miles behind, led by the infamous and notorious Kirsan of Ventura."

Youngblood's expression turned from one of disappointment to that of extreme satisfaction. "As I expected. Kirsan was unable to resist."

"What do we do now, Commander?" Major MaCleod asked.

"We turn and fully engage General Santiago. We cannot allow him the opportunity to detect our snare and alert Kirsan," Youngblood replied.

He raised his hand and brought the Praetorian Guard to a halt.

"Gentlemen, we have been tasked with an unbelievable objective. It is now our responsibility to ensure the success of this great endeavor," Youngblood said.

"No disrespect intended, sir, but we are so few and they are so many?" the young and apprehensive Captain LeClair asked.

"We have no choice, William. The Praetorian Guard must engage the advance guard and hold them at bay until the main force arrives. Upon their arrival, we will break and lead them into the snare set by General Cantrell and Colonel Fox," Youngblood said.

"I understand, Commander, but how do we know that General Cantrell, Colonel Fox, and my father have not been captured or defeated as we speak?" William LeClair asked.

"We don't know," Youngblood Hawke countered, acknowledging that the future was clouded with possibilities and risk.

The very experienced and battle-hardened Major MaCleod just nodded in agreement, fully understanding that the strategy outlined by their commander would not be accomplished without great risk and substantial loss of life.

❦   ❦   ❦

Sinclair Fox waited, not so patiently upon the hill, in the hopes that he would soon see some sign of his colleague. The wait was nerve-racking, considering the stakes, and the responsibility that his rank and station now carried.

A young lieutenant approached the distracted colonel, who personally watched the road from Ventura.

"Colonel Fox? Sir? We have a dispatch from General Cantrell. Colonel?" he asked.

"What? I'm sorry, good man. What is it you say?" Sinclair's attention returned to reality as he looked upon the puzzled face of the young officer.

"Colonel, we have a dispatch from General Cantrell," the young officer said.

"A dispatch?"

"Yes, sir. General Cantrell insisted that I deliver it to you with no delay," he responded.

"Excellent! Give it here, my good man," Sinclair ordered, who was now fully comfortable with the sound of his military rank and the respect that accompanied it.

Sinclair opened the dispatch to find the handwriting of his colleague and friend, Horatio Cantrell:

CONFIDENTIAL DISPATCH: COLONEL SINCLAIR FOX

Colonel Fox, "It goes without saying" that you have been entrusted with a mission that may very well determine the fate of mankind. Knowing your affiliation for the depths of the abyss, I would just like to remind you that if you were to distinguish yourself on that hill as a soldier and warrior, your subsequent trips to the abyss would be most enjoyable indeed. Your feats will introduce you to a level of wisdom and acclaim acquired by very few. The abyss would not only beckon you, but command your presence as well! I believe we have heard our commander quote the Prophet himself in saying that, "wisdom is a woman and a woman loves only a warrior." See you in Ventura, my friend. Mandamus Veritas!

Your Friend and Colleague, General Horatio Cantrell

Sinclair read the dispatch again as he laughed aloud, alarming the young officer who stood before him. "You scoundrel you!" he shouted.

"Colonel? Is something wrong?" the troubled lieutenant asked, searching for some sign of assurance.

"Ah yes, my lad! It is all wrong and that is what makes it so damned right!" Sinclair Fox said, as he dismissed the young officer with orders to remind the cavalry that they must be prepared to strike within a moment's notice.

The entire unit of Colonel Fox's cavalry stood in amazement as they watched their commander atop the hill, revealed only by his silhouette, engaging in an imaginary sword fight with the winds of fate. Colonel Sinclair Fox appeared to be in ample supply of his own brand of inspiration that had secured the loyalty and admiration of his men.

The moment of truth was coming and they were all feeling the overwhelming power of its approach.

CHAPTER 19

The Paradox of the End

Refuge, safe harbor, will it be?
The eye of the storm calls out to me!
Its allure the promise of eternal tranquillity.

The decision of a lifetime had just presented itself to Youngblood Hawke. He expressed his hasty plan to his trusted colleagues with a dramatic tone of confidence. The tone was intended to infect the Praetorian Guard with the necessary resolve required to successfully lure the mass into the awaiting trap. However, his tone veiled his true sense of self-doubt and paralysis. He considered the lessons of his experience, the vision of his wisdom, and the influence of his many teachers. His spirit continued to seek the inspiration of Sapphire for the answer to his eternal destiny. She would surely encourage him to move forward and accept his destiny, elevating himself to the next level. But Youngblood was solely responsible for the decision and the consequences resulting from his decision. It was the risk and mystery associated with ascension to the next level that was responsible for his paralysis. For he was fully aware that upon accepting this destiny, he would be leaving behind an existence that had become his reality, and pursuing an undetermined path riddled with possibilities of fortune and danger. Youngblood Hawke could not help but toy with the paradox of the moment as he asked himself, "Is this the beginning or is this the end?"

He knew that only time held the answer to that question, and as the moment passed, time no longer remained his friend. Internal conflict punished the warrior as the predator of time closed in on its prey.

The Eye of the Storm

Pursuing my quest, forever to be.
Following fate wherever it may lead.
Adventure, fortune, and discovery!

Overcome, suddenly, by a sapphire sea.
Tossed and thrashed about deaf to my pleas,
Lost in a storm of wonder and mystery.

Refuge, safe harbor, will it be?
The eye of the storm calls out to me!
Its allure—the promise of eternal tranquillity.

Is there no mercy for me?
No more suffering, I beg of thee!
Take me! Give me serenity! Or let me be!

—*Youngblood Hawke*

General Santiago's advance guard continued their pursuit, but he was well aware that he had no idea where the forces of Youngblood Hawke were or where they were headed. Unfortunately, at the moment, he did not have the luxury of complete command or the option to rely solely upon his military experience. He was acting under the directions of a politico, and could not help but feel he was leading his unit directly into a trap.

"General Santiago! General!" the approaching scout was filled with excitement as he came to an abrupt halt. "Sir, you are not going to believe this but a force of about twenty warriors is riding directly toward us!"

"What? Are you telling me that Hawke's forces are returning to engage us?" the puzzled general asked. "What is that lunatic up to now?"

"I don't know what he has planned, General, but it appears that he intends to engage us directly and attack!"

The general halted his advance guard and asked, "Did you see any additional forces or reinforcements following him?"

"No, sir, nothing at all," the scout responded, looking east, expecting the attacking force to reveal itself at any moment.

"Captain of the Guard! Assemble the men in formation and prepare to attack!" General Santiago ordered.

"Yes, General," the captain responded.

Turning to the scout, the general ordered, "You! You are to proceed directly to Kirsan and inform him of what is transpiring! Do you understand?"

"Yes, General," he replied as he departed in the direction of the main force.

The Praetorian Guard advanced toward their target and with the sound of an approaching storm, they thundered west. No words were spoken as the Select Warriors prepared themselves for the impending battle and the certain death that would soon fall upon their ranks. Their leader, Youngblood Hawke, led the charge with the determination of destiny itself. Major MaCleod clearly displayed his years of experience in battle as he rode with an unnatural degree of peacefulness about him. Captain LeClair's inexperience was invisible to the naked eye. The young captain's lack of battlefield familiarity was not revealed to his colleagues, for he appeared to be as determined and fearless as Major MaCleod, advancing in anticipation of what was to come. The remaining members of the Praetorian Guard focused upon the charge and appeared to be inspired by the courage being displayed by their leaders. However, they were well aware of what awaited them just ahead, and were prepared to enter the fire of combat as comrades in arms and warriors for truth.

Warriors of Truth

Against all odds, they pursue absolute truth,
Intellectual warriors and fact-chasing sleuths.
Living in the Limelight, overcoming all resistance,
Professional thinkers, the epitome of persistence.

Dismissing bias and prejudice, seeking what is true,
Defending justice and liberty, for many and the few.
They cry Integrity and Honor! This above all,
Attacking the enemies of truth, answering the call.

Alone in the darkness, seekers never losing sight,
Searching for the answers, hidden from the light.
Moments of brief victory, followed by lasting defeat,
Dedicated warriors of truth, they vow never to retreat.

They are one and they are many, woman and man,
Advocates of the truth, courageously taking a stand

—*Youngblood Hawke*

"Sir! A scout approaches at full gallop!" the Black Guard colonel proclaimed.

"Waste no time, Colonel. What does he have to report?" Kirsan demanded. "Where is General Santiago? More importantly, where is that criminal Youngblood Hawke?"

The Supreme Commander of the Black Guard was dressed in full battle garb, surrounded by his elite unit. He was still recovering from the embarrassment inflicted upon his camp by Youngblood Hawke and what he described as a band of criminals.

After receiving the scout's report, the colonel proceeded directly to Kirsan.

"Supreme Commander Kirsan, sir, the scout reports that General Santiago is preparing to engage Youngblood Hawke's forces! According to the scout, General Santiago is but a two miles east of our position!" the Colonel said.

"Outstanding! Well done! Well done, indeed!" Kirsan shouted.

Kirsan could hardly maintain his excitement as the crimson glow of his eyes intensified in anticipation of what he believed to be impending victory.

"Sir, I await your command," the colonel replied.

"Proceed immediately and at full gallop to assist General Santiago! That bloodthirsty titan will not steal the entire honor and glory for himself. This day will belong to Kirsan, and I will personally command the defeat of Youngblood Hawke!" Kirsan commanded.

"By your command, sir," the colonel responded as he ordered the Black Guard forces into combat, and what Kirsan believed to be his greatest hour.

❦   ❦   ❦

General Santiago's unit stood silent and ready as his troops began to see the distant cloud of dust and the sound of thunder approaching them from the east. The anxiety spread through the unit as man and horse became uneasy, with the continued advance of the ominous force making its way to them.

"Steady! Steady! Do not advance until I give the command," General Santiago ordered.

The Black Guard forces were lined across in two rows of twenty-five warriors. Their swords were drawn and resting upon their right shoulders, awaiting the order to charge and engage the approaching enemy. As the dust cloud thundered closer, the enemy forces became visible to the Black Guard. The only sound heard was the pounding of their mounts as they charged at full gallop. The enemy forces were assembled in a manner that did not disclose their numbers. Only the leader could be seen clearly as the dust cloud concealed the true size of their force. It was an intimidating site to even the most experienced soldier.

"Stand fast, gentlemen!" General Santiago barked, as he sensed the uneasy tension within his ranks.

Suddenly, the enemy force stopped and the dust cloud momentarily concealed the combatants. As the dust cloud cleared, the Select Warriors were revealed to their adversaries. They assumed the classic cavalry formation, in preparation to charge as they stood shoulder to shoulder. Without uttering a sound, the Select Warriors discharged their weapons from their scabbards. The snap of the steel shattered the silence and echoed across the battlefield that would soon ignite with the sounds of death. The moments that followed were almost mystical, as they appeared to halt time itself in a way that would mark the event to come as eternal, one that would surely change the course of time.

"Charge!" Youngblood Hawke commanded, as the Praetorians stormed toward their targets.

General Santiago replied in kind as he ordered his unit to engage the enemy. Suddenly the opposing forces crashed into each other with the might of a monstrous hurricane pounding against the rocky shores of a continent. The sound of steel upon steel resonated across the battlefield as the thundering charge of the warriors demanded the attention of nature itself. The adversaries converged upon each other and assimilated the other in a storm of igniting steel and bloodshed. The carnage was horrific as anonymous warriors fell in agony, only to be greeted by the specter of death. One of the first warriors to fall was a young Praetorian who had displayed the heart of a true warrior. His demise was instantaneous as his steel death warrant entered his chest and ejected him from his mount. Youngblood Hawke was witness to the grizzly site and did not allow it to go unpunished. He instantly reduced the young warrior's slayer to dust by the revenge of his katana. Captain LeClair's fate arrived in the form of two attackers as he was violently forced from his horse. Youngblood's attempt to recover William LeClair was interrupted by the raging battle that appeared to engulf the Praetorians like a firestorm.

Major MaCleod displayed his legendary bravado, yielding his battle sword in a portrait of heroism. MaCleod was no stranger to the field of battle, and death continued to pursue him with a vengeance. His apparent passion for the intoxicating effects of combat was clearly displayed by his face of battle. He was an army of one in many respects as the enemy gained an immediate respect and attacked him in numbers. No matter what the odds, Major Will MaCleod stood his ground, and reveled in the obvious compliment to his skills. The remaining Praetorians fought ferociously and with honor as their ranks dwindled in the face of the relentless attack by the Black Guard opposition.

Youngblood Hawke remained securely atop Veritas and continued to strike into the heart of the enemy's ranks. Confusion and the sounds of death engulfed the battlefield as man after man fell, spilling blood and memorializing what would soon become hallowed ground. The close combat called for a pragmatic response to every immediate threat. Youngblood Hawke continued to lead the Praetorians in an attempt to hold their ground, awaiting the main force led by Kirsan. The Praetorians were outnumbered two to one, and were now reduced to about fifteen bloodied warriors. Youngblood's katana and battle sword were applied with extreme prejudice as the two weapons worked harmoniously against their master's foes. Black Guardsmen with visions of grandeur attacked almost ceremoniously as they each attempted to make a name for themselves by killing a living legend. Their dreams were shattered one by one as Youngblood Hawke decimated their ranks.

The disorder was evident and the distractions many, but not enough to obstruct General Santiago's line of site, directly focused upon Youngblood Hawke. Youngblood was the prize, and there he stood waiting for the hand of justice to strike him down, befalling honor upon the hand responsible for his demise. The presence of the infamous General Raphael Santiago did not go unrecognized by Youngblood. While his attention was drawn to the immediate threats that confronted him, he remained keenly aware of the general and his actions.

"Will! Will! How are you holding up?" Youngblood Hawke cried out to his old friend and colleague.

"No wine nor woman has ever brought me as much pleasure, my friend," Will MaCleod replied, followed by a bellowing laugh that appeared to taunt his attackers.

"You are incorrigible!" Youngblood shouted, as he intercepted a blade intended for one of his Praetorians.

The momentum of the fight brought the two warriors side by side as the battle raged on.

"Do you see William? He fell instantly!" Youngblood said.

"His death will be answered by many more before this day is done!" Will MaCleod declared with the tone of vengeance, clearly present in his voice, and his sword imbedded in the chest of an attacker.

"We have to hold on just a little longer! Kirsan must give chase to our force as it retreats!" Youngblood said.

"You had better hope that we have a force remaining for him to give chase to," he responded.

The cold steel penetrated the warmth of the blood raging within Youngblood's veins, revealing an all too familiar pain. He turned to find General Raphael Santiago extracting his blade, preparing for another strike. However, the next attempt by the general was met by Youngblood's katana and immediately followed by the forceful blow of his battle sword. Santiago was unprepared for the power of his younger adversary, which pushed him back, causing him to pull on the reins of his horse. The wound inflicted by Santiago was of no consequence, and did not delay Youngblood Hawke's counter-attack. General Santiago was caught off-guard as he attempted to deflect the continued assault of the two swords wielded by the mysterious warrior. The Black Guardsmen surrounding the general responded immediately as they perceived the threat to their commander.

The dilemma facing their own commander did not go unnoticed by the Praetorians. Major MaCleod organized a powerful and uncompromising response, targeting General Santiago himself. The attack to their left flank distracted the Black Guardsmen enough to allow Youngblood Hawke to continue his fiery attack. Youngblood was within striking distance when he was alerted to the arrival of Kirsan and the main force.

"A reprieve has been issued for you at this hour!" Youngblood Hawke proclaimed.

"Your final hour approaches as we speak, Youngblood Hawke!" the relieved general said, as he was well aware that fate had just smiled upon his very existence.

"Praetorians! Praetorians! Retreat! Fall back, comrades!" Youngblood Hawke commanded as he disengaged General Santiago and rallied the remnants of the Praetorian Guard to fulfill their destiny.

"You heard the commander! Retreat!" Major MaCleod ordered, acknowledging the approach of Kirsan's forces.

Youngblood Hawke stopped briefly and saluted his adversary as a challenge to pursue him if he dared.

"Until the next time, General! Of course, fate will not be so kind when we meet again!" Youngblood Hawke warned.

Veritas charged east, leaving nothing but a trail of dust and a wake of death behind him. A grim reminder that the face of battle was an ugly and terrifying sight indeed.

❧   ❧   ❧

"General! General Santiago! Shall we pursue them, sir?" the Black Guard captain asked, filled with the excitement and peril of the moment.

General Santiago's military expertise demanded that he assemble his men and pursue what was left of the rebels at once. However, his political survival instincts instructed him to do otherwise. Kirsan was approaching at the head of the main force and he would demand to lead the expedition himself. Any attempt to intercede and displace Kirsan as the named victor could be fatal. Therefore, he ignored his military instincts and followed a philosophy of political subordination, noting the immediate approach of Kirsan.

"Assemble the men, Captain, but do not pursue the enemy at this time! We will await the orders of the Supreme Commander Kirsan!" General Santiago ordered.

"It shall be done, sir," the Captain acknowledged, as he gathered the men and attended to the wounded.

Kirsan's arrival was always met with a degree of pretentious ceremony. The advance guard assembled in his honor as the main force assumed the battle-field that had moments earlier, been alive with the sounds of combat.

"General Santiago, where is that criminal? Is he dead?" Kirsan demanded, as he surveyed the bodies strewn across the open field.

"No, sir, he was not killed or captured, but his final moment is near," Santiago responded, noting the dust cloud being kicked up by Youngblood Hawke's abrupt departure.

"Damn you! How did you let that criminal escape?" screamed Kirsan, filling his eyes with the crimson shade of hate.

"Supreme Commander Kirsan, I felt that the honor of securing his death should be your own," Santiago replied.

"Yes, indeed, my dear general. What of Horatio Cantrell? Is he among the dead?" Kirsan inquired with a noticeable degree of unease about him.

"Oddly enough, sir, he was not among the band of attackers. Personally, I find his absence disturbing, and advise caution in our pursuit."

"Caution? You are always advising caution. I suspect your caution is what restricts you from becoming a truly great leader," Kirsan commented in an obvious attempt to insult and humiliate his subordinate.

General Raphael Santiago ignored the comment and dismounted. He stood before Kirsan with all the grace of a military commander.

"There is an interesting member of the aristocracy among the enemy wounded," General Santiago noted.

"Who might that be?" the curious Kirsan asked, hoping that it was a prize.

"The young LeClair. I believe his name is William?" General Santiago responded.

"Yes, the son of the beloved man of the people, Jonathan LeClair, and brother-in-law of Horatio Cantrell. What a wonderful prize, indeed! His involvement will surely lead to an inquisition and the prosecution of his father for treason! Bring him to me!" Kirsan demanded with a sinister smile. "You have done well here, General Santiago, but this battle is far from over! I want Youngblood Hawke!" Kirsan exclaimed.

General Santiago approached Kirsan and advised, "He has no route of escape. His mounts are tired, and the remnants of his force are broken and running with fear. I would suggest that we pursue them immediately and end this insurrection once and for all!"

"So be it! It is time to hunt down and kill a Hawke!" Kirsan proclaimed, as he directed General Santiago to lead the main force in full charge after his nemesis.

The main force of the Black Guard remained powerful even after suffering substantial losses during the two attacks. Sixty Black Guard warriors had been slaughtered during the two confrontations. A number that did not go unnoticed by General Santiago. The advance guard lost half of its numbers during the direct confrontation with the enemy. It was a bloody and unyielding action that left many dead on both sides. He personally counted thirteen of the enemy dead on the field. The general would not dare state his observations to Kirsan, but he had a newfound respect for the general known as Youngblood Hawke. As they pursued the fleeing enemy force, General Santiago could not help but wonder if Hawke truly was fleeing for his life or if a deadly trap awaited them? The absence of the cunning and capable Horatio Cantrell worried the experienced commander.

❧   ❧   ❧

The anxiety level was undoubtedly taking its toll upon the inexperienced cavalry commander. Colonel Fox continued to pace back and forth, in anticipation of the impending battle. He constantly demanded briefings from his scouts and sentinels, seeking information on the whereabouts of his colleague and the Praetorian Guard.

"Where are they? They should have entered the pass by now. Is there any word from General Cantrell?" Colonel Fox inquired.

"No, sir, the last dispatch advised patience," the young captain responded.

"Patience? He has years of military experience and the best advice he has to offer is patience?"

Sinclair's personal cadre of officers remained silent as they listened to the ranting and raving of their commander. They had become accustomed to his strange ways. but also maintained great faith in his ability as a commander. In fact, they took great pride in the fact that their leader was a bit eccentric. Colonel Sinclair Fox's unpredictability was somewhat intriguing, and was now worn like a badge of honor by the entire unit. "Crazy like a fox!" was now the motto of the elite cavalry unit, and they took pride in being unconventional just like their rather unusual commander.

A scout rode up to the command tent and broke the ramblings of his commander. "Colonel Fox! Colonel! Riders…riders…approaching…from the west, sir!"

"I say, good man! Bravo! Bravo! How many? Come now! Spit it out!" the excited Sinclair Fox demanded.

"Approximately a dozen, sir," the scout replied, out of breath from what was obviously a demanding ride.

"A dozen? Is that all? Are they ours? Praetorians?" a puzzled Sinclair Fox asked.

"There is more, Colonel…they are…they are being pursued."

"How many?"

"Hundreds, Colonel! Hundreds, if not a thousand!"

"The mass? Tell me, man! Are they being pursued by the mass?" Sinclair Fox demanded with an obvious change in his tone, from that of anxiety to determination.

"Black Guards, sir! Without question, they are Black Guards!"

"Very well! It is time, gentlemen! You know what to do! Assemble the men and have them assume their positions!" Colonel Fox ordered.

"Yes, Colonel," the captain responded, as he directed the warriors to their concealed positions atop the hillside.

Colonel Fox pulled the scout aside, "You have done well, soldier. Now I have another important task for you to perform."

"Yes, sir, I shall not fail you," the excited young scout replied.

"Replace your mount with a fresh one and proceed directly to General Cantrell. Tell him what you have told me. Also, give him a personal message for me."

"Yes, sir."

"Repeat what I am to say to you exactly. Do you understand?"

"Indeed, I do."

Colonel Sinclair Fox recited the words for the young scout and then bid him farewell, as he instructed him to remain with General Cantrell's forces. The scout rode off wondering if he would ever see his odd commander again.

Assuming a position visible to all of his men, Colonel Sinclair Fox remained calm and steadfast, gazing out into the distance for the first glimpse of what could be the face of death itself. The unit watched their commander looking into the distance, engaged in what appeared to be a conversation with the heavens.

Suddenly he turned to the hillside with his sword raised, "Gentlemen and warriors! Heed my words and you shall be complete, *'Assume a virtue, if you have it not.'*[178] On this day you shall adorn the face of courage and display it clearly for your enemy to see! May God's speed be with you as you strike deep into the heart of the beast!"

The attention was immediately drawn away from the reluctant commander as the thundering approach of the beast could be heard in the distance.

❧   ❧   ❧

General Horatio Cantrell sat quietly in the command tent, listening to General Chang discuss the art of war with the young officers as they briefed him on the state of their forces. Cantrell's encampment was organized in classic military style, with sentinels posted on the perimeter. The mood of the entire camp was that of the calm before the storm. His men were instructed not to become too comfortable, noting that they would be called to action at a moment's notice.

The officers continued to discuss strategy with the veteran general, when suddenly they were distracted by the hurried approach of a rider. He rode from the direction of Colonel Fox's encampment and General Cantrell assumed that the rider was delivering an urgent message.

The scout was escorted to the command tent where he was met by a captain. The scout insisted upon speaking with General Cantrell directly, stating that he was following the orders of Colonel Sinclair Fox.

General Cantrell interrupted the debate, "Bring him here, Captain."

"Yes, General," the captain responded, now annoyed by the insistence of the scout.

"You have something for me?" the very focused and intimidating commander asked.

"A message from Colonel Fox, sir. A dozen riders approach the pass, being pursued by hundreds of Black Guards!"

"Very well. You are dismissed," the general instructed.

"I have a personal message from the colonel as well, General."

"What is it?" the curious Horatio Cantrell asked, knowing that any personal message from Sinclair Fox was bound to be interesting, if not amusing.

"Well, sir, he said…I must get this right…*'Ignorance is the curse of God, knowledge the wings wherewith we fly to heaven.'*[179] I believe that is correct,

218   The Quest for Truth

General. Oh yes, and then he instructed me to tell you that he would see you in the abyss?" the scout said.

"That sounds like Colonel Fox. I suspect that you have recited it correctly," Horatio said, shaking his head and grinning.

The scout was escorted from the command tent and joined Cantrell's forces in preparing for battle. Horatio Cantrell looked to General Chang, who had remained by his side at the request of Youngblood Hawke. The general gave him a wink and a nod, acknowledging that it was indeed time for battle. Horatio returned the nod and then gave the final orders to his officer corps, along with some words of advice.

"We have no choice this day but to win! Anything less would be a failure…the likes of which will haunt us until our dying day. But if we should fail, remember this, warriors, such failure will not be accompanied by dishonor. Our ghosts will not be haunted by the spirit of cowards. If our blood is to be spilled on this day, it will stain the battlefield with courage! May the spirit of Youngblood Hawke be with you! *Mandamus Veritas*!"

The strength and stamina of Veritas led the remaining Praetorians in a most fantastic retreat. The intensity and will of both riders and mounts was so great that Youngblood Hawke found it necessary to slow the pace of the withdrawal. The Black Guard continued pursuit of the remaining band of warriors. Kirsan led the chase, with the taste of blood seething from his soul. His prize lye just ahead, ripe for the taking, a crowning achievement for all to praise.

Youngblood Hawke and the Praetorians rode in virtual silence, knowing that their only mission now was to lure the great beast into the snare. A masterful plan, simple in design, yet complex in application. Youngblood Hawke could not help but wonder if he was the predator or in fact the prey?

What if Sinclair and Horatio were discovered and had already been defeated? What if I am being driven into a trap? he wondered to himself. The location and state of Jonathan LeClair's forces were all but unknown. *What if he was discovered or was unable to forge the river?*

The fate of William LeClair laid heavily upon Youngblood. He could not help but accept responsibility for his demise. He died valiantly, but that would be of little comfort to his father and sister. And what of Horatio? William was like a son to him, and his loss would surely be a striking blow to his old friend.

The questions and doubts began to fade as the Praetorians approached the pass. The river appeared tranquil and at peace as it flowed quietly but with all the force that nature had to offer. Its depths would not allow a crossing and therefore, on this day, it was allied with the Select. Youngblood searched for a sign that Sinclair and his forces were cleverly hidden on the hillside and prepared to strike. But the hillside revealed no indication that at the moment it concealed a unit of elite cavalry. The tall grass waved in harmony with the wind, providing no suggestion that its fields would soon be paved with blood.

Youngblood maintained faith that Colonel Sinclair Fox would soon rise from the grass and strike the flank of the Black Guard, as General Horatio Cantrell's unit revealed itself and led a direct attack into the heart of the beast. Of course, the river would do its part, but the success of the entire plan would fall upon the shoulders of General Jonathan LeClair. If he is unable to close the door of retreat, the Black Guard could very well fall back, and then organize a devastating counter-attack.

Youngblood Hawke and the Praetorians entered the pass and would soon begin their ascent up the hill with the hope that they would be met by Sinclair Fox's cavalry. Only time had the answer to his questions, and at the moment, time was not revealing its infinite knowledge.

CHAPTER 20

The Face of Battle

So true, demanding all of me,
My life, my love, my destiny.

The two scouts stood before General LeClair, attempting to describe the military force approaching from the north. General LeClair listened intently as one of the scouts drew a diagram in the sand, demonstrating where they were, in respect to his position. It was obvious that the advancing unit, estimated at approximately two hundred strong, were going to cross the river at the very location of his intended crossing. It was also very clear to General Jonathan LeClair that the approaching military force was a Black Guard unit.

"I suspect that they are returning from the Northern Kingdom. The tragic death of the royal family opened the door for Kirsan's intervention," LeClair said.

"A tragic event," the young lieutenant replied.

"Indeed. But at this moment that Black Guard unit is our problem," LeClair said. "We must forge that river now!"

"General? Couldn't we just charge the river and cross it ahead of them?" the lieutenant asked.

"No, Lieutenant. We cannot allow that unit to pursue our rear guard and bite away at it until nothing is left. Such a strategy will only place us between them and the rear guard of their main force," LeClair explained. "No, we must remove this force from the equation now."

"But how do you suggest we accomplish this task?" the skeptical lieutenant asked.

"Through deceit and deception," Jonathan LeClair replied, displaying a most delightful smile.

"Lieutenant, listen carefully, I want you to prepare thirty of our warriors for a little bit of play acting."

"Play acting?" the lieutenant asked.

"Yes. Drama, my lad, pure drama!" Jonathan LeClair declared.

Kirsan could barely contain his excitement as he cast his eyes upon Young-blood Hawke. The mass of Black Guards entered the valley, pursuing the remaining band of Praetorians who were fleeing up the hill.

"Look at that coward now!" Kirsan screamed.

The Black Guards had completely entered the valley and were positioned at the bottom of the hill where General Santiago had halted the large column.

"General Santiago, what are you waiting for?" Kirsan demanded.

Santiago stood silent with a suspicious gaze as he surveyed the hill and his surroundings. He watched the Praetorians climb the steep incline, and Santiago squinted from the brightness of the sun that was now setting on the crest of the hill. It was obvious that his thoughts were focused upon what may be waiting on the other side of that hill.

"Santiago! Get him now before he escapes!" Kirsan ordered impatiently.

General Raphael Santiago turned back to his commander and nodded in acknowledgment. He then reluctantly gave the command, ordering the advance guard to pursue the Praetorians up the hill. At least a quarter of the Black Guard forces began to navigate the hill in pursuit of the Praetorians. Youngblood Hawke was almost halfway up the hill when he suddenly halted his men. They stopped dead in their tracks and then turned to face the attacking mass.

"He is surrendering! He knows that there is no escape!" Kirsan bellowed in a premature celebration of victory.

General Santiago continued to monitor his forces climb the hill. He noted with immediate concern the abrupt halt and defiant stand of Youngblood Hawke. He was tempted to call a halt to the pursuit but knew that such an order would only infuriate Kirsan.

"Bring me his head!" Kirsan demanded from atop his mount as he and the remainder of the Black Guard force waited idle upon the road.

Youngblood Hawke remained cool, staring down upon the advancing attackers. The remnants of the Praetorian Guard had assumed a formation stretching across the crest of the hill with their commander as the centerpiece. Youngblood Hawke discharged his battle sword from its scabbard, signaling the warriors by his side to follow suit.

Surely this one cannot be preparing to strike? thought General Santiago. *He would not strike unless…*

Without warning the hillside erupted like a wave, as an entire cavalry unit appeared, masked slightly by the tall grass and the setting sun. Colonel Sinclair Fox assumed a position by the side of his commander as his unit remained at the ready, awaiting the command to attack. Kirsan's face dropped in disbelief, wiping the smug look from his face as he witnessed an army materialize before him. He was stunned and unsure of what to do as he looked to General Santiago for guidance.

"General Santiago! What? Do you see that? Retreat! Retreat!" Kirsan screamed in a panic.

"No! No! Continue the attack! Charge!" Santiago commanded, noting that the forces were now halted and in a state of confusion.

Youngblood Hawke exchanged glances with his friend and colleague, Sinclair Fox.

"By your command, sir?" Sinclair said, deferring the honor of command.

"Charge! Give them hell!" Youngblood Hawke ordered, giving way to a rapid descent upon the disorganized Black Guardsmen trapped upon the hillside.

The momentum gained by the Select Warriors as they traveled down the hillside overwhelmed the Black Guards. They struck them at full stride with the force of an avalanche. Black Guardsmen were discharged from their horses as the steel from their attacker's swords ripped through man and mount. The scene was horrific and chaotic as the Black Guard warriors fell one after one, tumbling down the hillside in a merciless slaughter.

"Do not let up!" Youngblood Hawke ordered, as he chased the enemy down and struck them with all the brutality he could muster.

Youngblood led the charge down the steep hillside with battle sword in one hand and the reins of Veritas in the other. The advantage of momentum and higher terrain was just too much for the opposition. Warrior after warrior fell victim to attack as the Select Warriors made their way deep into the Black

Guard ranks. Youngblood Hawke was covered in the blood of his adversaries, displaying the face of battle and the relentless determination of a warrior prince.

"Surely you jest? That cannot be the best that you have to offer?" Sinclair Fox said, as he deflected an attacker's blade and tormented him with insults.

Colonel Sinclair Fox found himself engulfed in the heat of battle. His mastery with a sword was almost entertaining to any onlooker who could spare a moment to notice. Kirsan was in a state of complete panic, retreating with his cadre of personal bodyguards to a rear position adjacent to the river.

"Where is Santiago?" Kirsan demanded.

General Raphael Santiago was no stranger to the unexpected on the battlefield. He was ignoring the ranting and raving of Kirsan, attempting to organize a counterattack. However, his forces were in an almost tragic state. Santiago was able to assemble approximately two hundred warriors when confusion once again broke out among the ranks. He turned to find a large force charging from the east.

"Horatio Cantrell!" Santiago declared, as he recognized the man leading the approaching force at full gallop.

Santiago remained calm yet fully aware that the tide had now turned against him and he was facing yet another formidable enemy. Santiago was now forced to reconsider his strategy. He had no choice but to commit his assembled strike force to confront Horatio Cantrell. The retreating unit being forced down the hill would have to fend for themselves. Santiago was counting on Kirsan to organize the remainder of the force to supplement his strike force and wage a counter offensive against the cavalry descending the hill. However, Kirsan was busy building a defense around himself, utilizing the river as protection to his rear guard and preparing for what appeared to be a retreat. Kirsan had requisitioned approximately three hundred warriors for his own personal defense. The ambush left a quarter of the force being slaughtered as they fled down the hillside and another quarter of the Black Guards engaging Horatio Cantrell. Almost a third of the force was standing by to defend Supreme Commander Kirsan, and what was left of the group found themselves in a state of complete confusion.

Youngblood Hawke and Sinclair Fox continued their offensive, chasing the Black Guards down the hill with a vengeance. They engaged the Black Guard with extreme prejudice, striking the retreating warriors with merciless devotion. The face of battle was now sharing the stage with the face of death.

Leaping over horse and man, the Select Warriors pursued the enemy with an almost cruel conviction. Will MaCleod was in many ways an army of one. Wielding his sword with the determination of an executioner, he became stronger and more determined with every strike. MaCleod was a natural predator, revealing his true self on the field of battle.

"Sinclair! Behind you!" Youngblood warned, as the attacker struck Colonel Fox from behind. "Damn you!" Youngblood cursed.

Sinclair felt the cold steel enter his side, sending a sharp and penetrating pain throughout his body. The impact caused him to double over and as he pulled on the reins of his mount, the incline of the hill brought him and his horse crashing down. The impact dislodged his sword from his hand, leaving him with no weapon. He was trapped under his horse and unable to reach his sword or escape the attacker who was now preparing to finish his kill. Youngblood discharged the katana from its scabbard and tossed it in the direction of Sinclair, who was helplessly awaiting his fate.

"Sinclair!" Youngblood screamed.

Sinclair reached out, catching the katana and deflected the attacker's sword as he attempted to strike its target. The attacker recovered and was about to strike again when he was abruptly pulled from his horse by the back of the neck. Will MaCleod maintained an iron grip and dragged the warrior for several yards before dropping him to the ground. The Black Guard warrior's attempt to get back upon his feet was interrupted by the back of MaCleod's fist. The impact spun the warrior violently and hurled him to the ground. The warrior's second attempt to gain a footing was designated his last by the business end of MaCleod's sword, that had now penetrated deep into the warrior's heart. Two of Sinclair's men pulled their commander from beneath his fallen mount and propped him atop another horse.

"I say, that was rather close!" Sinclair said, grimacing from the pain of his wound that continued to spew blood. "I am forever in your debt, gentlemen."

"We can discuss payment at a later time!" Youngblood responded, as Sinclair handed him the katana.

Sinclair nodded his head in acknowledgment as he maintained a steady position within his saddle and continued to fight alongside his colleague.

"That looks pretty bad, my friend. Perhaps you should fall back," Youngblood said, noting the seriousness of the wound and the fact that it had to be extremely painful.

"Fall back? I think not! Do you really believe I would allow you to bask in all of the glory?" Sinclair replied, obviously in great pain and struggling with his sword.

"Of course not, my friend," Youngblood Hawke acknowledged, recognizing that Colonel Sinclair Fox was aware of the inspiration he was extending to his men.

Sinclair's wound was slowing him down, but it was not incapacitating, and it was clear that he intended to continue the fight. And continue it he would, for this fight was far from over.

"What do you make of that, Major?" the Black Guard captain asked.

"I am not sure, Captain, but they appear to be surrendering," Major Constantine answered, now in command of the Black Guard unit returning from the Northern Kingdom.

"It is possible, if not highly probable, that they are the remains of the rebellion," the captain said. "Look at them. They can barely stand, and many appear to be wounded."

"That is possible, they may have fled the forces under the command of Supreme Commander Kirsan and General Santiago," Major Constantine noted, as he continued to eye the small band of approximately thirty warriors with suspicion.

"That would make perfect sense, Major. They must have been fleeing to the north when they realized that we have cut off their avenue of escape," the captain said. "Shall I dispatch a small force to take them prisoner?"

"No, we have no time for that, Captain. We shall round them up quickly and then provide a small security force to watch over them until we can return," Major Constantine ordered.

"Very well, sir," the captain acknowledged, as he gave the command for the entire unit to proceed to the river and take the surrendering rebels as prisoners.

The major led his Black Guard unit to the edge of the river and confronted the ragtag group of warriors. "Who is in command here?" he demanded.

"That would be me," the young lieutenant responded.

"And you are?" he asked.

"I am an officer under the command or should I say, formerly under the command of Youngblood Hawke," the lieutenant said.

"Formerly?" Major Constantine inquired.

"Yes, our commander was killed but a few hours ago in a most ferocious battle with the Black Guard," he explained.

"Tell me of this battle? Is it over?" Major Constantine asked.

"Very much so. Our forces were completely destroyed. We are all that is left and as you can see, we have no fight left in us," the lieutenant said. "As an officer and a gentleman, all I ask is for fair treatment of my men."

"An officer and a gentleman? You will be treated accordingly. Indeed, you shall be treated as rebels and as such you and your men will executed for treason," Major Constantine replied.

"I don't think so!" the lieutenant boldly announced, as he drew his sword from under his cloak and attacked the Black Guard commander.

Major Constantine's attempt to deflect the Select Warrior's assault was in vain. He was immediately struck from his mount and impaled upon his own sword. The Select Warriors reacted swiftly, following the example of their lieutenant. The level of violence inflicted upon the Black Guard was an extreme example of warfare. The Black Guardsmen were totally unprepared for the deceptive assault that had instantly killed their commander. The Black Guard captain attempted to rally his men and suppress the rebels when his attention was turned to the charge of Jonathan LeClair from the nearby tree line. Concealed within the trees, LeClair attacked at full charge with his entire force. Black Guardsmen were being pulled from their mounts by the Select Warriors, who had now infiltrated their disorganized ranks. The action erupted into a brawl as the opposing warriors fought man-to-man, in a struggle for existence. The river turned red from the blood of fallen warriors now littering its banks.

"Your ignorance shall be silenced forever!" General Jonathan LeClair cried out, wielding his sword as if it were blessed by a divine providence.

Jonathan LeClair knew that he had to destroy the Black Guard unit expeditiously and then proceed directly to the support of the primary forces. The future of their cause and the lives of many depended on his success.

"Fight men! Fight with all your heart and soul!" LeClair screamed, as he pressed on against the Black Guard.

Horatio Cantrell's advance was now stalled, finding himself engaged in a fierce struggle with the opposition led by General Santiago. He could only hope that Jonathan LeClair had initiated his attack against the Black Guard's rear flank. The charge of Youngblood Hawke and Sinclair Fox was clearly visible to Horatio, providing some reassurance that the plan was gaining ground. However, it was also clear that the battle was raging to a level of brutality that he had never witnessed before. Accompanied by General Chang, Horatio and his forces fought meritoriously as they attempted to break Santiago's ranks.

Kirsan's reserves remained out of the fray and disengaged. His lack of ambition was a blessing to the Select forces. Jonathan LeClair had not arrived to attack the rear guard. Therefore, Kirsan's forces were free to retreat, prepare a counterattack, or immediately engage Sinclair's cavalry. He could also effectively divide his force to support General Santiago as well.

Youngblood Hawke's elevated position allowed him the advantage of being able to survey the entire battlefield. A view that revealed Kirsan was a dangerous threat, positioned to change the course of the entire battle. He could only have faith that LeClair's unit had not been wiped out and that he would arrive soon.

"Where is LeClair?" Sinclair asked.

"That remains a riddle," Youngblood said as he continued to fight his way through the mass.

⁂

General Santiago was waging a successful defense against Horatio Cantrell's assault. But he knew that it was imperative that they launch a counterattack or risk being outflanked by Youngblood Hawke and the advancing cavalry.

"Colonel! We must get a message through to Kirsan!" Santiago ordered. "Tell him that he must organize a counter offensive immediately!"

"I will deliver the message myself, General," the colonel replied, as he forced his way through the tangled mass of bloodshed.

Youngblood Hawke and Will MaCleod led the remnants of the Praetorian Guards straight through the middle of the retreating enemy forces. The Praetorians fought side by side as they drove a wedge through the enemy's ranks. The confusion escalated as the Black Guards appeared to have no direction, focus, or command structure to organize a counterattack or strategic retreat. They attempted several times to stand and fight, but were continually defeated by the momentum of Colonel Fox's cavalry driving its way down the hill.

"Will! We have to break through and support Horatio's assault! His forces are stalled!" said Youngblood, as he swung his battle sword, striking man and steel indiscriminately.

"By your command," Will MaCleod said. "But what of that large force gathering by the river?"

"I see it! Press on, Will! Press on!" Youngblood ordered. His concern about that gathering mass of warriors was escalated by the fact that there was still no sign of Jonathan LeClair.

"I know of nothing but attack, my friend!" Will MaCleod said, just as he caught glimpse of what appeared to be a ghost on the battlefield.

"William!" Youngblood cried out, "You are alive! But how?"

"I was knocked unconscious and they believed me to be dead! It was just the device I needed to escape and join you here!" William LeClair replied.

"It is good to see you alive and kicking!" Youngblood said. "Now stay close! I don't want to lose you again."

"I intend to," he replied.

The battle raged on as the setting sun had now been replaced by the ghostly illumination of the moon. The night sky was vast and dark, yet alive with the power of distant stars that were randomly interrupted by drifting clouds. The battlefield was littered with fallen warriors and stained with the blood of both friend and foe. Steel striking steel continued to echo the sound of war as the specter of death pursued the victims of fate. The Select Warriors remained inspired by the sight of their commander as he led them against the enemies of truth in a bloody and fatal clash of ideology. The face of battle was now being worn in its most demonic state, dismissing the very existence of its creator, by striking at the very heart of humanity.

Kirsan maintained the security of his forces as he observed the battle from his position by the river. He was not blind to the fact that his command was in danger. However, he was a politico and not the strategic commander he wished to be. Santiago was the real soldier. A fact to which Kirsan was becoming increasingly aware. He did not know how or where to direct his forces. He was in a state of near panic as he watched the battle unfold before him. It was not the clear victory that he had envisioned.

"Supreme Commander!" the colonel said, as he approached Kirsan.

"Yes, Colonel, what is it?" Kirsan asked.

"General Santiago needs you to organize a counter offensive," the colonel said.

"Why yes, of course. Colonel…I will remain here with a small security force to block any attempt by the enemy to retreat. You will lead the counterattack in support of General Santiago. Now go!" Kirsan ordered.

"Yes, sir!" the colonel acknowledged, fully aware that Kirsan was ensuring only that he maintained an avenue of escape for himself.

The Black Guard colonel was no fool and was a seasoned veteran of many campaigns. He immediately dispatched one hundred Black Guardsmen in support of General Santiago. The remaining troops were quickly organized into a strike force and launched against the charging cavalry led by Youngblood Hawke and Sinclair Fox. The threat had now become a reality for the Select Forces as the reserves withheld by Kirsan were now committed on the battlefield.

The reinforcements reached Santiago just as Horatio Cantrell was about to break through his ranks. General Santiago acted swiftly as he responded to the threat and halted the enemy advance. However, Santiago's attempt at a counter-attack was thwarted by the resolve of Horatio Cantrell. Cantrell continued to press an attack and maintain Santiago in a defensive posture.

The Black Guard's counter offensive against the attacking cavalry appeared to be gaining ground. The momentum had faded as the cavalry led by Youngblood Hawke reached the bottom of the hill where they found themselves confronted by a second wave. The Select Warriors had, in fact, routed the initial attack force that had made its way up the hill. However, the casualties to their own ranks were not few. At least one third of Sinclair's unit lay dead or wounded upon the hill and the remainder was now faced with a larger threat. It was a threat that did not escape the attention of the Select Warriors.

"Further action would be futile," Sinclair said, as he continued to fight, despite the pain caused by his unattended wound. "We must retreat, for there are just too many."

"Have faith, Sinclair...truth will lead the way," Youngblood said.

Youngblood was also experiencing his own doubts of confronting such an overwhelming force as he questioned his own resolve.

Broken Beyond Repair?

Stand and fight, you coward!
Stop! Don't you dare run away.
Advance, move further forward,
Don't leave—you have to stay.

This battle is just beginning,
The end is nowhere in sight,

Remain—you may start winning,
No problem is solved by flight.

Never broken beyond repair,
There is nothing you can't mend,
Dismiss the sadness and despair,
This is the beginning, not the end.

—*Youngblood Hawke*

"The mass has become a powerful beast," Sinclair replied.

"Then we must kill the beast!" Youngblood Hawke commanded.

"How would you suggest we do that?" he asked.

By cutting off its ugly head!" Youngblood declared, as he pulled back on the reins of Veritas.

Discharging his katana from its scabbard, Youngblood led a charge into the ranks of the attacking Black Guards and made a run directly for Kirsan.

"Today is a good day to die!" Will MaCleod screamed, as he too charged into the depths of the mass, followed closely by Sinclair Fox and his cavalry.

The direct assault penetrated the ranks of the Black Guard, dividing them in two. They were totally unprepared for such a surgical strike. The attack pierced through their ranks like a spear driving itself through its intended target. Before the Black Guard could react, Youngblood had broken through and was now on a collision course with Kirsan and his personal security force.

Kirsan, with his back to the river, was now forced to respond. He was all on his own and could expect no assistance from General Santiago, who remained in check by Horatio Cantrell's forces. Within moments, Youngblood Hawke and his warriors were upon him, wearing the awesome face of battle.

"Retreat! Retreat!" Kirsan cried out, but his forces had no avenue of escape as the Select Warriors drew down on them.

Kirsan made an attempt to flee when Youngblood Hawke leaped from Veritas and dragged him to the ground. The two men were locked in a struggle as Youngblood pounded Kirsan with the hilt of his sword. Kirsan fell to the ground, but managed to drag his attacker down. The close combat was fought with hand and fist as they each attempted to beat the other into submission. Blood streamed from both of the men as they tore at each other's flesh and delivered every blow with devastating power. The anger and hostility escalated as the men struggled to break free and attack with the cold steel of their swords. They were engaged in a personal conflict, surrounded by the sounds of war and death. Oblivious to the carnage around them, the two adversaries pursued the other's mortality with the sole purpose of extinguishing it forever. The hatred was ignited within the darkness of Kirsan's heart and revealed by the crimson glow in his eyes. He was afire with the desire to kill Youngblood Hawke.

"You are a criminal and must be punished for your crimes!" Kirsan cried out, as he delivered blow after blow with his sword.

Youngblood Hawke deflected every attack with the grace of a mystical knight and champion. Wielding his battle sword in one hand, and the katana in the other, he unleashed every strike with unyielding force. Youngblood assumed the momentum of a siege engine as his advance pushed Kirsan into retreat. His eyes were illuminated by the sapphire storm that had now set in his eyes, revealing the power of truth as his source of inspiration.

"Come out of your cave! Reveal yourself!" Youngblood Hawke commanded.

Kirsan was forced to his knees as Youngblood Hawke continued his relentless attack. Youngblood's battle sword deflected Kirsan's last futile attempt to strike and dislodged it from his grip, now rendering him defenseless. Turning back to Youngblood Hawke, Kirsan was greeted by the sharp edge of the legendary katana pressing against his throat. The raging conflict around them appeared to disappear into another reality as the two men stared into each other's souls.

"Surrender! Surrender and I will spare your miserable life!" Youngblood Hawke demanded.

Youngblood Hawke stood victorious over Kirsan as he looked deep into the hate burning within his eyes, revealing the emptiness of a dark and lonely soul.

A Miserable Soul

A child of the aristocracy, is what he claims to be,
Condescending and dismissive, abrasive is he,
Compulsive and demanding, all the flaws of man.

Eccentric and odd, difficult to understand,
Confused as a thinker, never taking a stand,
Using gold and silver, to purchase loyalty.

Forever alone, a solitary man, no true friend,
A pathetic soul, miserable, forced to pretend,
Lost in a world, dreary, cold, and very alone.

Time will pass swiftly, this man will grow old,
No one will remember, his story to go untold,
An unfortunate destiny, a most sorrowful end.

—*Youngblood Hawke*

The crimson fire appeared to increase in Kirsan's eyes as he grinned and stared past Youngblood Hawke. Youngblood slowly turned as the pain rushed through his body and engulfed his mind, soul, and spirit. The dagger penetrated deep into his flesh, bringing him to his knees, as the katana fell from his hand. The sapphire tint of his eyes slowly diminished, releasing the life from his being.

The dagger continued to twist and turn, driving the pain deeper and deeper into the warrior's heart. Struggling in pain, Youngblood Hawke turned to face his executioner. The familiar eyes stared deep into his own, revealing a never-before-seen shade of crimson, deep within the assassin's soul.

"*E Tu Brute?*"[180] whispered Youngblood Hawke, as William LeClair drove the dagger deeper.

"Don't act surprised. You are a threat to my very existence and had to be stopped!" William LeClair explained, slowly removing the dagger from Youngblood's back.

"A threat? But why? Why would you see me as a threat?" Youngblood said as he struggled to speak while also seeking an answer to the betrayal.

"Not a birthright, but earned meritoriously," William LeClair replied. "Those are your own words. I am only protecting my birthright."

Kirsan picked himself up from the ground and said, "William, your loyalty here shall be rewarded very handsomely."

"Here is your reward!" shouted Sinclair Fox as he struck William LeClair down. Sinclair leaped from his horse and buried his battle sword deep into the shoulder of his former colleague, screaming, "You traitorous snake!"

Crying out in agony, William LeClair made a hasty retreat as Kirsan attempted to strike Youngblood with his sword. Youngblood found the strength to lift his katana and unleashed one last strike at Kirsan. The blade of the katana ripped across Kirsan's face, releasing a sporadic flow of blood as

Kirsan screamed in pain. Kirsan immediately fled and disappeared into his ranks, seeking protection from the vengeance of Sinclair Fox.

"They have killed Youngblood Hawke!" a Select Warrior shouted.

The news spread throughout the ranks of the Select Warriors, creating a wave of outrage. The Select Warriors exploded in rage, attacking the mass with horrific and unrestrained brutality. The conflict intensified beneath the midnight sky as a sapphire storm brewed violently above the battlefield, illuminated by the ghostly moonlight.

"Youngblood! What happened? I could not believe my eyes!" Sinclair rambled, as he tried to attend to Youngblood's wound.

"Sinclair, listen to me. Get me onto Veritas," he commanded.

"What? Are you mad? You are dying!" Sinclair said.

"Do as I say, Sinclair! That is an order!" Youngblood demanded.

"Very well," he replied.

"My friend, this fight is not over and I cannot let them down. They have sacrificed all to be one with me. I will not sentence them to a destiny of mediocrity," Youngblood Hawke explained, as he struggled to climb upon Veritas.

Youngblood Hawke gripped his katana and raised it in defiance for all to see.

"He is alive! Youngblood Hawke lives!"

The battlefield was alive with excitement and renewed hope as Youngblood Hawke rallied the Select Warriors and pursued the fleeing Black Guards. The news of Youngblood Hawke's death and resurrection reached Horatio Cantrell, inspiring him to personally lead a charge smashing into the ranks of General Santiago. Santiago's defensive line was broken, creating confusion and distention within his ranks. He lost complete control of his command as Cantrell's forces broke the back of his elite unit. Those who were unable to successfully flee the battlefield with General Santiago fell victim to the wrath of the Select Warriors.

The remnants of the Praetorian Guards, led by Major Will MaCleod, foiled Kirsan's attempt to counterattack by trapping him between Horatio Cantrell's forces and the river. The battle raged on as Youngblood Hawke remained firmly in his saddle, displaying the feared face of battle while struggling to hide the face of death.

The blood dripped from Kirsan's face, which had now been scarred by the legendary katana. He was blind in one eye and in great pain, but was briefly inspired with visions of victory as he eyed an approaching force from the west.

"Yes! Yes! Major Constantine with reinforcements!" Kirsan said with excitement.

But his excitement was soon extinguished when he realized that the approaching military force was not Major Constantine with a contingent of the Black Guard. His heart sank to new depths of despair when he learned that it was, in fact, General Jonathan LeClair, preparing to attack his rear guard.

"No! This cannot be happening!" Kirsan said.

"Supreme Commander Kirsan, we must retreat and regroup!" the Black Guard captain advised.

"Where is General Santiago?" Kirsan demanded.

"His forces have been completely routed," the captain replied.

"Is he dead?" Kirsan asked with desperation.

"I believe he organized a successful retreat," he responded.

"Yes, of course, an organized retreat," Kirsan said sarcastically.

"Supreme Commander Kirsan, we must go now," the captain advised, noting that they would soon be trapped and flanked on all sides, with no avenue of escape.

"So be it. I have but one consolation, having personally witnessed the execution of Youngblood Hawke. No mortal man could survive such a fatal wound. He will surely die, as will his quest. Call retreat, Captain!" Kirsan ordered.

Kirsan and the remnants of his elite Black Guard departed the battlefield as rapidly as they had arrived. The ground was stained with blood and strewn with the bodies of fallen warriors. A victory had been acquired on this day, but at what cost.

Youngblood Hawke rode tall upon his trusted friend Veritas, dismissing the pain that had now engulfed his very being. He slowly rode Veritas to the top of the hill where the cavalry had initiated its charge against the Black Guard. The army of Select Warriors remained silent as they watched their commander struggle to the crest of the hill. Upon reaching the top, he discharged his katana and raised it victoriously in the air. The sapphire storm continued to rage above the clouds, generating thunder and bolts of lightning, illuminating the darkened sky. The sun began to rise, signifying the beginning of a new day and perhaps a new era of enlightenment. Youngblood Hawke surveyed the battlefield, saddened by the horror of war displayed before him. His eyes began to swell as he shed a tear for his fallen comrades.

"Do not let this day be in vain. You have done a great thing here today. Truth has been revealed to you, and now you must defend it at all costs!"

Youngblood Hawke declared with all the energy he could muster, before falling from Veritas.

The army of Select Warriors bowed their heads in respect and sorrow as they realized their inspirational leader had now been delivered to another realm. Sinclair Fox remained by Youngblood's side, attempting to comfort his friend and colleague. An inner circle of colleagues that consisted of Horatio Cantrell, General Chang, William MacLeod, and Zacharia's son Remo joined him. Zacharia had met his own eternal fate earlier in the battle, fighting by his son's side.

Jonathan LeClair was devastated when he learned of his son's betrayal. He approached Youngblood and begged for his forgiveness. "Please forgive him," he asked.

Unable to muster the strength to speak, Youngblood nodded his head in acknowledgment.

The close friends and colleagues of Youngblood Hawke stood upon the hill, overlooking the battlefield that had proclaimed him a prince. He remained still and peaceful, drifting away toward a destination unknown. As they watched their commander, a mysterious sapphire glow cast itself upon him. His body appeared to absorb the strange light, revealing a faint spark within his eyes.

Sinclair Fox was mesmerized by the mystical glow of the sapphire light, as the figure suddenly became visible to him. The others did not see her, but she was clear to him. She knelt down beside the fallen warrior prince and held him in her arms, absorbing his pain.

"Sapphire," whispered Youngblood Hawke, "my dearest Sapphire."

"I am here," she replied with a warm smile, stroking his head as if to wash away the suffering.

"I have failed you," said Youngblood. "I have fallen short of my quest."

"Your quest is not over, my love, it has just begun," she replied.

"The riddle, it no longer remains a mystery to me," Youngblood said, struggling to speak.

"You have discovered the answer?" Sapphire asked.

"Yes, deep within the darkest confines of my heart," he replied.

"Tell me what wisdom you have uncovered, Youngblood Hawke," she asked.

Youngblood closed his eyes, and in a faint whisper, revealed the answer to the riddle...

My Destiny

So wonderful,
              A dream this has to be,
         Passion, love, and mystery.
    A warm place to rest my soul,
Peaceful, inviting, and all our own.

So powerful,
              Demanding secrecy,
         Painfully concealed from reality.
    Trapped in a world of its own design.
The heart suffering and confined.

So beautiful,
              Surely an angel is she,
         Sapphire eyes, calling out to me.
    Cry out her name for all to hear,
The truth be told I love her dear.

So true,
              Demanding all of me,
         My life, my love, my destiny.
    A promise of eternity together,
Hello, My Love, I Love You Forever.

—*Youngblood Hawke*

The solitary tear rolled down Sapphire's face as her warrior opened his eyes to gaze upon her one last time. Sapphire just smiled and rocked the dying warrior in her arms as he drifted closer to truth. She traveled deep into his soul and led him to the object of his eternal quest. Sapphire glanced at Sinclair, acknowledging his presence within her realm.

"What will become of him?" he asked.

"His destiny awaits him," she responded with a smile.

Sinclair remained captured by her beauty, and he admired her aura that revealed a mystical strength of innocence and simplicity. A sensation of peacefulness entered his soul, providing a degree of clarity he had never experienced before. As he was about to speak to the angelic spirit, a sapphire storm erupted violently over the battlefield in a swirling tunnel of lights and sounds. The celestial beauty was slowly drawn upward, toward the clouds, illuminating the hillside, as she was delivered to another realm. The heavens above literally exploded as if to announce the passing spirit of the warrior prince, forever to be known as Youngblood Hawke.

A Time of Clarity

High above the clouds,
    I think with such clarity,
Wrapped in my shroud,
    Dismissing my mortality.

Drowning in my thoughts,
    Yet, peaceful and free,
No longer overwrought,
    I ignore a painful reality.

So many words I write,
    A reflection of my soul,
Revealing a foresight,
    A philosophy I am told.

"To thine own self be true,"
    This is what William said,
Is that something I can do?
    Perhaps—when I am dead.

—*Youngblood Hawke*

The Select Warriors stood in awe as they watched the storm evaporate into the morning sky and disappear without a trace. The darkness had now been replaced by a new day.

Horatio approached Sinclair, who stood silent staring off into the horizon.

"Sinclair? Are you all right?" Horatio asked of his friend.

"Actually, I am quite well, considering…," he replied, as a faint smile became visible upon his face.

"It is over," Horatio said gravely.

"It is far from over, my dear Horatio," Sinclair replied.

"Yes, we have won this battle but Kirsan has escaped to the protection of the mass, and we have lost our inspirational leader. This rebellion is over," Horatio said.

Sinclair stood straight up and turned to face Horatio and the army of Select Warriors, "The rebellion is not over. In fact, it has just begun!" he declared.

"But Youngblood Hawke is dead, as is his quest. He no longer exists to lead!" a warrior shouted from the ranks.

"Alas! But you are wrong. The spirit of Youngblood Hawke lives! He lives within each and every one of us. He had faith in us and our noble cause. My friends, we all have the potential to become Youngblood Hawke. We must continually struggle and seek accession to the next level. Our desire to understand will ignite the spirit of Youngblood Hawke that lies dormant deep within our souls. This rebellion has not ended. No, my friends, it has just begun. The path to truth has been revealed to each of us, and it can no longer be ignored. The beast will return and try to destroy us. It will relentlessly hunt us as prey, seeking to imprison us within its cave of darkness. Fear not, for the spirit of Youngblood Hawke shall forever lead us from the darkness and into the light of truth!" Sinclair said.

Horatio Cantrell and the entire army of Select Warriors silently pondered the words of Sinclair Fox. They stood motionless as they honored the bravery and sacrifice of their fallen comrades and recalled the great deeds that they had witnessed on this fateful day.

"He deserves the funeral of a great warrior prince," young Remo announced, as he wiped the tears from his eyes.

"Indeed, he does," Sinclair replied, "and he shall, when destiny commands it."

"You will take him to a place where he will be honored?" General Chang asked.

"It goes without saying, General," Sinclair replied.

"Where are you taking him?" Horatio asked.

"To the Noble House," Sinclair Fox declared, in a tone that demanded no further inquiry from Horatio, who wondered how Sinclair had learned of its location.

Recruiting the assistance of Horatio Cantrell and Will MaCleod, Sinclair carefully placed Youngblood's body upon Veritas. Veritas displayed a majestic and almost royal air as his former master was laid across his back. The legendary katana was prominently displayed on the right side of Veritas' saddle, for all to see.

Sinclair Fox approached Horatio Cantrell and presented him with the faithful battle sword of Youngblood Hawke and said, "He would want you to have this. Use it as an inspirational beacon of truth, my friend."

"Indeed, I will," Horatio responded, as he fought back the tears.

The Select Warriors opened a passage within their ranks and lined the path with swords drawn in honor of their esteemed commander. Veritas was led down the hill by young Remo, following Sinclair Fox in a solemn journey through a gauntlet of honor and reverence. Horatio Cantrell watched Sinclair Fox disappear into the distance as he accepted command of the Select army. What lay ahead remained a riddle, but it was a date with destiny he could no longer deny.

Epilogue

The story of Youngblood Hawke continued to resonate in the collective conscience of the population. Some time had passed since the legendary battle between the mass and the Select Warriors, inspiring a paradigm shift among the thinking class. The rebellion and struggle against the powerful and dark forces of Kirsan continued under the command of General Horatio Cantrell. The rebellion was slowly gaining ground as the mass and the Select fought for the minds and hearts of the people. Pockets of resistance formed within the four kingdoms. The Northern Kingdom was especially active under the command of Remington Fox and Reginald Quartermain. The spirit of Youngblood Hawke remained alive and thriving among the Select Forces as their ranks swelled with would-be philosophers, soldiers of fortune, and professional adventurers. The legendary warrior's spirit had become a virtual paragon of excellence and freedom against the mass.

The father and son traveled the dark road returning from their hunting trip. The night sky was vibrant with stars and a bright full moon illuminated the countryside.

"Look at the moon, Father," the boy said. "It has the oddest shade to it."

"Yes, it does. It is a Sapphire moon, or what some call, a Youngblood Hawke moon," he replied.

"A Sapphire Moon and Youngblood Hawke moon?" the boy asked.

"Yes, they are actually one and the same."

"One and the same?" the boy continued.

"It is said that the warrior, Youngblood Hawke, displayed a deep sapphire glow within his eyes. A reflection of his soul, perhaps? It is also said that a sapphire moon illuminated the battlefield when Youngblood Hawke led the Select Warriors against the Black Guard," the father explained.

"Father, please tell me of this battle."

"It was a great and profound battle, my son. A battle that may very well change the course of humanity."

The boy listened intently as his father spoke of the legendary battle and the Select Warriors led by Youngblood Hawke.

A Sapphire Moon

A mystical moon drifts across the sky,
Dismissing the clouds and all below,
Magically illuminating the countryside,
Casting an ominous sapphire glow.

Such a night is a reflection of the past,
The subtle reminder of a love now lost,
A romance so passionate it didn't last,
An eternal memory preserved at all costs.

What was so special of this particular night?
A man and a woman realized their fate.
Hidden desires exposed by the moonlight,
Revealing a love that could no longer wait.

The mystery of such a night, you cannot dismiss
So just close your eyes, and gaze at the moon,
Simply dream of a true love, and then make a wish,
Your fate may be realized—not a moment too soon.

—*Youngblood Hawke*

"Legend also has it that on such a night, when the moon casts its sapphire glow, the great warrior prince rides his battle horse Veritas in search of truth," the father added, as his son's eyes opened wide with excitement.

"Do you believe it, Father? Does he ride on this night?"

"I believe he does. I truly believe that he does," the father replied, as they continued their journey.

With Veritas He Does Ride

The story of a legend, mythology we are told,
Reality he must be, a man so brave and bold.
Knowledge is his prey, the truth he does stalk,
A predator is he, the warrior Youngblood Hawke.

Made of flesh and blood, aware of his mortality,
Traces of a tender heart, capable of great brutality.
Accepting every challenge, mastering every test,
A soldier of fortune, a man with a vision quest.

An intimidating presence, with an icy cold stare,
Confront him if you must, defy him if you dare.
Many suffered his attack, agonizing in defeat.
Always leading the charge, never calling retreat.

Armed with truth, the sword of justice by his side,
Shielded within his armor, with Veritas he does ride.
Inspiring so many others, preparing them for the fight,
Battling the armies of darkness, searching for the light.

Standing in absolute solitude, always prepared to defend,
Attending to his mission, a quest with no definitive end.
Concealing an ancient secret, the true object of his desire,
Youngblood Hawke seeks only the love of his Sapphire.

—*Youngblood Hawke*

🍁   🍁   🍁

The solitary warrior approached the majestic structure noting its mythical presence elevated above its surroundings, within the picturesque rolling hills outside the City of Ventura. The mystical glow of the moon illuminated the temple as he traveled slowly along the road lined with statues of great warriors, philosophers, and kings. He stopped momentarily to examine the latest addition, resembling the image of a legendary warrior prince.

The warrior dismounted his horse and ascended the steps leading up to the large oak and iron door. Upon reaching the door, he entered in a manner that would suggest a certain familiarity. The two doors slowly opened for the warrior as he entered the temple and followed the long hallway lined with burning torches that led into the main chamber. The warrior gazed up into the seemingly endless ceiling that reached deep into the darkness.

Upon entering the center of the chamber, he stood in the middle of the triangular mosaic, reflecting the inscription: VE RI TAS. Suddenly, the three figures appeared before him, curious as to who would be visiting at such a late hour. The ancient sages appeared to be studying the young warrior and talking among themselves in a faint whisper.

"Does the journey ever end?" the solitary warrior asked.

"The beginning is an end," a sage replied.

"And the end a beginning," said the warrior. "I have traveled a long and hard path to that which I seek. I have fought mighty beasts, slain fierce dragons, and climbed the highest mountains, yet, I still have not found what I am looking for."

The eldest sage moved closer to the warrior, who continued to remain hidden within the shadows, "*It appears there is a narrow path which brings us safely to our journey's end, with reason as our guide. As long as we have a body, and this evil can mingle with our soul, we shall never completely attain what we desire, namely, truth. For the body is forever wasting our time with its demands.*"

"My body has been beaten and subjected to great pain and suffering," the warrior said.

"*Whenever it is ill it hinders us in our pursuit of real being. It fills us with passions, desires, fears, and all kinds of imaginings and foolishness,*" the eldest sage continued.

"Distractions, indeed," the warrior agreed.

"*It is always preventing us from thinking properly. The body alone, and its desires, cause wars, social divisiveness, and battles: for the origin of all war is the desire for wealth, and we are forced to pursue wealth because we are enslaved by the wishes of the body. On account of this, we have no leisure for philosophy. Even if we manage to free ourselves from the body for a while, and try to examine some matter, it hinders us at every step of our inquiry, causing confusion and trouble and panic, so that we cannot see the truth for it,*" the eldest said.

The solitary warrior just listened and nodded his head in agreement as the sage continued.

"Truly we have learned that if we are to have any pure knowledge at all we must be freed from the body," the eldest sage continued.

"The body in many ways confines the spirit and imprisons the soul," the warrior noted.

"The soul by itself can see things as they truly are. Only after we are dead, it seems, can we gain the wisdom that we desire and for which we claim to have a passion. But this cannot happen while we are alive, as my argument shows. For if it is impossible to have pure knowledge while we have a body, one of two things must be true: either we can never gain any true knowledge, or we can only gain it after we are dead. For then, and only then, will the soul exist by itself, separate from the body," the eldest sage said.

"Are you saying that absolute truth cannot be found within this realm of reality?" the warrior asked.

"While we live we come closest to true knowledge if we have no use for or communion with the body beyond what is necessary, and if we are not defiled by nature," answered the sage. *"We must live pure of the body until God releases us. When we are pure and released from the follies of the body we shall dwell, I imagine, with others who are pure like ourselves, and we shall of ourselves know all that is pure,"*[181] the eldest sage replied.

"Is humanity capable of reaching such a level of existence, and if it can be reached, can it be maintained?" the warrior asked. "I ask you this question, aware that you will not answer. For your thoughts and words are wise, but also confined to this realm and therefore, you are unable to answer."

The mysterious warrior intrigued the three sages as they peered through the darkness, in an attempt to link a face with the familiar philosophy.

The warrior continued to respectfully address the three sages, "Your words are very wise and you have provided guidance to me and many who have come before me. The words and wisdom of your philosophy will continue to guide generations of future adventurers traveling the path to truth. I shall forever be in your debt, but the answer I seek is not inscribed within this temple. My quest demands that I seek the next level."

"Your journey has taken you farther than you think, warrior," the eldest sage remarked. "You have learned much."

"I know nothing except the fact of my own ignorance,"[182] the warrior said, quoting the all too familiar words of the eldest sage. "However, my journey has revealed much to me."

"Who are you?" the eldest sage inquired, his curiosity now piqued.

"Who I am is of little consequence," he replied.

"Explain," the youngest sage asked.

"The answer to that question is in the eyes of the beholder," the warrior replied.

The three sages listened as the warrior continued.

"All things of this earth are relative. I have learned that my own perspective supersedes all others as it relates to my own destiny. You will see me as you choose to see me, and I will be who I choose to be. I must be fully self aware, while also conscious of how others perceive me. Understanding that how I perceive myself will influence the perspectives of those around me," the warrior said.

"Do you know who you are, warrior?" the youngest sage inquired.

The warrior smirked and slightly shook his head.

"I know where I am, I know what I am, and I am fully aware of who I am. But why I am remains a tormenting riddle," the warrior replied with an eerie tone of self-confidence.

The three sages were startled by the warrior's familiar answer, prompting them to once again ask, "Who are you?"

"I know only that my thirst for knowledge remains unsatisfied. Perhaps the relative purpose of my existence is to pursue the absolute nature of my existence? My quest is far from over," the warrior continued.

The solitary warrior stepped out of the shadows and into light as he removed the hooded cloak that concealed his identity.

Slowly he lifted his head, revealing the piercing radiance of his sapphire eyes and declared, "I am Youngblood Hawke!"

The End, and a New Beginning

The Poetry of Youngblood Hawke

Forbidden Knowledge

Traveling my own path,
A relative truth revealed,
An epiphany of sorts,
No longer concealed.

Truth now confronts me,
I ask—What do I do?
Many paths to destiny,
Now forced to choose.

My future is unclear,
Only the past is mine,
Now aware of my fears,
I live one day at a time.

Absolute truth is hidden,
Unreachable and obscure,
Perhaps I am forbidden,
To possess a truth so pure.

—*Youngblood Hawke*

The Ignorance of the Young

Ignorance and youth, what a truly wonderful blend,
Living life clueless, they have no need to pretend.
Fooling only themselves, they think they are clever.

Pursuing the moment, and the illusion of fun,
Staring at the clouds, and frolicking in the sun.
Laughing and playing, believing it will last forever.

Caring only about today, forgetting their tomorrow,
Unaware of a future, filled with pain and sorrow.
Simple and carefree, trusting things will get better.

What fools are the young, unappreciative of youth.
Dismissing life's lessons, and running from the truth.
Turning away from reality, and the advice of elders.

One day they will awaken, by then it will be too late,
Their time will have passed, having sealed their fate.
Left with wisdom and old age, what a terrible waste.

—*Youngblood Hawke*

Alone and Confused

In search of life's answers, I can no longer pretend,
My life a proverbial puzzle, a maze without end.
From the very beginning, I was alone and confused,
A virtual powder keg of emotion, unable to defuse.

Time passed so slowly, maturing from a boy to a man,
In preparation of my future, and all life would demand.
Entering the world, with raw excitement and ambition,
I ignored the menacing power of fear and inhibition.

No longer imprisoned, mind and spirit wandering free,
Dismissing a painful past, in pursuit of a new reality.
Level after level, I conquered more difficult heights,
Fleeing the cave of darkness, seeking intellectual light.

In command of a world, reserved for the very few,
Yet, I found myself lacking, unaware of what to do.
Detachment and distraction, questions so profound,
Inflicted with paralysis, I was chained and bound.

Suddenly and without warning, a truth was revealed,
The meaning of my existence, no longer concealed.
A vision to tomorrow, the very image of potentiality,
Unveiling the answers to the questions of my destiny.

—*Youngblood Hawke*

The Path of the Damned

Tragically inflicted with the desire to understand,
The questions of life, the very meaning of existence,
Asking what is the profound purpose of destiny's plan?
Surely such a question is the reflection of ignorance.

So frail and pathetic is this creature we call man,
Yet gifted with the power of a creative intelligence,
Faithfully searching for truth and all it commands,
Confronted by legions of opposition and resistance.

Burdened by so many perilous and earthly demands,
A servant of nature, forever subject to its influence,
So naïve and idealistic, heroically taking a stand,
Encumbered by a soul and guided by a conscience.

This poor being travels the path of the damned,
Led hopelessly astray by fate's cruel indifference.

—Youngblood Hawke

The Beast

What is it that pulls me?
Forever dragging me down,
The power of gravity,
Bringing me to the ground.

Struggling against its power,
Fighting day after day,
More difficult by the hour,
Impossible to break away.

This mighty beast lives inside,
Against it I have no chance,
From this monster I can't hide,
For it is my own ignorance.

—Youngblood Hawke

The Fate of Mankind

A fate worse than death?
        Life, some would say.
Better to die young,
    Than to die of old age.

Some will burn brightly,
        While others fade away.
A few achieve greatness,
    But most will just obey.

A truth will be revealed,
> Without further delay.
The promise of tomorrow,
> Yet, a reflection of today.

The weakness of mortality,
> Humanity runs astray.
An undetermined destiny,
> Forced to live day to day.

—*Youngblood Hawke*

The Mass Man

He is the ultimate fool,
> Following all the rules,
That others have set for him.

He will always obey,
> Without further delay,
Avoiding any hint of sin.

He renders no resistance,
> Content with his existence,
Unaware of a future so dim.

He needs no goal or plan,
> No, not the mass man,
Knowing he can never win.

—*Youngblood Hawke*

The Riddle

I know where I am, what I am,
And am fully aware of who I am,
Yet, why I am remains a riddle.

This is my puzzle, my own mystery,
Pursuing the question of my destiny,
The answer hidden by the hand of fate.

Forever searching, the ultimate test,
Day and night, leaving no time for rest,
I must find the answer, before it's too late.

Time is my enemy, obstructing my path,
A reminder, I will fall victim to its wrath,
Such is the dilemma, the nature of my quest.

—*Youngblood Hawke*

A Vision of Beauty

Look into my eyes, what do you see?
Determination, ambition, and potentiality.
A man with a quest, a future to unfold.

Look into my soul, what do you see?
Loneliness, despair, a desire to be free.
A solitary spirit, lost and out of control.

Look into my heart, what do you see?
Desire, passion, romance, and fantasy.
A lover in waiting, one to behold.

Now I turn to you, what do I see?
Clarity and truth, a vision of beauty.
An image of true love and my destiny.

—*Youngblood Hawke*

Time Alone

Peaceful, reflective, and surreal,
A silence that surely can't be real,
Quietly we sit, we think, and stare.

Such a time is needed to heal,
Our own thoughts—how we feel,
Reminding us why we still care.

These moments we tend to conceal,
For it is often the truth they reveal,
Accept such moments if you dare.

—— *Youngblood Hawke*

The Reluctant Adventurer

The distant horizon tempts me,
Forever calling out my name,
Gazing out—What do I see?
The allure of fortune and fame.

So far away it appears to be,
A promise of another life,
The spirit desiring to be free,
Dismissing all pain and strife.

A ship suddenly drops from view,
Falling from the edge of reality,

Traveling from the old to the new,
Following the stars seeking destiny.

A ship and crew seek a heroic tale,
Now traveling a course set by fate,
The winds of change fill their sail,
As an unknown future lies in wait.

How I wish to be one of the crew,
Pursuing adventure and mystery,
A journey reserved for a select few,
Such courageous souls—so unlike me.

—*Youngblood Hawke*

The Great One

Behold the Emperor! He thinks and stares,
Approach and ask, why? No one dares,
It is said that he contemplates our destiny.

A visionary—he remains deep in thought,
Confronting the riddle of the Gordian Knot,
Discharging his solution—defining our fate.

To the east he leads us to final victory,
Conquering all who would be his enemy,
So swift and exact, his dream cannot wait!

Spreading the light of Hellenic ideology,
It is in our blood that he writes his history,
Liberator or tyrant? Better left to debate.

Centuries to come will speak of his name,
Many more will attempt to achieve his fame,
For they too wish to be known as *"The Great!"*

—*Youngblood Hawke*

The Questions of Humanity

So many profound questions, no time for delay,
Society and culture, a proverbial state of decay,
Searching for answers, the truth we are told.

Philosophers and poets, questions of destiny,
Revealing nature's truths, a relative reality,
The value of knowledge, the purpose of a soul.

The temptation of wealth, the fear of poverty,
The pursuit of true love, a quest for immortality,
A desire to remain young, the right to grow old.

A need to be free, the demands of conformity,
The potentiality of man, the flaws of humanity,
The cruelty of time, the allure of silver and gold.

The fate of civilization, the lessons of history,
The hope of possibility, the comfort of mediocrity,
The meaning of life, an unknown future to unfold.

—*Youngblood Hawke*

A Warning

A knight in shining armor?
Now don't you be fooled,
More a rogue without honor,
The very definition of cruel.

Yes, charming and handsome,
Also so very brave and bold,
Appearing kind and wholesome,
Claiming a heart of pure gold.

Be careful my beautiful princess,
For your heart he will surely take,
Return to the safety of your fortress,
At once! Before it is too late.

—*Youngblood Hawke*

The Wild One

So violent and aggressive,
Dangerous—out of control,
A hatred dark and deep,
His heart empty and cold.

Such a blinding ambition,
Freely selling his soul,
Trading duty and honor,
For mere silver and gold.

He desires with such envy,
For his story to be told,
A vision of his greatness,
Daring, brave, and bold.

Soon his time will come,
The grim future to unfold,
A foolish spirit so young,
Destined never to grow old.

So behold his greatness!
His spirit does swiftly run,

To the cover of his hatred,
Beware of this Wild One!

—*Youngblood Hawke*

A Most Elusive Prey

Love and Truth, arguably one and the same.
Sharing a destiny, differing only in name.
Dismiss one, and the other would remain.

An eternity spent together, a history to reveal.
The secrets of humanity, profoundly concealed.
Pursued by so many, always refusing to yield.

Possessing the power of vision, the gift of clarity.
Blessed with eternal life, in command of reality.
In defense of the other, unleashing fear and brutality.

Love and Truth, the proverbial partners in crime,
Enjoying an abstract existence, impossible to define.
Eluding capture and the understanding of mankind.

—*Youngblood Hawke*

Just Another Day

Darkness slowly arrives,
The clouds run for cover,
Day disappears with the sun.

This day I did survive,
It was like all the others,
So thankful that it is done.

The pain I cannot deny,
Waiting, suddenly it is over,
Another day has just begun.

—*Youngblood Hawke*

What is Love?

What is Love? But a poisonous blend,
A mixture of passion and romance,
An infliction to which we must attend,
The outcome often left up to chance.

What is Love? Not so innocent and pure,
Coming to us cleverly disguised as a friend,
Beware of the power of its intoxicating allure,
Promising a beginning, it will deliver an end.

What is Love? Sadly it is just an idea,
Fully aware, but we continue to pretend,
Created by humanity to dismiss our fears,
A broken promise, we will forever defend.

—*Youngblood Hawke*

If Only For A Moment

If only for a moment, I could feel your tender touch,
I would thank the stars, for giving me just this much,
For surely such a gift, would be sent from up above.

If only for a moment, I could hold your lovely hand,
The woman that you are, I might begin to understand,
A mystery to unravel, all that I have dreamed of.

If only for a moment, I could hold you in my arms,
You would soon realize, I could never do you harm,
The object of my desires, you are the one that I adore.

If only for a moment, I could experience your kiss,
Please let it last forever, this would be my only wish,
Your lips, so sweet, would leave me wanting more.

If only for a moment, you would look into my eyes,
A lonely soul you would find, much to your surprise.
A heart filled with sadness, just waiting for your love.

—*Youngblood Hawke*

A Difficult Journey

What is life, after all?
    A tangled thicket,
Obscuring your view.

An impassable path,
    A maze of sorts,
Forever delaying you.

Impossible to travel,
    Slowing your progress
Difficult to break through.

Such is your journey,
    So difficult at times,
Yet, you must continue.

—*Youngblood Hawke*

Seeking New Heights

The heights of success are almost mystical when viewed from the depths of mediocrity. Represented as a majestic mountain, its summit is barely visible to the naked eye. To many who dwell in the valley, it can only be seen with imagination and wonder. To some, it cannot be seen at all.

The summit towers high above the clouds of insecurity and fear. The majority has no desire or ambition to scale its steep cliffs. For them, the perils are too real, the risk of falling too great. However, a select few are unable to resist the summit's powerful and intoxicating allure. The select accept the challenge of the mountain. Prepared and unprepared, planned and unplanned, as a member of a team, and often a solitary climber, they all share the same quest.

Every minute, every hour, of every day, a new expedition departs. Climbers, beware! This treacherous mountain is loyal to none. Many dedicated climbers have fallen and many more remain stranded, unable to climb higher and reach new heights. What torture it must be to clearly see the summit, but remain unable to reach it?

How can a climber get so close, yet remain so distant from the object of his desire? Paralysis can inflict the climber with the power of a plague. The symptoms are clearly defined: inadequate supplies and provisions, the absence of a strategic plan, the lack of resolve and vision, and the inability to control fear. This disease can be avoided and is not always fatal. It can be overcome by some but for many it is the end. The tragic and unforgiving end of a life's dream.

Why do they climb this mountain riddled with danger? The simple answer resonates within our collective conscience. Echoing from the depths of reality, our minds, hearts, and souls understand that humanity demands no less. The climber of mountains seeks the next level of existence, maintaining faith that the summit is near and within reach.

A very select few will break through the clouds and reach the summit. A truth may be revealed to those who succeed. They may realize that success was achieved when the courage was found to actually begin the journey. The pain, the suffering, and sacrifice endured during the climb will become revered memories. Their past life in the valley will no longer be treated with contempt. In fact, it will remain a humbling reminder of who we are and where we come from. The climber will begin a new life, high above the clouds, upon the heights of this proverbial mountain.

One must take care, for living at such heights can be as difficult as it is rewarding. The perils of the mountain do not disappear upon reaching the summit. The dangers are enhanced, as the winds of competition and change grow stronger. The elements of nature will work harmoniously to push them from the heights. More and more climbers will come, friend and foe alike, seeking a place on this majestic mountain. The summit will become crowded as the majority seeks to secure their positions. Vision and ambition will be replaced by mediocrity and fear.

A select few will become restless and begin to once again look up into the clouds. A fateful few will see through the clouds and catch glimpses of an even higher summit. They will realize that the next level calls out to them. Such climbers will embark on a new expedition into the heights of human potentiality, inspiring others to follow and join in their quest. They will continue to climb higher and higher, never looking down, always seeking the next level. The future of humanity demands no less.

—Youngblood Hawke

A Fool's Quest

Will this tribulation ever end?
A fool's quest, cleverly disguised,
In God's name, we often pretend,
A destination never to be realized.

A cynical thought, you so often say.
Open your eyes! What do you see?
Suffering and pain rules the day,
Closing your eyes, ignoring reality.

Oh what a cute faithful little clown!
Hoping and praying, always in pain.
Unaware you are chained and bound,
Seeking forgiveness, hiding your shame.

Break those chains! Open your eyes!
Life is a journey, not a trial or test,

Pursue the truth; expose all the lies,
Such is the nature of humanities quest.

—Youngblood Hawke

The Race

My life runs a gauntlet,
Ignorant of the fact it will fail,
Against the powers of nature,
So meek, so weak, and so frail.

Setting sail so boldly,
Weathering every storm,
So often thrown off-course,
Battered, beaten, and worn.

Running the path to destiny,
Pursued by fate's evil twin,
A mad dash against time,
It is a race I can never win.

If only I could rest a moment,
Some time to catch my breath,
A chance to stop and realize,
That I am racing to my death.

—Youngblood Hawke

A Daily Reminder

ell me, why do I hate you so?
For so many years, taunting me,
Yet, who you are, I do not know,
Show me mercy, just let me be.

Day and night, living inside of me,
rom you I have no place to hide,
Bringing so much pain and misery,
Forcing me to live this tragic lie.

Who are you? Such a miserable soul,
Reveal yourself, disclose your identity.
Wait! I know you, eyes angry and cold,
It is my own image in the mirror I see.

Now I understand this fatal connection,
Forever bound, you will never let me go,
The horror of an image, my own reflection,
A daily reminder of why I hate you so.

—*Youngblood Hawke*

True Understanding

You tell me you understand,
There is no need to explain,
Compassion and comfort,
Sympathy—feeling my pain.

Do you truly understand me?
The deep sadness of my soul,
The suffering and heartache,
Such a memory to behold.

Into the depths of your heart,
So very deep you should go,
Scars of torment and anguish,
Revealing a common sorrow.

Are you beginning to understand?
Only empathy allows you to see,

Your own woeful tears must flow,
To share my pain and cry with me.

—*Youngblood Hawke*

Refuge Within

I must withdraw and escape,
To the confines of my mind,
To a most spiritual state,
Peaceful, reflective, sublime.

From reality I must hide,
The daily trial and grind,
A calmness deep inside,
The only refuge I can find.

Retreating to relative safety,
So solitary—alone and cold,
Hidden in virtual obscurity,
Such a lost and lonely soul.

—*Youngblood Hawke*

Drifting To You

I suffer in a world of complete totality,
Wallowing within the great depths of my own reality,
        Yet my mind drifts to you.

In vain, I commit myself to this mundane neutrality,
So keenly aware of time's punishing brutality,
        Yet my mind drifts to you.

Responsibilities abound, problems profound,
More and more aware of my own mortality,
　　　Yet my mind drifts to you.

Crisis, scandal, disaster all around,
Turmoil and calamity are the only sounds,
　　　Yet my mind drifts to you.

This quest must come to an end,
For only then, will time become my friend,
As I spend an everlasting eternity,
　　　Drifting with you.

—*Youngblood Hawke*

A Virtual Prison

Life—such an elaborate web,
Reaching out so distant and far,
Yet, we remain within bounds,
Self-confined to where we are.

Why do we live so afraid?
Fear is not what we need,
Tangled in our complex web,
A life we have chosen to lead.

We trap and confine others,
Our web does not discriminate,
In every direction it restricts us,
Holding us in this limited state.

A virtual prison of our own design,
Nothing but an abstract boundary,

Imaginary walls keep us confined,
Tragically—we choose not to be free.

—*Youngblood Hawke*

Sentenced to Life

Why do you punish me?
I have committed no crime.
Suffering in my humanity,
Facing the brutality of time.

I am a prisoner of fate,
Serving a life sentence.
Locked in a solitary state,
Confined to my existence.

Waiting alone in my cell,
I plead for my release.
Trapped in a living hell,
Begging for some peace.

One day you may forgive,
Freeing me from my chains.
Perhaps then I will live,
Freed from my sins and pain.

—*Youngblood Hawke*

Lost in the Realm of Reality

Lost in a world of chaotic conformity
    My heart and soul grow weary,
Longing for a time of relative sanity.

I awaken from my dreams
    An angel appears before me.
Is this a dream or reality?

This vision, such clarity!
    Touching me momentarily,
Continuing to elude me.

Eternity was revealed to me,
    Dismissing reality,
Forgiving the weakness of my mortality

Could it possibly be?
    Is this my destiny?

—*Youngblood Hawke*

With Or Without You

With or without you,
    My mind wanders,
To a destination unknown.

With or without you,
    My spirit retreats,
Creating a world of its own.

With or without you,
    My soul seeks comfort,
For a place to call home.

With or without you,
    My heart aches,
Desiring a love of its own.

With or without you,
    My life will continue,
Desperate, dark, and alone.

—*Youngblood Hawke*

The Exceptional Being

Surrounded by many,
I remain standing alone,
A self-imposed exile,
No place to call home,

A dark and lonely heart,
The most desperate soul,
Ruled by fear and doubt,
In command and control.

The moment is coming,
I can no longer pretend,
The world is watching,
This is surely the end.

—*Youngblood Hawke*

Taunted By True Love

Romance, passion, the heart's desires be told.
The allure of happiness punishes my soul.
The suffering and pain of an unknown destiny,
Pursuing so many yet choosing me.

True Love as written in the days of old,
Teasing, taunting, demanding to be told.

All that I have dreamed of delivered to me.
What game is this? Fate toying with humanity?

Slowly detached, my mind loses control,
Wandering in the wilderness alone and cold.
A soul mate, friend, and lover is she,
An alternative universe, an escape from reality.

Time will pass, and all will grow old,
Capture what is yours! Lovers be bold!
Searching for answers, my quest will be,
Ignoring the truth, for the answer lies within me.

—Youngblood Hawke

A Reflection of A Man

The spirit of a warrior, I am sworn to protect.
No life of my own, only exile and neglect.
The weight of responsibility, chained to my neck.

The mind of a philosopher, wandering and free.
In search of the truth, wherever it may lead.
The ultimate riddle, tempting and taunting me.

The heart of a poet, desperate, alone, and cold.
Dreaming of romance, passionate and bold,
A lasting true love, a story to be told.

The soul of a fool, forever living in pain.
A punishing ignorance, driving me insane.
This cry for help, I can barely contain.

My spirit, my mind, my heart, my soul.
A warrior, a philosopher, a poet, and a fool.
I am unlike any other, an exception to the rule.

—*Youngblood Hawke*

The Select Warrior

My armor is robust, my weaponry deadly.
Fearing nothing that dares to confront me.
Rendering my sword upon demand,
Restrained as a man in solitude I stand.

A soldier and philosopher of sorts,
An adventurer and mercenary by creed.
Haunted by the desire to understand,
Freed from the shackles of the mass man.

Commonality replaced by nobility,
Not a birth rite but earned meritoriously.
Command of the truth wherever it may stand.
In defense of honor and the Select man.

Relentless pursuit of an ancient ideology,
Emptiness and loneliness has unto now defined me.
Shrouded by my quest, cloaked in darkness,
A self-imposed exile from the majority.

Mastering a world of unlimited potentiality,
Honor, fortune, and the allure of glory.
Sacrifice all and you shall be one with me.
Risk nothing and mediocrity will be your destiny.

—*Youngblood Hawke*

Looking Toward the Sky

Heaven—a clear blue sky,
Clouds floating and drifting,
Above this barren wasteland,
And humanity asking why?
A lonely creature is man,
This state he cannot deny,
Searching for the truth,
Living such a mortal lie,
Walking and wandering so,
Hopelessly he does try,
Unaware of where to go,
And having no idea why.

—*Youngblood Hawke*

The Eye of the Storm

Pursuing my quest, forever to be.
Following fate wherever it may lead.
Adventure, fortune, and discovery!

Overcome, suddenly, by a sapphire sea.
Tossed and thrashed about deaf to my pleas,
Lost in a storm of wonder and mystery.

Refuge, safe harbor, will it be?
The eye of the storm calls out to me!
Its allure—the promise of eternal tranquillity.

Is there no mercy for me?
No more suffering, I beg of thee!
Take me! Give me serenity! Or let me be!

—*Youngblood Hawke*

Warriors of Truth

Against all odds, they pursue absolute truth,
Intellectual warriors and fact-chasing sleuths.
Living in the Limelight, overcoming all resistance,
Professional thinkers, the epitome of persistence.

Dismissing bias and prejudice, seeking what is true,
Defending justice and liberty, for many and the few.
They cry Integrity and Honor! This above all,
Attacking the enemies of truth, answering the call.

Alone in the darkness, seekers never losing sight,
Searching for the answers, hidden from the light.
Moments of brief victory, followed by lasting defeat,
Dedicated warriors of truth, they vow never to retreat.

They are one and they are many, woman and man,
Advocates of the truth, courageously taking a stand.

—*Youngblood Hawke*

Broken Beyond Repair?

Stand and fight, you coward!
Stop! Don't you dare run away.
Advance, move further forward,
Don't leave—you have to stay.

This battle is just beginning,
The end is nowhere in sight,
Remain—you may start winning,
No problem is solved by flight.

Never broken beyond repair,
There is nothing you can't mend,

Dismiss the sadness and despair,
This is the beginning, not the end.

—Youngblood Hawke

A Miserable Soul

A child of the aristocracy, is what he claims to be,
Condescending and dismissive, abrasive is he,
Compulsive and demanding, all the flaws of man.

Eccentric and odd, difficult to understand,
Confused as a thinker, never taking a stand,
Using gold and silver, to purchase loyalty.

Forever alone, a solitary man, no true friend,
A pathetic soul, miserable, forced to pretend,
Lost in a world, dreary, cold, and very alone.

Time will pass swiftly, this man will grow old,
No one will remember, his story to go untold,
An unfortunate destiny, a most sorrowful end.

—Youngblood Hawke

My Destiny

So wonderful,
              A dream this has to be,
        Passion, love, and mystery.
    A warm place to rest my soul,
Peaceful, inviting, and all our own.

So powerful,
              Demanding secrecy,
        Painfully concealed from reality.

Trapped in a world of its own design.
The heart suffering and confined.

So beautiful,
       Surely an angel is she,
     Sapphire eyes, calling out to me.
   Cry out her name for all to hear,
The truth be told I love her dear.

So true,
        Demanding all of me,
    My life, my love, my destiny.
   A promise of eternity together,
Hello, My Love, I Love You Forever.

—*Youngblood Hawke*

A Time of Clarity

High above the clouds,
    I think with such clarity,
Wrapped in my shroud,
    Dismissing my mortality.

Drowning in my thoughts,
    Yet, peaceful and free,
No longer overwrought,
    I ignore a painful reality.

So many words I write,
    A reflection of my soul,
Revealing a foresight,
    A philosophy I am told.

"To thine own self be true,"
    This is what William said,

Is that something I can do?
    Perhaps—when I am dead.

—*Youngblood Hawke*

A Sapphire Moon

A mystical moon drifts across the sky,
Dismissing the clouds and all below,
Magically illuminating the countryside,
Casting an ominous sapphire glow.

Such a night is a reflection of the past,
The subtle reminder of a love now lost,
A romance so passionate it didn't last,
An eternal memory preserved at all costs.

What was so special of this particular night?
A man and a woman realized their fate.
Hidden desires exposed by the moonlight,
Revealing a love that could no longer wait.

The mystery of such a night you cannot dismiss
So just close your eyes and gaze at the moon,
Simply dream of a true love and then make a wish,
Your fate may be realized—not a moment too soon.

—*Youngblood Hawke*

With Veritas He Does Ride

The story of a legend, mythology we are told,
Reality he must be, a man so brave and bold.
Knowledge is his prey, the truth he does stalk,
A predator is he, the warrior Youngblood Hawke.

Made of flesh and blood, aware of his mortality,
Traces of a tender heart, capable of great brutality.
Accepting every challenge, mastering every test,
A soldier of fortune, a man with a vision quest.

An intimidating presence, with an icy cold stare,
Confront him if you must, defy him if you dare.
Many suffered his attack, agonizing in defeat.
Always leading the charge, never calling retreat.

Armed with truth, the sword of justice by his side,
Shielded within his armor, with Veritas he does ride.
Inspiring so many others, preparing them for the fight,
Battling the armies of darkness, searching for the light.

Standing in absolute solitude, always prepared to defend,
Attending to his mission, a quest with no definitive end.
Concealing an ancient secret, the true object of his desire,
Youngblood Hawke seeks only the love of his Sapphire.

—*Youngblood Hawke*

A Warrior Indeed!

A warrior's mind is forever free,
    No longer shackled in chains,
Pursuing an unknown destiny,
    Searching for fortune and fame.

A warrior's spirit is wildly alive,
    Riding boldly into the night,
Doing what it must to survive,
    Always prepared for the fight.

A warrior's heart is never soothed,
    Growing old and forever alone,

Close to love but once removed,
    True love he has never sewn.

A warrior's soul is dark & cold,
    Trapped & imprisoned by fate,
Waiting for his future to unfold,
    Forbidden to enter heaven's gate.

—*Youngblood Hawke*

Endnotes

1. *Kung Fu Meditations & Chinese Proverbial Wisdom*, Ellen Kei Hua, Thor Publishing Company, 1991, meditation number 17.

2. *The Book of Five Rings*, Miyamoto Musashi, translation by Thomas Clearing, Barnes & Noble Books, New York, 1993, Page 71.

3. *Kung Fu Meditations & Chinese Proverbial Wisdom*, Ellen Kei Hua, Thor Publishing Company, 1991, meditation number 17.

4. *Kung Fu Meditations & Chinese Proverbial Wisdom*, Ellen Kei Hua, Thor Publishing Company, 1991 Ventura, California. The Tao, pronounced "Dow," refers to the way. "When you have found the Tao you can find peace in all things."

5. *Kung Fu Meditations & Chinese Proverbial Wisdom*, Ellen Kei Hua, Thor Publishing Company, 1991. *Chung ts'ai* is meditation.

6. *Kung Fu Meditations & Chinese Proverbial Wisdom*, Ellen Kei Hua, Thor Publishing Company, 1991, meditation number 10.

7. *Kung Fu Meditations & Chinese Proverbial Wisdom*, Ellen Kei Hua, Thor Publishing Company, 1991.

8. *Socrates, Ideas of the Great Philosophers*, William S. Sahakian, Mabel Lewis Sahakian (Socrates), Barnes & Noble Books, 1993, page 33.

9. *Socrates in 90 Minutes*, Paul Strathern, Ivan R. Dee Publisher, 1997, page 23.

10. *Socrates in 90 Minutes*, Paul Strathern, Ivan R. Dee Publisher, 1997, page 24.

11. *Aristotle: Ideas of the Great Philosophers*, William S. Sahakian, Mabel Lewis Sahakian (Aristotle), Barnes & Noble Books, 1993, page 33.

12. *Aristotle: The Desire to Understand*, Jonathan Lear, Cambridge University Press, 1988, page 168.

13. *Aristotle: Ideas of the Great Philosophers*, William S. Sahakian, Mabel Lewis Sahakian, (Aristotle), Barnes & Noble Books, 1993, page 34.

14. *Socrates: Ideas of the Great Philosophers*, William S. Sahakian, Mabel Lewis Sahakian (Socrates), Barnes & Noble Books, 1993, page 32.

15. *Plato's Republic*, 1996 Barnes & Noble Books, copyright by Robin Waterfield, page 327.

16. *Plato's Republic*, 1996 Barnes & Noble Books, copyright by Robin Waterfield, page 328.

17. *Plato's Republic*, 1996 Barnes & Noble Books, copyright by Robin Waterfield, page 240. A reference to Plato's "Allegory of the Cave."

18. *Plato's Republic*, 1996 Barnes & Noble Books, copyright by Robin Waterfield, page 240.

19. *Plato's Republic*, 1996 Barnes & Noble Books, copyright by Robin Waterfield, page 240.

20. *Plato's Republic*, 1996 Barnes & Noble Books, copyright by Robin Waterfield, the "Allegory of the Cave." Chapter four provides a descriptive and enhanced version of Plato's "Allegory of the Cave" as an example of human suffering in respect to ignorance, fear, and the lack of a desire to understand.

21. *Plato's Republic*, 1996 Barnes & Noble Books, copyright by Robin Waterfield, page 228.

22. *Plato's Republic*, 1996 Barnes & Noble Books, copyright by Robin Waterfield, page 228.

23. *Plato's Republic*, 1996 Barnes & Noble Books, copyright by Robin Waterfield, page 228.

24. *Aristotle Ethics*, Penguin Press, 1976, translated by J.A.K. Thomas, page 117.

25. *Aristotle Ethics*, Penguin Press, 1976, translated by J.A.K. Thomas, page 116.

26. *Aristotle Ethics*, Penguin Press, 1976, translated by J.A.K. Thomas, page 122.

27. *Socrates, Ideas of the Great Philosophers*, William S. Sahakian, Mabel Lewis Sahakian (Socrates), Barnes & Noble Books, 1993, page 28.

28. *Plato's Republic*, 1996 Barnes & Noble Books, copyright by Robin Waterfield, page 240.

29. *Aristotle Ethics*, Penguin Press, 1976, translated by J.A.K. Thomas.

30. William Shakespeare, *Hamlet*.

31. Homer, *The Odyssey*.

32. *The Globe Illustrated Shakespeare: The Complete Works*, Crown Publishers, 1979, New York.

33. *Alexander the Great and His Time*, 1993 Barnes & Noble, New York, Agnes Savill, page 31.

34. *The Globe Illustrated Shakespeare: The Complete Works*, Crown Publishers, 1979, New York.

35. The Dialogues of Dr. Richard F. Grego, professional philosopher.

36. *The Tormentor of Fools*, Brandon A. Perron, poem number 15.

37. *The Age of Analysis*, The New American Library, Jean-Paul Sartre, 1955, New York, Morton White, page 124.

38. *The Age of Analysis*, The New American Library, Jean-Paul Sartre, 1955, New York, Morton White, page 124.

39. William Shakespeare, *Hamlet*.

40. *The Age of Analysis*, The New American Library, Jean-Paul Sartre, 1955, New York, Morton White, page 130.

41. *The Age of Analysis*, The New American Library, Jean-Paul Sartre, 1955, New York, Morton White, page 130.

42. William Shakespeare. *Hamlet*.

43. William Shakespeare, *Hamlet*.

44. William Shakespeare, *Hamlet*.

45. William Shakespeare, *Hamlet*.

46. William Shakespeare, *Hamlet*.

47. *The Prince*, Niccolo Machiavelli, Barnes & Noble Books, New York, 1994, Chapter V, page 18.

48. *The Prince*, Niccolo Machiavelli, Barnes & Noble Books, New York, 1994, Chapter VI, page 19.

49. *The Prince*, Niccolo Machiavelli, Barnes & Noble Books, New York, 1994, Chapter VI, page 20.

50. *The Prince*, Niccolo Machiavelli, Barnes & Noble Books, New York, 1994, Chapter VI, page 21.

51. *The Prince*, Niccolo Machiavelli, Barnes & Noble Books, New York, 1994, Chapter VI, page 21.

52. *The Prince*, Niccolo Machiavelli, Barnes & Noble Books, New York, 1994, Chapter VI, page 21.

53. *The Prince*, Niccolo Machiavelli, Barnes & Noble Books, New York, 1994, Chapter VII, page 22.

54. *The Prince*, Niccolo Machiavelli, Barnes & Noble Books, New York, 1994, Chapter VI, page 22-23.

55. *The Prince*, Niccolo Machiavelli, Barnes & Noble Books, New York, 1994, Chapter IX, page 33.

56. *The Prince*, Niccolo Machiavelli, Barnes & Noble Books, New York, 1994, Chapter X, page 36.

57. *The Prince*, Niccolo Machiavelli, Barnes & Noble Books, New York, 1994, Chapter VII, page 40-41.

58. *A Nietzsche Reader*, Penguin Classics, selected and translated with an introduction by R.J. Hollingdale, Penguin Books, New York 1977, page 278.

59. *The Book of Five Rings*, Miyamoto Musashi, translation by Thomas Clearing, Barnes & Noble Books, New York, 1993, Page 91.

60. *The Book of Five Rings*, Miyamoto Musashi, translation by Thomas Clearing, Barnes & Noble Books, New York, 1993, Page 91.

61. *The Prince*, Niccolo Machiavelli, Barnes & Noble Books, New York, 1994, Chapter XIV, page 48.

62. *The Prince*, Niccolo Machiavelli, Barnes & Noble Books, New York, 1994, Chapter XV, page 51.

63. *The Prince*, Niccolo Machiavelli, Barnes & Noble Books, New York, 1994, Chapter XVII, page 55.

64. *The Prince*, Niccolo Machiavelli, Barnes & Noble Books, New York, 1994, Chapter XVIII, page 57.

65. *The Prince*, Niccolo Machiavelli, Barnes & Noble Books, New York, 1994, Chapter XVIII, page 58-59.

66. *The Prince*, Niccolo Machiavelli, Barnes & Noble Books, New York, 1994, Chapter XIX, page 60.

67. *The Prince*, Niccolo Machiavelli, Barnes & Noble Books, New York, 1994, Chapter XXI, page 72.

68. *The Prince*, Niccolo Machiavelli, Barnes & Noble Books, New York, 1994, Chapter XXII, page 75.

69. *The Prince*, Niccolo Machiavelli, Barnes & Noble Books, New York, 1994, Chapter XXIII, page 77.

70. *The Prince*, Niccolo Machiavelli, Barnes & Noble Books, New York, 1994, Chapter XXIII, page 78.

71. *Socrates in 90 Minutes*, Paul Strathern, Ivan R.Dee, Publisher, Chicago 1997, page 24.

72. William Shakespeare, *Hamlet*.

73. *The Age of Analysis*, William James, Introduction by Morton White, Mentor Books, New York, 1955, page 172.

74. *The Age of Analysis*, William James, Introduction by Morton White, Mentor Books, New York, 1955, page 172.

75. *The Revolt of the Masses*, Jose Ortega, W.W. Norton & Company, New York & London, 1957.

76. *The Age of Analysis*, William James, Introduction by Morton White, Mentor Books, New York, 1955, page 165.

77. *The Revolt of the Masses*, Jose Ortega, W.W. Norton & Company, New York & London, 1957.

78. *The Age of Analysis*, William James, Introduction by Morton White, Mentor Books, New York, 1955, page 166.

79. *The Revolt of the Masses*, Jose Ortega, W.W. Norton & Company, New York & London, 1957.

80. *The Revolt of the Masses*, Jose Ortega, W.W. Norton & Company, New York & London, 1957.

81. *The Revolt of the Masses*, Jose Ortega, W.W. Norton & Company, New York & London, 1957.

82. *The Revolt of the Masses*, Jose Ortega, W.W. Norton & Company, New York and London, 1957.

83. *The Revolt of the Masses*, Jose Ortega, W.W. Norton & Company, New York and London, 1957.

84. *The Revolt of the Masses*, Jose Ortega, W.W. Norton & Company, New York and London, 1957.

85. *The Revolt of the Masses*, Jose Ortega, W.W. Norton & Company, New York and London, 1957.

86. *The Revolt of the Masses*, Jose Ortega, W.W. Norton & Company, New York and London, 1957.

87. *The Revolt of the Masses*, Jose Ortega, W.W. Norton & Company, New York and London, 1957.

88. *The Revolt of the Masses*, Jose Ortega, W.W. Norton & Company, New York and London, 1957.

89. *The Revolt of the Masses*, Jose Ortega, W.W. Norton & Company, New York and London, 1957.

90. *The Revolt of the Masses*, Jose Ortega, W.W. Norton & Company, New York and London, 1957.

91. *The Revolt of the Masses*, Jose Ortega, W.W. Norton & Company, New York and London, 1957.

92. *My Heart Cries*, Brandon A. Perron, poem number 7.

93. *The End of History and the Last Man*, Francis Fukuyama, Avon Books, A Division of the Hearst Corporation, New York, New York, 1992, page 289.

94. Friedrich Nietzsche, *Thus Spoke Zarathustra: A Book For None and All*, translated with Preface by Walter Kaufmann, Penguin Books, 1978, page 42.

95. Friedrich Nietzsche, *Thus Spoke Zarathustra: A Book For None and All*, translated with Preface by Walter Kaufmann, Penguin Books, 1978, page 42.

96. Friedrich Nietzsche, *Thus Spoke Zarathustra: A Book For None and All*, translated with Preface by Walter Kaufmann, Penguin Books, 1978, page 42-43.

97. Friedrich Nietzsche, *Thus Spoke Zarathustra: A Book For None and All*, translated with Preface by Walter Kaufmann, Penguin Books, 1978, page 43.

98. Friedrich Nietzsche, *Thus Spoke Zarathustra: A Book For None and All*, translated with Preface by Walter Kaufmann, Penguin Books, 1978, page 43.

99. Friedrich Nietzsche, *Thus Spoke Zarathustra: A Book For None and All*, translated with Preface by Walter Kaufmann, Penguin Books, 1978, page 152.

100. Friedrich Nietzsche, *Thus Spoke Zarathustra: A Book For None and All*, translated with Preface by Walter Kaufmann, Penguin Books, 1978, page 153.

101. Friedrich Nietzsche, *Thus Spoke Zarathustra: A Book For None and All*, translated with Preface by Walter Kaufmann, Penguin Books, 1978, page 152.

102. Friedrich Nietzsche, *Thus Spoke Zarathustra: A Book For None and All*, translated with Preface by Walter Kaufmann, Penguin Books, 1978, page 49.

103. Friedrich Nietzsche, *Thus Spoke Zarathustra: A Book For None and All*, translated with Preface by Walter Kaufmann, Penguin Books, 1978, page 44.

104. *A Nietzsche Reader*, Penguin Classics, Selected and Translated with an introduction by R.J. Hollingdale, 1977, page 281.

105. *A Nietzsche Reader*, Penguin Classics, Selected and Translated with an introduction by R.J. Hollingdale, 1977, page 198.

106. Friedrich Nietzsche, *Thus Spoke Zarathustra: A Book For None and All*, translated with Preface by Walter Kaufmann, Penguin Books, 1978, page 46-47.

107. Friedrich Nietzsche, *Thus Spoke Zarathustra: A Book For None and All*, translated with Preface by Walter Kaufmann, Penguin Books, 1978, page 41.

108. *A Nietzsche Reader*, Penguin Classics, Selected and Translated with an introduction by R.J. Hollingdale, 1977, page 91.

109. *A Nietzsche Reader*, Penguin Classics, Selected and Translated with an introduction by R.J. Hollingdale, 1977, page 91.

110. *A Nietzsche Reader*, Penguin Classics, Selected and Translated with an introduction by R.J. Hollingdale, 1977, page 274.

111. *A Nietzsche Reader*, Penguin Classics, Selected and Translated with an introduction by R.J. Hollingdale, 1977, page 274.

112. *A Nietzsche Reader*, Penguin Classics, Selected and Translated with an introduction by R.J. Hollingdale, 1977, page 274.

113. *A Nietzsche Reader*, Penguin Classics, Selected and Translated with an introduction by R.J. Hollingdale, 1977, page 253.

114. R.G. Ingersoll

115. William Shakespeare, *Measure for Measure*, I.iv.77 (Lucio to Isabella)

116. *Plato's Republic*, 1996 Barnes & Noble Books, copyright by Robin Waterfield, page 131.

117. *Plato's Republic*, 1996 Barnes & Noble Books, copyright by Robin Waterfield, page 131.

118. *Plato's Republic*, 1996 Barnes & Noble Books, copyright by Robin Waterfield, page 214.

119. *Plato's Republic*, 1996 Barnes & Noble Books, copyright by Robin Waterfield, page 214-215.

120. *Plato's Republic*, 1996 Barnes & Noble Books, copyright by Robin Waterfield, page 215.

121. *Plato's Republic*, 1996 Barnes & Noble Books, copyright by Robin Waterfield, page 53.

122. *Plato's Republic*, 1996 Barnes & Noble Books, copyright by Robin Waterfield, page 53.

123. *Plato's Republic*, 1996 Barnes & Noble Books, copyright by Robin Waterfield, page 53.

124. *Plato's Republic*, 1996 Barnes & Noble Books, copyright by Robin Waterfield, page 53.

125. Aristotle, *Ethics*, translated by J.A.K. Thomson, Penguin Classics 1955, page 66.

126. *Nicomachean Ethics*, VII3, II47a, II14.

127. *Aristotle: The Desire to Understand*, Cambridge University Press1988, Jonathan Lear, page 181-182.

128. *Aristotle: The Desire to Understand*, Cambridge University Press1988, Jonathan Lear., page 180.

129. *Aristotle: The Desire to Understand*, Cambridge University Press1988, Jonathan Lear, page 175.

130. *Aristotle: The Desire to Understand*, Cambridge University Press1988, Jonathan Lear., page 164.

131. *Aristotle: The Desire to Understand*, Cambridge University Press 1988, Jonathan Lear, page 160.

132. Hamlet, Act III, scene I, line 55, William Shakespeare.

133. *The Prophet*, Kahlil Gibran, The Kahlil Gibran Pocket Library, published by Alfred A. Knopf, Inc., November 2000, page 14.

134. William Shakespeare, *Measure for Measure*, I.iv.77 (Lucio to Isabella).

135. Friedrich Nietzsche, *Thus Spoke Zarathustra: A Book For None and All*, translated with Preface by Walter Kaufmann, Penguin Books, 1978, page 41.

136. *The Book of Five Rings*, Miyamoto Musashi, translation by Thomas Clearing, Barnes & Noble Books, New York, 1993, page 71.

137. *Kung Fu Meditations & Chinese Proverbial Wisdom*, Ellen Kei Hua, Thor Publishing Company, 1991 Ventura, California.

138. *Kung Fu Meditations & Chinese Proverbial Wisdom*, Ellen Kei Hua, Thor Publishing Company, 1991 Ventura, California.

139. William Shakespeare, *Julius Caesar* II ii.32 (Caesar to Calphurnia).

140. *Unorthodox Strategies: 100 Lessons in the Art of War*, translated by Ralph D. Sawyer, 1998 Barnes & Noble Books, page 47. A tactical principle from *Wu Tzu*.

141. *Unorthodox Strategies: 100 Lessons in the Art of War*, translated by Ralph D. Sawyer, 1998 Barnes & Noble Books, page 47. A tactical principle from *Wu-Tzu*.

142. *Unorthodox Strategies: 100 Lessons in the Art of War*, translated by Ralph D. Sawyer, 1998 Barnes & Noble Books, page 66. A principle from *Sun-tzu's* Art of War.

143. *Unorthodox Strategies: 100 Lessons in the Art of War*, translated by Ralph D. Sawyer, 1998 Barnes & Noble Books, page 66. A principle from *Sun-tzu's* Art of War.

144. *Unorthodox Strategies: 100 Lessons in the Art of War*, translated by Ralph D. Sawyer, 1998 Barnes & Noble Books, page 69. A principle from *Sun-tzu's* Art of War.

145. *Unorthodox Strategies: 100 Lessons in the Art of War*, translated by Ralph D. Sawyer, 1998 Barnes & Noble Books, page 71. A principle from *Sun-tzu's* Art of War.

146. *Unorthodox Strategies: 100 Lessons in the Art of War*, translated by Ralph D. Sawyer, 1998 Barnes & Noble Books, page 79. A principle from *Three Strategies*.

147. *Unorthodox Strategies: 100 Lessons in the Art of War*, translated by Ralph D. Sawyer, 1998 Barnes & Noble Books, page 93. A principle from *Sun-tzu's* Art of War.

148. *Unorthodox Strategies: 100 Lessons in the Art of War*, translated by Ralph D. Sawyer, 1998 Barnes & Noble Books, page 24. A principle from *Sun-tzu's* Art of War.

149. *Unorthodox Strategies: 100 Lessons in the Art of War*, translated by Ralph D. Sawyer, 1998 Barnes & Noble Books, page 25. A principle from *Sun-tzu's* Art of War.

150. *Unorthodox Strategies: 100 Lessons in the Art of War*, translated by Ralph D. Sawyer, 1998 Barnes & Noble Books, page 25. A principle from *Sun-tzu's* Art of War.

151. *Unorthodox Strategies: 100 Lessons in the Art of War*, translated by Ralph D. Sawyer, 1998 Barnes & Noble Books, page 115.

152. *Unorthodox Strategies: 100 Lessons in the Art of War*, translated by Ralph D. Sawyer, 1998 Barnes & Noble Books, page 118. A principle from *Questions and Replies.*

153. *Unorthodox Strategies: 100 Lessons in the Art of War*, translated by Ralph D. Sawyer, 1998 Barnes & Noble Books, page 26. A principle from *Sun-tzu's* Art of War.

154. *Unorthodox Strategies: 100 Lessons in the Art of War*, translated by Ralph D. Sawyer, 1998 Barnes & Noble Books.

155. *A Nietzsche Reader*, Penguin Classics, Selected and Translated with an introduction by R.J. Hollingdale, 1977, page 159.

156. William Shakespeare, *King Lear*, I, 280 (Cordelai to Goneril and Regan).

157. William Shakespeare, *Measure for Measure*, Act II, Scene I, Line 38.

158. William Shakespeare, *Hamlet*, Act V, Scene I.

159. William Shakespeare, *Henry VI*, Act 2, Scene IV, Line I29 (Suffolk to his captors).

160. *The Book of Five Rings*, Miyamoto Musashi, translated by Thomas Cleary, Barnes & Noble Books, New York, 1997, page 19.

161. *The Book of Five Rings*, Miyamoto Musashi, translated by Thomas Cleary, Barnes & Noble Books, New York, 1997, page 102.

162. William Shakespeare, *Julius Caesar*, Act II, Line 36 (Caesar to Calphurnia).

163. William Shakespeare, *Twelfth Night*, Act II, Line I45 (Malvolio, quoting letter).

164. *Unorthodox Strategies: 100 Lessons in the Art of War*, translated by Ralph D. Sawyer, 1998 Barnes & Noble Books, page 115.

165. William Shakespeare, *Macbeth*, Act I, Line 60 (Lady to Macbeth).

166. William Shakespear, *Hamlet*, Act I, Verse I66 (Hamlet to Horatio).

167. *Unorthodox Strategies: 100 Lessons in the Art of War*, translated by Ralph D. Sawyer, 1998 Barnes & Noble Books, page 208-209. A principle from *Sun-tzu's* Art of War.

168. *A Nietzsche Reader*, Penguin Classics, Selected and Translated with an introduction by R.J. Hollingdale, 1977, page 274.

169. *A Nietzsche Reader*, Penguin Classics, Selected and Translated with an introduction by R.J. Hollingdale, 1977, page 274.

170. *A Nietzsche Reader*, Penguin Classics, Selected and Translated with an introduction by R.J. Hollingdale, 1977, page 274.

171. William Shakespeare, Romeo and Juliet II.ii.I (Romeo)

172. Ancient Roman Legion sworn to protect the Emperor and the City of Rome.

173. *Unorthodox Strategies: 100 Lessons in the Art of War*, translated by Ralph D. Sawyer, 1998 Barnes & Noble Books, page 102.

174. *Henry IV*, Part 2, III.i.3I (King Henry IV).

175. William Shakespeare, *King Henry V*, King Harry to his men before battle.

176. *A Nietzsche Reader*, Penguin Classics, Selected and Translated with an introduction by R.J. Hollingdale, 1977, page 91.

177. William Shakespeare, *Pericles*, II iii.45 (Pericles).

178. William Shakespeare, Hamlet III.ivI60 (Hamlet to Getrude).

179. William Shakespeare, *Henry VI*, Part 2 IV, vii.73 (Lord to Jack Cade).

180. William Shakespeare, *Julius Caesar*. The last words of Julius Caesar as he was betrayed and assassinated by his colleague, Brutus, and other members of the Roman Senate.

181. *Socrates in 90 Minutes*, Ivan R. Dee, Chicago, Paul Strathern, 1997, pages 68-70.

182. *Socrates in 90 Minutes*, Ivan R. Dee, Chicago, Paul Strathern, 1997, page 24.

0-595-29951-2

Printed in the United States
35619LVS00003B/97-108